Also by C. J. Tudor
Available from Random House Large Print

The Other People

THE
BURNING
GIRLS

THE BURNING GIRLS

A NOVEL

C. J. TUDOR

RANDOM HOUSE
LARGE PRINT

Published in the United States of America by Random House Large Print in association with Ballantine Books, an imprint of Random House, a division of Penguin Random House LLC.

Cover design: Elena Giavaldi
Cover images: Marzufello/Shutterstock (flames), courtesy of the author (church)
Title page art: iStock.com/MorePics

The Library of Congress has established a Cataloging-in-Publication record for this title.

ISBN: 978-0-593-29512-0

www.penguinrandomhouse.com/
large-print-format-books

FIRST LARGE PRINT EDITION

Printed in the United States of America

10 9 8 7 6 5 4 3 2 1

This Large Print edition published in accord with the standards of the N.A.V.H.

For Neil, Betty and Doris.
The tall, the cute and the furry.

THE
BURNING
GIRLS

BURNING GIRLS:

Twig dolls peculiar to the small Sussex village of **Chapel Croft**. The dolls are made to commemorate the **Sussex Martyrs**—eight villagers who were burned at the stake during **Queen Mary**'s purge of **Protestants** (1553–8). Two of the martyrs were young girls. The **Burning Girls** are set alight in a ceremony held every year on the anniversary of the purge.

PROLOGUE

What kind of man am I?

It was a question he had asked himself a lot lately.

I am a man of God. I am His servant. I do His will.

But was that enough?

He stared at the small whitewashed house. Thatched roof, bright purple clematis crawling up its walls, bathed in the fading glow of the late-summer sun. Birds chittered in the trees. Bees buzzed lazily among the bushes.

Here lies evil. Here, in the most innocuous of settings.

He walked slowly up the short path. Fear gripped his belly. It felt like a physical pain, a cramping in his gut. He raised his hand to the door, but it opened before he could knock.

"Oh, thank God. Thank the Lord you came."

The mother sagged at the doorway. Lank brown

hair stuck to her scalp. Her eyes were shot through with blood and her skin was grey and lined.

This is what it looks like when Satan enters your home.

He stepped inside. The house stank. Sour, unclean. How could it have come to this? He looked up the stairs. The darkness at the top seemed thick with malevolence. He rested his hand on the banister. His legs refused to move. He squeezed his eyes tightly shut, breathing deeply.

"Father?"

I am a man of God.

"Show me."

He started to ascend. At the top, there were just three doors. A boy, slack-faced, in a stained T-shirt and shorts, peered around one. As the black-clothed figure approached, the boy pulled the door shut.

He pushed open the door next to it. The heat and smell hit him like a physical entity. He placed a hand over his mouth and tried not to gag.

The bed was stained with blood and bodily fluids. Restraints had been tied to each bedpost, but they hung loose. In the middle of the mattress a large leather case lay open. Sturdy straps held the contents in place: a heavy crucifix, a Bible, holy water, muslin cloths.

Two items were missing. They lay on the floor. A scalpel and a long serrated knife. Both slick with blood. More blood pooled, like a dark, ruby cloak, around the body.

He swallowed, his mouth as dry as the summer fields. "Dear Lord—what has taken place here?"

"I told you. I told you that the devil—"

"Enough!"

He spotted something on the bedside table. He walked over to it. A small black box. He stared at it for a moment and then turned to the mother hovering in the doorway. She wrung her hands and stared at him pleadingly.

"What shall we do?"

We. Because this was upon him too.

He looked back at the bloody, mutilated body on the floor.

What kind of man am I?

"Get cloths and bleach. Now."

WELDON HERALD,
Thursday, May 24, 1990
MISSING GIRLS

Police have appealed for help in the search for two missing Sussex teenagers: Merry Lane and Joy Harris. The pair, who are believed to have run away together, are both aged 15. Joy was last seen at a bus stop in Henfield on the evening of 12 May. Merry disappeared from her home in Chapel Croft a week later on 19 May, after leaving a note.

Police are not treating their disappearance as suspicious but are concerned about the girls' welfare and are appealing for them to get in touch with their families.

"You won't be in trouble. They're worried. They just want to know you're safe and you can always come home."

Joy is described as slight, around 5 foot 5 inches tall, with long, light blonde hair and delicate features. She was last seen wearing a pink T-shirt, stone-washed jeans and Dunlop Green Flash trainers.

Merry is described as thin, 5 foot 7 inches tall, with short, dark hair, and was last seen wearing a baggy grey jumper, jeans and black plimsolls.

Anyone who sees them should report the sighting to Weldon Police on 01323 456723 or call Crimestoppers on 0800 555 111.

ONE

"It's an unfortunate situation."

Bishop John Durkin smiles, benevolently.

I'm pretty sure that Bishop John Durkin does everything benevolently, even taking a shit.

The youngest bishop to preside over the North Notts diocese, he's a skilled orator, author of several acclaimed theological papers and, if he hadn't at least tried to walk on water, I'd be amazed.

He's also a wanker.

I know it. His colleagues know it. His staff know it. Secretly, I think, even he knows it.

Unfortunately, no one is going to call him on it. Certainly not me. Not today. Not while he holds my job, my home and my future in his smooth, manicured hands.

"Something like this can shake the faith of the community," he continues.

"They're not shaken. They're angry and sad. But

I won't let this ruin everything we've achieved. I won't leave people now when they need me the most."

"But do they? Attendance is down. Classes canceled. I heard that the children's groups may move to another church."

"Crime scene tape and police officers will do that. This is not a community that has any love for the police."

"I understand that—"

No, he doesn't. The closest Durkin gets to the inner city is when his driver takes a wrong turn on the way to his private gym.

"I'm confident it's only temporary. I can rebuild their trust."

I don't add that I need to. I made a mistake and I need to make amends.

"So now you can perform miracles?" Before I can answer or argue, Durkin continues smoothly. "Look, Jack, I know you did what you thought was best, but you got too close."

I sit back stiffly in my seat, fighting the urge to fold my arms like a sulky teenager. "I thought that was our job. To build close ties with the community."

"It is our job to uphold the reputation of the Church. These are testing times. Everywhere, churches are failing. Fewer and fewer people are attending. We have an uphill battle even without this negative publicity."

And that is what Durkin really cares about. The newspapers. PR. The Church doesn't get good press at the best of times and I've really screwed things up. By trying to save a little girl and, instead, condemning her.

"So, what? You want me to resign?"

"Not at all. It would be a shame for someone of your **caliber** to leave." He steeples his hands together. He really does that. "And it would look bad. An admission of guilt. We have to give careful consideration to what we do next."

I'm sure. Especially considering my appointment here was his idea. I'm his prize show-dog. And I had been performing well, turning the once-derelict inner-city church back into a hub of the community.

Until Ruby.

"So, what do you suggest?"

"A transfer. Somewhere less high profile for a while. A small church in Sussex has suddenly found itself without a priest. Chapel Croft. While they nominate a replacement, they need an interim vicar."

I stare at him, feeling the earth shift beneath my feet.

"I'm sorry, but that's not possible. My daughter is taking her GCSEs next year. I can't just move her to the other end of the country."

"I've already agreed to the transfer with Bishop Gordon at the Weldon diocese."

"You've **what**? **How**? Has the post been advertised? Surely there must be a more suitable local candidate—"

He waves a hand dismissively. "We were chatting. Your name came up. He mentioned the vacancy. Serendipity."

And Durkin can pull more strings than frigging Geppetto.

"Try and look on the bright side," he says. "It's a beautiful part of the country. Fresh air, fields. A small, safe community. It could be good for you and Flo."

"I think I know what's best for me and my daughter. The answer is no."

"Then let me be blunt, Jack." His eyes meet mine. "This is not a fucking request."

There's a reason why Durkin is the youngest bishop to preside over the diocese and it has nothing to do with his benevolence.

I clench my fists in my lap. "Understood."

"Excellent. You start next week. Pack your wellies."

TWO

"Christ!"

"Blaspheming again."

"I know, but—" Flo shakes her head. "What a shithole."

She's not wrong. I pull the car to a halt and stare up at our new home. Well, our spiritual home. Our **actual** home is next door: a small cottage that would be quite pretty if not for its alarming off-kilter bearing, which makes it look like it's trying to slope away, quietly, brick by brick.

The chapel itself is small, square and a dirty off-white. It doesn't look much like a place of worship. There's no high-pitched roof, cross or stained glass. Four plain windows face the front: two up, two down. Between the two upper windows is a clock. Florid writing around it proclaims:

"Redeem the Time, for the Days are Evil."

Nice. Unfortunately, the "e" has worn off the

end of "time," so it actually reads, "Redeem the Tim," whoever he is.

I climb out of the car. The muggy air immediately shrink-wraps my clothes to my skin. All around us, there's nothing but fields. The village itself consists of about two dozen houses, a pub, general shop and village hall. The only sounds are birdsong and the occasional buzzing bee. It sets me on edge.

"Okay," I say, trying to sound positive, and not full of dread, like I feel. "Let's go and take a look inside."

"Aren't we going to look at where we're going to live?" Flo asks.

"First the house of God. Then the house of his children."

She rolls her eyes. Communicating that I'm impossibly stupid and tiresome. Teenagers can communicate a lot with eye rolls. Which is just as well, seeing as oral communication hits something of a brick wall once they turn fifteen.

"Besides," I say, "our furniture is still stuck in traffic on the M25. At least the chapel has pews."

She slams the car door and slouches along grumpily behind me. I glance at her: dark hair, cropped into a ragged bob, nose ring (hard fought for and taken out for school), and a hefty Nikon camera slung almost permanently around her neck. I often think my daughter would be a dead ringer for Winona Ryder's role in a remake of **Beetlejuice.**

A long path leads up to the chapel from the road. A battered metal mailbox stands just outside the gate. I've been told, if no one is here when we arrive, that this is where I will find the keys. I flip up the lid, stick my hand inside, and . . . bingo. I pull out two worn silver keys, which must be for the cottage, and a heavy iron thing that looks like it should open something from a Tolkien fantasy. I presume this is the key to the chapel.

"Well, at least we can get in," I say.

"Yay," Flo deadpans.

I ignore her and push open the gate. The path is steep and uneven. Either side, tilting headstones rise up from the overgrown grass. A taller monument stands to the left. A bleak grey obelisk. What look like bunches of dead flowers have been left at its base. On closer inspection, they're not dead flowers. They're tiny twig dolls.

"What are those?" Flo asks, peering at them and reaching for her camera.

Automatically, I reply, "Burning Girls."

She crouches down to snap some shots with her Nikon.

"They're something of a village tradition," I say. "I read about it online. People make them to commemorate the Sussex Martyrs."

"The who?"

"Villagers who were burned to death during Queen Mary's purge of the Protestants. Two young girls were killed outside this chapel."

She stands, pulling a face. "And people make creepy twig dolls to remember them?"

"And on the anniversary of the purge, they burn them."

"That is **way** too **Blair Witch**."

"That's the countryside for you." I give the twig dolls a final contemptuous glance as I walk past. "Full of 'quaint' traditions."

Flo pulls out her phone and takes a couple more pictures, presumably to share with her friends back in Nottingham—**Look at what the crazy yokels do**—and then follows me.

We reach the chapel door and I stick the iron key into the lock. It's a bit stiff and I have to push down hard to get it to turn. The door creaks open. **Properly** creaks, like a sound effect in a horror movie. I shove it open wider.

In contrast to the August sunshine, it's dark inside the chapel. It takes my eyes a moment to adjust. Sunlight peters in through the grimy windows, illuminating a cloud of dust motes floating thickly in the air.

It's an unusual layout: a small nave; barely enough room for half a dozen rows of pews facing a central altar. Either side, a set of narrow wooden stairs leads up to a balcony where more pews look down upon the proceedings, like a tiny theater, or gladiator's pit. I wonder how the hell it ever passed a fire inspection.

The whole place smells stale and unused, which

is odd, considering it was used regularly until a few weeks ago. It also manages, like all chapels and churches, to feel both stuffy and cold at the same time.

At the bottom of the nave, I notice that a small area has been cordoned off with a couple of yellow safety barriers. A makeshift sign is hung on one of them:

"Danger. Uneven flooring. Loose flagstones."

"I take it back," Flo says. "Total and utter shithole."

"It could be worse."

"How?"

"Woodworm, damp, beetle infestation?"

"I'll be outside." She turns and stomps from the building.

I don't follow. Best to just let it lie. There's little I can say to console her. I've uprooted her from the city she loves, the school where she felt settled, and brought her to a place with nothing to offer except fields and the aroma of cow shit. It's going to take some work to win her over.

I stare up at the wooden altar.

"What am I doing here, Lord?"

"Can I help you?"

I swivel round.

A man stands behind me. Slight and very pale, his chalky pallor accentuated by oily black hair, slicked back from a high widow's peak. Despite the warm weather, he wears a dark suit over a collarless grey shirt. He looks like a vampire on his way to a jazz club.

"Sorry, never had a direct reply before." I smile and hold out a hand. "I'm Jack."

He continues to stare at me suspiciously. "I'm the warden of this church. How did you get in here?"

And I realize. I'm not wearing my collar and he's probably only been told that "Reverend Brooks" is arriving today. Of course, he could have looked me up online, but then, he also looks like he still uses an ink and quill.

"Sorry. Jack Brooks. Reverend Brooks?"

His eyes widen slightly. The tiniest hint of color touches his cheeks. I admit, my name causes confusion. I admit, I enjoy it.

"Oh, goodness. I'm so sorry, it's just—"

"Not what you expected."

"No."

"Taller, slimmer, better looking?"

And then a voice shouts: "MUM!"

I turn. Flo stands in the doorway, white-faced and wide-eyed. My maternal alarm shrills.

"What is it?"

"There's a girl out here. She's . . . I think she's hurt. You need to come. **Now.**"

THREE

The girl can't be more than ten. She wears a dress that might have once been white, her feet are bare . . . and she's covered in blood.

It has turned her blonde hair a dirty russet, streaked her face with crimson and stained the dress a deep maroon. As she staggers up the path toward us, her feet leave small, bloody footprints.

I stare at her, frantically trying to work out what could have happened. Has she been hit by a car? I can't see one on the lane. And there's **so much** blood. How is she still standing?

I approach her carefully and crouch down.

"Hi, sweetheart. Are you hurt?"

She raises her eyes to mine. Startling blue, shiny with shock. She shakes her head. Not hurt. Then where's all the blood come from?

"Okay. Can you tell me what happened?"

"He killed her."

Despite the heavy heat of the day, a chill snakes down my spine.

"Who?"

"Pippa."

"Flo," I say carefully. "Call the police."

She takes out her phone and stares at it in disbelief. "No signal."

Shit. Déjà vu comes over me so hard I feel sick. Blood. A little girl. Not again.

I turn to Jazz Vampire, who is hovering by the door. "I didn't get your name?"

"Aaron."

"Is there a landline inside, Aaron?"

"Yes. In the office."

"Can you go and use it?"

He hesitates. "The girl—I know her. She's from the Harper farm."

"What's her name?"

"Poppy."

"Okay." I smile reassuringly at the girl. "Poppy, we're going to get some help."

Aaron still hasn't moved. Maybe shock, maybe just indecision. Either way, it's not helpful.

"Phone!" I bark at him.

He slinks back inside the church. I can hear the sound of a car engine accelerating. I glance up, just as a Range Rover tears around the corner and abruptly squeals to a halt outside the chapel gate, tires screeching on gravel. The door flies open.

"**Poppy!**"

A heavy-set man with sandy hair jumps out and pounds up the path toward us.

"Oh God, Poppy! I've been looking everywhere for you. What were you thinking, running off like that?"

I straighten. "Is this your little girl?"

"Yes. She's my daughter. I'm Simon Harper—" Said as if it should mean something. "Who the hell are you?"

I bite hard on my tongue. "I'm Reverend Brooks, the new vicar. Care to tell me what's going on here? Your daughter is covered in blood."

He scowls. He's a few years older than me, I'd say. Broad, not fat. A bullish face. I get the impression he's not used to being challenged, especially by a woman.

"This is not how it looks."

"Really—'cos it looks like the **Texas Chainsaw Massacre**." This from Flo.

Simon Harper flicks her an irritated glance then turns back to me. "I can assure you, **Reverend,** it's all just a misunderstanding. Poppy, please come here—" He holds out his hand. Poppy cowers behind me.

"Your daughter said someone had been killed?"

"**What?**"

"Pippa."

"Oh, for Christ's sake." He rolls his eyes. "This is ridiculous."

"Well, we can always let the police decide what's ridiculous—"

"It's **Peppa,** not Pippa . . . and Peppa is a **pig.**"

"I'm sorry?"

"The blood is **pig's** blood."

I stare at him. Sweat tickles my back. A tractor chugs slowly along the road. Simon Harper sighs heavily.

"Could we go inside—clean her up? I can't take her back in the car like this."

I glance over at the ramshackle cottage.

"Walk this way."

My first time inside our new home. Not quite the housewarming I expected. Flo brings in a couple of plastic chairs from the garden and we sit Poppy down. I locate a cleanish-looking cloth and half a bottle of liquid soap under the sink. I also spot a flashlight and a spider the size of my fist.

"I'll have a look in the car," Flo says. "I think there're some wet wipes and a sweatshirt of mine that Poppy could wear."

"Good thinking."

She trots back outside. She's a good girl, I think, despite the attitude.

I run the cloth under the tap and crouch down next to Poppy. I wipe at the blood on her face.

Pig's blood. How did a little girl get covered in pig's blood?

"I know this looks bad," Simon Harper says, in an attempt at a conciliatory tone.

"I don't judge. Rule number one of the job."

Also, a lie. I clean blood from around Poppy's forehead and ears. She begins to look more like a little girl and less like a refugee from a Stephen King novel.

"You said you were going to explain?"

"I own a farm. Harper's Farm. It's been in the family for years. We have our own slaughterhouse on site. I know some people struggle with that . . ."

I don't rise. "Actually, I think it's important to know where our food comes from. My last parish, most of the kids thought meat grew in buns from McDonald's."

"Right . . . well, exactly. We've tried to bring both our children up to understand the farming process. Not to be sentimental about the animals. Rosie—that's our older daughter—has always been fine with that, but Poppy is more . . . sensitive."

I get the feeling that "sensitive" is a euphemism for something else. I smooth back Poppy's hair. She stares at me blankly with those brilliant blue eyes.

"I told Emma . . . that's my wife . . . she never should have let her name them."

"Who?"

"The pigs. It made Poppy happy . . . but then, of course, she got attached, especially to one."

"Peppa?"

"Yes."

"This morning we took the pigs to slaughter."

"Ah."

"Poppy wasn't supposed to be home. Rosie was taking her to the playground . . . but something must have happened. They came back early and the next thing I know Poppy is standing there. . . ."

He breaks off, looking bewildered. I imagine a child running into such a horrific scene.

"I still don't understand how she got covered in blood?"

"I think . . . she must have slipped and ended up on the floor. Anyway, then she ran away, and you know the rest. . . ." He looks at me. "You have no idea how bad I feel, but it's a farm. It's what we do."

I feel a small sliver of sympathy. I rinse the cloth out and use it to wipe the last of the blood from Poppy's face. Then I fish in the pocket of my jeans for a hair bobble and wind Poppy's sticky hair up into a ponytail.

I smile at her. "I knew there was a little girl in there somewhere."

Still nothing. It's a little disconcerting. But then, trauma can do that. I've seen it happen before. Being a vicar in an inner city is not all cake bakes and rummage sales. You meet a lot of troubled people, old and young. But abuse is not confined to city streets. I know that too.

I turn to Simon. "Has Poppy got any other pets?"

"We have some working dogs, but they're kept in kennels."

"Perhaps it would be a good idea for Poppy to have a pet of her own. Something small, like a hamster, she could care for?"

For a moment I think he might accept my suggestion. Then his face closes again.

"Thank you, Reverend, but I think I know how to deal with my own daughter."

I'm on the verge of pointing out that the evidence would suggest otherwise when Flo reappears in the kitchen, holding baby wipes and a sweatshirt with a picture of Jack Skellington on it.

"Will this do?"

I nod, feeling suddenly tired. "Fine."

We stand at the door and watch as father and daughter—Flo's sweatshirt flapping around Poppy's knees—climb into the four-by-four and drive off.

I sling an arm around Flo's shoulders. "So much for the peace of the countryside."

"Yeah. Perhaps it **will** be fun here after all."

I chuckle and then I spot a ghostly figure in black walking toward the cottage holding a large rectangular box. Aaron. I'd completely forgotten about him. What on earth has he been doing all this time?

"I presume the police are on their way?" I ask.

"Oh, no. I saw Simon Harper pull up and thought it wasn't necessary."

Did you, now? Simon Harper obviously wields influence here. In many small communities, there's a family who others defer to. Out of tradition. Or fear. Or both.

"And then I remembered," Aaron continues. "I was supposed to give you this when you arrived."

He holds out the box. My name is printed neatly in bold type on the front.

"What is it?"

"I don't know. It was left for you at the chapel yesterday."

"By whom?"

"I didn't see. I thought perhaps it might be a welcome gift."

"Maybe the last vicar left it?" Flo suggests.

"I doubt it," I say. "He's dead." I glance at Aaron, realizing that might have sounded insensitive. "I was sorry to hear about Reverend Fletcher. It must have been a shock."

"It was."

"Had he been ill?"

"Ill?" He looks at me oddly. "Didn't they tell you?"

"I heard his death was sudden."

"It was. He killed himself."

FOUR

"You should have told me."

Durkin's voice is barely audible at the other end. "Delicate . . . —ation . . . best not . . . details."

"I don't care—I should have known."

"I didn't . . . personal . . . sorry."

"Who does know?"

"Few people . . . church warden . . . found him . . . the parish council."

Which probably means pretty much everyone in the village. Durkin is talking again. I hang further out of the upstairs bedroom window—the only place I can get a workable signal on my phone—and gain a magical third bar.

"Reverend Fletcher . . . mental health issues. Fortunately, he had already agreed to resign before it happened, so officially he wasn't the residing vicar anymore. . . ."

So, in other words, not the Church's problem. Durkin's lack of empathy verges on pathological. I often think his skills would be better put to use in politics rather than the Church, but then, perhaps there isn't so much difference. We both preach to the converted.

"I should have known. It affects how I run things here. It affects people's perception of the chapel and the vicar."

"Of course. I'm sorry. It was an oversight."

It bloody well wasn't. He just didn't want to give me another reason not to come.

"Is that all, Jack?"

"Actually, there's one more thing—"

It shouldn't matter. If death is simply a release to a higher plane, the circumstances should not be an issue. But they are.

"How did he do it?"

A pause, long enough for me to know—having known Durkin a long time—that he is wondering whether to lie. Then he sighs.

"He hanged himself, in the chapel."

Flo is kneeling on the floor in the living room, taking things out of boxes. Fortunately, there aren't that many. When the removal van eventually arrived, it took the two tattooed young men all of twenty minutes to unload our worldly possessions. Not much to show for half a lifetime's work.

I flop on to the worn sofa, which only just fits

in the cramped living room. Everything in the cottage is tiny, low and wonky. None of the windows open properly, making it unbearably warm, and I have to keep remembering to duck through the doorway between the kitchen and the living room (and I'm not exactly Amazonian).

The bathroom is olive green and speckled with mold. There's no shower. Heating is provided by an oil-fired boiler and an ancient-looking log burner, which probably needs a safety check, or we'll gas ourselves come winter.

In the spirit of counting our blessings, the house is rent free. We can do our best to make it our own. Just not right now. Right now, I want to eat, watch some TV and sleep.

Flo looks up. "I hope today's events haven't blinded you to what a dump this place is."

"No, but tonight I'm too tired and hungry to feel depressed about it. I don't suppose there's such a thing as a takeaway nearby?"

"Actually, there's a Domino's in the next town. I googled it on the way here."

"Hallelujah. Civilization. Shall we see what's on Netflix?"

"I thought BT hadn't connected the broadband yet?"

Bugger.

"Stuck with normal TV, then."

"You'll be lucky."

"What? Why?"

She gets up and sits on the sofa next to me, slipping an arm around my shoulders.

"What's wrong with this picture, Michael?"

I smile at the **Lost Boys** reference. At least some of my cultural influences have rubbed off.

"No TV aerial. Do you know what it means when there's no TV aerial?"

"Oh God." I throw my head back. "Really?"

"Yup . . ."

"What have we got ourselves into?"

"Hopefully not the murder capital of the world."

"Vampires, I can deal with. One thing I do have is crosses."

"And a mysterious box."

The box. I'd been so furious at Durkin for not telling me about the circumstances of Reverend Fletcher's death that I'd almost forgotten what kicked it all off in the first place. I look around.

"I'm not sure where I left it."

"In the kitchen."

Flo hops up and returns with the box, which she plonks down next to me. I eye it dubiously.

Reverend Jack Brooks.

"So?" Flo brandishes a pair of scissors.

I take them and slit open the masking tape sealing the box. Inside, something is wrapped in tissue. A small card rests on top. I take it out.

But there is nothing covered up that will not be revealed, and hidden

that will not be known. Accordingly, whatever you have said in the dark will be heard in the light, and what you have whispered in the inner rooms will be proclaimed upon the housetops.

Luke 12:2–3

I glance at Flo and she raises her eyebrows. "Bit melodramatic."

I put the piece of card down and peel away the tissue paper, revealing a battered, brown leather case.

I stare at it. Goosebumps skitter up my arms.

"So, are you going to open it?" Flo says.

Unfortunately, I can't find a reasonable excuse not to. I lift the case out and lay it on the sofa. Something clunks around inside. I undo the clasps.

"But there is nothing covered up that will not be revealed."

The interior is lined with red silk, the contents held in place by straps: a leather-bound Bible, a heavy cross featuring a prostrate Jesus, holy water, muslin cloths, a scalpel and a large serrated knife.

"What is it?" Flo asks.

I swallow, feeling a little sick. "An exorcism kit."

"Whoah." Then she frowns. "I didn't know you used knives for an exorcism?"

"Usually, you don't."

I reach forward and take hold of the knife's worn bone handle. It feels cool and smooth in my grip.

I lift it out of the case. It's heavy, the jagged edges sharp and covered in rusty brown stains.

Flo leans forward. "Mum, is that—"

"Yes."

It's turning into something of a theme today.

Blood.

FIVE

Moonlight. You wouldn't think it could be different, but it is.

He holds out his fingers, lets it play on his hands, trickle down to the grass. **Grass**. That's new too. Inside, there was no grass. Nothing soft. Not even the stiff and scratchy bedding. The moonlight was always filtered through narrow windows, partially obscured by the buildings looming all around. And when it fell, it landed hard. On concrete and steel.

Here, the light sprawls out freely, uncontained. It bathes—yes, **bathes**—the park around him in silver. It nestles gently next to him on the grass. So what if the grass is sparse and patchy, littered with rubbish, cider bottles and cigarette butts? To him, it's paradise. The garden of fucking Eden. His bed tonight is a bench and his luxury bedding cardboard and a sleeping bag he stole from a drunk. No honor among thieves or beggars. But to him it's a four poster with silk sheets and duck-down pillows.

He is free. After fourteen years. And this time, he isn't going back. He's finally got himself clean, done their rehab program. Kicked the drugs, behaved like a good boy.

It's not too late. That's what the counselors told him. **You can still build a life for yourself. You can put this behind you.**

All lies, of course. You can never leave your past behind. Your past is a part of you. It trails at your heels like a faithful old dog, refusing to leave your side. And sometimes, it bites your arse.

He chuckles to himself. **She** would have liked that. She used to tell him he had a way with words. Maybe, but he also had a way with his fists and his boots. He couldn't stop the anger. It clouded everything. Snatched away his words and replaced them with a thick blood-red haze that thrummed in his ears and filled his throat.

You have to control your anger, she told him. **Or the bitch wins.**

At night, in his cell, he would imagine her beside him, her hand stroking his hair, whispering, calming him. Helping him through the confinement and the withdrawal symptoms. He casts his eyes around in the darkness, searching for her. No. He is alone. But not for much longer.

He pulls the sleeping bag up to his chin, rests his head on the bench. It's a mild night. He's happy sleeping outside. He can stare at the moon and the stars and look forward to tomorrow.

What was that song, about tomorrow? Only a day away, or something.

They used to sing that sometimes.

I wish we were **orphans, like Annie,** she would say. **Then we could get away from this place.**

And she would snuggle up to him. All bony limbs and tangled hair that smelt like biscuits.

He smiles. **Tomorrow, tomorrow, I'm coming to find you.**

SIX

Sunday-morning service is the headline performance of a vicar's week. If you're going to draw a crowd—and by a crowd, I mean double figures—then you'll get them on a Sunday.

In my old church in Nottingham, which had a largely black congregation, Sundays meant full formalwear: hats, suits, little girls with tight curls and large bows. **Like Ruby.**

It made the day feel special. It made **me** feel special. Particularly as I knew, if you looked a little closer, those outfits were often a little threadbare or tight around the waist. My congregation came from the poorest areas in the city and yet they made the effort. It was a matter of pride to turn out properly dressed on a Sunday morning.

Even in some of my other churches, Sunday morning saw bums on pews, quite literally in some cases. Still, you take what you can get in this business.

Of course, it can be disheartening, but I always try to remind myself that if one person gets a little comfort from my words, that's a win. The Church isn't just for those who believe in God. It's for those who don't have anything to believe in. The lonely, lost and homeless. A place of refuge. That's how I found it. When I had nowhere to go, nowhere to turn. Someone reached out to me. I never forgot that kindness. Now I try to pay it back.

I'm not sure what to expect from the congregation here. Small villages tend to be more traditional. The church plays a bigger role in the community. But the congregations also tend to be older. It's funny how many people acquire faith with their first set of dentures.

Not that I'm actually taking the service today. I don't officially start for another two weeks. This morning, the headliner is Reverend Rushton from Warblers Green. We've already exchanged a few emails. He seems kind, dedicated and overworked. Like most rural priests. He currently divides his time between three churches, so covering Chapel Croft is something of an ask, or as he put it:

"God may be omnipresent but I've yet to master being in four places at once."

It explains some of the urgency of my appointment. But not all.

The strange parcel has left me feeling uneasy. I didn't sleep last night. The silence kept jolting me awake. No comforting wail of distant sirens or drunks shouting outside the window. The events of the day kept resurfacing in my mind: Poppy, her face streaked with blood. The serrated knife. Ruby's face. Merging into Poppy's. Blood linking them all.

Why did I agree to come here? What do I hope to achieve?

I finally heave myself out of bed at just past seven. A cockerel is crowing noisily outside. Bloody marvelous. After making myself a coffee, I give in to temptation and dig out my rolling tin and tobacco from where I stuffed them, underneath a tea towel, in a kitchen drawer.

Flo keeps on at me to give up smoking. I keep on trying. But the flesh is weak. I roll the clandestine ciggie at the table, then chuck an old hoodie over my vest and joggers and smoke it outside the back door, trying to put my feelings of gloom to one side. It's already warm, despite the cloudy skies. A fresh day. New challenges. One thing I always give thanks for. Tomorrow is not guaranteed. Each day is a gift, so use it wisely.

Of course, like most vicars, I don't always practice what I preach.

I finish my cigarette and head upstairs for a lukewarm bath. Then I dry my hair and try to make myself look presentable. My hair is still, mostly, dark. I don't have too many wrinkles, but then, my face is cushioned from carrying a few extra pounds. I look, I suppose, like any other harried mid-forties mum. Verdict—it will have to do.

I trudge back downstairs. Flo is up, surprisingly, curled on the sofa in the living room, with a cup of tea and a book. The latest Stephen King, from the looks of it.

"So, how do I look?"

She glances up. "Worn out."

"Thanks. Aside from that?"

I've gone for jeans, black shirt and collar. Just to let people know who I am but also that I'm off duty.

"I'm not sure about the black."

"I'm saving the neon and fishnets."

"For when?"

"Christmas Eve?"

"Break them in gently."

"That's the plan."

She smiles. "You look great, Mum."

"Thanks." I hesitate. "What about you?"

"What about me?"

"Are you okay?"

"I'm fine."

"Really?"

"Could we not do this again, Mum? **No,** I don't hate you. **Yes,** I'm pissed off about leaving Nottingham. But it's only temporary, right? Like you say—it is what it is."

"Sometimes, you're too grown up for your own good."

"One of us has to be."

I want to go and wrap my arms around her and hug her tight. But she's got her nose buried back in her book.

"Are you coming this morning?"

"Do I have to?"

"Up to you."

"Actually, I thought I might go and have a look around the graveyard. Take some photos."

"Okay. Have fun."

I try to quell the small pang of disappointment. **Of course** she doesn't want to come and listen to a dry, dusty service in a small, fusty chapel. She's fifteen. And I don't believe you should force your beliefs upon your children.

My mum tried. I remember being dragged along to services when I was small, fidgeting and itching in my best, often-washed dress. The pews were hard, the chapel cold and the priest in his black robes made me cry. Later, religion became one of Mum's crutches, along with gin and the voices in her head. It had the opposite effect on me. I escaped as soon as I had the chance.

Belief should be a conscious choice, not something you're brainwashed into when you're too young to understand or question it. Faith isn't something you pass down like an heirloom. It's not tangible or absolute. Not even for a priest. It's something you have to keep working at, like marriage or children.

You have wobbles. Naturally. Bad things happen. Things that make you question whether there **is** a God and, if there is, why he's such a bastard. But the truth is, bad things do not happen **because** of God. He is not sitting in his heavenly control room, thinking of ways to "test" our faith, like some celestial Ed Harris in **The Truman Show**.

Bad things happen because life is a series of random, unpredictable events. We'll make mistakes along the way. But God is forgiving. At least, I hope he is.

I grab my hoodie off the back of a kitchen chair and stick my head back into the living room. "Right. I'd better go."

"Mum?"

"Yes?"

"What are you going to do about that case?"

I really don't know. It's shaken me more than I like to admit. Certainly, more than I can admit to Flo. **Where has it come from? Who could have left it? And why?**

"I'm not sure. Maybe I'll have a word with Aaron about it."

She pulls a face. "He gives me the creeps."

I want to tell her not to be so harsh but, actually, he gives me the creeps too. I'm not quite sure why. You meet a fair few oddballs and loners in my line of work. But there's something about Aaron. Something that invokes feelings I'd rather forget.

"Let's talk about it later, okay?"

I shrug my arms into the hoodie.

"Okay—and Mum?"

"What?"

"You might want to wear a different hoodie. That one stinks of smoke."

SEVEN

Aaron is standing at the back of the chapel talking to a plump, curly-haired vicar when I walk in. It's half past nine and the first worshippers haven't arrived yet.

For some reason, perhaps the way they both turn quickly, I immediately get the impression they are talking about me. Maybe paranoid. Maybe not. And why wouldn't they be talking about me? I'm the newbie. But it makes me uncomfortable. I force a smile.

"Hello. Not interrupting, am I?"

The curly-haired vicar beams. "Reverend Brooks. I'm Reverend Rushton—Brian. We finally meet in person!"

He holds out a pudgy hand. He's a short, stout man with mottled, corned-beef-colored skin that speaks of a fondness for the fun things in life. His eyes are bright and mobile, dancing with mischief.

Were it not for the clerical collar, I'd have put him down as a pub landlord or perhaps Friar Tuck.

"We—and especially me—are so glad to have you here at last."

I shake his hand. "Thanks."

"So, how are you settling in? Or too soon to say?"

"Good, although it always takes a while to adjust. You know how it is."

"Actually, no. I've been at Warblers Green since I was a curate. Almost thirty years now. Very lazy, I know. But I love this parish and, of course"—he leans in conspiratorially—"there's a rather good pub next door."

He chortles, his laugh low, dirty and contagious.

"Can't fault you on that one."

"It must be quite a change from Nottingham."

"It's certainly that."

"Try and bear with us poor yokels. We're not all bad once you get to know us. And we haven't burned any newcomers in a wicker man recently. Well, not since Solstice."

He chortles again, face turning even redder. He takes a handkerchief out of his pocket and dabs at his brow.

Aaron clears his throat. "The theme of today's service is new friends and beginnings," he says in a funereal drone that couldn't sound less friendly. "Reverend Rushton thought it appropriate."

"No pressure on you to do or say anything," Rushton adds. "We'll do all that officially later. But it's good you're here." He winks. "News of your arrival has spread. Everyone is keen to see the new lady vicar."

I tense. "Great."

"Well, we'd better get ourselves ready then." Rushton stuffs the handkerchief back in his pocket and claps his hands together. "Our audience will be arriving soon!"

Aaron moves toward the altar. I sit down on a pew near the front.

"Oh." Rushton half turns in a way that's a little too casual. "Aaron tells me that you met Simon Harper and his daughter yesterday."

So **that's** what they were talking about.

"Yes. It was quite an introduction."

He pauses, choosing his next words carefully.

"The Harper family have lived in the area for generations. Their ancestry goes all the way back to the Sussex Martyrs . . . I don't know whether you've heard of the martyrs?"

"The Protestants who were killed during the reign of Mary I."

He beams. "Very good."

"I looked it up online."

"Ah, well, you'll hear a lot about them in this area. Simon Harper's ancestors were among the martyrs burned at the stake. There's a monument to them in the graveyard."

"We saw it. Someone had left Burning Girls all around it."

His bushy eyebrows rise. "Burning Girls? You really **have** done your research. Some people find them a bit macabre, but we're very proud of our burnt martyrs here in Sussex!" He chortles again. Then his face grows more serious. "Anyway, as I was saying, the Harpers are what you might call 'stalwarts of the community.' Very well respected here. They've done a lot for the village and the church over the years."

"In what way?"

"Donations, fundraising. Their business employs a lot of locals."

Money, I think. **What it always comes down to.**

"I was thinking of calling around to see them," I say. "Check Poppy is okay."

"Well, it couldn't hurt to acquaint yourself with the Harpers." He eyes me shrewdly. "And anything else you want to ask me about, anything at all, I'd be happy to help."

I think about the leather case sitting on the table in the kitchen. The strange card. Does Rushton know something? Perhaps. But I'm not sure now is the time to mention it.

"Thank you." I smile. "If I think of anything, I'll be sure to do that."

The service passes quickly. The church is almost half full, which is probably just curiosity but still a sight I'm unused to. Even in my previous church, which was well attended by city standards, I was lucky to see a quarter of the pews filled. And not all of the congregation here are elderly. I spot a dark-haired man in his forties sitting alone at the end of a row and a few families, although not the Harpers, so obviously their support is limited to the financial kind.

Throughout the service I can feel eyes upon me. I tell myself it's understandable. I'm new. I'm a woman. They're seeing the dog collar, not me.

Rushton is a warm, ebullient speaker. Humorous in just the right places and not too heavy on biblical text. That may sound odd, but people don't come to church to hear from the Bible. For a start, it was written thousands of years ago. It's a little dry. The best vicars translate the Bible in a way that reflects the lives and concerns of their congregation. Rushton has it spot on. If I wasn't so aware of being watched, I'd have taken notes.

Although I've been a practicing vicar for over fifteen years, I still feel like I'm learning. Perhaps, as a woman, I'm conscious of how much harder it is to be taken seriously. Or perhaps all adults feel like that at times. Like we're just playing at being grown-up, but inside we're still children, shuffling around in oversized clothes, wishing someone would tell us that monsters don't exist.

Rushton keeps the service short and sweet. Soon, the congregation starts to file out. Rushton stands at the chapel entrance, shaking hands and making small talk. I hang back, not wanting to intrude. A few people ask how I'm settling in. Others remark how nice it is to have a fresh face at the church. Some markedly ignore me. That's fine too. Finally, the last fluffy white head totters past and I breathe a sigh of relief. First public display over. Rushton pulls out his car keys.

"Right, got to get to Warblers Green by eleven thirty, so I'll catch you tomorrow."

"Tomorrow?"

"Parish meeting. Nine a.m., here at the chapel. Just to run through all the boring administrative stuff."

"Oh, of course."

I must have forgotten. Or maybe no one mentioned it. The whole relocation has been so swift, almost suspiciously so, like Durkin couldn't wait to get rid of me.

"Maybe we can catch up less formally at some point too, over a coffee or, better still, a pint?" Rushton continues.

"Sounds good."

"Excellent. I've got your number. I'll Whats App you."

He grabs my hand again and pumps it vigorously. "I'm sure you'll fit in here very well."

I smile. "I already feel at home."

He trots down to his bright yellow Fiat. I wave him off and walk back into the chapel. Aaron has collected the prayer books and disappeared back into the office. I'm not quite sure what Aaron's skill sets are, but silently disappearing and reappearing have got to be up there.

I stand there for a moment, just taking in the chapel. There's always a feeling once the congregation have left, like a slow exhalation of breath before a well-deserved rest. The presence of all those souls leaves an echo behind.

Except the chapel isn't empty. Not quite. There's a figure sitting in a pew at the front. I thought everyone had gone and wonder why Aaron hasn't moved them on. Not that God has a kicking-out time, but very few churches can afford to leave their doors open all day. In the inner city this would be an invitation for drunks, drug addicts and prostitutes. Here, I imagine it's more likely to be foxes, bats and rabbits.

I walk slowly down the aisle toward the figure. Barely more than a shadow in the dim light.

"Excuse me?"

The figure doesn't turn. It's small, no more than a child, but no one would forget to take their child home with them, would they?

"Are you okay?"

The figure still doesn't turn. And now I realize that I can smell something. Faint but unmistakable. Smoke. Burning.

"Reverend?"

I jump and spin around, squinting against the bright shaft of sunlight from the door. Aaron stands behind me. Again.

"Je—Could you **stop** doing that?"

"Doing what?"

"Sorry. Never mind. Who's the child?"

"What child?"

"The—" I turn to point out the figure in the front pew.

I blink. The pew is empty, except for a black coat slung over the back, left behind by one of the parishioners. The hood is sticking up and, in the dim lighting, if you squinted, you might just mistake it for a person.

Aaron does something odd with his lips. It takes me a moment to realize that he is smiling.

"I believe that's Mrs. Hartman's coat. She's always forgetting it. I'll drop it off to her later."

He walks over, picks the coat up and slings it over his arm. I feel my cheeks start to color.

"Right. Thanks. Sorry. It looked just like . . ." I trail off. I'm sounding stupid. I need to regain some authority. "Why don't I drop the coat off to Mrs. Hartman?"

He frowns. "Well, she lives all the way down Peabody Lane, out near Harper's Farm."

My ears prick up. I hold out my hand. "That's no problem at all."

EIGHT

Joan Hartman lives in a quaint whitewashed cottage down a narrow country track just wide enough to fit a car. Luckily, the only traffic I meet coming the other way is a family of pheasants who glare at the car with bright orange eyes before waddling off into the undergrowth.

"Wings. God gave you wings!" I mutter.

I pull up outside the cottage and climb out of my car, clutching Joan's coat. The door is around the side. I push open the gate and walk along a path fringed by lupins and hollyhocks. Usually, with elderly parishioners, it takes at least three hefty knocks to summon them to the door. To my surprise, I've only just raised my hand when the door swings open.

Joan Hartman squints up at me through eyes cloudy with cataracts; five foot nothing, with a dusting of floury-white hair, wearing a purple dress and leaning heavily on a cane.

"Hello," I say, thinking I'll probably need to refresh her memory. "I'm—"

"I know," she says. "I hoped you'd come."

She turns and trots back into the cottage.

That seems to be my invitation to enter. I follow her, pulling the door shut behind me.

It's dark and welcomingly cool inside. The windows are small and leaded, the walls thick stone. The front door leads straight into a kitchen that's so low-beamed my head brushes the warped wood. There are quarry tiles on the floor, an old range and a perfunctory cat sleeping in a tattered basket.

Joan shuffles through the kitchen and down a step into the living room. This is also low-beamed, and long, stretching the entire width of the back of the house, with French doors leading out to the garden. A huge bookcase takes up all of one wall, its shelves packed tightly with battered spines. The only other furniture is a sagging sofa and a high-backed chair skirting a large coffee table. A bottle of sherry stands on the coffee table with two glasses. Two.

I hoped you'd come.

Joan eases herself down into the high-backed chair. I stand awkwardly, still clutching the coat.

"I'm sorry to bother you, but you left this at the church."

"Thank you, dear. Just pop it down anywhere.

Would you mind pouring me a sherry? Help your-self to one too."

"That's very kind, but I'm driving."

I pour Joan a large sherry and hand it to her.

"Sit," she says, gesturing at the sagging sofa.

I look at the squishy velour. I'm pretty sure, if I sit, I may never get up again. Still, I lower myself down, knees shooting up to my chin.

Joan sips her sherry. "So, how are you finding it here?"

"Oh. Fine. Everyone has been very welcoming."

"You came from Nottingham?"

"That's right."

"Must be quite a change?"

The cataracts can't dull the inquisitiveness in her eyes. I change my mind about the sherry. I lean forward—with some difficulty—and pour a small measure.

"I'm sure I'll get used to it."

"Did they tell you about Reverend Fletcher?"

"Yes. It's very sad."

"He was a friend of mine."

"Then I'm sorry for your loss."

She nods. "How do you like the chapel?"

I hesitate. "It's very different from my previous church."

"It has a lot of history."

"Most old churches do."

"You've heard of the Sussex Martyrs?"

"I've read about them."

Undeterred, she continues: "Six Protestant martyrs, men and women, were rounded up and burned at the stake. Two young girls—Abigail and Maggie—took refuge in the chapel. But someone betrayed them. They were caught and tortured, before being killed, right outside."

"That is some history."

"Have you seen the twig dolls by the memorial?"

"Yes. People make them to commemorate the martyrs."

Her eyes gleam. "Not quite. The story goes that the ghosts of Abigail and Maggie haunt the chapel, appearing to those in trouble. If you see the burning girls, something bad will befall you. That's why the villagers originally made the dolls. They believed they could ward off the girls' vengeful spirits."

I shift uncomfortably in the squishy seat. It's making the small of my back sweat.

"Well, every church needs a good ghost story."

"You don't believe in ghosts?"

I remember the figure I thought I saw. The smell of burning.

Just a coat. Just my imagination.

I shake my head firmly. "No. And I've spent a lot of time in graveyards."

Another low chuckle. "Reverend Fletcher was fascinated by the story. He started to research the history of the village. That's how he became interested in the other girls."

"Other girls?"

"The ones who went missing."

"I'm sorry?" I stare at her, a little thrown by the barrage of questions and sudden changes in conversational direction.

"Merry and Joy," she continues. "Fifteen years old. Best friends. Disappeared without a trace, thirty years ago. The police decided they ran away. Others weren't so sure, but they were never found, so nothing could be proved."

Sweat is trickling down to my backside. "I don't seem to remember the case."

She cocks her head to one side, like a bird. "Well, you would have been young yourself. And there wasn't twenty-four-hour news like there is now, no social media." She smiles sadly. "People forget."

"But not you?"

"No. In fact, I'm probably one of the last who does remember. Joy's mother, Doreen, suffers from dementia. And Merry's mother and brother left the village. Almost a year to the day after Merry disappeared. Just went. Didn't take a thing with them."

"Well, grief can make people do strange things."

I put down my sherry glass. It's empty. Time to make my excuses.

"Thank you so much for the drink, Joan, but I should really get back for my daughter."

I start to extract myself from the sofa.

"Don't you want to know about Reverend Fletcher?"

"Maybe another—"

"He thought he knew what had happened to Merry and Joy."

I freeze, half bent over. "Really? What?"

"He wouldn't tell me. But whatever it was, it troubled him deeply."

"You think that's why he committed suicide?"

"No." Her milky eyes glint and I understand two things—Joan did not leave her coat in the chapel by mistake. And I am in more trouble than I thought.

"I think that's why he was killed."

NINE

Flo loads new film into her camera. The weight of the heavy Nikon feels reassuring in her hands. Like a shield. She'll need a new darkroom here. Mum mentioned there was a cellar, or maybe the outhouse around the back of the cottage. She'll check them both out later.

In their old house, the darkroom had been her refuge. Flo always felt calm and content when she was developing her photos. It was her space, even more so than her bedroom, which Mum would still enter sometimes with only the briefest of bloody knocks.

Her mum knew never to enter the darkroom without permission in case she ruined Flo's photos. The **"Do Not Enter"** sign slung on the door actually seemed to mean something. Sometimes, when Flo wanted to be alone, she would just stick the sign on the door and sit in the darkness, not developing. Just taking time.

She's never told her mum this. There are plenty of things she hasn't told her mum, like the time she smoked weed at Craig Heron's house or the time she got wasted and let Leon finger her in the bathroom at a party, which hadn't been much fun, in all honesty (for either of them) but at least meant they could both boast about it and not feel like total virgins. Flo is pretty sure Leon is gay, but she's been happy to go along with it until he is ready to come out.

She doesn't keep this stuff secret because her mum is a vicar. She keeps it secret because she's a **mum** and, however much Flo loves her and however close they are, there are some things you just can't share with your mum.

The vicar stuff is just a job. Same as any job, in Flo's book. Like being a social worker or a doctor. Mum talks to people about their problems. She organizes youth groups and school fetes and coffee mornings and goes to meetings with people she doesn't really like. The only difference is that she wears a different type of uniform.

But then, everyone wears uniforms, Flo thinks. Even in school, and **despite** the official uniform, the type of bag you carry, your jacket or shoes define who you are. Rich or poor. Cool or uncool.

Flo is glad she has always been an outlier (that's what her friend Kayleigh christened them). One of the kids who doesn't belong to any particular group. Not popular but not really picked on either. Mostly, just invisible.

Of course, she's had **some** shit because of her mum's job, but she usually just shrugged it off and the bullies soon got bored. The best defense against bullies is to make yourself uninteresting.

But then there had been the little girl. Ruby. Mum and the church had been splashed all over the papers. That's when things had taken a turn for the worse. There had been graffiti on their front door, the windows in the church were smashed and someone even came to the house, calling Mum really vile names.

Flo never told her mum about the names **she** had been called at school or the messages she had received on Snapchat. She didn't want to worry her more. So, Flo keeps her secrets. She's pretty sure Mum keeps hers too.

As Flo has gotten older, she's noticed stuff. Like how Mum never talks about her family. She's always said Flo's grandparents are dead. But there are no photos of them. Nor any of Mum when she was younger. And Mum doesn't have any social media accounts. Not even Facebook.

"Real friends are more important than virtual followers," she always says. **"One good friend is worth a dozen hangers-on."**

Flo gets that. She's not one for measuring her life in likes on Insta. She's always been happier on the outside, looking in. Perhaps another reason why she likes photography. But sometimes, she can't help wondering if there's something else. Something Mum is hiding from her. Or hiding **from.** Occasionally, Flo has thought about asking, prodding a little. But there's never been a right time. And now, with the move and everything, it's definitely not the right time.

Film loaded, Flo slings the camera around her neck and saunters out of the house. She gazes around the graveyard. The uneven headstones run almost up to their front door, which is pretty cool. The church in Nottingham didn't have a graveyard. It was bang in the center of the city, surrounded by narrow terraced streets, with just a tiny area of grass outside, usually covered in dog shit and used needles; the occasional drunk sleeping it off on the church's doorstep.

The chapel is more traditional, except it isn't. It's not like the ones on TV, at least not British TV. It looks like something out of a painting. What was that one with the old woman and a man holding a pitchfork? She can't remember. But that's what it looks like, anyway. And it's a dump, no argument. But it's also kind of spooky and weird. It should make for some good photos, she thinks, especially in black and white. If she tints them, she can make it look really Gothic.

She wanders between the headstones, the overgrown grass brushing her legs. Most are so old the inscriptions have worn away. But there are a few where she can just make out the names and dates. People had short lives back then. So much hardship and disease. Most were lucky to hit their forties.

She snaps a few of the inscriptions. Then she walks around to the back of the chapel. The land slopes up here and there are more graves, some a little newer and better kept, but the grass is still overgrown, thick with dandelions and buttercups. She takes a few shots of the back of the chapel. The sun is high, and the building is mostly coming out in silhouette.

She wipes an arm across her forehead. The last two weeks have been humid and close. She didn't sleep well last night. She misses her old room; it might have been a bit damp, but it had been big, and she'd got it how she liked it with posters of her favorite bands, films and TV shows on the walls.

Her room here is small and stuffy. The tiny window sticks halfway, hardly letting in any air. Worst of all, it has a sloping roof, which she keeps forgetting and bashing her head on. Still, as her mum is fond of saying: "It is what it is."

And what it is, she thinks, is shit.

She swishes her way back through the long grass down to the rear of the cottage. The outhouse is a ramshackle brick building tacked on to the kitchen, probably once an outside toilet. Mum said she thought it had electricity but, looking at it now, Flo is doubtful. She pushes open the rotting wooden door. The smell of urine assaults her nostrils, swiftly followed by a shout of:

"**Shit!**"

She blinks in the gloom. A lanky figure is hastily doing up his fly. Their eyes meet. He turns and tries to shove past her. But years of self-defense classes (which her mum insisted she take from the age of seven) have taught Flo to react quickly. And not to bother with the fancy stuff. She grabs his shoulders, knees him in the crotch and shoves him hard.

He hits the ground outside and rolls over, clutching his groin.

"Owww. My balls."

Flo folds her arms and stares down at him.

"Who the fuck are **you** and what are you doing, pissing in our outhouse?"

TEN

I leave Miss Marple sipping her sherry, feeling even more out of sorts than when I set out this morning.

Of course it's nonsense. Just the meanderings of a mind with too much time to fill. I enjoy **Midsomer Murders** as much as anyone but, in reality, people do not go around knocking off village vicars because "they know too much."

Real life isn't like that. I know from pastoral visits to prison that real crimes aren't clever or complicated. They're opportunistic and poorly thought out. Murderers very rarely "get away with it" and, if they do, it's usually because of luck rather than planning. Killing someone is almost always a desperate act, with no thought of the consequences. For your life, or your soul.

I accelerate up to thirty. I'm so preoccupied I almost drive straight past the wooden sign for Harper's Farm.

"Bugger."

I brake hard, reverse and pull on to a long gravel track. It winds up between fields to a handsome red-brick, slate-roofed farmhouse perched at the top of a hill. The house has been extended and modernized, with a huge double-height window and large conservatory offering views across the countryside all the way to the Downs. It's breathtaking.

I park up next to a battered truck and Simon Harper's Range Rover and climb out of the car. My nostrils are immediately assaulted by the smell of manure and something slightly rotten. A herd of brown cows graze in one field and sheep are dotted around another.

Close by, another area has been turned into a paddock for two glossy brown horses. To the left of the farm, along a muddy track, I can see more barns and a modern warehouse-type building which, I presume, is the slaughterhouse.

I'm not sentimental about animals. I abhor cruelty, but I eat meat and I understand that it doesn't just drop down from heaven, or Tesco. An animal has to die and the best we can do is ensure the animal has a good life and a swift, painless death. In many ways, the fact that the slaughterhouse is on site is good. But the thought of a little girl stumbling inside still makes me feel uncomfortable. And **how** exactly did she just "stumble" inside? I think again about Poppy's blank stare, Simon's aggressive bluster. Embarrassment? Or guilt?

I crunch across gravel to the farmhouse's front door. This is exactly the type of thing Bishop Durkin would advise me against doing. Poking my nose in. Making a nuisance of myself. On the other hand, this is why I became a priest. To protect the innocent. There are things that people will tell a priest that they won't confess to the police, or even a social worker. Also, a white collar gives you access that other people don't get. It's almost as good as a warrant card.

I raise my hand and knock briskly. I can hear voices and then the door swings open. A willowy teenage girl leans against the doorframe, nonchalant in cropped jeans and a vest top, blonde hair pulled carelessly back into a loose ponytail.

She has an older sister, Rosie.

"Yes?"

"Hello, I'm Jack Brooks—the new priest in charge at Chapel Croft."

She continues to regard me silently.

"There was an incident with your sister yesterday. I just thought I'd drop by and check she's okay."

She sighs, steps back from the door and calls out: "Mu-um?"

"What is it?" A female voice echoes down the stairs.

"Vicar. About Poppy."

"Tell her I'm just coming."

She flashes me a quick, insincere smile. "She's just coming." And then she turns on one pedicured foot and slinks off back down the hall, no invite in, nothing. Fine. I step inside.

The hall is huge and the massive window bathes the room in light. A wooden staircase winds around to a balconied landing on the first floor. I guess the business must be doing well.

"Hello?"

Another willowy blonde descends the staircase. For a moment, I wonder if there's a third sister. As the figure gets closer, I reprise my opinion. The woman is older and, despite what looks like some subtle cosmetic work, you can never really defeat the aging process. She's probably in her forties, like me. Still, the resemblance to her elder daughter is startling.

"Hi," I say. "I'm Reverend Brooks. Jack."

The woman glides across the quarry floor. I feel immediately lumpen and scruffy in her presence.

"Emma Harper. Nice to meet you. I heard all about the little misunderstanding yesterday." She smiles. "I'm so sorry you got caught up in it."

"No problem. I was happy to help. I just wanted to see if Poppy is okay."

"Of course, she's fine. Come on through. I'm sure she'd like to say hello. Coffee?"

"Thanks," I say. "That would be lovely."

Emma is gracious and nice . . . and yet? Is she a little **too** gracious and nice? Or am I just judging her because of her husband?

I follow her through to the kitchen, which is

straight out of **Grand Designs**. Huge island, granite worktops, shiny appliances. The whole caboodle. It blends into the glass conservatory which houses a long table and benches, comfy sofas and a hanging egg chair.

I feel a stab of envy. I'll never live somewhere like this. I'll probably never even own my own home. If I'm lucky, the Church will let me continue to live in the house I end up in, in exchange for occasional help with services and administration. If I'm unlucky, I'll be out on my ear, forced into the rental market with no savings or equity.

Such is the life of a vicar. Of course, we live in our accommodation rent and mortgage free. If you're savvy, you can save a modest deposit. But vicars earn around half the average wage in the UK and, with a teenage daughter, money does not go far. At present, my savings might buy me a mobile home near a dump.

"You have a beautiful home," I say.

"Oh." Emma glances around as if noticing it for the first time. "Yes, thank you."

She walks over to a sleek-looking coffee machine that probably cost more than my car. The green-eyed monster grumbles.

"Cappuccino, latte, espresso?"

I fight the urge to say, **Nescafé**.

"Just black, thanks. No sugar."

"No problem."

As the coffee machine gurgles, I walk across to

the trifold doors and peer out. Part of the field has been fenced off into a garden area with a wooden climbing frame, slide and a trampoline, upon which Poppy is bouncing. Up, down, up, down, hair flying. Yet her face, when she turns, is blank. No smile or expression of pleasure. The sight is slightly disconcerting.

"She'll do that for hours." Emma pads over and hands me a mug of coffee.

"She must enjoy it."

"It's hard to say. Often with Poppy, it's hard to say how she feels about things." She turns to me. "Do you have children, Reverend?"

"Just the one. Florence, Flo—she's fifteen."

"Ah, the same age as my older daughter, Rosie. Is Florence going to Warblers Green Community College?"

"Yes."

"Oh, good. We should get them together."

"That would be nice."

I can't see the pair getting on. But you never know.

"So, is your husband a vicar too?"

"He was." I swallow. "He died when Flo was very young."

"Oh, I'm so sorry."

"Thank you."

"You've brought Flo up all on your own? That must have been tough."

"Being a parent is tough full stop."

"Tell me about it. If I'd known what hard work Poppy would be compared to Rosie, I might have stuck at one—" She catches herself. "Not that I'd be without her. Shall we sit down?"

We walk to the table and perch on the benches. Stylish, but not very comfortable.

"How has Poppy been?" I say, steering the conversation back to the reason for my visit. "She seemed quite upset yesterday."

"Oh, well, yes. It was all very unfortunate."

"It must be difficult stopping the children getting attached to the animals."

"Yes. Simon showed Rosie the slaughterhouse when she was about Poppy's age."

"He did?"

"It's part of their heritage. Our livelihood. Rosie wasn't fazed. She's not like Poppy."

"She was looking after Poppy yesterday?"

"Yes, she's very good with her. But Poppy can be difficult. Poor Rosie was in pieces."

"I'm still a little puzzled as to how Poppy got covered in blood."

She smiles tightly. "There's a lot of blood in a slaughterhouse."

I get it. But it still doesn't really answer my question. I glance out of the window and see that the trampoline has been deserted. The kitchen door swings open and Poppy walks in.

"Hi, sweetheart," Emma says.

Poppy spots me sitting at the table.

"Hi, Poppy. D'you remember me, from yesterday?"

A nod.

"How are you?"

"I'm getting a hamster."

My eyebrows rise.

"Great."

"It was Simon's idea," Emma says. "But remember you have to clean it, Pops. Mummy isn't doing it."

"Nor Daddy," a deep voice booms from behind us.

I turn. Simon Harper stands in the doorway in a frayed jumper, stained jeans and heavy socks. He walks over to the kitchen, grabs a glass and fills it with cold water from the fridge. He doesn't seem surprised to see me, but then he's probably spotted my car outside. The sticker on the back—"**Vicars do it with reverence**"—is a bit of a giveaway. Not mine, I hasten to add. Like most things, I inherited the car from a predecessor.

"Reverend Brooks. Nice to see you again."

His tone suggests otherwise.

"I hope you don't mind me popping round— I just wanted to see how Poppy was."

"She's fine, aren't you, Pops?"

Poppy nods obediently. Her father's presence seems to have switched her back to mute.

He looks at Emma. "You should have called to let me know we had a visitor."

"Sorry, I thought you were busy."

"I could have found time."

"Right, well, I didn't think—"

"No. You didn't."

The words hang in the air, sharp with accusation. I glance between them, and then I stand before I say something someone in my position shouldn't.

"Emma, thank you for the coffee. It was nice to meet you. Good to see you again, Poppy."

"I'll see you out," Simon says.

"There's no need."

"I'd like to."

We walk out into the hall. As soon as we're out of earshot he says:

"You didn't need to come here, checking up on us."

"I wasn't."

He lowers his voice. "I know about you, Reverend Brooks."

I tense. "Really?"

"I know where you come from."

I try to keep my face composed but I can feel sweat dampening my underarms. "I see."

"And I'm sure you mean well, but you're not in Nottingham now. This is not some inner-city shit-hole where we go around abusing our kids. We're not like those people."

"**Those** people?"

"You know what I mean."

"No." I stare at him coldly. "Perhaps you'd like to elaborate?"

He scowls. "Just look after your flock and I'll look after mine, okay?"

He holds the door open and I walk stiffly out. It slams behind me. **What a twat.**

I walk over to my car, the afternoon heat heavy on my back. And then I stop. Two deep, jagged lines have been scored along the paintwork on the passenger side, forming an upside-down Christian cross. I stare at the occult symbol, the sweat cooling on my body. I'm pretty sure it wasn't there when I left this morning, although I didn't check. I look around. The driveway is empty. But I feel like I'm being watched. I glance up, squinting against the sun. Rosie leans out of an upstairs bedroom window. She smiles and waggles her fingers in a mocking wave.

Be Christian. Be Christian.

I smile back. Then I give her the finger, climb into my car and pull off in a spray of dirt.

ELEVEN

The boy is around her own age. Thin, dressed in skinny jeans, a hoodie with a skull on the back and Docs. His hair is dyed black and long. It falls over his face as he lies on the ground, squirming.

"I asked you a question."

"Look, I'm sorry. I just come up here some-times and—"

"And what?"

"I . . . like to look . . . and draw stuff."

"What sort of stuff?"

"Just stuff." He pulls a battered sketchbook out of his back pocket with some difficulty and hands it to her, his arm jerking. Flo takes it and flicks through. The pictures are mostly charcoal, graves and the church, but intermingled with odd graphic monsters and strange ghostly figures.

"These are really good."

"You think?"

"Yes." She snaps the book shut and hands it back to him. "You still shouldn't have been using our outhouse as a toilet."

"**You** live here now?"

"My mum's the new vicar."

"Look, I just really needed to, you know, **go**, and I don't like to . . ." He gestures toward the graves. His arm twitches and trembles even more violently. "It seems wrong to do it out here."

Flo regards him for a moment more, weighing him up. He seems genuine and she actually feels a little sorry for him, what with the odd, involuntary spasms. She holds out her hand. He takes it and she heaves him up.

"I'm Flo."

"W-Wrigley."

Even as he says it, his whole body convulses.

"Is that some kind of joke?"

"N-no, it's my surname. Lucas W-wrigley."

"Oh."

"Yeah. The irony, right? It's like I'm doing half of the bullies' work for them. 'Look, it's **wriggly** Wrigley.'"

"That sucks."

"That's bullies for you. None of them is going to win any points for imagination."

"True."

"It's called dystonia, by the way. The twitching and stuff. The doctors say it's neurological. Something wrong in my brain."

"They can't do anything for it?"

"Not really."

"That's rough."

"Yep." He glances at the camera around her neck. "You're a photographer?"

She shrugs. "I try. I was thinking of turning the outhouse into a darkroom."

"Cool."

"Yeah—that was before I realized it's being used as a toilet."

"Sorry."

She waves a hand. "I might look at the cellar instead."

"You just moved in?"

"Yesterday."

"What d'you think of it here?"

"Honestly?"

"Yeah."

"It's a dump."

"Welcome to the shit end of nowhere."

"You live in the village?"

"Yeah, over the other side, with my mum. You?"

"Just me and my mum too."

"So, are you going to Warblers Green Community College?"

"I guess so."

"Maybe I'll catch you in school then."

"Maybe."

"Okay. Cool."

Conversation momentarily exhausted, they

stand, looking at each other. His eyes are an odd silvery green, she notices. Almost feline. They'd be cool to photograph. She could really bring out the strange flecks. And then she wonders why she is thinking about his eyes so much.

"Right, well, see you."

"See you."

Wrigley starts to turn, then pauses and looks back. "You know, if you like taking photos, I could show you a really cool place?"

"Yeah?"

"There's this old, abandoned house, over the fields that way." He points with a wavering arm. "It's creepy as hell."

Flo hesitates. Wrigley is weird, but weird isn't necessarily bad. And, if it wasn't for the strange twitching, he'd actually be kind of cute.

"Okay."

"Are you around tomorrow?"

"Well, my diary is packed . . ."

"Oh."

"Kidding. I'm free. What time?"

"I dunno. Two?"

"Okay."

"There's an old tire swing in the field past the graveyard. I'll meet you there."

"Fine."

He grins at her from under his hair before loping jerkily away. **Wrigley**. Flo shakes her head.

Hopefully, she hasn't just agreed to meet the village's resident psycho.

She snaps a few photos, but she's losing enthusiasm. She starts to wind her way back down toward the chapel. Her foot catches on something and she almost goes flying. She just manages to regain her balance in time and stop her camera from smashing on to the headstone in front of her.

"Shit."

She looks back to see what tripped her. A toppled headstone, submerged in the undergrowth, half covered in moss, the inscription almost worn away. She raises her camera to take a photo and then frowns. It seems a bit blurry. She fiddles with the focus. Still not quite right. She turns to try and refocus the camera on something else in the distance and almost jumps out of her skin.

A young girl stands a few feet away.

She's naked. And on fire.

Orange flames flicker around her ankles and lick at her legs, blackening the skin and stretching up to her smooth, hairless pubis. That's how Flo knows it's a girl. It would be hard to tell otherwise.

Because she's missing both her arms and her head.

TWELVE

Damn. I accelerate along the narrow lanes, cursing Simon Harper, his family and myself.

Fair to say, my tenure here is not turning out to be the quiet idyll Durkin intended. In fact, things couldn't get much worse if I stood naked in the middle of the village and sacrificed a few chickens. Or pheasants. They seem intent on committing suicide beneath my wheels anyway.

Still, I should know from experience that things can **always** get worse.

I park outside the chapel, stomp up to the cottage and let myself in. I'm immediately seized by the quiet.

"Flo?"

No reply. I frown. She mentioned taking some photographs in the graveyard. I wonder if she's still outside, around the back. I'm just about to go and look when I hear a creak from upstairs.

"Flo?"

I climb up the staircase. Her bedroom door is open. She isn't in there. I try the bathroom door. Locked. I bang on it.

"Flo. Are you okay?"

No reply, but I can hear movement.

"Flo—talk to me."

"Wait!" Urgent, annoyed.

I wait. After a few more seconds there's the sound of the bolt being drawn across. I take this as my cue and gently push the door open.

"Quickly," Flo hisses, and I immediately understand why.

A flattened cardboard box has been used to obscure the bathroom's tiny window. Photographic equipment covers every available surface and most of the cracked-lino floor. The small room stinks of developing chemicals. Her battery-powered safelight is propped on top of the bathroom cabinet. The shower curtain has been shoved to one side and the rail is being used as a drying line. Wet photos are clipped to it with clothespins from the laundry basket. While I was out, Flo has turned the tiny bathroom into a makeshift darkroom.

I watch as she carefully takes a sheet of photographic paper out of the wash tray and hangs it on the shower rail.

"What are you doing, sweetheart?"

"What does it look like?"

"It looks like I'm out of luck if I need to pee."

"I have to get this film developed."

"Can't it wait?"

"No. I need to see the girl."

"What girl?"

"The girl in the graveyard." She adjusts a photograph on the clothespin and regards the row of black-and-white images.

She's made the graveyard, with its higgledy-piggledy headstones, look hauntingly beautiful. But I can't see a girl in any of the pictures.

"I don't see anyone."

"I **know**!" She turns in frustration. "But she was definitely there. She was on fire, and she had no head or arms."

I blink at her. "I'm sorry?"

She tilts her chin at me defiantly. "I get how it sounds."

"Right—"

"It sounds nuts, right?"

"I didn't say that." I pause. "You think you saw, what, some sort of ghost?"

A shrug. "I don't know what she was. She looked real. Then she was gone."

The shrug is too casual. She's trying to keep it together and not sound hysterical, but I know my daughter. She's scared. Whatever she saw, it's shaken her.

"Okay," I say gently. "Could there be another explanation?"

"I **know** what I saw, Mum. That's why I tried to take some photos—I knew no one would believe me."

"Well, what about a statue or some kind of—I don't know—weird trick of the light?"

I'm grasping now. Flo folds her arms and narrows her eyes.

"It was a girl, on fire, without a head or arms. That's some frigging trick of the light." She turns and squints back at the photos. "But why hasn't she shown up on film?"

"I've no idea."

But Joan's words suddenly come back to me.

The burning girls still haunt the chapel. If you see the burning girls, something bad will befall you.

I look around at the detritus littering the bathroom. "Look, why don't we go downstairs and come back to this later?"

She huffs dramatically. "Okay. Fine. I'm done, anyway."

She allows me to guide her out of the bathroom.

"Why were you so long?" she asks as we go downstairs.

"Parish visits."

"Who were you visiting?"

"Simon Harper."

"I thought you were supposed to be keeping your head down here?"

I feel a wince of guilt. "I am. Come on. I'll make us a late lunch."

"You've been shopping?"

Crap. With everything else, it totally slipped my mind. I am a terrible mum.

"I'm sorry, I forgot. Don't suppose you fancy pizza, for a change?"

"Works for me."

We walk into the living room. It's only two o'clock, but the sky has clouded over and it feels gloomy and dark. Through the window I can just see the tips of headstones amid the overgrown grass. We stand and stare out at the graveyard.

"D'you think she could be one of the girls you told me about?" Flo asks. "The ones who were killed for being martyrs."

I'm reluctant to feed this fixation but, on the other hand, she saw **something**: "Some villagers believe the girls haunt the chapel—but that's just folklore."

"But it's possible?"

I sigh. "It's possible."

She loops an arm around my waist and leans her head against my shoulder. **She'll be too tall to do this soon,** I think sadly. **Dear God, I know she has to grow up, but does it have to be yet? Can't I hold on to her, protect her, just a little bit longer?**

"Mum?"

"Yes."

"Is it better or worse that we both now believe that a burning, headless and armless girl is haunting the graveyard?"

I squeeze her shoulders, trying to batten down my disquiet. "Let's not dwell on that."

I do dwell on it, of course. More so than Flo, who is now snoring away heavily in her room, lanky teenage limbs tangled in her **Nightmare Before Christmas** duvet.

We cleaned up the makeshift darkroom. I told her I would investigate the cellar as an alternative tomorrow. The outhouse is no good, apparently. No electricity, not light-proof.

In the evening we microwave leftover pizza and potato wedges and watch old comedy DVDs. **Black Books. Father Ted.** I follow Flo up to bed at just past midnight.

As always, before I settle down under the covers, I sit, cross-legged, and I pray. I'm not sure if God hears me. In a way, I hope he's got better things to do than listen to my ramblings. But I get comfort from our nightly chats. They're an outlet for my fears, my worries and my joys. They calm my soul and clear my mind. They remind me who I am and why I became a priest.

Tonight, I struggle. I can't seem to find the words. My head feels muddy and disorganized. As if coming here has shaken loose all the bits that I normally keep carefully in place and I don't know where anything is anymore.

I mumble some perfunctory "thank yous" and praise then turn off my light and lie on my side. But, predictably, I can't sleep. It's too hot and stuffy in the small room. And I've never been a good sleeper. I don't like the dark. I don't like the silence. Mostly, I don't like time alone with my thoughts. All the prayers in my repertoire cannot quite stop the things that prey upon my mind from crawling out of their dark corners, looking to feast.

I stare up at the lumpy ceiling, willing my eyelids to droop, for sleep to start to pull me down into oblivion, but my mind stubbornly resists.

She was on fire, and she had no head or arms.

If you see the burning girls, something bad will befall you.

Folklore, urban legend. Rubbish. But I still feel a wedge of discomfort sit heavily in my stomach.

Flo isn't prone to flights of fancy. She is pragmatic, sensible, reasoned. She wouldn't make something like this up. So, what's the alternative? Some kind of apparition?

As a vicar, I believe in a continued existence after death. But ghosts? Physical entities that remain tied to this earth, seeking revenge or resolution? No. I've never seen anything that could convince me of that. More to the point, I don't **want** to see anything to convince me of that. I would rather keep those that haunt me metaphorical, rather than physical.

I sit up, flick on the bedside light and swing my legs out of bed. The wooden floor feels cold and rough beneath my feet. **Rugs,** I think, mentally adding another expense to the list of "things to make the cottage vaguely comfortable."

I shove my feet into my threadbare slippers and pad out on to the landing. I switch on the hall light and make my way downstairs.

In the kitchen, I yank open a drawer and fumble under the tea towel for my rolling tin and papers. My fingers scrabble around but come up empty. I curse under my breath. **Flo**.

Fortunately, I have a contingency plan. I duck into the living room. Most of my books are still in boxes, but I've taken a few out to stick on the battered bookcase, including a thick leather-bound Bible. It looks like a church relic, but I actually picked it up from a rummage sale. Instead of containing the word of God, it's hollow. A good hiding place for a flask, if you are so inclined or, in my case, a spare rolling tin, a packet of Rizlas and a lighter.

I walk back into the kitchen, roll a cigarette and open the door. The night air is heavy and thick with the familiar cloying smells of evening primrose, moonflower and jasmine. **Night flowers.** I remember the scent drifting through my bedroom window when I was a child.

I draw hard on the cigarette, banishing the memory, sucking in the nicotine, but it's doing little to soften the sharp edges of my anxiety. I'm too aware of the quiet, the dark, my clamoring thoughts.

The dark here is different than the city. There, it's softened by streetlights, the glow from shops, passing cars. This is true dark. The dark we lived with before fire and electricity. Hungry dark, full of hidden eyes. **Here lies evil,** I think, and then wonder where that came from. My brain is really going overboard tonight.

I raise the cigarette to my lips . . . and pause. There's a light in the chapel.

What the—

It flickers from an upper window. Could it be a reflection of car headlights? No, this window faces the cottage, not the road. And there it is again. A small light bobbing about upstairs. A faulty bulb? Dodgy wiring? Or an intruder?

I stare at the light, torn. Then I stub out my cigarette, walk back into the cottage and open the cupboard under the sink. I remember seeing a flashlight in here yesterday. Chances are, it's out of batteries, but there's no way I'm going out there in the pitch black with just my phone light. I switch on the flashlight. A sturdy beam of light shoots out.

I grab my keys and walk along the narrow path from the cottage to the chapel, flashlight trained in front of me. A small inner voice tuts that this is exactly the sort of thing people in horror films do.

Stupid people who inevitably die in gruesome ways before the titles kick in. I try to ignore that voice.

I reach the door to the chapel. I locked it last night. I remember twisting the heavy key. It had stuck, and I'd had to lean on it with all my weight to get it to turn.

Now, the door is ajar.

I hesitate, then push it open further. I step inside. The flashlight illuminates a small triangular section of the church. Darkness presses in on either side. Where are the light switches? I swivel to my right and feel around. And now the darkness is behind me. Where are the bloody switches? My fingers brush plastic.

The lights hum and stutter into life. The bulbs are dim and jaundiced, coated in dust and cobwebs. They don't do an awful lot to alleviate the gloom. The church looks empty. But that's the problem with churches. They're full of nooks and crannies where you can crouch and hide.

"Hello? Anyone here?"

No reply, surprisingly. I grip the flashlight tighter. It's sturdy enough to make a half-decent weapon. In my other hand, I hold the hefty key. I wedge it between my fingers, sharp edge poking out. Just like I used to do in the city at night.

I spotted the light upstairs, so I climb the steps at the side of the chapel to the upper balcony. It's even darker up here. Only two lights provide illumination. And there's that strange smell again. Smoky, charred. I swing the flashlight around. Nothing but the rows of wooden pews. I move along them, poking the flashlight into the dark areas in between. But no one is hiding.

At the far end of the balcony, there's a small, narrow door. A storeroom, I guess. I walk forward, clutching the key, flashlight held out in front of me. I reach the door and yank it wide open. A pile of pew cushions topples out.

I leap back, heart jumping. And then I allow myself a chuckle of relief. **Just pew cushions, Michael**.

I peer back into the cupboard. It's tiny, jammed with more cushions and prayer books; no room for anyone to hide in there. I bend and pick up the cushions, realizing now that they are blackened and scorched, like they've been set alight. Odd, but it might explain the smoky smell. I shove them back inside and shut the door. As I do, I hear a noise from below me. A creak, like the chapel door opening. My heart catapults into my mouth. I scurry back along the pews and down the steps, being careful not to twist my ankle.

At the bottom, I swing the flashlight around the nave. I can't see anyone. I pause and swing it back, toward the altar. The reading lamp is on. I'm sure it wasn't before.

I walk down the aisle toward it. There's something on top of the altar. A Bible. Small and blue. The type given to children at Sunday School.

It's been left open and a passage highlighted: **2 Corinthians 11:13–15.**

> **For such are false apostles, deceitful workers, transforming themselves into apostles of Christ. And no wonder! For Satan himself transforms himself into an angel of light. Therefore, it is no great thing if his ministers also transform themselves into ministers of righteousness, whose end will be according to their works.**

I stare at the words, feeling a coldness wash over me. And then I pick up the Bible. One corner is blackened, as if by a flame. I flick back to the very first page. When I attended Sunday School, we were made to write our names on the inside cover of our Bible. And sure enough, there's a name. Written in blue ink, now almost entirely faded away. I trace my fingers over the ghostly letters:

Merry J. L.

They lay in the long grass behind the house. Hidden in the swaying fronds. Bible study was finished. They had a few moments to themselves before they had to head home.

Merry fumbled in her jeans and pulled out a crumpled cigarette and a Bic lighter. "Want to share?"

"I can't. The reverend is coming around for tea."

"Why?"

"Mum wants me to take extra Bible lessons."

"Extra? With old Fudface?"

"No. The new one. Have you seen him?"

Merry shrugged. "Yeah."

"He looks a bit like Christian Slater."

"Still a God-botherer."

"You shouldn't say that."

"Why?"

"God might hear you."

"There is no God."

"D'you want to go to hell?"

"You sound like my mum."

Joy leaned over and gently touched the bruise around her friend's eye.

"Does it hurt?"

"Yes. Get off."

"Do you hate her?"

"Sometimes. Sometimes I wish she was dead. Mostly, I just wish she was different."

They lay in silence for a while. Then Joy stood. "I have to go. I'll call you later?"

"Okay."

Merry sat up and watched her friend skip off through the grass. She glanced back at the house. She could hear her mum screaming inside. She picked up the Bible and lighter. She held the flame near the corner, watching the leather blacken. Then, before it could catch, she threw the Bible back on to the grass, lay down and lit the cigarette.

I don't care if I go to hell, **she thought.** It can't be worse than this.

THIRTEEN

I fasten my shirt and adjust the white collar. I smooth my vestment. Then I walk from the vestibule and up to the altar. I stare out at the congregation. The worshippers sit, bent forward, heads bowed, faces in shadow.

"Welcome," I say, and one by one the figures raise their heads toward me.

I see my husband, Jonathon, first. Smiling. Always smiling. Even on his worst days. Even now, when his head is caved in on one side, hair matted with blood and brain matter. Next to him is Ruby. Of course. She stares up accusingly. Her face is bruised and swollen from where they beat her with their fists, boots and her own wooden toys. She holds a stuffed bunny. The one I found her with. She loved that bunny, except, as I watch, I realize that it's a real rabbit she's clutching. Eyes never leaving mine, she bends her head and bites a chunk from one of its ears.

I step back, heart thudding, and something brushes the top of my head. I look up. Reverend Fletcher hangs from the balcony above me, feet twitching in a macabre death dance.

"If you see the burning girls," he gasps between cracked and blackened lips, **"something bad will befall you."**

I bite back a scream. More faces peer up at me from the pews. Some, I recognize. Some, I barely remember. Two figures rise and begin to shuffle down the center of the aisle toward me. Halfway, they burst into flames. But still they keep coming.

I stumble backward. A cold hand falls on my shoulder. I understand my mistake. I smell his rancid breath and hear a voice . . .

"Mum. **MUM!**"

I flail, breaking the waters of sleep like a drowning woman breaking the surface of a dark and fetid lake.

"**Mum**. Wake up!"

I tear my eyes open and focus blearily on Flo, who is holding my shoulders and looking worried and angry.

"Jesus, you scared me."

"I . . . I—"

"You were having some kind of nightmare."

A dream. Just a dream. Awareness creeps in. I'm

curled on the sofa, in clothes that stink of sweat and cigarette smoke. I swing my legs around to get into a sitting position. Daylight is edging in through the curtains.

Flo sits back on her heels. "Mum?"

"I . . . erm . . . couldn't sleep. I came down for a cigarette and saw a light in the chapel. So, I went to take a look—

"You went out on your own in the middle of the night?" Flo stands and glares at me, hands on hips. "Mum, that is **so** stupid. You could have been attacked, killed."

"Okay, okay. There was no one there."

"What about the light?"

"I don't know. A dodgy bulb. My imagination."

"And that's all?"

"Yes."

"Why are you sleeping on the sofa? You stink of cigarettes."

"I suppose I must have lain down here for a bit and then nodded off."

She continues to regard me suspiciously. Then she sighs and shakes her head. "Fine. Want some coffee?"

"Yeah, thanks. . . . Actually, what time is it?"

"Almost nine o'clock."

Nine o'clock. Nine a.m. Monday morning. Meeting time. **Damn.**

· · ·

"Good morning, everyone. Apologies for being a bit late."

I smile at the small group in front of me, trying for my own version of Durkin's benevolent beam. I'm not quite sure it's cutting it. The fact that I'm panting, red-faced and still fumbling to do up my clerical collar probably isn't helping.

Reverend Rushton stands. "Shall I do the introductions?"

"Thank you," I say gratefully. **Damn collar.**

We're crammed into a tiny office off the main chapel, which seemed cramped when devoid of people and now, with the whole parish team gathered in it, seems Hobbit-like.

Paperwork is piled everywhere. A cork board overflows with safety notices, parish newsletters and orders of service. Even the walls are cluttered, with historical photos of the chapel and its previous clergy: a much younger Rushton; a severe-looking man with a shock of dark hair (**"Reverend Marsh,"** a label underneath reads) and Reverend Fletcher—a good-looking man in his fifties with grey hair and a neat beard. Next to Fletcher, there's a lighter square patch where a picture seems to have been removed. I wonder why.

There is barely enough room for a desk and two chairs. Probably just as well that our "team" consists of just five people, of whom only four are here this morning.

"This is Malcolm, our lay reader," Rushton says.

An angular bespectacled man nods and smiles.

"Aaron, you know."

We nod at each other briskly.

"Our administrator, June Watkins, sadly, has become too ill to keep up with the work. Fortunately, we have someone to fill in temporarily—"

Right on cue, the door opens and a tall, striking woman in a flowing dress, with a mane of white hair piled messily into a bun, walks in, holding a flask and a stack of plastic cups.

"Hello, everyone. I left the coffee in the car."

I stare at her as she puts the flask and cups down on the desk.

"Most of you know Clara," Rushton says. "She'll be helping on a voluntary basis, an angel sent from the heavens."

Clara looks around and smiles. "He **has** to say that—I'm his wife!"

Her eyes fall on me. She holds out a hand. "Jack? Nice to meet you. What's that short for?"

"Err . . . Jacqueline."

Her grey eyes gleam. "A lovely name. Both of them."

"Thank you."

"So, a small team, as you see," Rushton finishes.

A very small team. But then, these days, there is simply not enough demand for every rural church to have its own vicar, let alone a dedicated warden or staff. In addition to Chapel Croft and Warblers Green, Rushton and I will oversee two other small churches in the parish—Burford and Netherton—dividing our time between them as best we can.

"It's good to meet you all," I say, trying to compose myself. "As I'm sure you know by now, my name is Jack Brooks and I'll be working as the interim priest here until a new long-term incumbent is found."

"Do you know when that might be?" Malcolm asks, perhaps a little hastily.

"Afraid not," I say. "So, best to presume you'll be stuck with me for a while."

"No 'stuck' about it," Rushton interjects. "We're delighted to have you. And anything we can do to help you settle in, just ask."

"Yes, of course." Clara nods. "I think we're ready for a fresh start, after . . . well, you know."

I was wondering who would be first to bring it up.

"I was very sorry to hear about Reverend Fletcher."

"We just wish we had known what he was going through," Malcolm adds. "I mean, we knew he was under stress, but to take his own life . . ."

"Those intent upon taking their own lives are good at hiding it from their closest friends and family," I say. "Suicide is a tragedy for everyone."

"And a sin."

I stare at Aaron. "I'm sorry?"

"Life is a gift from God. Only he has the power to take it away." His eyes meet mine, defiant.

I keep my voice calm. "That has not been the view of the Church of England for a long time, Aaron."

"So, we choose to ignore the word of the Bible?"

"There is no explicit condemnation of suicide in the Bible and, while I'm the vicar here, I'd prefer not to hear such talk in this chapel."

I hold Aaron's gaze and I'm pleased when he drops his eyes.

"So . . . anyway"—Rushton clears his throat—"life, as they say, must go on. Shall we proceed with the business of the coming week?"

We do. I'm relieved to find myself falling back into the normal routine, not too dissimilar from my previous parish. Coffee mornings, a village fete, a youth group, three upcoming weddings and four funerals. Although I'm not officially on duty for another two weeks, it's agreed that I should start to make myself known at a few church events.

"Oh, and of course there's still the matter of the repairs to the chapel floor."

"I saw some of the flagstones were broken. What happened?"

"Oh, just wear and tear. We'll be getting someone to take a look soon. In the meantime, Jack, please make sure no one goes near the area. The last thing we need is someone suing us for a broken ankle."

"Right."

"Good. Well, I think we're done. Anything else you want to add?"

Rushton turns his ruddy face toward me. I consider. Obviously, asking who might be leaving me strange, creepy messages is up there. But until I know more, I don't think it would be wise to say anything. Yet.

"Erm, no. I think we've covered everything."

"Excellent. I cannot tell you what a relief it is to have you on board to share the load."

"I'm glad to help."

Everyone starts to move, gathering their things. Malcolm clasps my hand in his bony one as he leaves. "Lovely to have you here, my dear."

Aaron pointedly ignores me, busying himself shuffling his notes.

I really want to get away myself, but I sense Clara watching me as she shrugs her arms into a long, multicolored cardigan. "I hear you have a daughter, Jack?"

"Yes."

"How old?"

"Fifteen."

"A difficult age."

"Well, I've been lucky so far. Do you have children?"

"We were never blessed," Rushton says. "But we

seem to have acquired many godchildren over the years. And Clara used to teach, so we've always had young people in our lives."

I nod, politely, thinking, **A teacher. Of course**.

"How long have you been married?"

"We recently celebrated our twenty-eighth anniversary."

They're an odd match. Tall, elegant Clara and short, dumpy Brian. Not that I want to be judgmental.

"Congratulations."

"You're a widow?" Clara says, reminding me how much I hate that word.

"My husband died, yes."

"You've raised Flo all alone."

"Like I said, I've been lucky. She's a good girl."

"And how is she settling in?" Rushton asks. "I'm afraid there's not a lot to do in the village for the youngsters."

"Well, she likes photography. We were actually thinking of turning the cellar into a darkroom."

"Ah."

"Is there a problem with the cellar?"

"No. It's just there are still quite a few of Reverend Fletcher's things down there," Clara says. "I sorted through as much as I could—"

"He didn't have any family?"

"Sadly not. He bequeathed everything to the Church and the items we could donate, such as furniture, clothes, his laptop, we did. But there was a lot of—"

"Junk," Rushton says, less tactfully. "To be fair, it's not all Reverend Fletcher's. A lot is general church stuff. We didn't know what to do with it, so it's still in the cellar."

"Well, looks like I shall have plenty to keep me busy over the coming weeks."

Something else occurs to me.

"Is Reverend Fletcher buried here? I feel I should pay my respects."

"Actually, no," Rushton says. "He's buried in Tunbridge Wells. Near his mother."

"He didn't want to be buried here," Aaron suddenly chips in from behind me.

I turn. "Oh. Why?"

"He said that the chapel had become corrupted."

"Corrupted?"

"As Malcolm mentioned," Clara interjects, "Reverend Fletcher had been under a lot of stress."

"He wanted it exorcized," Aaron continues. "That was just before—"

"Aaron!" Rushton says sharply.

Aaron shoots him a strange look. "She should know."

"Know what?"

Rushton sighs. "Shortly before his death, Reverend Fletcher tried to burn the chapel down."

FOURTEEN

"Not the first time someone has tried that, of course." Rushton sips his latte.

We're sitting at a table in a corner of the village hall, which, according to a bright, handwritten sign on the door, is: **"Open for coffee Mondays, Wednesdays and Fridays 10–12."** Clara has joined us. Aaron, unsurprisingly, has not.

I'm surprised how busy it is. In Nottingham, the coffee mornings were generally only attended by the truly faithful or the homeless. I suppose most other people feared they would get a religious lecturing or, worse, crap coffee.

The patrons here are older but well dressed. There are a couple of mums with babies. Even the coffee is half decent. I'm pleasantly surprised. Which is the first pleasant surprise I've had since I came here.

"So, what happened?" I ask.

"Catholic separatists. Descendants of Queen Mary's Marian persecutors. They burned the old chapel to the ground in the seventeenth century. Destroyed everything, including most of the parish records. The current chapel was rebuilt by Baptists some years later."

"Sorry, I meant what happened with Reverend Fletcher?"

"Oh. Well, fortunately, he didn't get that far. Aaron found him before the fire could really catch hold."

"What was Aaron doing there?"

"It was late at night. Aaron happened to be passing and saw a light in the chapel. He found Reverend Fletcher standing over a pile of lit pew cushions."

"He said someone had broken into the chapel," Clara says, shaking a second packet of sugar and emptying it into her coffee. Obviously, her figure isn't maintained by dieting.

"Could they have?" I say, thinking about the unlocked door and the light I saw last night.

"No sign of a break-in. Aaron and I are the only other people with keys to the chapel," Rushton replies.

"Right." I make a mental note of this. "Could it have been left unlocked?"

Rushton sighs. "Matthew—Reverend Fletcher— had been behaving oddly for a while."

"In what way?"

"He claimed to have seen apparitions," Clara says.

I tense. "What sort of apparitions?"

"Burning girls."

Icy fingers grip my scalp.

"They're something of a local legend," Clara says, a glint in her eye. "Two young girls, Abigail and Maggie, burned at the stake along with six other martyrs in the sixteenth century."

"I know," I say. "At least, some of it."

"Jack has been doing her homework," Rushton says. "She even knew about the dolls."

"Really?" Clara's eyebrows rise. "Where did you hear about those?"

There's something about her searching gaze that makes me feel uncomfortable.

"Oh, online."

"A lot of people find them a bit ghoulish."

"Can't imagine why."

She smiles. "Small villages have their ways."

"I wouldn't really know."

"You grew up in Nottingham?"

"Yes."

"You don't have much of an accent, if you don't mind me saying."

"Well, my mum was from the south."

"Ah, that explains those soft vowels." She sips her coffee casually, but I don't think anything about her questions is casual.

I turn back to Rushton. "Just because Reverend Fletcher thought the chapel was haunted, it doesn't necessarily make him unstable. I've known a few priests who believe in apparitions."

"It wasn't just that," Rushton says. "He'd become increasingly paranoid. Obsessive. He believed that someone was out to get him. That he was being threatened. He claimed that Burning Girls had been left in the chapel and pinned to the door of the cottage."

"Did he go to the police?"

"Yes. But he had no proof."

"Did anyone have any reason to threaten him?"

"No," Clara says. "Matthew had been the vicar here for almost three years. He was well liked."

"But in the last year, he had lost his father and mother," Rushton says. "A close friend had been diagnosed with cancer. He was wrestling with many personal issues. He handed in his resignation shortly after the fire in the chapel. I think he accepted things were getting on top of him."

I consider. The Church is still a long way behind other institutions in recognizing mental illness. We're not encouraged to talk about it and, possibly because the majority of priests are male, it's seen as some kind of failing.

Prayer is a useful medium for focusing the mind. But it is not a magic cure-all. God is not a therapist or a psychiatrist. We still need the support of other people and sometimes those people are professionals. I often wonder, if my husband had sought help sooner, if things might have been different.

I reach for my coffee and take a gulp. It doesn't seem to taste quite as good now.

I choose my next words carefully. "Did anyone suspect that Reverend Fletcher's death might **not** have been suicide?"

"No. Of course not. Who would say that?"

"One of the parishioners mentioned something—"

Rushton rolls his eyes. "Joan Hartman." He waves his hand, indicating I don't need to deny or confirm. "Joan is quite a character, but I wouldn't take what she says too seriously."

"Because she's old?"

"No. Because she's isolated, imaginative and reads far too many crime novels." Rushton leans forward. "Jack, can I offer a bit of advice?"

I want to say no. Generally, when people ask if they can offer advice, it's as welcome as a pile of horse shit. But I smile and say: "Of course."

"Don't get bogged down with the past. Your arrival is a fresh start. A chance to put the tragic circumstances of Reverend Fletcher's death behind us. And, as you can see, there is plenty here to keep you busy."

I keep the smile glued in place. "I'm sure you're right."

He places his chubby hand over mine and gives

it a squeeze. "Talking of which, we should get back. I have to meet with the Bakers to talk about their father's funeral."

He gets up from the table. Clara follows.

"See you later. And remember what I said."

"I will. Bye."

I watch them walk from the hall, exchanging goodbyes with a few of the other patrons. I think about getting another coffee, then glance at my watch. Nope. I should really go and do some shopping. Woman and daughter cannot live on pizza alone.

I'm just standing up when I hear the crash. I turn. An elderly lady at another table lies on the floor, surrounded by broken crockery and dregs of coffee. A few people glance over and a couple start to rise, but I'm closest. I hurry over and kneel down, taking her hand.

"Are you okay? Have you hurt yourself?"

She seems a little dazed. I wonder if she's hit her head.

"It's all right. Take a moment," I say.

She stares at me. Her eyes focus.

"Is that you?"

I try to pull my hand away, but she digs her fingers in.

"Where is she? Tell me."

"I'm sorry. I don't—"

And then a warm, soothing voice says:

"It's okay. She gets confused sometimes."

A young woman with short hair, dressed in dungarees and a T-shirt, crouches down next to me and speaks gently to the elderly lady.

"Doreen? You had a bit of a fall. You're in the village hall. Are you okay?"

"Village hall?" The old lady's grip slackens. The woman eases her hand away from mine.

"Shall we get you sitting up?"

"But I need to get home. She'll be expecting her tea."

"Of course, but first, how about we get you some water?"

"I can do that," I say.

I walk over to the serving hatch.

"Can I get a glass of water?"

By the time I bring the water back the old lady is sitting on a chair, looking a little less dazed.

"Here you go."

She takes the paper cup in a wavering hand and sips from it.

"I'm so sorry. I don't know what came over me."

She smiles, embarrassed. And I remind myself that old age is not a disease but a destination.

"That's okay," I say. "We can all have a dizzy moment."

"Do you have anyone who can take you home, Doreen?" the short-haired woman asks.

Doreen. Why is that name familiar? **Doreen.** And then it comes to me. The conversation I had with Joan:

"Joy's mother, Doreen, suffers from dementia."

Joy's mother. I stare at her. Doreen must only be
in her early seventies, but she looks closer to ninety.
She's so frail. Her face is like flaccid dough, hair
spider-web fine and spun into wispy curls.

"I was going to walk, dear."

"I'm not sure that's a good idea," short-haired
woman says.

There's a pause, during which I could make a
perfectly reasonable excuse about having to go
shopping and get back to my daughter. Instead, I
hear myself say:

"I can give Doreen a lift home."

Short-haired woman smiles at me. "Thank you."
Then she glances back at Doreen. "That's okay, isn't
it, Doreen? If the nice lady drives you home?"

Doreen looks at me. "Yes. Thank you."

Short-haired woman sticks out a hand. "I'm
Kirsty. I run the youth group and help out here
when needed."

"Jack." I shake her hand. "The new vicar."

"I guessed. The dog collar kind of gave it away."

I glance down. "Ah. Yes. That's the thing with
dog collars. They're a bit like tattoos. You forget
you've got one until people give you odd looks."

She laughs and hitches up the arm of her T-shirt,
revealing a bold tattoo of a leering skull.

"Amen to that."

.   .   .

Doreen lives on a narrow lane off the high street. Packed with higgledy-piggledy terraces, most brimming with window boxes and hanging baskets.

I would have known Doreen's house even if Kirsty hadn't given me the address. The brick is dirty, the small front garden overgrown and the windows grimy and dark. Grief and loss hang over the place like a widow's veil.

I pull up outside. Doreen hasn't spoken much on the short journey, sitting, twisting a handkerchief around in her gnarled hands. I let the silence be. Sometimes, trying to fill a silence just makes it heavier.

I climb out of the car and hold the door for her, helping her out and then guiding her up the path to the front door. She fumbles in her handbag and brings out a key.

"Thank you again, dear."

"No problem."

She opens the door. "Would you like to come in for a cup of tea?"

I hesitate. I really shouldn't. I shouldn't even be here. I need to go shopping, then get back to Flo and finish sorting out the cottage. On the other hand, I look at the forlorn terrace. Something twists inside.

I smile. "That would be lovely."

The hall is dark and smells of stale cooking and damp. The patterned carpet is threadbare. An old dial phone sits on a chipped side table under a large picture of the Virgin Mary. Her mournful eyes follow us into a dingy kitchen that looks un-touched since the mid-seventies. Cracked linoleum, Formica worktops and sagging green cupboard doors. A tiny semicircular table is wedged against one wall, two chairs tucked in either side. A cross hangs directly above it and two plaques: **"As for me and my house, we will serve the Lord"; "Be still, and know that I am God."**

Doreen sheds her jacket and shuffles toward the kettle.

"Would you like some help?"

"My mind might not be what it once was, but I can remember how to make a cup of tea."

"Of course."

And the elderly have their pride. I pull out a chair and sit down beneath God's soundbites while she makes tea in a proper teapot.

"So, you're the new vicar?" She brings the teapot over with shaking hands.

"Yes. Reverend Brooks. But please call me Jack."

She walks back over to the cupboard and returns with two slightly stained cups and saucers.

"No sugar."

"That's fine."

She eases herself into the seat opposite. "Oh dear. I forgot the milk."

"Shall I get it?"

"Thank you."

I walk over to the small fridge and pull it open. Inside, there's nothing but a couple of ready meals, some cheese and a half-pint of milk. I take out the milk. It went out of date a day ago. I take a quick sniff and bring it over anyway.

"Here we go." I add a splash to both brews.

"We never had lady vicars in my day."

"No?"

"The Church wasn't a place for women."

"Well, times were different then."

"Priests were always men."

I hear this view a lot, especially from older parishioners. I try not to take it personally. We don't always move at the same pace as progress. Life, at some point, starts to leave us behind. We struggle along with our walking frames and mobility scooters but, ultimately, we'll never catch it up. If I make it to seventy or eighty, I'll probably find myself staring at the world around me with the same sense of bewilderment, wondering what the hell happened to all the things I thought were true.

"Well, things change," I say, sipping my tea and fighting a grimace.

"Are you married?"

"Widowed."

"I'm sorry. Any children?"

"A daughter."

She smiles. "I have a daughter. Joy."

"That's a lovely name."

"We called her Joy because she was such a happy baby." She reaches for her tea, hand trembling slightly. "She went away."

"Oh?"

"But she's coming home. Any day."

"Well, that's good."

"She **is** a good girl. Not like that other one." Her face darkens. "A bad influence, that one. Bad."

She shakes her head, eyes clouding, and I can see her drifting away from me, slipping through those invisible gaps in time.

I swallow. "Do you mind if I just use your bathroom?"

"Oh. No. It's—"

"I'll find it. Thank you."

I walk out of the room and up the narrow staircase, past more biblical quotes on the wall. The bathroom is on my left. I shut myself inside, flush the loo and splash my face with some cold water. Being in this house is getting to me. Time to leave. I walk back out on to the landing and pause. There's a door to my right. A small sign tacked on the front reads: **"Joy's room."**

Do not do it. **Get down those stairs, make your excuses and go.**

I gently push the door open.

This room, like the rest of the house, is frozen in time. A time when Joy still lived here. It doesn't look as if it has been touched since she disappeared.

The bed is neatly made with a faded floral bed cover. At its foot is a small dressing table. A brush and comb are arranged on top. Nothing else, no jewelry or makeup.

A plain wardrobe stands in one corner and beneath the window a low bookcase is stuffed with dog-eared paperbacks. Enid Blyton, Judy Blume, Agatha Christie, plus a few more turgid titles such as **Jesus in Your Life**, **Christianity for Girls** and, wedged on top of them, on its side, a large, leather-bound Bible.

I walk over to the bookcase and pull out the Bible. It's light. Far too light to contain the word of the Lord. I sit down on the edge of the bed and open it. Like my Bible, there is a hidey-hole inside. But unlike mine, this one is self-made. The middle pages have been hacked out with scissors or a knife to create a small space, just big enough to hold a few precious, secret things.

I take them out carefully, one by one: a pretty shell fashioned into a brooch. A packet of Juicy Fruit chewing gum. Two cigarettes and a mix tape. Of course. Swapping mix tapes. It's what best friends did, along with clothes and jewelry.

The writing on the inlay card is tight and crammed. It always was when you tried to write the titles and bands in such a small space. The Wonder Stuff, Madonna, INXS, Then Jericho, Transvision Vamp. I smile fondly. Those were the days.

I put the cassette to one side and take out the final item. A photograph of two girls, arm in arm, smiling into the camera. One girl is winsomely beautiful, with wide blue eyes and blonde hair in a long plait. A teenage Sissy Spacek. The other girl is brunette, hair cut into an unflattering bowl. She's very thin, her eyes dark hollows in her face, and her smile is guarded, more like a wince. Both wear silver necklaces with letters dangling from them. M for Merry. J for Joy.

"Fifteen years old. Best friends. Disappeared without a trace."

A chair scrapes across the floor downstairs. I jump. I replace the items in the Bible and put it back in the bookcase where I found it.

The photograph still lies on the bed. I stare at it. **Merry and Joy. Joy and Merry.**

Then I pick it up and slip it into my pocket.

"You know, when you're sixteen you can leave home. No one can stop you."

They were sitting on the bed in Joy's bedroom. Merry wasn't often invited in. But Joy's mum was out shopping.

"We're not sixteen for almost a year."

"I know."

"Where would we go?"

"London."

"Everyone goes to London."

"So where?"

"Australia."

"The water goes the wrong way around the plughole there."

"Really?"

"Yeah—I read it somewhere."

Joy nudged up the volume on her small stereo. They were playing the mix tape Merry had made her. Madonna blared out—"Like a Prayer."

"I love this song," Joy said.

"Me too."

"Oooh." Joy suddenly turned. "I got you something."

"What?"

She reached into her bookcase and pulled out the hefty black Bible. She had carved out a secret compartment inside. Merry knew this was where Joy hid things she didn't want her mum to see. She opened it up and took out a small paper bag. She held it out.

Merry took it and tipped the contents on to the bed cover. Two silver chains fell out. One with the letter M dangling from it. One with a letter J.

"Friendship necklaces," Joy said.

Merry held one up, letting the letter catch the light.

"They're beautiful."

"Let's put them on."

She smiled at her friend.

"I've got an idea—"

The front door slammed downstairs. Their eyes met.

"Shit."

"Joy Madeleine Harris. Are you playing that heathen music up there?"

Joy leaped from the bed and ejected the tape from the stereo. She stuffed it in the Bible. Footsteps marched up the stairs. Nowhere to go. The bedroom door burst open.

Joy's mother stood framed in the doorway, a slight woman with a haze of golden hair and fierce blue eyes. She was smaller than Merry's mum, and less prone to violence, but she was still scary when she was mad. She glared at Merry.

"I should have known."

"Mu-um," Joy said pleadingly.

"I've told you. She's not welcome here."

"She's my friend, Mum."

"I'd like her to leave."

"But—"

"It's okay," Merry said. "I'm going."

She snatched up the necklace, face burning, and hurried from the room.

On the landing, she glanced back. Joy's mum had picked up the stereo. She walked over to the window and dropped it through. There was a dull crash. Joy buried her face in her hands.

Merry clenched her fists.

Leave. Now. **If only they could.**

FIFTEEN

"Just running a quick errand, then going shopping. If hungry, money in kitty jar."

Flo looks at her mum's text—which she has sent three times, presumably because the first two wouldn't go through—and glances at the clock. Already after eleven.

Mum's timekeeping can be haphazard at the best of times and this morning she was really out of sorts. Something happened last night, and although Flo believes her mum when she says she saw a light in the chapel, she gets the feeling that there's more to it. Mum probably thinks that she's protecting her, but Flo often feels like saying, **You're not protecting me when you keep stuff from me, you're just worrying me.**

That's the problem with mums. Despite them saying they want to treat you as an adult, Flo knows that when her mum looks at her, she still sees a six-year-old girl.

After her mum had rushed out of the door, still fumbling with her dog collar, Flo searched the kitchen cupboards for something for breakfast, coming up with half a packet of digestives and a pack of cheese-and-onion crisps, which she demolished while finishing the King book (definitely one of his best). But her stomach is rumbling again. Also, she has the nagging feeling that she's wasting the day. No TV, no internet. She needs to get up and **do** something.

She could take a look in the cellar, see if it's any good for a darkroom, but she isn't wild about the thought of creeping around a dark, cobwebby space right now. Although she is loath to admit it, she's still a little freaked out by what she saw in the graveyard yesterday.

Of course, in daylight, with a night's sleep behind her, the memory is growing less distinct, her mind working hard to rationalize it. Perhaps it **was** a trick of the light. Perhaps it was someone playing a joke. It all happened so quickly. She could have been confused, her eyes fooling her. And if there really **had** been something there, the camera would have captured it.

Flo has never believed in ghosts. Because of her mum's job she's been around graveyards and death more than most kids her age. She has never felt there was anything remotely scary or spooky about them. The dead are dead. Our bodies just lumps of flesh and bone.

On the other hand, she could kind of get on with the idea that we leave imprints upon the world, a bit like a photographic image. A moment captured in time by a combination of chemicals and conditions.

Her stomach grumbles again. Okay, enough dwelling on ghosts. She wanders into the kitchen and picks up the glass kitty jar on the windowsill. It's filled with loose change and a few pound coins. She empties seven quid's worth out. There's a small shop in the village and it's only about a fifteen-minute walk.

She stuffs the change into her pocket and lets herself out of the house, locking the door behind her and stuffing the key in her pocket. And then she hesitates. Her camera. There might be some cool things to photograph on the way. She darts back inside, picks it up and slings it around her neck.

The pavement leading to the village is narrow. At times, it dissolves completely into overgrown grass and stinging nettles. Hardly any traffic passes. The drone of farming machinery and the occasional mournful moo of a cow are the only sounds. It feels weird everywhere being so quiet.

She stops a couple of times to snap photos. A derelict barn, a lightning-scarred tree. Pretty soon, she can see the beginnings of habitation. A village hall to her right surrounded by playing fields, an ancient-looking children's playground, where a mum pushes a toddler on a swing.

Further on, there's a small primary school on her left and the houses start to nudge up closer together, a couple of side streets running off in both directions. She passes a whitewashed pub, abundant with hanging baskets. **"The Barley Mow,"** the sign proclaims.

The village shop is next door to it. Carter's Convenience Store. She shoves the door open. It jangles with an old-fashioned bell. A middle-aged woman with a thick helmet of grey hair sits behind the counter. She stares at Flo as she walks in.

Flo smiles. "Morning."

The woman continues to stare at her, as if she has two heads. Finally, she summons up a gruff: "Morning."

Flo tries to ignore the feeling of being watched as she wanders around the shop. People are suspicious of teenagers, especially if you look a bit different. She sees it all the time. The worried glances older people give you, as though every single teen harbors a secret desire for their handbag. She often wants to shout out, **We're just young. We're not all muggers, you know.**

She buys a loaf of bread, butter, a bar of chocolate and a Diet Coke. That should sustain her until Mum gets back from the supermarket. The woman serves her quickly, as if eager for Flo to leave the shop. **You and me both**, Flo thinks.

She eats the chocolate bar sauntering along the pavement and washes it down with a swig of Coke. She's almost at the village hall when it occurs to her that she might be able to get a half-decent phone signal in the village. She takes out her phone. Three bars. A miracle. And enough to message Kayleigh and Leon. She glances around. The mum and toddler have gone. The playground is deserted. She walks in and sits down on a rickety bench near the roundabout. Then she takes out her phone and brings up Snapchat.

She's barely started typing when she hears the gate to the playground creak. She glances up. Two teens walk in. A glossy blonde girl in skinny jeans and a tight vest and a well-built dark-haired boy in a T-shirt and shorts. Not her tribe. And straight-away, something about their swagger tells her that this could be trouble. But it's too late to get up and walk away. Not without looking lame. This is the stuff that parents don't understand. The everyday minefield of being a teen. Trying to avoid situations that could blow up in your face.

Flo keeps her head down as the pair sit on the swings nearby, but she can't concentrate. She can feel them watching her. And, sure enough, the girl calls out:

"Hey! Vampirina."

Flo ignores her. She hears the swings squeak as

they get up and walk over. Beefy Boy sits down next to her, deliberately invading her space. He smells of cheap body spray and vaguely masked BO.

"You deaf?"

Great. So, they're really going to do this.

She glances up at him and says politely, "My name isn't Vampirina."

"Should be. Goth."

"I'm not a Goth."

Blondie looks her up and down.

"What are you, then?"

"Minding my own business."

Don't rise. Don't give them anything to work with and they usually get bored.

"You're new here."

"Nothing gets past you."

Blondie regards her curiously. Then she clicks her manicured fingers. "**Wait**. Is your mum the new vicar?"

Flo feels her cheeks flush.

Blondie grins. "She is, isn't she?"

"And?"

"That must suck?"

"Not really."

"So, you're some religious nut?"

"Yes. That's exactly what I am. A Goth religious nut."

Beefy Boy gestures at her camera. "What's that antique shit round your neck?"

She tenses. "A camera."

"What's wrong with your phone?"

"Nothing."

"Give us a look, then."

He reaches for it. Flo clutches the strap and jumps up. Immediately, she regrets it. She's shown a weakness. Something that makes her vulnerable. She spots the gleam in Beefy's eyes.

"What's your problem?"

"Nothing. Why don't you and Taylor Swift just get out of my face?"

He stands. "Let me have a look at your camera then."

"No."

It happens quickly. He lunges forward. Instinctively, Flo shoots out a hand. It smashes into his nose. He screams and clutches at his face. Blood spurts out between his fingers, staining his white T-shirt crimson.

"Mmm . . . whuu fuuuck."

"Tom!" Blondie gasps. "You've broken his nose, you crazy bitch."

Flo stares at them, frozen, hand still half out-stretched.

"I'm sorry," she mumbles. "I—"

The door to the village hall swings open. A dumpy dark-haired woman sticks her head out.

"What's going on out here? Oh, my goodness, Tom—you're bleeding."

Flo opens her mouth to defend herself, but before she can say anything Blondie steps forward.

"Just a nosebleed, Mrs. C. Have you got any tissues?"

"Oh, of course, Rosie. Yes, yes. Come inside."

Tom stumbles toward the village hall, still holding his spurting nose, shooting Flo an evil look as he goes.

Blondie turns to Flo and hisses, "Get the fuck out of here."

"But—"

"I said"—she smiles poisonously—"**run, Vampirina.**"

Flo doesn't wait to be told again. She runs. As fast as she can, one hand hanging on to her precious camera. She doesn't stop till she's almost back at the chapel. Then she slows, bends over and tries to catch her breath. What the hell has she done? What if he reports her for assault? Mum will freak. And then she remembers the look in Blondie's eyes.

Run, Vampirina.

Flo knows that look. It's the look a cat gets when it's tormenting a mouse. Toying with its prey.

This isn't over. This is just the start.

SIXTEEN

The supermarket is busy, probably because it's the only one within about thirty miles. I hurry around as quickly as I can, but one of the disadvantages of a clerical collar is that you can't be rude to people or barge them out of the way when they block you in with their trolley, ram you with a pushchair or jump the queue (although my visit does reconfirm my belief that self-service tills **are** the work of the devil).

It's a forty-minute journey home, along more twisty country lanes. The Romans forgot their rulers when they came to Sussex. I can feel the photograph in my pocket. I shouldn't have taken it. But something about it tugged at me. I round the bend, hearing the shopping topple and bottles crash. And then I hit the brakes.

"**Crap!**"

A battered MG is pulled up on the verge, rear end

sticking out on to the narrow lane. A dark-haired man in jeans and a T-shirt is crouched alongside it, attempting, unsuccessfully, to get the car up on to a jack. I only just avoided hitting him.

I consider winding down the window and telling the man to move his car. He could cause an accident or get himself killed. On the other hand, he looks like he's really struggling and . . . **be Christian**.

I sigh, pull my car up behind him and climb out. "Need a hand?"

The man straightens. He looks hot, annoyed and vaguely familiar. Late forties, weathered face, dark hair peppered with grey. And then I remember. He was at the service yesterday.

He offers me a rueful smile. "Could you pray for me to get better at changing a tire?"

"Nope, but I could help you set that jack up properly."

A small flash of surprise. "Oh. Okay. I mean, thanks. That would be great. I'm really rubbish at car stuff."

I walk over. He steps back and I bend down and reposition the jack under the car. I pump it up.

"Tire iron?"

"Oh, yes."

He picks up a rusty tire iron from the ground and promptly drops it on his foot.

"Ouch." He clutches at his toes.

I bite back a smile. "You really **are** rubbish at this, aren't you?"

"Thanks for the sympathy. Very Christian."

"I'll say a prayer for your big toe later. Are you okay?"

"My ballet-dancing days are over, but otherwise"—he puts his foot down gingerly—"fine."

I pick up the tire iron, fit it on to the nuts and pop them off quickly, one by one. Then I ease off the tire. I lay it down on the grass and wipe my hands on my jeans.

"Spare?"

"What?"

"Spare tire?"

"Right." He walks round to the back of the car. His face falls. "Crap."

"What?"

"I forgot. I don't have one."

I stare at him. "**You don't have a spare**."

"Well, I did." He glances at the tire I've just taken off. "That's it."

Christ.

"I don't suppose you're a member of the AA, RAC . . . any breakdown service?"

He looks even more sheepish.

"Okay. Well, you could call a garage and wait here . . ."

"I really need to get back home."

"Where d'you live?"

"Just outside of Chapel Croft."

"In that case, I can give you a lift."

"Thank you. That's really kind."

He locks the MG and follows me over to my car.

"I don't think I got your name?" I say.

"Oh, Mike. Mike Sudduth."

He sticks out a hand. I shake it. "Jack Brooks."

"I know. The new vicar."

"Word travels fast."

"Not much to talk about here."

"I'll bear that in mind." I glance back at his car, abandoned on the verge. "Will your car be okay?"

"Not like it's going anywhere."

"True, but what if someone hits it?"

"They'd be doing me a favor."

I eye the MG with its numerous dents and scrapes. "Also true."

I climb into my car. Mike opens the passenger door. He frowns, staring at the upside-down cross scored into the paintwork.

"Do you know someone has vandalized your car?"

"Yep."

He slides in and does up his seatbelt. "It doesn't bother you?"

It bothers me, but I'm not about to admit it.

"Just kids. Thinking they're being clever."

"By carving Satanic graffiti?"

"I'm sure I did worse as a teenager."

"Such as?"

I start the engine. "You really don't want to know."

. . .

It's only about another fifteen minutes back to Chapel Croft. I stick some music on—The Killers.

"So, how are you finding things here?" Mike asks as Brandon laments that there is no motive for this crime and Jenny was a friend of his.

"Well, it's only been a couple of days so—"

"Reserving judgment?"

"I suppose."

"When do you officially start?"

"A couple of weeks. The diocese usually gives you some time to settle in first, to get to know the parish."

"Well, if you want to get to know your parish, the Barley Mow is a good place to start. You'll find most of them in there on a Sunday afternoon. They serve a passable roast and a very fine selection of wines and ales." He flashes me a quick glance. "Or so I'm told."

"Not a drinker?"

"Not anymore."

"Have you lived here long?"

"I've only lived in Chapel Croft for a couple of years. I used to live over in Burford. I moved here after my wife and I split up."

"Oh."

"No, it's fine. It is for the best. And I still see a lot of my son. You have children?"

"One daughter. Flo. She's fifteen."

"Ah, the teenage years. How does she feel about your job?"

"Like most teenagers, she thinks her mum is pathetic and embarrassing most of the time."

He chuckles. "Yeah, Harry's twelve, so he's only just getting to that stage."

"Well, you're probably lucky. From what I gather, boys are easier. They simply retreat into their rooms. Girls, they'll push all the boundaries whenever they can."

I smile, but he doesn't return it. In fact, his face stiffens, something I can't quite read in it. I'm not sure whether to speak again when a smart red-brick house draws into view.

"Here we are," he says.

"Okay."

"Oh, and . . ." He reaches into his pocket and pulls out a crumpled card. "This is my number—if there's anything you'd like to know about the village, then I can point you in the right direction."

I look at the card. **Michael Sudduth. Weldon Herald.**

"You're a reporter."

"Well, if you can really call it that. Mostly cake bakes and flea markets, but occasionally we get a bit of excitement, when someone steals a mower."

I feel myself tense. A reporter.

"Right. Well, thanks for the card."

"And thanks for helping with the tire."

He climbs out of the car, then turns back.

"You know, if you fancy doing an interview,

about coming here, a female take on being the new vicar, I'd love to do a—"

"No."

"Oh."

I glare at him. "Is that why you came to the service yesterday? To sound me out?"

"Actually, I come to the chapel every Sunday."

"Really?"

"Yes. For my daughter."

"I thought you had a son."

"I do. My daughter died. Two years ago. She's buried in the graveyard at the chapel."

My face flames. "I'm sorry. I didn't realize—"

He gives me a dark look. "Thanks for the lift. But maybe work on that whole 'reserving judgment' thing."

He slams the car door shut and walks up to the house without a backward glance.

Great. Well done on those people skills, Jack.

I sit in my car for a moment, wondering whether I should go after him and apologize. Then I decide it's best to leave it for now. I'll probably only make things worse.

I open the glovebox and chuck Mike's card inside. As I do, a folded piece of paper falls out. I pick it up . . . and curse.

I'd forgotten this was in here. Or rather, I had tried really hard to forget this was in here.

As a priest, I talk a lot about honesty, but I'm a

hypocrite. Honesty is an overrated virtue. The only real difference between a truth and a lie is how many times you repeat it.

I didn't agree to this tenure just because of Durkin's ultimatum. It wasn't even Ruby or my own need to make amends. It was because of this.

Nottingham Prison Service. Notice of early release.

I shove the letter back in the glovebox and slam it shut.

He's out.

And I can only pray that this is the last place he will look for me.

SEVENTEEN

"This is how much I love you." That's what Mum would whisper. **"Even when you have been so wicked."**

And then she would lower him into the hole. No food. No water. Staring desperately up at the small circle of sky, birds circling overhead.

The cries of the crows take him back. **A murder,** he thinks. A murder of crows. He looks up at the old building. It was an asylum back in Victorian times. A grand and ornate structure on the outskirts of Nottingham, surrounded by rolling green lawns. Then, in the 1920s, it was converted into a hospital. But at some point, the doors had closed for the final time, the big, arched windows were boarded up and the building and its grounds left to rot.

He knows this because it had been his home, for a while, after he ran away. He squatted with the other homeless. Druggies, alcoholics, people with mental health problems. Kind of ironic, really. He begged in the day, bringing in enough to buy a bit of food and water. The others were kind to him, for the most part, taking pity on a youngster.

Then another group moved in. Five young men and women with long hair and piercings. They wore baggy trousers and multicolored tops and sat around at night smoking funny-smelling cigarettes and talking about "politics" and the "fattest regime."

Fascist regime, he had realized years later.

"They're not like us," one of the older drunks, Gaff, had told him.

"How?"

"Got homes. Folks. Just don't want to live there."

"Why?"

"Think they're fucking rebels, don't they?" Gaff had said witheringly, honking a great glob of blood-speckled spit on to the ground.

He had been shocked. That someone would choose this life, living among rubble and bird droppings, with no heat or light, when, at any time, they could just go home. To parents who cared for them. And then he had felt angry. Like the newcomers were somehow mocking him.

One of the group—a skinny dreadlocked man called Ziggy—he particularly disliked. Ziggy came and tried to talk to him sometimes. Sat too close. Offered the funny cigarettes. Once or twice, he tried them. He didn't really like how they made him feel. Kind of out of it and even hungrier. Later, he got over this. Being "out of it" became a way of life.

"Why are you talking to me?" he had asked Ziggy.

"I'm just being nice."

"What for?"

"My parents are rich, y'know. They send money."

"So?"

"You need money."

"Yeah."

"So, if you're nice to me, maybe I'll give you money."

Ziggy had winked at him, grinning a yellow-toothed grin.

A few nights later, he had woken up to a strange noise. A weird moaning, groaning sound. He sat up. Ziggy stood over him, hands in his trousers, rubbing them viciously up and down.

"What are you doing?"

Ziggy had grinned. "Suck me off. I'll give you a tenner."

"What?"

Ziggy moved closer, shoving his trousers down, bringing out his erect penis, surrounded by curly ginger hairs.

"C'mon, man. Just a quick suck."

"No."

Ziggy's face had changed. "Do it, you little shit."

Blood roared in his ears. Red suffused his vision, blinding him. He rose up and shoved Ziggy away. Stoned, Ziggy stumbled and fell backward, crashing to the ground.

"Shit, man!"

He had looked around. Bits of rubble and broken bricks were strewn all over the place in the falling-down asylum. He grabbed a bit of brick, raised it and brought it down on Ziggy's head. Again, and again, till Ziggy stopped moving.

He stepped back. The rage had receded, but he could still see red. All over the ground, the brick and Ziggy's matted dreadlocks.

He could hear her voice:

What have you done?

"He wanted me to suck him," he said dully. "I'm sorry."

You can't stay here. You have to leave. Tonight.

"What about him?"

He had looked at Ziggy. His head was all mushy and strangely lopsided, but he was breathing, faintly.

You can't leave him like that.

He shook his head. "I can't go to the police . . ."

No. I said you can't leave him like that. **He could identify you.**

Ziggy had groaned; one blue eye stared helplessly through the blood.

He understood. **She** always knew what to do.

He had stepped toward Ziggy and raised the brick.

The crows caw. He closes his eyes. He is not that boy anymore. Nor is he the substance-addicted young man who spent most of his twenties in and out of prison for various petty crimes—drugs, assault, theft. He's changed. They all told him so. The counselors. The parole board. But it's not enough. He needs to hear it from **her**.

She wrote to him, after she left the first time. That was how he knew where to look for her. But Nottingham is a big city. And when he finally found her again, the anger took hold, he did the really bad thing and messed it all up.

She only came to visit him in prison once. His letters were returned unopened. He doesn't blame her. She had her reasons. And he has forgiven her.

Now she just has to do the same. And then they can be together again. Like before.

He'll show her.

This is how much I love you.

EIGHTEEN

Flo walks downstairs as I'm putting away the last of the shopping. Straightaway, I notice that she seems tense.

"Hey. How's it going?"

"Okay."

"What have you been up to?"

"Took a walk to the shop."

"Anything interesting to report?"

"Nope." She scrapes a chair across the floor and sits down without meeting my eyes. "How did your errand go?" she asks.

"All right."

"Anything interesting to report?"

I pause with a bag of peas in my hand, thinking about Joy's mother, the photograph in my pocket and my encounter with Mike Sudduth. I shake my head. "Nope." I shove the peas in the freezer. "After lunch I thought we could maybe take a look at the cellar for your darkroom. But it needs clearing out. Apparently, there's a lot of junk down there."

"Oh. Right."

Not quite the enthusiastic reaction I was hoping for.

"I thought you wanted a new darkroom?"

"I do. But I was planning to go and take some more photos after lunch. Wrigley says there's this—"

My head snaps around. "Whoah, rewind. Who's Wrigley?"

She looks down, fiddling with the zip on her hoodie. "Someone I met yesterday."

"You didn't mention meeting anyone yesterday."

"I forgot."

"Right. Well, I'm going to need a little more information."

"He's just a boy, okay?"

No, it was not okay. But I couldn't say that. And it wasn't as if I didn't want Flo to have friends who were boys. **Boy. Friend.** I would just rather they stayed separate nouns for as long as possible.

"So, Wrigley—that's an odd name?"

"It's his surname. His first name is Lucas."

"Okay. And how did you meet him?"

"I met him in the graveyard. He draws pictures. He's really good."

"He draws pictures of graves. Nice."

"I take photos of them."

"Obviously a match made in heaven, then."

"Mu-um." She rolls her eyes so hard I'm surprised

smoke doesn't come out of her ears. "It's not like that. Okay?"

"Okay," I say, not believing her for a second. "So, what did Wrigley say?"

She hesitates.

"This place?" I prompt.

"Yeah—" Another hesitation. "These really pretty woods."

"Right."

She scowls at me. "Don't say it like that."

"What?"

"You know."

"Look, I'm not sure I want you wandering around the woods with a boy you barely know."

"So, you'd rather I went on my own?"

"No."

"But you don't want me going with a friend who knows the area."

Oh, she's good, my daughter. I don't want her going at all. But she's fifteen. She needs her freedom. She also needs friends here. And forbidding her is only going to make her want to do it more.

I sigh, heavily. "Fine. You can go—"

"Thanks, Mum."

"**But** . . . be careful. Take your phone. In case you fall down a ditch or something."

"Or get attacked by a mad cow?"

"That too." I eye her suspiciously. "And I want to meet this Wrigley."

"Oh God. Mum."

"That's the deal."

"**I've** only just met him."

"Doesn't have to be right now, but I want to know who my daughter is seeing."

"I'm not . . . oh, for God's sake, fine."

"Good."

"Great."

"And you're not making this up to get out of helping me clean the cellar?"

"Would I lie to you?"

"You're fifteen. So, yes."

"Like you never lie?"

"Of course I don't. I'm a vicar."

She shakes her head, but I see a hint of a smile. "Vicar or not—you are so going to hell."

"You have no idea. Now, what d'you want for lunch?"

I stand at Flo's bedroom window and watch her amble up through the graveyard at the rear of the cottage, all skinny legs and attitude, camera slung around her neck. My stomach tightens into a hard knot. She's hiding something from me. But then, I can hardly berate my daughter for keeping secrets.

I walk downstairs. The photograph shifts in my pocket. I take it out and look at it again. Merry and Joy. One blonde, one dark. Both slight, dressed in baggy jumpers and leggings, friendship necklaces glinting around their necks.

Joy is the more beautiful. Doll-like, with her

pale blue eyes and flaxen hair. The girl next to her is not so obviously pretty. Her smile is less open, her eyes guarded. A face that already speaks of lost hope, fear, suspicion.

What became of you?

I tuck the photo away in my Bible hidey-hole and stand in the living room, feeling lost. I consider rolling a cigarette and then change my mind. I need to do something more productive, and better for my lungs. I told Flo I would clean out the cellar, so I might as well make a start.

I retrieve trash bags and rubber gloves from the kitchen cupboard and advance upon the cellar door, which is under the stairs in the nook between the kitchen and living room.

I stare at it. What's that line from **Donnie Darko**? Something about, of all the endless combinations of words in history, "cellar door" is the most beautiful.

True. Yet I don't believe anyone has ever approached a cellar door without a frisson of foreboding. A door that leads down into darkness, a room hidden in the earth. I tell myself not to be stupid and yank it open. A smell of mold and a cloud of dust billow out. I cough and wipe my nose on my sleeve. I spot a limp piece of string hanging near the door. I tug on it. A small puddle of yellow light spills over the uneven steps, like a urine stain. It will have to do.

I make my way gingerly downward, slightly

crouched over because of the low ceiling. Fortunately, at the bottom, the ceiling rises, and the cellar spreads out before me. I stare around.

"Christ!"

When Rushton said there was a lot of junk, he wasn't joking.

Box after crumpled cardboard box, yellowing newspapers and broken furniture fill almost every inch of the large cellar. I shine the flashlight around, revealing more boxes and unidentifiable mounds covered in old sheets. I don't know where to start. Maybe the best thing would be to call a house-clearance company and let them deal with it.

On the other hand—I eye the boxes mutinously—how much would a clearance company charge to deal with this? Several hundred pounds. The Church won't contribute, I'm broke and I'm not sure that fund-raising to empty the new vicar's cellar of crap will rank highly on the parish council's agenda.

I sigh and approach the least intimidating stack. First, I'll deal with the boxes, because, I reason, most of those will be full of stuff for recycling. And there's always the chance I might unearth some long-lost treasure that could turn out to be worth thousands.

Half an hour later, it's apparent I won't be troubling **Antiques Roadshow** any time soon. Instead, I have dumped numerous ancient copies of the **Church Times** into black sacks. I have ditched old newsletters and sermons, and plastic cups and paper plates no doubt intended to be used at fetes and other events but long since devoured by mold. One box contains a pile of old Christmas hats, streamers and rotting crackers.

I shuffle over to another box. This one appears to be full of DVDs. Reverend Fletcher's, I presume. **Star Wars** (originals), **Blade Runner,** the **Godfather** trilogy, **Ghostbusters**. Fletcher had good taste in films. And then I spy **Angels and Demons** lurking at the bottom (well, I guess everyone has a guilty pleasure). The next box is full of CDs. Mostly Motown and soul. A few generic pop compilations. Some old eighties stuff. Alison Moyet, Bronski Beat, Erasure. Okay. Eclectic. But, as someone who has a penchant for playing My Chemical Romance loudly in the car, who am I to judge?

A third box is full of books. It occurs to me that Clara said she had cleared out most of Reverend Fletcher's stuff. She doesn't seem to have done a very good job.

I take some of the books out. Bulky hardbacks. C. J. Sansom, Hilary Mantel, Ken Follett, Bernard Cornwell. Huge nonfiction tomes about history, local legends, superstitions.

It's clear to see where Fletcher's interests lay. And for the first time, I feel like I'm getting more of a picture of my predecessor. You may not be able to judge a book by its cover, but you can certainly judge a person by their books. I think I would have liked Fletcher. If he'd still been alive, we would probably have enjoyed chatting over a coffee.

I pull out a few more paperbacks. And frown.

The Witching Class. A Shower of Spells. The Coven Seekers.

These don't quite sit with the others. I flip one over and read the blurb. Some kind of YA series about a school for witches—**Mallory Towers** meets **The Craft.**

The author's name is Saffron Winter. It rings a distant bell. Was she the YA author whose books were being made into films (although that doesn't really narrow it down)?

I flick to the back of the book. There's a small black-and-white photo of a woman who looks to be about my age, with a mass of curly dark hair and a knowing smile. I wonder why authors' photos always make them seem so smug. **Look, I wrote a book. Aren't I clever?**

And then I see there's a piece of paper sticking out of the pages, obviously used as a marker. I slip it out. It looks like an old to-do list:

Summer fete—volunteers?
Coffee morning, new kettle
Speak to Rushton re: plans
Aaron
Sainsbury's click and collect

I stare at it, feeling suddenly sad. It's just a mundane day-to-day list. But those are often the things that are the most poignant. I remember a parishioner who had recently lost her husband telling me it wasn't the funeral or the wake or even the news of his death that broke her. It was when an Amazon delivery for some books he had pre-ordered turned up.

"He had been looking forward to reading them so much, and now he never will."

Those pristine, unthumbed pages. That was what had caused her to collapse, howling, on to the floor.

But then, we all make those small investments in our future. Tickets to a concert, dinner reservations, a holiday booking. Never letting ourselves imagine we might not be here to enjoy them; that some random event or encounter might snatch us from existence. We all take a punt on tomorrow. Even though every day is actually a leap of faith, a step out over the abyss.

I wipe my arm across my forehead. The air down here is both damp and stuffy. There must be air bricks somewhere, but they have probably been clogged by dirt and blocked by more of the omnipresent boxes. I've filled three rubbish sacks already and still barely made a dent upon the metropolis of cardboard.

Time for a break. I'll take the sacks upstairs, make a coffee and then tackle some more later.

I pick up two sacks. I'm feeling dirty and dusty and . . .

"Bugger."

As I heave the sacks around, one catches the corner of another teetering pile of boxes. I see them about to collapse a moment before it happens, but I'm powerless to stop it. I drop the sacks, grabbing for the wobbling boxes, but it's no good. The whole lot comes piling down, sending me crashing into the mound of rubbish on the ground, my fall thankfully broken by the bin bags full of magazines. My elbow still connects hard with the rough cellar floor. I curse and cup the throbbing bone, rubbing at it viciously.

"Crapping hell."

I curse again and ease myself up, still rubbing at my bruised elbow. I look around. Fortunately, most of the toppled boxes don't contain anything breakable or skull-crushing—just more old newspapers and magazines. I scramble to my feet and start to stuff them into the black sacks. As I do, I notice something. Another box. It stands out because it's newer and unmoldy. It is sealed with brown tape. It must have been stuffed in one of the older boxes. Hidden? I slide the box across the cellar floor toward me, get my nonexistent nails beneath the edges of the brown tape and eventually manage to peel it off and open the flaps.

The first thing I see is a folder, secured with

an elastic band. Scribbled on the front—**"Sussex Martyrs."** I lift it out. It's bulky, paper bulging out of the sides. There's another folder underneath. This one is lighter. Scribbled on the front: **"Merry and Joy."** Reverend Fletcher really **had** been interested in the village's history. This looks like a lot of research.

I look back inside the box. There's something else at the bottom. Something small, rectangular and black. I reach in and take it out.

It's an old portable tape recorder, with a cassette still inside. I stare at it, feeling sick. Written on the label in neat, precise handwriting:

"Exorcism of Merry Joanne Lane."

NINETEEN

Wrigley is already there, skinny frame wedged into the tire swing, rocking back and forth. He raises a hand as Flo approaches, arm jittering from side to side. She fights her way through the tangled grass toward him.

"Hey."

"You came."

"Why wouldn't I?"

"Thought you might have changed your mind about meeting the village's resident weirdo."

"Don't give yourself so much credit. You've not met my mum."

He hops off the swing. "How weird can she be? She's a vicar, right?"

"Exactly."

They fall into pace alongside each other. A track has been worn into the field, leading toward a small copse of trees.

"What about your mum?" Flo asks.

A shrug. "What about her?"

"Just asking."

"She's all right, but she can be a bit intense."

"Yeah?"

"I had a pretty shit time at my last school. It's why we moved. Mum is kind of overprotective."

"I guess that's her job."

"It's embarrassing."

"That's mums for you."

"Right."

They reach an overgrown stile. Despite his weird twitches, Wrigley jumps over it easily. Flo struggles a little, not being used to stiles and with the heavy camera around her neck. Wrigley proffers a trembling hand and, reluctantly, she takes it. She hops off the other side, quickly retracting her hand.

"So, you ever get any crap about your mum being a vicar?"

Flo thinks about the graffiti on their old house. The smashed windows at the church. The messages on social media.

Bitch. Cunt. Child killer.

"Not really. Most people didn't care."

"Yeah, well, watch out here."

"Why?"

"Small village. In some parts of the world, they're yelling, 'Revolution, revolution!' Here, they're yelling 'Evolution, evolution! We want our thumbs!' "

Flo looks at him, surprised. "Bill Hicks?"

He turns and grins. "You know it."

"Mum's a fan. She got me into a load of eighties and nineties stuff."

"Cool. Favorite film?"

"Well, **The Lost Boys** is a classic. What about you?"

"**The Usual Suspects**."

"Keyser Söze?"

" 'The greatest trick the devil ever pulled is pretending he didn't exist.'"

They smile at each other. Then both quickly look down again.

"Anyway," he says. "Just warning you. A lot of the kids are, like, totally inbred."

"Harsh."

"But true."

"Yeah, well, I can look after myself."

He shrugs again, and his whole body convulses. "Just giving you a heads up."

They wander along an uneven track through the trees, so narrow they have to slip into single file. Flo finds herself watching Wrigley's jerky progress, thinking that it reminds her of something. And then she has it—Edward Scissorhands. He has the same kind of awkward clockwork motion. There's something weirdly appealing about it.

Stop it. **No odd crushes**. **You don't really know anything about him.**

Which probably means that following him through dark woods to an abandoned house isn't necessarily the smartest idea.

"Just over here," Wrigley says. "There's a bridge over a stream."

They cross the bridge; the path rises up and the small copse ends at another stile. Wrigley hops over. Flo manages to clamber over it with a little more dignity this time. She jumps down.

"Whoah!"

Ahead of them, she can see the shell of an old building. It stands stark and aloof, bricks blackened, windows hollowed out. If someone wanted to find the perfect creepy house for a horror movie, then the location scout would wet themselves at this.

"Cool, isn't it?" Wrigley says, moving beside her.

"Yeah."

Flo raises her camera and starts snapping. There is something really ominous about the building, even through a lens. If the chapel possesses a kind of Gothic melancholy, this place exudes . . .

Evil.

The word slips, like a sliver of ice, down her neck. Stupid. Crazy. She doesn't even believe in evil. No such thing. Just fucked-up people doing fucked-up things.

"Is this the only way to get to it?" she asks, feeling a bit discomfited.

"There's a track from the road that way." He

waves past the fields. "But it's, like, totally grown over. Plus, someone put a gate up—to stop kids getting in." He grins.

"Right."

"C'mon. Just wait till you see inside."

"Inside?"

He is already loping awkwardly ahead. "The whole place still has furniture and all sorts of shit in there. Like the people just upped and left."

He leaps over a crumbling stone wall into the garden. **It's just a building,** she tells herself. **An empty, creepy building.** She scrambles to catch up, hops over the wall and looks around.

The grass is knee high and choked with weeds and brambles. In one corner, a rusted swing is half collapsed. A child's ancient trike is all but submerged in stinging nettles. Children lived here once. A family. It's hard to imagine. She looks up at the desolate building, trying to picture it with windows, a brightly painted front door, maybe purple flowers crawling up the walls.

She raises the camera again. She can't quite get the right angle. She takes a couple of steps backward. And then a couple more. Wrigley suddenly grabs her arm, yanking her to the side so hard she stumbles and almost falls.

"Jesus! What the fuck are you doing?" She pulls her arm away and glares at him, heart hammering.

"The well!"

"What?"

"You almost fell down the **fucking** well."

He points to the spot where she was just standing. And now she sees it: a raised circle of uneven stones, almost entirely camouflaged by the grass and weeds. She moves forward and peers cautiously over the lip. A long drop into darkness. Another step and she could have toppled straight down. She looks back at Wrigley, feeling stupid.

"I'm sorry. You just scared me . . ."

"Why? What did you think I was going to do?"

"Nothing."

"Attack you? Murder you?"

"Of course not."

"Perhaps that's what weirdos like me do, right?"

"Don't be so stupid. I'm **sorry**. Okay?"

He stares at her from under his long fringe, eyes unreadable. Then he grins. "If I really wanted to murder you, I wouldn't have told you about the well." He turns and shambles away. "C'mon."

Flo hesitates for a moment. She glances back at the well. **Fucker**. And then she follows him.

TWENTY

Blood throbs in my ears, heart expanding and contracting, expanding and contracting. **Exorcism. Merry Joanne Lane.** The name in the Bible. **Merry J. L.** The old leather case. I press eject, but the cassette is stuck. I fumble but can't get my nails around it. I need a small screwdriver or a pen.

I stand. The thudding in my ears grows louder. And then I realize—it's coming from above me. I glance up. Someone is knocking at the front door. Crap.

Reluctantly, I close the recorder and drop it back into the box, along with the folders. Then I hurry up the stairs and pull the door open.

Aaron stands outside, oily hair gleaming in the faint sunshine, dressed in his usual black suit and grey shirt ensemble.

"Aaron. What are you doing here?"

"I just came by to . . . Are you all right?"

I'm suddenly aware of how I must look: breathless and covered in dust. I brush at my smock, trying to regain some dignity.

"Fine. I was just sorting some boxes in the cellar."

"I see. Well, I have a message from Reverend Rushton."

"He couldn't call?"

"I was passing by."

Aaron seems to do a lot of passing by. I remember what Rushton said again: **"Aaron and I are the only other people with keys to the chapel."**

"I noticed that someone has vandalized your car," he adds. "Most unpleasant."

"Yes, I know," I say impatiently. "What's the message?"

"Reverend Rushton was supposed to be meeting a young couple tomorrow morning to talk about their upcoming marriage, but he's double-booked himself. As you'll be the residing vicar when they marry, he thought that you could chat to them instead."

"Okay. Have you got their details?"

"Yes. I wrote them down."

He takes out a folded sheet of paper from his pocket and hands it to me.

"Thanks."

We stare at one another. I will him to go away. He remains, standing patiently, like he's waiting for something—the Second Coming, perhaps.

I sigh. "Would you like to come in for a cup of coffee?"

"Thank you, but I'm afraid I don't drink caffeine."

"Oh. Well, I don't have any decaf." **Because what's the point?** "But I may have some mint tea at the back of a cupboard?"

"That would be fine, thank you."

Great. He follows me into the kitchen.

"Have a seat," I say.

He pulls out a chair and perches on the edge, like he might set off an ejector button if he sits further back.

I set the kettle to boil and get out some mugs. "So, we haven't really had a chance to chat, have we?"

"No."

"How long have you been the warden here?"

"Officially, about three years."

"Forgive me for saying, but you're very young for a warden?"

Most wardens tend to be retired and, despite the old-fashioned clothes, Aaron can't be more than mid-thirties.

"Maybe so, but I've been helping at the chapel since I was a child."

"Were your family very involved with the chapel?"

He gives me an odd look. "My father was the vicar here for over thirty years."

"Your **father**?"

"Reverend Marsh."

Marsh. I never asked Aaron's surname. But now, I can see the resemblance to the picture in the office. The same dark hair, sharp features.

"You seem surprised?" Aaron says.

"I, erm, no, I just didn't realize."

I turn and plop a teabag into one mug and spoon coffee somewhat unsteadily into the other. "So, I suppose this was your family home?"

"Yes. Until my father retired."

The thought that Aaron grew up here, has his own memories of this place, makes me feel awkward, like I am somehow intruding.

"And do your mother and father still live in the village?"

"My mother died when I was six. Cervical cancer."

"I'm sorry. And your father?"

"My father is very ill. That's why he retired."

"I see. Is he in the hospital?"

"I care for him at home. He has Huntington's. There's nothing the hospital can do for him."

"Oh, that's awful."

And it really is. Huntington's is a horrible, cruel disease that gradually robs people of their movement, their cognitive thought, their ability to talk, to eat and eventually to breathe. It is incurable and relentless. And worse, it's hereditary, with a child having a 50 percent chance of acquiring the defective gene from their parent.

"You're his sole carer?"

"There are nurses who come in. But mostly, yes."

I regard Aaron with more sympathy. It's tough being a carer. You have to put your own life on hold. It isolates you from people, makes it impossible to hold down a job. I suppose that's how Aaron ended up being a churchwarden—something he can work around his father's care that gives him a purpose. I realize I feel sorry for him, and then think that he probably doesn't want my pity.

"Well, I'm very grateful for your help and dedication to the chapel, especially with all the other demands on your time."

"Thank you. It's always been a part of my life."

"And your father's?"

"Yes."

"You must know a lot about its history?"

"You mean the Burning Girls?" He offers a thin smile. "Everyone in the village knows about them. Although, I imagine, to an outsider, it seems rather a strange custom."

"Oh, I don't know. I've experienced stranger."

"My father didn't really like the burning of the effigies. He felt it was pagan, but you can't change a tradition that's taken place in a village for hundreds of years."

"Well, if that was the case, we'd still be burning witches and using leeches to cure mental illness."

He gives me an odd look.

"Sorry." I wave a hand. "I just find that 'tradition'

is often used to defend things we'd otherwise rightly condemn." **Especially in the Church**. I bring the drinks over to the table and sit down opposite him.

"There was actually something else I wanted to ask you—"

"Yes?"

"The box you gave me when I arrived. Do you have any idea who might have left it?"

"No. Why? What was in it?"

"An exorcism kit."

"**What?**"

He seems genuinely shocked, and I don't think Aaron is any kind of actor.

"It looks quite old. I'm wondering where it could have come from."

"I don't know. Have you asked Reverend Rushton?"

"No. Would he know who left it?"

"Well, he knows all the church business. He's been the vicar at Warblers Green for a long time."

"How long?"

"It must be close to thirty years."

"He knew your father?"

"Yes, my father trained him as a curate after . . ." He falters, catches himself.

"After what?" I prompt.

"After the previous curate left."

I think about the space on the wall in the office. Like a picture had been taken down and no one had got round to replacing it.

"Oh. Where did he go?"

"I really don't know. I'm sorry—what does this have to do with anything?"

"I'm just curious as to why someone would leave me an old exorcism kit? It feels like some kind of message."

"As I've said, I have no idea. None of us even knew you were taking over here until a few days ago. It was all done rather hastily. But then, the whole business was a shock."

It strikes me that people keep saying Reverend Fletcher's suicide was a shock. But they're also very keen to tell me he was having some kind of breakdown. Something doesn't tally.

"Were you and Reverend Fletcher close?"

"Matthew and I were colleagues."

Colleagues? And yet, I note the use of Reverend Fletcher's first name.

"You were the one who found him?"

His faint color all but evaporates.

"Sorry," I say. "I didn't mean to—"

He waves a hand. "It's fine. It was just very . . . unpleasant."

An understatement, I'm sure. I move quickly on.

"I wish I knew a little bit more about him. What was he like?"

I sense him softening a little. "He was a good man. Kind, generous. Full of life. Everyone in the village liked him and he was very enthusiastic about the parish and the chapel."

"I understand he was interested in its history?"

"Yes. The martyrs, mainly."

"Did he ever mention the names Merry and Joy?"

"The girls who disappeared?"

"You've heard of them?"

A small twitch of annoyance. "It's a small village. Things like that don't happen every day."

"But it was a long time ago. You must have been very young."

He sighs. "Reverend Brooks . . . Matthew and I discussed church matters. Anything else, you'd be better off talking to Saffron Winter."

Saffron Winter. It takes a moment and then it comes to me. The name on the books. The author.

"She's a writer," Aaron says, interpreting my frown as a lack of familiarity with the name. "She moved here fairly recently. Matthew had become quite friendly with her in the months before he died."

There's a definite note of disapproval in his voice. Which immediately makes me think that Saffron Winter would be someone I'd like. It explains the books in the cellar as well. I make a mental note to look her up . . . when we have internet.

I sip my coffee and try to soften my voice. "Aaron, do you mind if I ask—did Matthew seem suicidal to you?"

A look crosses his face. Something I can't quite interpret.

"I think," he says slowly, "Matthew didn't need to . . . do what he did."

"Perhaps he felt there was nowhere he could turn."

"He could have turned to God."

"God doesn't have all the answers."

"It doesn't make suicide the right answer."

"No, not always."

He tilts his chin up defiantly. "My father is dying, Reverend. He can't talk. He struggles to eat. Soon his nervous system will shut down completely. He **knew** what was coming. But he never considered killing himself."

"Not everyone is that strong."

Or selfish. Condemning his son to years trapped, caring for him. I wonder if the reason Aaron is so angry at Fletcher for killing himself is because his father didn't.

"Aaron—"

He makes a show of looking at his watch. "I'm sorry. If you'll excuse me, I should probably get home."

He stands abruptly and knocks into the table. His tea, almost untouched, slops over the rim of the mug.

"Sorry."

"No problem."

"Just a little clumsy."

I think about the odd stiffness of his motions.

The almost robotic sense of control. The refusal of caffeine, a stimulant. And I remember that Huntington's is hereditary.

He knew what was coming.

I nod. "Of course."

I see Aaron to the door and watch him walk down the road. An odd man. That doesn't necessarily mean a bad man. But he knows more than he's saying.

He **knew** Merry and Joy's names right away. He also caught himself when he was talking about Rushton's predecessor.

I wonder, what else does he know?

TWENTY-ONE

The building stinks. Urine, shit, stale smoke, weed. In a way, Flo thinks, it makes the place feel less creepy. It might have been unlived in for years, but it hasn't been unoccupied. People, probably teenagers, have been using this space. Of course. If there's an abandoned building, one thing you can count on is that teenagers will use it as a place to hang out, smoke, drink, take drugs and have sex.

Downstairs, there are two rooms. A kitchen and what must have been the living room. The kitchen is just a shell. Both the range and the sink have been ripped out at some point. The tiled floor is cracked. Cupboard doors hang open, revealing a few ancient rusted tins and rat droppings.

The living room hasn't fared much better. A sagging, mold-encrusted couch sags in one corner, springs sticking up like unruly hairs. A sideboard leans drunkenly in another, drawers long gone for firewood. The floor is strewn with smashed pictures and ornaments.

Flo raises the camera and snaps away. She crouches down to get close-up pictures of the shattered ornaments. Angels and Jesus figures. Crosses and religious artifacts. This is good stuff.

Wrigley hovers nearby, jigging from foot to foot, his body unable to contain its twitches and jerks. She's noticed that the spasming is worse when his mind is unoccupied. She takes a little longer over the photos. She hasn't quite forgiven him for the well incident.

"You ready to see upstairs?" he asks.

"Is it much different from downstairs?"

"Way better."

Flo eyes him suspiciously. "Okay."

She follows him up a rickety staircase. It creaks alarmingly. Flo thinks about rot and woodworm. A landing at the top leads to three more rooms. She pokes her head into the bathroom. Small and dirty, the sink and bath streaked with something unpleasant and unidentifiable. She beats a hasty retreat and crosses the landing, treading carefully around holes in the floorboards. Forget ghosts— she'd like to avoid plunging to **her** death.

The first bedroom is bare of furniture. A few pictures still hang wonkily on the walls, faded and water damaged, but she can just make out biblical scenes and quotes:

"Honor your father and your mother, so that

you may live long in the land the LORD your God is giving you."

"Children, obey your parents in everything, for this pleases the Lord."

"Submit yourselves therefore to God. Resist the devil, and he will flee from you."

"Guess your mum would feel at home here," Wrigley says, idly poking his finger in a hole in the wall and dislodging a small pile of rubble.

"I doubt it," Flo says, snapping some of the pictures. "She doesn't like to bring her work home with her."

In fact, Flo thinks, without the dog collar, you'd never guess Mum was a vicar. Sometimes, Flo wonders how she ended up getting into the priesthood. Mum doesn't talk about it much, usually brushing it off with talk of a "calling," but once she let slip that she didn't have a great childhood and someone from the Church had helped her.

She wanders across to the window and peers out. She can just make out the well, a gaping mouth at the very far edge of the overgrown garden. Beyond it, the shadowy woods lurk. From here, they look even closer to the house. Like the trees are creeping up when no one is looking. She fights back a shiver. Something white catches her eye near the trees' dark folds. A figure? She raises the camera again. Click, click.

"So, ready to see what's behind the final door?"

She jumps. Wrigley stands behind her, jittering.

"I'm breathless with anticipation."

He smirks. "It's good. Trust me."

She isn't sure she does, but she follows him back across the landing to the second bedroom. Wrigley pushes open the door.

She steps inside and looks around. "Holy fuck."

The room is large. A bed still stands in the center, topped by a stained and moldy mattress. Flo doesn't like to think what might have taken place on it, fuelled by cans of cider and the numerous discarded joints lying around.

But that's not what makes her gasp. It's the walls. Covered in flaking wallpaper and plastered with graffiti. Not your usual **"Kerry is a slag"** and **"Jordan fucks bumholes"** graffiti. This is far weirder.

Pentagrams, upside-down crosses, evil eyes, weird inscriptions in what looks—to her untrained eye—like Latin, as well as strange stick figures, goat's heads, the Leviathan cross. A lot of it is crude, but the effect, over and over again, covering every wall and even some of the floor, is skin-crawling in its sheer magnitude.

She walks around the room. Up close, you can see that the drawings and inscriptions are layered, newer ones overlapping older, more faded ones. People, kids, have been doing this for years. And taking it seriously. No one has interspersed the symbols with an errant penis or a jokey scribble.

"Totally **Blair Witch,** right?" Wrigley says, and

reaches out a hand to touch the walls. Flo has the strongest urge to tell him not to.

She fumbles for the camera again.

"So, what is this? Satanic worship? You come up here and sacrifice goats?"

"Not me. I like goats. I come up here to draw pictures."

"Then who did all of this?"

"Dunno. This stuff has been appearing here for eons. More keeps getting added."

"But why? Did something bad happen here?"

He wanders around, kicking up dust with his boots. Then he sits down on the edge of the stained mattress.

"Okay, story is that the family who lived here, the daughter disappeared. Along with her best friend. Some reckoned they ran away, some reckoned they were murdered. But no one could ever prove it.

"Then, like, a year after the girl who lived here disappeared, so did her mum and brother. Just vanished one night. Poof! Never seen again, and the house was left to rot."

"A whole family just disappeared?"

"Yeah. A few years ago, another family were going to buy the house, but then their little girl died in an accident. People say that the place is cursed, haunted, jinxed. Call it what you will."

Flo snorts. "Doesn't mean it's anything to do with the devil."

"Don't you think that some places are just rotten? Like black spots in the earth. Bad stuff keeps happening there."

Flo lowers the camera. She wants to say no, she doesn't believe in any of that crap, but actually, she remembers an occasion when she was taking some photos in the Rock Cemetery in Nottingham.

She'd walked around it before, but this time found herself in a different part, an area shielded by trees in the shadow of a small rocky outcrop. It was a pretty spot and yet something about it just felt off. She had taken a couple of photos, but all the time she was aware of the **offness,** like an itch at the back of her neck. She left more quickly than she intended, but the feeling clung to her, like the dregs of a nightmare.

The next day she had mentioned it to Leon, whose eyes had widened. **"You know, a girl was murdered there a couple of years ago."**

She had called bullshit—Leon had a taste for the melodramatic—but later googled it to see if it was true. She found the story. A sixteen-year-old girl had been raped and murdered on her way home from a night out, her body dumped in the cemetery. The photo showed the same distinctive rocky outcrop.

She shrugs now. "I'm not really superstitious."

"I think some kids come up here, hold seances, do Ouija boards, all that sort of shit."

"Not you?"

"I'm not first pick for any club, not even the worshippers of Beelzebub. Besides, that stuff is rank. Treating death like it's a game. If someone you loved died, you wouldn't want a bunch of drunk morons tormenting them for fun, would you?"

She thinks about her dad. She was just a toddler when he died, and Mum never really talks about him. She guesses it's still too hard. But she gets what Wrigley means. Death isn't something you play with. The dead deserve peace and respect. She feels herself warming to him again.

"I guess not," she says.

He rises abruptly. "So, you done?"

"Err, yeah."

She's barely replaced the cap on her camera lens before Wrigley is stomping downstairs. She gives the bedroom a final glance and starts after him. Something crunches underfoot. She looks down, expecting to see a bit of broken bottle. Instead, she realizes, it's a photo frame.

She bends down, curious. The frame still holds an old picture, weathered and faded. She can just make out two children. A dark-haired teenage girl and a younger boy. She stares at it for a moment, and then a sharp **crrrack** makes her jump. **Shit**. What was that? Another **crrrack,** this time followed by the thunder of wings and a chorus of harsh caws. Gunshots, she thinks.

"Wrigley?"

She hurries down the stairs and out into the

sunshine, the bright light momentarily blinding her. She blinks and then spots him, crouching down, holding something in his hands.

"What's going on?"

He turns, and she recoils. He's cradling a large crow. Its feathers gleam like oil in the sunlight, sharp beak gaping slightly. One eye has been blown away, the socket a raw mass of gore. The other still gleams with a faint, terrified light. As she watches, the bird twitches and the eye dims to darkness.

Wrigley stands, whole body jittering with anger. His face is pale and taut. He yells into the woods:

"You killed one. Are you happy now?"

Silence. Enormous in the aftermath of the echoing shots and terrified bird cries. Flo stares across to the woods. Pretty earlier, sunlight dappling the forest floor with gold. Now, they seem thick with threat.

"Wrigley," she starts to say. "I think—"

Another shot rings out. A roof tile jumps from the building and shatters at their feet. Wrigley stumbles backward, clutching at his face. Flo can see blood running down his cheek.

"Wrigley?"

He moves his hands away. There's a nasty gash just above his eye. It looks shallow, but it's hard to tell with all the blood.

"We need to get out of here." She turns, and then stops.

Two figures have emerged from the woods. The

tall blonde and the boy from this morning. Rosie and Tom. **What are the fucking chances?** An air-gun swings from Tom's hand. Even better.

Wrigley lets out a low breath. "Fuckers."

"You know them?"

"Rosie Harper and her cousin, Tom. Total twats."

"I ran into them this morning."

"How did that go?"

"Not well."

"Not surprised."

Harper, she thinks. Why does that ring a bell? And then it clicks. The little girl and her dad. Could Rosie be her sister?

The duo draws closer. She can see now that Tom's nose is swollen, bruises forming beneath his eyes. They jump over the broken-down wall.

Rosie smiles. "Well, look, it's Vampirina and wriggly Wrigley."

Wrigley stares at her darkly. "Look, it's the morons who kill innocent animals for fun."

"Just shooting some vermin."

Tom grins. "Nasty graze, Wrigley."

"How's your nose?" Flo says sweetly. "Painful?"

The grin fades. "You're lucky you ran, you psycho bitch."

Wrigley turns to her. "**You** did that?"

"It was an accident."

"So, what are you two doing here?" Rosie asks. "Fucking?"

"What's it got to do with you?" Flo says, staring at her hard.

"Well, seeing as my dad just bought this land, plenty. You're trespassing."

"Fine. We were just leaving anyway." Flo grabs Wrigley's arm. "C'mon."

They start to move. Tom raises the airgun.

"We didn't say you could go yet."

Flo stands still, heart thudding.

Tom gestures at the camera. "Give me that piece of shit around your neck. Then you can go."

Show no fear. Show no fear.

"No."

Wrigley steps forward. "Just leave her alone."

"Stay out of it, retard. Unfinished business." Tom aims the gun at Flo's chest. "I **said,** give me your camera."

Flo grasps the strap. Blood pulses in her throat.

Give him the camera. It's not worth it. That's what her mum would say.

But it **is** worth it. To her.

She lets her hands fall. "Go fuck yourself."

He grins. "Bitch."

And pulls the trigger.

TWENTY-TWO

We all have our hiding places. Not just physical ones. Places deep inside where we put away the things we don't want others to see. The less palatable parts. **Our St. Peter's box,** I call it. The one we pray he won't find when we're trying to sneak in through the pearly gates.

I take my smoking tin and papers out of the hollowed-out Bible on the bookcase, roll a cigarette and stand outside the kitchen door, inhaling deeply, savoring the nicotine hit. We all have our vices too. Addictions, needs, desires. Again, some more palatable than others.

I think about the small black tape recorder. **Exorcism of Merry Joanne Lane.** The Church hardly has a glorious track record when it comes to the treatment of women. Exorcism is no exception. It's no coincidence that the majority of exorcisms were carried out upon young women. Women who might have been depressed, suffering mental illness or simply displaying "wanton willfulness" by not doing what a husband or father instructed them.

All manner of "undesirable" female behavior could be ascribed to demonic possession and therefore "cured" by abusive and violent exorcisms. All performed in the name of God.

The Church of England has, over the years, taken a more moderate approach. Pastoral care over violent expulsion of evil. Although it would probably surprise many people if they knew that, even now, in these days of scientific advancement, many dioceses have a **Deliverance Ministry.** Basically, a specialist team called in to deal with paranormal experiences. These might often be in conjunction with mental health advisers, but their presence is real and recognized. Even regular priests can occasionally be called to investigate incidents of demonic possession or haunting.

I remember a visit I made as a curate with my mentor, Reverend Blake—a heavy-set, balding man with a fierce gaze and a fiercer Mancunian accent. I was twenty-seven, three years into my training, and we had been called to see a young woman in the Meadows area of Nottingham.

I expected the usual. Drug abuse, alcoholism, perhaps domestic abuse. But that wasn't it (although I suspected that drugs or alcohol might still be involved). The young woman we were visiting believed that her flat was possessed, haunted. She wanted us to perform an exorcism.

"Do you believe in God?" Blake had asked me.

We were sitting in his car, a beaten-up Honda Civic, grabbing a quick McDonald's on our way to a grim tower block where the woman lived.

I stared at Blake over my quarter pounder, wondering if this was a trick question. Up until now, I had known all the right answers. Or rather, I had learned them. Night after night, studying while also working part time. I had passed everything so far with flying colors. Because I was good at exams, good at debating. Good at saying what people wanted to hear. I had learned fast and hard. But I couldn't lie to or bluff Blake. He knew me too well. He ought to. He had rescued me from the streets when I was sixteen.

"I have faith," I said.

"And nothing could shake your faith?"

The quarter pounder lodged uncomfortably in my throat. I reached for my Coke and took a swig. The straw gurgled in the plastic cup.

"I don't believe so."

"So, in a way, it doesn't matter if God exists or not, as long as we have faith that he does?"

I frowned, unsure how to reply.

He smiled. "It's okay. I'm not trying to engage you in some religious Schrödinger's cat–type debate."

"Then why are we discussing this?"

"Because I sense your skepticism about our visit today."

He was right. As usual.

"I just feel uncomfortable about it."

He nodded, wiping his mouth with a paper napkin and chucking it into his empty container of fries.

"Because?"

"It sounds as if this woman needs the care of mental health professionals, counseling, maybe medication."

"And what if those haven't helped?"

"But exorcism? Really?"

"You don't believe in demonic possession?"

"No."

He raised his eyebrows.

"I believe that evil exists," I said. "In the hearts of all men and women. Our dark side, if you will. External demons—no, I don't believe in that."

"But this young woman does. She believes absolutely. She is desperate and she has turned to us for help. Should we turn her away?"

"No, of course not."

"Jack, our belief is not the point. **She** believes it, and the human mind is a powerful thing."

"Aren't we just enabling her delusions?"

"Do you pray for God's help in times of trouble?"

"Yes."

"Even though you know he's probably not going to drop everything just to deal with your problem?"

I made a noise of assent.

"But it provides comfort?"

"Yes."

"Our job is to perform the exorcism rites. Whether the demons are real or not, the exorcism will provide comfort. The young lady will believe that the demon is gone and that her flat is cleansed. God has triumphed. Faith, to an extent, is a placebo. If you believe it works, it works."

"I suppose," I said doubtfully.

He winked. "Good. Now, let's go bust some ghosts."

I feel a sadness settle over me. Blake died five years ago. Time. It's scary when you think about it. I stub my cigarette out and walk back into the kitchen. The box from the cellar sits on the table. I take the tape recorder out and press play, without much hope. Predictably, nothing happens. I turn it over. The screws to the battery compartment are coated with rust. I try to eject the tape again, but to no avail. The mechanism is stuck, and the tape looks like it's caught up inside.

Okay. I rifle through the drawers, looking for a screwdriver or a pen. I finally find what I'm looking for in a Tupperware box I seem to have labeled "Keys." There are no keys in the box. Instead, there are paperclips, Blu-Tack, clothespins, an old pair of headphones and, buried underneath, a small silver screwdriver. I pluck the screwdriver out triumphantly and start trying to dislodge the tape.

I manage to loosen it and then, suddenly, it pops out . . . and the tape snaps.

"Damn!"

I'm still staring at the broken cassette, wondering if I can remember how to fix it—Scotch tape?—when the front door slams, hard enough to shake the cottage. I quickly drop the cassette and tape recorder back into the box, dump it on the floor and shove it under the table with my foot.

I turn. Flo stands in the doorway with her arm around a skinny teenage boy whose face is streaked with blood. Her hair is disheveled and the Nikon around her neck is smashed.

She stares at me and utters the words guaranteed to strike dread into every parent's heart:

"Mum—don't be mad."

TWENTY-THREE

"An airgun? Christ. I thought it was in Nottingham we had to worry about guns, not here."

I dab at Wrigley's head. Cleaning blood off someone for the second time in three days.

"I know," Flo mutters.

"Did you see who was shooting?"

"No, too far away."

I want to contradict her. I don't know much about airguns, but I don't think they have a particularly long range.

"We need to report this to the police."

"It was just an accident."

"How do you know? You could have been killed. The pair of you."

"Owww," Wrigley moans.

I am dabbing a bit too hard at the wound,

not that I'm blaming him for this or anything. Not totally.

"Sorry."

I chuck the bloody cloth at the sink. The wound is shallow, but head wounds bleed like bastards. I have retrieved the first-aid box from the bathroom upstairs. I dab on some antiseptic and stick two large dressing plasters on his head. I tilt his chin up to regard my work. He's actually a good-looking young man. I wonder what the story is with the odd jerking and twitching. Some kind of neuro-logical condition?

"There. That should do you, for now."

"Thanks, Reverend. I really appreciate it. My mum's not as cool about this sort of stuff as you."

I stare at him. "**Cool?** I'm not **cool** about it. I am very far from **cool** about it." I turn to Flo. "Some loon is wandering around the countryside firing off airguns. You could both have been killed. How many times do I have to say this?"

"We're fine," Flo says, impatiently.

"That's not the point."

I pick up the Nikon from the table. The lens is completely shattered. The pellet has lodged in the back, where it bulges slightly against the metal.

"Look at this. A few more millimeters and that could have pierced your heart."

I feel sick even as I say it.

"Mum, you're being melodramatic."

"No, I'm not."

"He wasn't aiming for my heart. He was aiming for the camera."

"**He?** I thought you said you didn't know the idiot who shot at you."

"We don't. I just said 'he' because, you know, turn of phrase."

I stare at both of them helplessly. There is more going on here. But, with teens, you can't drag it out of them. Sometimes, you have to play the long game. I could threaten. I could ground Flo. I could ban TV, the internet (if we had any). But if she doesn't want to tell me, she won't.

We all have our secrets. Teenagers more than most. I kept plenty from my own mother. And even with all the cruelties she inflicted, she never broke me.

"Promise me one thing," I say. "You won't go wandering around the woods again."

They glance at each other. Flo looks back at the camera.

"Now my camera's ruined there's not much point."

"We promise, Reverend Brooks," Wrigley says.

Flo sighs. "Promise."

"Okay. Right." I glance at the clock. Almost six o'clock. The afternoon has evaporated.

"Wrigley—do you want to stay for dinner?"

"I should probably get back home."

"Do you want a lift?"

"No, it's okay. I can walk."

"You sure? Where do you live?"

"Just over the other side of the village. It's fine. But thank you."

"Okay."

I walk him to the door.

"Thanks again, Reverend," Wrigley says. "I just want you to know—"

I hold up a hand. "Actually, there's something I want **you** to know." I pull the door half closed behind me. "I may have Reverend in front of my name, but don't let the dog collar fool you. First and foremost, I am a mother. If any harm ever comes to my daughter because of you, I will make it my mission in life to screw yours up beyond belief. Do I make myself clear?"

Just for a moment, the manic twitching seems to pause. He looks at me with eyes that are a distinctive silvery green.

"Crystal."

And then his whole body convulses again. He turns and stutters down the pathway. I watch him go, feeling uneasy. Then I close the door and walk back inside.

Flo is slumped at the kitchen table, holding the broken Nikon in her hands. She glances up as I enter.

"So, I suppose now Wrigley's gone you're really going to lay into me."

I sit down beside her and shake my head. "No."

I hold out my arms, like I used to when she was

a child having a tantrum. Comfort always dispels rage more quickly than shouting does. She sinks into my body and I hold her. After a while she raises her head. "I'm sorry, Mum."

"I know." I smooth her hair. "It's not your fault."

She looks at the camera. "I can't believe my camera is ruined."

"It's fixable. Unlike you."

"It will cost a fortune."

"We'll sort it, somehow."

We sit for a while and then I hear Flo's stomach rumble. "Hungry?"

"Yeah. A bit." Another low grumble. "A lot."

"How about I make us a stir fry and we stick a DVD on?"

"Okay."

"What d'you fancy?"

"Something trashy and retro."

"**Breakfast Club. Pretty in Pink?**"

She rolls her eyes. "Purleese. The cool girl chooses the idiot jock over the kind, lovely best friend?"

"Okay. You choose."

"**Heathers?**"

The beautiful girl falls in love with a psychopathic maniac.

"Okay."

She pads upstairs to get changed. I open the fridge and take out a selection of vegetables. Peppers, mushrooms, onions. I dump them on to a chopping board and grab a large knife.

I've just started chopping when Flo reemerges in a baggy pair of shorts and a black vest. She looks thin and tired and achingly beautiful. I want to wrap her up in my arms and never let her out of the house again.

She walks over to the fridge and takes out a Diet Coke. "Mum, what do you think of Wrigley?"

I try to keep my voice light. "Well, we didn't exactly meet in the best circumstances."

"It wasn't his fault."

"Okay. Well, he seems nice enough. What's with the twitching?"

"Dystonia. It's like something is wired wrong in his brain."

"Right." I select a large red pepper. "Question is—what do **you** think of him?"

A shrug. "He's okay. Y'know."

I do. I grip the knife tighter, trying to tell myself that he's just a boy. Probably harmless. Not all young men are predatory.

She wanders back and pulls out a chair.

"What's this?" she asks, looking down.

Crap. The box is still on the floor under the table.

"Oh, just some stuff that belonged to Reverend Fletcher. He was researching the history of the village. Pretty boring."

And yet she still reaches inside and lifts out a folder.

"Who are Merry and Joy?"

"Oh, just—**owww!** Bugger!"

She spins around. "Mum, you've cut yourself."

I've sliced my finger open with the sharp knife. Blood drips from the cut.

"Here." She grabs the plasters from the first-aid box and brings one over.

"Thanks, sweetheart."

I run my finger under the tap, dry it then wrap the plaster tightly around it.

"You should be more careful, Mum."

I raise an eyebrow. "Pot. Kettle?"

"Yeah, yeah."

"Why don't you go and find that DVD?"

"Okay."

She wanders out of the kitchen. I can hear her rummaging through the DVDs in the living room. I pick up the folder from the table, drop it back in the box and shove the box in the cupboard under the sink. Out of sight.

I hold up my finger. It hurts like hell. I cut it deeper than I meant to, but at least it provided a distraction. By the time Flo has found the DVD, I'm chucking vegetables into the wok and all talk of Merry and Joy has been forgotten.

TWENTY-FOUR

He continues his pilgrimage. From the old asylum down into the city. He slept rough here for a while, under the arches by the canal and in the underpass near the old shopping center.

Both are still popular spots. Early evening, and he can see sleeping bags piling up, cardboard boxes at the ready. Some bad stuff happened here too. An old drunk tried to steal from him, and he had to defend his things. He remembers how the drunk's body floated in the canal before the weeds and the weight of the rubble in his pockets dragged him down into the filthy water.

He walks on toward the Market Square. It's crammed with people. In the summer months, the square is turned into "The Beach." A grubby area of sand and a large paddling pool in the center of the city for families to pretend they are at the seaside. There is a bar, fairground rides and stalls selling food and drinks. Tepid lager in plastic cups. Greasy burgers and fried onions squeezed into anemic baps.

He stands near the edge of the crowds, not getting too close. So much noise, so many people, lights. He inhales the smells of popcorn, doughnuts and hotdogs, his rumbling stomach reminding him he hasn't eaten since the day before. Children scream and laugh on the rides.

He feels an old yearning in his heart. As a child, he never went to a fair, never experienced the dizzying spin of the waltzers or tasted the sweet, sugary rush of candyfloss. Mum regarded such pleasures as sinful. Even before he ended up on the streets, food was often basic or out of date, a "treat" getting through the day without incurring a beating.

Only when he escaped did he understand that his life was not like other children's. He would watch them sometimes as they skipped past, smiling, hand in hand with parents who kissed and cuddled them, smoothed their hair. All the while he huddled in cardboard, careful to keep away from prying eyes in case anyone questioned why a young boy was sleeping rough.

He starts, suddenly noticing that one of the mums is watching him suspiciously, phone in her hand. He realizes how he must look. A stooped figure in secondhand clothes, clean but not exactly well kept, staring at children. He flushes. He is not a good man, but he is definitely not **that** type of man. More to the point, he can't have her calling the police. He can't go back to prison. He has things he needs to do.

He hurries away, driving himself onward even though the day is starting to weigh down on him. He's hungry and thirsty, but he only has loose change in his pocket. Fortunately, where he is heading next should solve that problem.

The sounds of the fair fade away behind him. His feet take him from the city center, through darker, narrow terraced streets. Bins overflow, dogs bark, heavy bass throbs. The smell of cannabis and the threat of violence hang heavy in the air. Some things never change. Eventually, he reaches his destination. He looks up.

A large building, brick blackened by the city grime, stained-glass windows shielded with heavy iron grates, the spire reaching up against the grey evening sky.

St. Anne's Church.

The doors are open, light spilling out on to the pathway. A few homeless mill outside, smoking. A handwritten sign propped on the gate reads: **"Monday Night Soup Kitchen. Eat, drink, stay/pray a while."**

He smiles, walks up the path and through the open doors.

The church is warm, brightly lit and smells of rich, hearty cooking. His stomach grumbles again. Food will be good, but that's not the only reason he's here. His eyes scan the church hungrily. Four volunteers in aprons stand behind a long trestle table, dishing out stew and curry from large metal pans. Where is she? And then he sees a figure step out from the back of the church, dressed in a dark suit and a white clerical collar.

The figure walks toward him and smiles, revealing dazzling white teeth.

"Hello. Can I help you?"

He stares at the burly black vicar.

"Who are you?"

"I'm Reverend Bradley." The priest holds out a hand. "And I'm happy to welcome you to our church."

"No." He shakes his head. This isn't right. This is not how he imagined it. How he planned it. "Where's the other vicar?"

"I'm afraid she left."

"Where did she go?" He can't control the desperation in his voice.

The vicar frowns. "I don't know."

He's lying, he thinks. **The fat black vicar is lying.** He knows where she is. He just doesn't want to tell him.

The priest is still holding out a hand. "Are you all right?"

He fights down the anger, and then shakes the liar's hand. It's large and surprisingly soft. "Yes. Just tired and hungry."

"Why don't you go and help yourself to some food? I can especially recommend the chicken curry."

He forces a smile and nods subserviently. "Thank you."

He joins the queue and accepts some of the food. Then he takes his plate and sits on the edge of a bench, forking it into his mouth. It smells good, but he barely tastes it. He'll have to come back here later, he thinks, when the liar is alone. Then he'll make him tell him what he needs to know. The priest might be large, but he's out of condition. It shouldn't take long.

He catches himself, shakes his head. No. He mustn't hurt the priest. He's changed. He is not that man. Controlling anger is not weakness. It's strength.

But he needs to find her.

Then only hurt him just enough.

Just enough. He considers. Controlling anger is not weakness. Perhaps he could do that. He smiles. All right.

And try not to enjoy it.

She huddled in the cellar, in the darkness.

Above her, she could hear Mum moving around, Songs of Praise playing loudly. This was her punishment for blaspheming on a Sunday. Or so Mum said. In truth, it was just another one of her mind games. Favoring one child, punishing the other. At least, now they were older (and bigger), they were spared the worst punishment. The well. Lowered down. Left for hours.

The cellar wasn't so bad. Apart from the dark. And the rats.

She thought about the plan. To escape. Since they had first discussed it, she had seen less of Joy. Her mum was trying to keep them apart. And now, two evenings a week, Joy was taking extra Bible lessons with the new priest.

Joy had hurried past her the other day, barely saying hello. There was something different about her. A flush to her cheeks. A secrecy in her smile. Merry was worried. What was going on? Was it the priest?

Lots of the girls had a crush on him. But Merry didn't like him. Whenever he read stuff from the Bible, especially all the sin and damnation stuff, his eyes got kind of glassy and his face got red. She swore once she had seen a hard-on in his pants.

Upstairs, she heard her mum turn the television up.

From the corner, there was a rustling. Her eyes strained in the darkness. She hated the dark. Hated how vulnerable it made her feel. She tried to summon up comforting words from an old childhood book. Reciting them to herself.

"Darkness is fun, darkness is kind. Darkness—"

Her mother's voice rose: "Then sings my soul, my Savior God, to Thee. How great Thou art, how great Thou art."

The rustling drew closer.

TWENTY-FIVE

"Shit!"

I open my eyes. My vest is stuck to me, clammy with sweat, my bedclothes kicked off on to the floor. The bedroom takes form around me. **My** bedroom in the cottage. Another nightmare.

I sit up and reach for the water on my bedside table. I swig it down. I can see silvery daylight edging around the curtains. The cottage is silent and stuffy. I glance at the clock: 6:13 a.m. I'm not going to get any more sleep, so I might as well get up. I have my wedding consult this morning so an early start can't hurt.

I sling on my joggers and creep down the creaky stairs. The cottage smells of the veggie stir fry I made for dinner. Afterward, Flo and I curled up on the sofa with a large packet of M&Ms and watched **Heathers** until I realized that she had drifted off to sleep on my shoulder. I left her like that for a while, relishing the closeness. When she was little, she would curl up on my lap while we watched films together. Just the two of us. Like it's always been.

Flo's dad died when she was just eighteen months old. She doesn't really remember him. He was attacked by an intruder at his church. During a struggle he fell and hit his head. I told Flo as soon as she was old enough to understand. I also told her what a good dad he was and how much he loved her. Which is true. Mostly. But like many things, it's a version of the truth. A story told so many times I almost believe it myself.

Eventually, at just past midnight, I nudged Flo awake and we both trudged wearily up to bed. Our dirty plates are still sitting in the sink. Flo's broken camera lies on the kitchen table. I wander over and pick it up. I have no idea how much it will cost to fix, but I'm pretty sure it will be more than the £6:50 I have in savings.

Looking at it again, my stomach tightens. The young think they're invincible but, as you grow older, especially as you become a parent, you see danger everywhere. Flo knows who shot the airgun. I'm sure of it. Wrigley too. But for some reason they don't want to tell me. And what about Wrigley? I can't decide. Am I wary of him because I would be wary of **any** boy Flo brought home, or is there something else?

I sigh and stare out of the kitchen window at the chapel. I feel the strongest urge to pray. Obviously, as a vicar, that's not unusual. I pray every night and, sometimes, randomly during the day. These aren't "on my knees, hands clasped" kind of prayers. More like short conversations. Stuff I need to get off my chest.

God's a good listener. He never judges, never interrupts, never jumps in with a better story. And, even if I'm talking to myself most of the time, getting the thoughts out there is good therapy.

Some days, a little like the urge to smoke, prayer is more of a compulsion than on others. Like this morning. The tendrils of the dream are still clinging to me. Things I'd rather not remember. Bad memories are like splinters. Sometimes painful, but you learn to live with them. The problem is, they always work their way up to the surface eventually.

The key to the chapel is lying on the kitchen worktop. I pick it up and let myself out of the cottage. The clouds part and the sun gleams in the sky. I stare out over the graveyard and my eyes alight on the monument. I walk over to it.

There are more twig dolls arranged around the bottom today. When we arrived, there were half a dozen. Now, there look to be around ten or twelve. Some are dressed in scraps of clothing. It makes them look even more creepy. The stuff of children's nightmares. I can imagine them coming to life at night, shuffling themselves up on their stick legs, marching toward the cottage, slipping in through cracks in the open windows . . .

Stop it, Jack. You're not a child anymore. I fight down a shudder and turn my attention to the monument. There is an inscription near the top:

> **In memory of the undernamed Protestant Martyrs, who, for their faithful testimony to God's truth, were, during the reign of Queen Mary, burned to death in front of this chapel on 17 September 1556. This Obelisk, provided by Public Donations, was erected AD 1901.**

Underneath, a list of names:

> **Jeremiah Shoemann**
> **Abigail Shoemann**
> **Jacob Moorland**
> **Anne Moorland**
> **Maggie Moorland**

Abigail and Maggie. The burning girls. I touch the letters carved into the stone. It's cold, yet to absorb the warmth of the day.

Beneath the girls' names:

> **James Oswald Harper**
> **Isabel Harper**
> **Andrew John Harper**

The Harpers. Of course. What did Rushton say—Simon could trace his history all the way back to the Sussex Martyrs. Bully for him. Yet something about the monument has made me feel melancholy. Deaths in the name of religion always do. People fighting over who has a greater claim on God. You might as well fight over who owns the sky or the sun. And I'm sure, without God, people would.

I turn away from the monument and its congregation of twig dolls and walk across to the chapel. I stare up at the weathered white building. "**Redeem the Tim, for the Days are Evil**." Okay. I need to make peace with this place if this is ever going to work. I unlock the door and push it open.

The sun streams in through the windows, casting splashes of gold and red across the pews. I've always loved the effect of sunlight through stained-glass windows.

And then I remember. The windows here aren't stained glass.

I blink and look around. Splashes of red on the glass, a bitter, metallic smell. I walk down the aisle, unease growing, along with a horrible sense of déjà-vu.

"Drip, drip. You don't take my Ruby."

There's something on the floor by the altar. Something large, black and red.

I feel bile rise in my throat.

A crow. Mangled and battered, wings broken, body twisted.

It must have become trapped and panicked, bashing itself against the windows in a desperate attempt to escape. I crouch down beside the dead bird. And then I notice something, half hidden under its battered body. I move the crow aside with a small grimace.

My scalp contracts. Another twig doll. This one dressed in black with a scrap of white around its neck. **A clerical collar**. A folded piece of paper has been pinned to the doll's chest. A newspaper clipping. I pull it off and unfold it. My own face glares back at me: **"Vicar with Blood on Her Hands."**

I feel a vein pulse in my head. **How? Who?** Then I hear a noise behind me. The creak of the chapel door. I jump up and spin around.

A figure stands in the doorway, haloed by the morning light. I squint as they walk down the aisle toward me. Tall, slender. White hair tied in a bun, clad in running leggings and a bright fluorescent top. Clara Rushton. I stuff the doll and the clipping in my pocket.

"Morning, Jack! You're up early."

"I could say the same."

"Practicing your sermons?"

"Actually, clearing up a dead crow."

She glances toward the altar. "Oh my. Poor thing."

"I was wondering how it got in."

"Well, there are a fair few holes in the roof. We've had pigeons before, the odd sparrow. Never a crow." She looks at me sympathetically. "Not the best start to the day."

"Not really. And it's not even seven o'clock." I glance at her running gear. "Are you always out this early?"

"Yes, Brian thinks I'm mad, but I enjoy the peace of the dawn. Do you run?"

"Not even for a bus."

She chuckles. "I was just cooling down when I saw the door was open so I thought I'd pop my head in."

It seems a bit presumptuous. Nosy, even. A bit like Aaron and his "passing by." Almost like they're keeping an eye on me.

"Well, don't let me keep you," I say. "I need to clear this mess up in here."

"There's some cleaning equipment in the store cupboard in the office," Clara says. "And four hands are better than two. Why don't I help?"

I can't think of a reason to refuse. "Thanks."

Of course, she's trying to be helpful. But as I follow her toward the office, I can't help wondering how long she was standing in the doorway, watching me.

Forty minutes later, we've cleaned the blood off the windows and the dead crow has been disposed of in the trash can around the side of the chapel.

"There!" Clara looks around. "Much better."

And it is. In fact, cleaning some of the grime

from the windows has made the whole nave seem brighter, less gloomy and fusty.

"Thanks," I say again. "I really appreciate it."

She waves a Marigold-clad hand. "No problem. We all look out for each other here in Chapel Croft."

"Well, that's good to know."

She smiles. She must be in her mid-fifties, but she could pass for younger, even with the white hair. It's true that some women grow into their looks, gaining beauty as the years pass.

"You know, maybe you need something to take your mind off all of this?" she says now. "Why don't you come to the pub with Brian and me tonight? It's quiz night."

She must catch the look on my face.

"Not a fan of quizzes?"

"Not so much."

"What about red wine?"

"Well, that I can get on board with."

"Good. We could do with a new member of our team."

"Who else is on it?"

"Me, Brian and Mike Sudduth. I'm not sure if—"

"I've met him."

"Oh, right. He works for the local paper." Her eyes light up. "You know, maybe he could do a piece on you—"

"I don't think so," I say, a little too quickly.

"No?"

"I'm really rather boring. Not a lot to write about."

"Oh, I'm sure that's not true, Jack." Her tone is teasing. "I bet you have some stories to tell."

I hold her gaze. "I'll save them for **Jackanory**."

She laughs. "Very good. Anyway, if you change your mind, Mike's very nice, although he's had a tough couple of years—" She pauses. "Do you know about his daughter?"

"Yes. He told me."

"Heartbreaking. She was such a lovely little girl. Only eight."

I feel a tug in my heart, thinking about Flo at that age. So innocent, just starting to form her personality. To have her snatched away. A lump rises in my throat.

"What happened?"

"A tragic accident. She was playing in a friend's garden. They had a rope swing. Somehow Tara got the rope twisted around her neck. By the time anyone realized, it was too late."

"How terrible."

"They tried to resuscitate her, but Mike and his wife had to make the decision to turn off the life support."

"That's awful."

"Yes. It drove the families apart. The mothers had been good friends. Afterward, Fiona never spoke to Emma again."

"Emma as in Emma **Harper**?"

"Yes, it happened at her house. Poppy and Tara were best friends. It devastated all of them. Poppy didn't utter a word for over a year. She still barely talks now."

I think about our encounter outside the church. About Poppy's strange muteness. Now, it starts to make more sense. To see her best friend die like that. Horrific.

I shake my head. "I can only imagine the pain. To go to play at a friend's house and never come back."

"And, of course, Fiona blamed Emma."

"That's understandable, but you can't watch children every minute."

"Emma wasn't there."

"What?"

"She'd popped out to the shops. Only down the road, but—"

"She left them alone?"

"No. She left Poppy's sister in charge. Rosie. She was the one watching them when Tara died."

TWENTY-SIX

I have married hundreds of hopeful couples (and many hungover ones). I have buried the bodies of the young, the old and the barely born. I have anointed the soft, downy heads of countless babies and consoled the victims of terrible traumas. I have visited prisons, served in soup kitchens and judged numerous baking contests.

But I don't think that will make any difference to Emily and her fiancé, Dylan.

The young woman regards me suspiciously: "You **are** a proper vicar?"

"I've been a practicing vicar for over fifteen years."

She frowns. "Have you finished practicing now?"

Dear God, it really is going to be a long morning. I force a smile. "Yes, I have."

"Only"—she grips Dylan's hand. He's a sturdy

young man with a beard and floppy hair—"we want this to be a very **traditional** wedding."

"Of course," I say. "This is your wedding. It can be anything you want. That's what we're here to discuss today."

They glance at each other. "We really liked the other vicar," Dylan says now.

"He's a very good priest," I say neutrally. "But you want to get married on September the 26th and Reverend Rushton isn't available that day. Besides, I am the presiding vicar at Chapel Croft."

"Right."

"You do want to be married here in this chapel?"

"Yes. Our parents were both married here. So, you know, it's—"

"Tradition?"

"Yes."

"Okay, well, why don't you tell me a little more about yourselves?"

Silence. More nervous glances. I sigh and put down my pen.

"Or how about you tell me what's bothering you?"

"It's not that we don't think you'll do a good job," Emily says.

"We're sure you're qualified and all that," Dylan adds.

"Good."

"It's just the photos," Emily says.

"The photos?"

"Well"—she looks me up and down—"I just don't think you're going to look right in the photos."

I set the kettle to boil and get out some bread for toast. I have sent Emily and Dylan away to reflect upon what is most important about their special day: the wedding in the chapel or the fact that I don't have a penis (although I may not have worded it quite like that).

The meeting has not helped my mood. The twig doll and the newspaper clipping are troubling me. I'm not easily scared, or intimidated. But I have Flo to think of. I don't want a repeat of what we went through in Nottingham.

I stuffed them both in the bottom of the bin, but I wonder who else knows. Who might have read the story in the paper or online? It's not hard to look up. My first thought was Simon Harper. He strikes me as vindictive, and a bully. But I'm not sure he's that imaginative. So, who else? Only Rushton, Aaron and I have a key to the chapel. But is that true? Keys can go missing, be copied, borrowed. I think about Clara, standing at the chapel door, watching me.

I slam the bread into the toaster. Although, now I keep seeing the dead crow, its blood smeared over the chapel windows, my appetite has somewhat diminished.

I'm just searching for the marmalade when Flo trots downstairs. I glance at the clock. Ten thirty.

"Morning. How did you sleep?"

She yawns. "Okay."

"Want some toast?"

"No, thanks."

"Coffee?"

"No."

She opens the fridge and takes out some milk.

"Any plans for the day?"

"I thought I might go into Henfield."

Henfield is the nearest small town to Chapel Croft.

"Oh, right. What for?"

"Drugs. Booze. Maybe some porn."

I stare at her. She shakes her head. "What's with all the questions?"

"Sorry. You're right. Why should I care what my only daughter does? It's not like she almost got herself killed yesterday."

She glares at me. "Are you ever going to let that drop?"

"Maybe when you're thirty, or forty."

She pours the milk into a glass. "Actually, I'm going into Henfield because they've got a photography shop."

"Really?"

"Yeah. I googled it, and they do repairs."

"You got some reception on your phone upstairs?"

"Just. When **are** BT coming, by the way?"

"I don't know. I'll chase them." I relent. "D'you need a lift?"

"Nope. I downloaded the bus timetable."

"Oh. Okay."

Sometimes I am proud that my daughter is so practical, mature and self-sufficient. Other times I wish she needed me, just a little bit more. Fifteen is when you start to lose them. Although, really, I think you start to lose them from the moment they slip from your body and take their first breath.

"Will you be all right catching the bus on your own?"

She gives me a withering look. "I **have** caught buses before. It's only a fifteen-minute journey."

"I know, but—"

"I've got it. I almost got myself killed. I'll try not to annoy any homicidal pensioners on the bus."

"Well, they have been known to pack."

A small smile. "I'll be fine, Mum. I just want to get my camera fixed. Okay?"

"Okay."

"And, no offense, but I really need to get out of this house for a bit. Somewhere I can actually get some internet access. I haven't been able to catch up with Leon and Kayleigh properly. I just need some time back in civilization. Well"—she considers—"semi-civilization."

Of course she does. Guilt sucker-punches me in the stomach. I've uprooted my daughter from a bustling city and dumped her in the middle of nowhere. For what? To make amends. Because Durkin gave me little choice. Because of my own guilt? I might tell myself we are safe here, but I'm more worried about Flo than ever.

I force a smile. "Okay. But any trouble, call me and I'll come and pick you up, okay?"

"Mum, I'm going to a camera shop and then I'm going to find a café that has wifi. There won't be any trouble."

"Fine." I hold my hands up in surrender. "Have you got enough money for the bus fare and coffee?"

"Actually, could you lend me a tenner?"

I sigh. No trouble, she said.

After Flo has gone I make a coffee, resist the temptation of a cigarette and take Fletcher's box back out from beneath the kitchen sink.

I look at the broken cassette. Scotch tape. I'm pretty sure that's what I need to fix it, but I'm also pretty sure we don't have any. I put the cassette to one side and lift out the file entitled **"Sussex Martyrs."**

Plenty of villages have a dark past. History itself is stained with the blood of the innocent and written by the ruthless. Good does not always triumph over evil. Prayers do not win battles. Sometimes, we need the devil on our side. The problem is, once you have him riding shotgun, he's hard to get rid of.

I sit and start to plow through the sheets of

paper. Some have been printed from the internet. Others seem to have been scanned from books. The text is scholarly, dry and packed with dates and historical references about the reign of Queen Mary and the purge in general. I'm halfway through the folder before I find any specific references to Chapel Croft. A very old article, by the looks of it, perhaps taken from some kind of journal. The print is bad, and the language is archaic, but Fletcher has summarized and made his own notes at the side.

> **Village stormed, martyrs hauled from beds and rounded up. Those who recanted branded but released. Those who refused convicted of heresy and burned at the stake. Two young girls, Abigail and Maggie, hidden in the chapel. Betrayed. Dragged out. Girls' punishment even more barbaric. Maggie's eyes put out. Abigail dismembered and beheaded before both burnt.**

I swallow. Dismembered and beheaded.

"She had no head or arms."

There is no way that Flo could have known that. I reach for my coffee. It's gone cold, but I swig it anyway. Fletcher's notes here read: "Betrayed by **whom?**"

The next piece of paper is larger, folded several

times. I open it and lay it flat on the table. It takes me a moment to work out what I'm looking at. Architectural plans of the chapel, or rather, the church that stood here before the chapel was built. Again, old and much faded.

I squint at the drawings. The footprint of the building is the same. I can make out the nave, the vestry. But there are other parts that I can't configure in my mind. Areas that look like they have changed over time. Another store cupboard? A cellar? I didn't think the chapel had a cellar. Vaults, perhaps? I stare at it thoughtfully then I carefully put all the pieces of paper back in the folder and close it.

I turn to the second folder. "**Merry and Joy.**" The urge to smoke is now so strong my hands feel twitchy. I open the folder and begin to flick through the printed newspaper stories. There aren't as many as you would imagine. The disappearances didn't garner much national interest. Which is unusual. Merry and Joy were young, white and female. Without wanting to sound cold, those are the girls the newspapers and media normally care about. From the start, the police treated the case as that of two runaways. Appeals were made for the girls to come home, to contact their mothers. There never seemed to be any suspicion that they might not be in a position to do so. And the sad fact is— something I know all too well from my work with the homeless—the police are more likely to spend time looking for dead girls than live ones.

The local newspaper seems to have run stories about the girls for a lot longer, but eventually even these progress from the front page to smaller articles to filler pieces.

The same school photos of the girls have been used in all the papers. Not particularly good photos. Blurry, old. Both girls look younger than in the photo I found in Joy's room. I wonder if that hampered the search.

And then, finally, I find a longer article. This one seems to have been written sometime after the girls' disappearance. And not for a newspaper. I squint. At the top of the page, in small print, a header reads: **Sussex Stories—Local Mysteries and Legends. March 2000. Issue 13.**

I start to read:

The Mysterious Case of the Sussex Runaways

Merry and Joy were the best of friends. Inseparable, many used to say. They grew up together, went to school together, played together, rode their bikes together. And during one week in the spring of 1990, aged fifteen, they disappeared together.

Oddly, there were no frenetic searches. Villagers did not beat bushes. Divers did not dredge the rivers and streams. It was presumed, almost from the start, that both girls had run away. The police inquiry was perfunctory, to say the least, and the case failed to really catch the attention of the national newspapers. To understand why the girls' disappearance was given so little heed it's probably best to start with the village in which they grew up.

Chapel Croft is a small hamlet in East Sussex. Its main features are farming and the church. It's a religious area; Protestant, with a bloody history of martyrdom.

During the religious persecutions of Queen Mary in 1556, eight villagers were burned at the stake, including two young girls. A memorial stands in the chapel graveyard. Each year, on the anniversary of the purge, small twig dolls called **Burning Girls** are set alight to commemorate the martyrs who died.

It would be fair to say, like many small villages, Chapel Croft is an insular place, inward-looking and protective of its church and its traditions.

Both Merry and Joy's families were

religious. Both had lost their fathers at an early age. But there the similarities ended. Joy grew up in a strict but loving household. Doreen was a good mother. Joy was her only child, and her daughter was her life.

Merry, on the other hand, grew up in far more chaotic surroundings. Her mother, Maureen, was devout and yet also an alcoholic. Merry and her brother didn't always attend school. Their clothes were dirty and second-hand. Often Merry had unexplained bruises.

Nowadays, these would probably be seen as warning signs of abuse and neglect. But in a small village a decade ago, people still believed that you let families take care of their own problems.

Reverend Marsh, the parish priest at the time, later confessed that he regretted not doing more: **"It was obvious that there was something ill about the household. Perhaps if someone had stepped in, a tragedy could have been avoided."**

Perhaps, indeed. The only respite for Merry from the miseries of home appears to have been her friendship with Joy, and the time that they spent together. However, that too was about to be threatened.

Joy's mother had never been happy about her daughter's relationship with Merry. She didn't think Merry was a "suitable" friend. Both girls already attended Bible lessons with Reverend Marsh. But it was agreed that Joy would take extra lessons as a means to "keep her on the right path."

Joy's lessons were with a young trainee priest at the chapel, the curate, Benjamin Grady. Grady was young—only twenty-three—and ambitious, a handsome man, outwardly charming. A lot of the village girls developed a crush on him. Did he also catch the eye of Joy?

Joy was a beautiful girl, and there were certainly rumors, unsubstantiated, that she had been seen attending the chapel at night, at times other than the scheduled lessons. However, a few weeks before her disappearance, Joy abruptly stopped attending her classes with Grady.

Could heartache or unrequited love be the reason Joy ran away? Or was it something more sinister? Grady, after all, was an adult, in a position of power.

The police spoke to Grady. But when Joy was last spotted, at a bus stop in Henfield, Grady had an alibi. He was preparing a service with Reverend Marsh.

Joy was never seen again.

The police visited Merry's house to ask her about her best friend's disappearance but were informed that she was "ill." For some reason, they never called back.

Less than a week later, Merry vanished.

This turn of events only reinforced the police view that Joy had run away. Joy had packed a bag. Merry had left a note: **I'm sorry. We have to get away. I love you.**

The use of the word "we" certainly made it seem as though the girls had planned to run away together. Perhaps the intention had always been to make their escape separately and meet up again later. Concerns for the girls' safety changed to appeals for them to get in touch.

Of course, they never did.

Oddly—perhaps coincidence, perhaps not—just after Merry disappeared,

Grady also left the village suddenly. There's no record of him ever working as a priest again. Of course, he could have abandoned the Church, perhaps even adopted a new name. But why?

Even more strangely, almost a year to the day after Merry ran away, her mother and younger brother disappeared, leaving their home and taking nothing with them. Again, neither has been heard of since.

No one in Chapel Croft really wants to talk about the girls. Joy's mother suffers from dementia and still believes her daughter is on her way home. It seems cruel to deprive her of this notion.

Perhaps Merry and Joy really did escape to better lives. Perhaps they met less pleasant fates. Perhaps they just don't want to be found.

But one can't help feeling that someone, somewhere, must know what happened to the two best friends, the Sussex runaways. Merry and Joy. Their names inseparable still.

I sit for a moment, fighting different emotions. Partly sorrow. Partly anger. I stare at the byline on the piece. Something clicks. I flick back through the newspaper stories, looking for the name of the reporter who covered the disappearances for the local paper. It's the same. **Of course**.

Once a reporter, always a reporter.

J. Hartman. Joan.

TWENTY-SEVEN

"I'd say you're looking at maybe £100, plus parts."

The man in the camera shop looks at her sympathetically.

Flo sighs. "Right."

"Not what you wanted to hear?"

"No, but what I expected."

"Sorry, love."

"Thanks anyway."

"Maybe if you ask your mum or dad nicely?"

"Yeah, maybe."

She walks to the door.

"Oh, hang on."

She turns back. He holds out a film canister. "Took the film out for you. Don't think it's damaged."

"Oh. Thanks."

She pockets the film canister. At least she hasn't

lost the photos. Small consolation. How the hell is she going to find a hundred quid?

She walks despondently out of the shop, the bell jangling cheerily behind her and only serving to heighten her black mood. **Fucking airgunslinging, crow-shooting bastard yokel.** She'd felt a bit bad about busting Tom's nose, but now she hopes it remains crooked. She hopes he has bad sinuses for the rest of his rotten life.

Not Christian, she imagines her mum telling her, but screw it. Fat lot of good her religion has done her so far. Turfed out of their home. Forced to move to this shithole. Yeah, devotion to God was really paying off.

She spots a café across the street and crosses the road. Right now, she could do with catching up with Leon and Kayleigh and just feeling normal for once. She walks inside. The café is busy, but she spots a table by the window. She slings her hoodie over the back of the chair, joins the queue for coffee and takes a mocha and a muffin back to her seat.

She sips her drink and connects to the wifi. A full signal. Hallelujah. She opens up Snapchat. Flo isn't really a huge fan of social media. She doesn't like how everyone pretends they have an amazing life or how they filter their faces a zillion times so they don't even look human. It's all false and fake. She doesn't even like taking photos with her phone and would rather use her Nikon (although that's not going to happen again any time soon), but Kayleigh and Leon are on Snapchat and it's the only way to stay in touch with her friends.

She misses them. And she'd rather see them in person. She tries not to get down about it but, sometimes, it's hard. When Mum first told her about the move, she was angry. They had argued, doors slammed—the lot. Okay, she **knew** they needed to leave the church at St. Anne's. All the stuff going on, it was getting too much. Mum was tense and worried all the time. It was tough.

But why **here**? Why not another church in Nottingham? Or somewhere that wasn't hundreds of miles away? The only thing she's holding on to is that it won't be for long. Mum is just the interim vicar here. When they get a permanent one, they can move back to Nottingham, and hopefully all the other stuff will have died down.

She does a scan of recent posts, smiling at some of her friends' selfies. She finds the photo she took of the creepy twig dolls and messages: "What the locals do for 'fun' (screaming face). Send news of civilization." She waits for the replies, sipping her mocha and staring idly out of the window.

A figure catches her eye. Standing by the bus stop a little further up the street. A skinny teenager all in black: jeans, hoodie, long black hair. **Wrigley?** She squints. The window is inlaid with the name of the café and a picture of coffee cups, so her view is distorted. But it looks a lot like him.

Something about the way he is standing. Staring. Watching her? A bus pulls up, blocking her vision. When it pulls away, the figure is gone.

She frowns. She can't be sure it was him. He can't be the only skinny boy in Sussex who likes to dress in black. And why **shouldn't** he be here? Henfield is the nearest town to Chapel Croft, after all. Nowhere much else for anyone to go.

She turns back to her mocha. As if to prove her point, a shadow falls over the table. She looks up.

"**Seriously?**"

Rosie smiles. "Hey, Vampirina."

Flo glares at her. "Are you stalking me?"

Rosie smiles and pulls out the other chair.

"You wish."

"What are you doing here?"

"Meeting some friends. We're getting our nails done. Mum's treat."

"Wow. Lucky you."

"Not really. That bitch will pay for anything if it gets me out from under her feet. What about you?"

"Wondering when I last went somewhere and you **didn't** show up."

"Small place, Vampirina. You'll find it's hard to escape people here."

"I'm starting to sense that." Flo folds her arms. "What do you want?"

"Actually, I want to apologize."

"Really?"

"Really."

"You're not just worried that I might have re-ported you to the police?"

"Have you?"

"Not yet."

Rosie glances at the broken Nikon. "You know, I could pay for you to get that fixed."

"I don't need your money."

"Fine."

"Is that it?"

"There's no reason we can't be friends."

"There are plenty."

"So, you prefer to hang out with wriggly Wrigley? Don't you find all that twitching kind of repulsive? Or does it turn you on?"

"Fuck you."

"So, you like him then?"

"I only just met him."

"Want to see a picture of his dick?"

Flo stares at her. Rosie laughs.

"I sucked him off once. For a bet."

"I don't believe you."

"Why? You think he's special? Trust me—he's just like any other boy. He doesn't care where he sticks it. Grow up."

Flo shrugs. "Like I care." Even though she does. Kind of. There'd been something about him. Or so she'd thought.

"Got a nice picture, which I've shared every-where. You're probably the only person in this vil-lage who hasn't seen it. Quite big, actually."

"You're sick."

"What. You don't like dick? Is pussy more your thing?"

"Just fuck off."

"Actually, I came over to give you a friendly warning."

"Yeah?"

"Has Wrigley told you about his last school?"

"Like I said, I only just met him."

"He got kicked out."

"So?"

"Aren't you curious as to why?"

"I'm curious as to why I should believe a word you say."

"He tried to burn it down. Almost killed a girl."

"Bullshit."

"Look it up. The school is in Tunbridge Wells— Ferndown Academy."

"Like I said, I don't care."

Rosie stand and shrugs. "Your funeral. But if I was you, I'd stay the hell away from Wrigley." She winks. "If you know what's good for you."

Flo watches her sashay off, willing someone to accidentally throw hot coffee in her face. She looks down at her phone. There's a message from Kayleigh. Her thumb hovers over it. Then she opens Safari and types in "Ferndown Academy."

TWENTY-EIGHT

"You used to write for the local paper."

Joan totters over to the table with two mugs of coffee. They wobble somewhat precariously in her twisted hands, but she manages to make it without spilling a drop.

"That's right."

"Why didn't you tell me before?"

"Give someone all the answers, they won't ask questions."

"But maybe I would have taken what you said about Reverend Fletcher more seriously."

She feigns surprise. "You mean you didn't? Perhaps you thought it was just the ramblings of a mad old lady?"

"I'm sorry."

"Don't be. I'm used to it. When you're old, no matter what you have accomplished in your life, people only ever see your age." She winks. "Of course, you can use it to your advantage too. I haven't carried a shopping bag to my car in years."

I smile. "The girls' disappearance must have been a big story for the local paper."

"At the start. But, gradually, that changed."

"Why?"

"Small villages are strange places. Backward, in some ways. Oh, I know people don't like to hear it, but it's true. They're resistant to change. Families have lived here for generations, and they have their ways."

I sip my coffee.

"Everyone knows everyone," she continues. "Or rather, they like to think they do. The fact is, they know what they want to know and believe what they want to believe. Anything that threatens their community, their traditions, their church, they close ranks to protect it."

She's right. And not just villages. Any small community. It happens in cities too. It's how some areas become ghettos. Us and them. However bad the "us" are, you still protect your own.

"Did someone tell you to stop writing about the girls?"

"Not directly. But my editor certainly discouraged me from asking too many questions. I think the police officer in charge, Inspector Layton, didn't want to be seen as incompetent, and the church was a big influence in the community. To suggest any wrongdoing was almost heresy."

"By wrongdoing, do you mean by Benjamin Grady, the curate?"

"Yes."

"Did you know him?"

"I knew **of** him. I lived over in Henfield back then. I only spoke to him once, properly, after Joy's disappearance."

"And?"

She hesitates.

"I didn't care for him . . ."

"Why?"

"There was just something about him. I couldn't put my finger on it. However, I know that a lot of the village girls were rather keen on him."

"It often happens. Girls developing crushes on priests. Of course, most would never abuse their position."

She nods. "Grady was certainly aware of his physical attributes. And Joy was a beautiful girl."

"That makes it seem romantic," I say tightly. "He was an adult in a position of power. She was fifteen."

She nods. "Yes."

"Was he ever considered a suspect in Joy's disappearance?"

"Not seriously. The police spoke to him, of course. But when Joy was last seen by a witness, Grady had an alibi. He was preparing a service with Reverend Marsh."

"The witness couldn't be wrong?"

"Her description tallied with what Joy's mother said she was wearing."

"Who was the witness? It's not mentioned in any of the reports."

"Clara Rushton."

I stare at her. "As in Reverend Rushton's wife?"

"Yes, although back then she was still Clara Wilson. She taught at the secondary school."

"I know . . . I mean, she mentioned it." I consider. "So, she knew the girls **and** Grady?"

"Yes. In fact, Clara and Grady grew up together in Warblers Green. Then Grady went away to university and theological college. When he returned, Clara helped out a lot at the chapel. Reverend Marsh didn't drive, so Clara would often run errands for the church."

"You really did your research."

She smiles. "Oh, I always do."

Something about the way she says it suddenly makes me wonder if she's done her research on me. I continue quickly: "So, it's **possible** Clara might have covered for Grady?"

"But how would she have known what Joy was wearing that evening?"

"Maybe she saw her earlier, when Grady didn't have an alibi?"

"Maybe. But to lie and pervert justice?"

"Perhaps he manipulated her?"

"Possibly. As I said, Grady was well aware of his looks. Clara may have had a crush. But back then she was rather overweight, awkward with her height. I think I might have some pictures somewhere."

She starts to rise, easing her frail body up out of the seat. I had almost forgotten her age as we talked; her mind is still so sharp. She walks out into the hall. I wait, wondering about poised, elegant Clara who was once awkward, overweight Clara. But then, the years change us all. For better, and for worse.

When Joan returns, she's clutching two old photos. She holds them out. I take them and stare at the pictures. The first shows a much younger Clara. Plump, dark-haired, barely recognizable. Her face is serious, her attire dated. It's obviously a photo taken for the school where she worked. I can picture it pinned up in the entrance hall. Her name beneath it. **Miss Wilson.**

I place the photo on the coffee table and look at the second one. I catch my breath.

Grady. He is sitting, facing the camera. Straight-backed, hands clasped on his lap, smiling, almost mockingly. His face looks smooth and feminine. Prominent cheekbones, full lips. Blond hair swept back from a high forehead. A handsome man and yet . . . even in these static pictures, something makes my skin crawl.

"Did you notice the ring?" Joan asks.

She leans forward and taps the photo with one crooked finger. Feeling obliged, I peer at it more closely. Most priests don't wear jewelry, except for a cross. But a large silver signet ring encircles one of Grady's fingers. I can just make out a figure on the front and words in Latin. I swallow, my mouth feeling dry.

"Unusual, isn't it?" Joan says. "The Latin is part of the prayer of St. Michael. I had to get a magnifying glass to make it out. Do you know it?"

I nod. **"Sancte Michael Archangele, defende nos in proelio.** St. Michael, protect us in battle. It's a prayer of protection. Against the forces of darkness."

I lay the photo on the coffee table, fighting the urge to rub my hands on my jeans.

Joan is staring at me curiously. "Are you all right, my dear?"

"Yes. Fine. It's just, I'm not sure what I can do. I'm a vicar, not a detective. And this all happened a long time ago."

"True. But finding out what Matthew knew would be a start."

She lowers herself back down into her chair. I sense it causes her pain. Arthritis, or maybe osteoporosis. I wait.

"Do you really believe someone killed him?"

Eventually, she settles and says: "I saw him a few days before he died. He didn't seem like a man who was suicidal. If anything, he seemed to have a new sense of purpose."

"The suicidal are good at hiding it."

"You say that as if you know from experience."

I hesitate and then find myself saying: "My husband, Jonathon, tried to commit suicide. More than once."

"I'm so sorry, my dear."

"He suffered from depression. He would have good days, which were great, but the dark spells . . . they were really bad."

"That must have been difficult."

I think about the hours he spent slumped in front of the TV. The paranoia which once involved him taking a sledgehammer to his own phone. The day he was found walking barefoot along the side of a dual carriageway. Some afflictions you can see. But depression is a crippling illness of the mind that twists the person you love into someone you don't even recognize.

"I was about to ask for a divorce when he died," I confess, feeling the old guilt. Even with God's support, I couldn't cope. Not with a small child. Not when I worried every day that his illness might endanger our daughter.

"He finally took his own life?" Joan asks gently.

"No." I smile bitterly. "He was murdered, by an intruder at the church. Somewhat ironic."

"Oh my goodness. How awful. Did they catch the person responsible?"

I think about the letter in the glovebox.

"Yes. He was sentenced to eighteen years."

She places her wrinkled hand on mine. "You've been through a lot."

"I don't normally tell people about Jonathon. I suppose I've tried to put it all behind us. I don't even use my married name any more."

"Well, you see, we reporters are good at getting stuff out of people."

"Very true."

And confessing one truth can be a good way to deflect from others.

Joan sits back and pulls her cardigan slightly tighter around her shoulders. I remind myself that she's in her eighties and we've been talking for a while. All this must be a strain.

"I should go. You're tired."

She waves a hand. "I'm eighty-five. I'm always tired. Has anyone mentioned Saffron Winter to you?"

"The writer? Yes, Aaron mentioned that she and Reverend Fletcher were friends."

"If you want to know more about Matthew, you should talk to her. They were close."

"Close as in romantically?"

"He never said as much, but I got the impression that there was **someone** important in his life."

Interesting. My phone buzzes in my pocket. I think about ignoring it, then check and see that the caller is Durkin.

"Sorry, would you mind if I just—"

"No, go ahead. You might find the reception is better outside."

"Thank you."

I stand and walk through the kitchen and out into the garden.

"Hello."

"Jack. Did you get my message?"

"Sorry, I haven't checked my voicemails."

Durkin sounds tense, not his usual smooth-as-a-polished-sandworm self. It immediately sets me on edge.

"Is there a problem?"

A deep sigh. "Actually, I have some rather upsetting news and I thought you should be first to know."

"Okay."

"You know Reverend Bradley?"

"Yes, my replacement. What about him?"

"He was attacked last night, in St. Anne's Church."

"How is he?"

A pause. The sort of pause that only ever precedes terrible news.

"I'm afraid he's dead."

TWENTY-NINE

He rests his head against the window of the train. The motion is soothing. The cool glass eases the throbbing in his skull.

It's almost two hours to London, and then he needs to change to catch another train to Sussex. From there, he'll have to check buses or maybe walk.

He was lucky that the fat priest had plenty of cash in his wallet. It paid for the train tickets and there was still a little left. He had slept in the church last night. It was clean and not too cold. It even had a small bathroom to wash off the blood.

The fat priest had told him what he wanted to know pretty quickly. He couldn't really remember now why he felt the need to keep hitting him so much and so hard. Maybe it was the way the priest looked at him; the way he told him softly that he forgave him for his sins. Perhaps it had reminded him a little too much of his mother.

This is how much I love you.

"Tickets, please."

He starts and glances up. Instinctively, his fists clench. Fight or flight. Attack or escape. No, he reminds himself. He has his ticket in his pocket. It's fine. He has every right to be on this train. He just has to act normal. Keep a clear head. Remember why he is doing this. Otherwise it will all be for nothing.

The ticket inspector draws closer. He sits up straight, ticket at the ready, trying to control the shake in his hand.

"Good morning, sir."

"Good morning."

He hands over his ticket. The inspector clips it, starts to hand it back, then pauses.

Panic grips him. What is it? Has he said or done something wrong? Can the inspector see the guilt on his face or blood on his hands?

The inspector smiles and hands him the ticket. "Have a good journey, Reverend."

Ah. Of course.

He relaxes, fingers touching the white collar.

The fat priest had known his fate the moment he told him to strip. He saw the terror in his large brown eyes and the damp stain on his underwear.

The suit is a little large but not so much that anyone will question it. He smiles back.

"God bless you, sir."

THIRTY

"You're sure you don't want to come tonight?"

Flo gives me a disparaging look. "Err, a pub quiz? No, thanks."

"You'll be okay here on your own?"

"Well, as long as you put me in my play pen."

"Funny."

"I'll be fine. Okay?"

But she doesn't look fine. Nose stuck back in a book, my daughter looks pale, preoccupied and unhappy.

I sit on the sofa next to her. "Look, I'll try to find some money to get the camera fixed. Maybe I could apply for a credit card."

"I thought you said credit cards were the work of the devil?"

"Well, many things are the work of the devil and I still do them."

"It's fine, Mum. It's not the camera."

"Then what's bothering you?"

"Nothing, okay?" She uncurls from the sofa. "I'm going upstairs."

"What about dinner?"

"I'll make something later."

"Flo?"

"Mum, just leave it, will you? I'm not one of your parishioners. If you want to know what's wrong, just take a look around you."

She stomps up the stairs and the bedroom door slams, rocking the whole cottage.

Okay. Well, perhaps I had that coming. I slump on to the sofa and rub my head. I can feel a headache coming on. The last thing I want is to go to a pub quiz. On the other hand, I could really do with a drink. I keep thinking about Reverend Bradley. **Attacked. Dead**.

Durkin told me the police are working on the theory that it was an intruder, perhaps one of the homeless men from the soup kitchen. Bradley's wallet had been taken, and his clothes.

But I have a bad feeling. St. Anne's was my old church. Was he looking for me? Did Reverend Bradley get in his way?

No. I am putting two and two together and panicking myself. It was fourteen years ago. He wouldn't have been given an early release unless he had shown remorse; proved he was a changed man. Why would he look for me now?

But I know the answer. I left him behind. And I never went back.

I stand. Enough. Perhaps the best thing to do is to give Flo some space, go out and take my mind off things for a few hours. I trudge upstairs, shower and get changed. I inspect myself in the full-length mirror propped against the wall. Jeans, black shirt, Docs. I start to pull my hair into a ponytail then change my mind and wedge it behind my ears. I grab my hoodie. It's still muggy, but it might be cool walking back later.

I knock gently on Flo's door. "Okay, I'm going."

No reply. I sigh. "Love you."

I wait and a muffled voice calls back:

"Don't get too drunk."

I smile, feeling a little comforted. Just normal teenage stuff. It will pass. Maybe all of this will pass. On the other hand, a little insurance couldn't hurt. I walk back into my room, open the wardrobe and take out the battered leather case. I undo it and lift out the bone-handled knife. I stare at the rusty stains. Then I carry it over to my bed and stick it under the mattress.

If he finds us, I'll be ready.

The Barley Mow is brightly lit. I haven't been to a pub in a long while. I don't drink that often. The occasional red wine at home, but that's about it. As a vicar, you can't really be seen doing tequila shots at the bar. Plus, I don't like feeling out of control. Losing myself, being unsure of what I might say.

I reach the door. Seven thirty-seven. I hesitate and touch my dog collar. A nervous tic. A gesture of comfort, reassurance. I can always choose not to wear it. There are occasions when I don't. But the thing about a dog collar is that it also acts as a shield. People see the dog collar, but they don't really see **you**.

I push the door open. Pub smells. Wheat, food, old furniture, stale sweat. The sounds of laughter and the clinking of glasses. Someone in the back kitchen yelling something unintelligible. I walk in and quickly survey my surroundings. It's a habit, like touching my dog collar. Assess the situation. Work out your opponents and friends. Look for exits.

The pub is cozy and low-beamed. To my left is the bar and a small area of seating. To my right, a large open fire, currently unlit, more tables and chairs and a couple of worn leather sofas. The walls are brick and adorned with a number of "humorous" plaques.

Money can't buy happiness, but it can buy beer.

Alcohol may not solve your problems, but neither will water.

Dogs welcome, children tolerated.

There are copper pans and irons hung around

the fire and stacks of logs. Most of the crowd are older; a few have dogs. It's that sort of pub.

There's one crowd of younger males to my left, congregating around the bar, talking to one of the staff serving, a stocky young man with two black eyes and a swollen nose. He glances up as I walk in and says something to one of the other lads. They laugh. I try to ignore it, but I feel my jaw clench.

"**Jack,** over here!"

I turn at the sound of Rushton's voice. He waves at me from a round table in the corner. Clara is sitting next to him, but no sign of Mike Sudduth yet. I squeeze my way over to them, stepping over a couple of dogs en route. There's a pint of ale in front of Rushton and a red wine in front of Clara. As soon as I reach the table Rushton gets to his feet and envelops me in a warm hug.

"So glad you made it. What can I get you?"

"Erm." I think about asking for a Diet Coke and then I think, sod it. "Glass of red wine, please. A Malbec or a Cab Sav, if they have one."

"No problem."

He trots off and I pull out one of the spare stools and sit down opposite Clara. This evening her hair is down; a shimmering snowy cloak draped over her shoulders. I think about the old pictures Joan showed me. Frumpy Clara. Handsome Grady.

Could she have lied for him?

"So, how are you?" she asks warmly.

"Oh, fine."

"How did your wedding consultation go?"

"Nothing a sex change or a false beard can't sort out."

She laughs. "They'll come round. Some people are just a bit narrow-minded."

"I know. Not my first rodeo."

"Of course."

Rushton returns, clutching a large glass of red, and with Mike Sudduth in tow.

"Look who I bumped into at the bar!"

He beams and places my wine in front of me.

"Cab Sav. And I understand you've met Mike, so no introduction is necessary."

"No." I smile politely. "How's the car?"

"Four-wheeled again. Thanks for your help."

"No problem. And about what I said—"

"Don't worry about it." He sits down on the stool next to me and places a glass of orange juice on the table. "So, what's your specialist subject?"

I stare at him blankly for a moment. "Oh, the quiz."

"Clara is our general knowledge expert," Rushton says. "I'm sport."

"What's yours?" I ask Mike.

"TV and film."

"Okay." I sip at my wine. "Well, I like to read."

"Good. Books it is then."

"I might be a bit rusty."

Rushton chuckles. "Not to worry. It's only a bit of fun."

Mike and Clara exchange glances.

"What?"

"Don't let him fool you with talk of fun," Mike says. "Quiz night is a serious business."

"Now you're worrying me."

"It's okay," Clara says. "It's only a matter of life or . . ."

She pauses, eyes drawn to the door. I turn. There's a gust of cool night air as two people enter. Simon and Emma Harper. I glance at Mike. His face is set, jaw tense. The pain in his eyes is almost tangible. He looks down, suddenly intent upon the quiz sheet on the table.

"So, team name," Rushton says quickly. "I think we should have a new one now we have a new team member."

"Definitely," Clara agrees. "Fresh start, and all that."

They look at me expectantly. This is another reason I hate pub quizzes.

"Erm . . ."

"The Four Musketeers," Rushton volunteers.

"The Holy Trinity," Clara says.

"Trinity means three," I remind her.

"Ah."

"Four Horsemen of the Apocalypse," Mike suggests.

Pestilence, War, Famine and Death.

I smile. "Sounds good."

We lose. Badly and predictably. A dour-faced group of men in wellies and Barbour jackets calling themselves (rather ironically) The Jolly Farmers win, although I suspect the fact that there were a suspiciously large number of questions about tractors may have helped.

However, unexpectedly, I do have fun. Rushton and Clara are good company and Mike is drily amusing. I start to relax a little.

"My round." Mike stands.

"Pint of Speckled Hen for me," Rushton says. Clara gives him a look. "Well, maybe just a half."

Mike glances at me. "Same again?"

I consider. I've had one large glass. I should probably have a soft drink or . . .

"Okay," I hear myself say.

He nods and heads to the bar. I realize I could do with using the loo.

"Just popping to the ladies." I squeeze out from my seat.

They are tucked behind the bar. A slant-ceilinged room with two loos, a small washbasin and mirror. I'm just flushing when I hear the door from the bar open. I emerge and find myself face to face with Emma Harper. For some reason, I have the distinct impression that she has followed me in here. We smile at each other in that awkward way you do when you bump into someone in a toilet.

"Hello."

"Hi."

I turn on the tap to wash my hands, expecting Emma to disappear into one of the cubicles. She doesn't. She comes and stands beside me, smoothing her hair in the mirror. Up close, in the harsh fluorescent light, there's shiny tightness to her skin—a facelift? Fillers?—and her nose has the chiseled sharpness of a nose job. Not that the lighting is doing my doughy complexion any favors. I turn the tap off and reach for the paper towels.

"I didn't expect to see you in here," she says. Her voice sounds a little slurred.

"Clara invited me. For the quiz."

"Did you enjoy it?"

"Yes." I screw up the towel and chuck it in the bin. "Even though quizzes aren't really my thing."

"Me neither, but it's something of a village tradition." A lopsided smile. "Simon's big on tradition. They all are around here."

"You're not from around here?"

"Me? No. I met Simon at uni in Brighton. We lived there for a few years. Moved back here after we married."

"Oh, why was that?"

"The farm. His father was retiring. He wanted Simon to take it over."

"Right. And you were okay with that?"

"I didn't have much choice. I was pregnant with Rosie—and what Simon wants, Simon gets."

The bitterness is hard to miss. Alcohol, the great truth serum.

"What about you?" she asks.

"Oh, I'm settling in."

She takes a lipstick out of her pocket and starts to apply it. "You seem to be getting on well with Mike."

"I try to get on with all my parishioners," I say steadily.

"I suppose you've heard about what happened, with his daughter?"

"Yes. And I'm sorry. The death of a child is a tragedy. For everyone."

She stares at me in the mirror. Her pupils are constricted. The hand holding the lipstick shakes slightly. Maybe it's more than a few drinks. Pills, perhaps?

"It wasn't my fault."

"I know."

"Do you?"

"It sounds like a terrible accident."

"I shouldn't even have been watching Tara that afternoon. I was doing Mike a favor. He called and begged me to pick her up from school."

"Why?"

A small smile, more like a sneer.

"Because he was drunk. Too drunk to drive. And not for the first time."

I remember Mike saying that he didn't drink anymore. The glass of orange juice. "So, he had an alcohol problem?"

"He was an alcoholic. It was getting so bad Fiona was thinking of leaving. She gave him one last chance. If he blew it, she'd be gone, with Tara. He couldn't bear the thought of losing Tara."

The irony claws at my throat.

"So, you agreed to cover for him?"

"I was just trying to help. I know I shouldn't have left Rosie to watch the girls, but it was only a few minutes . . ."

"You can't blame yourself."

Although, going out, leaving another child in charge, was careless. Rosie could have only been thirteen herself. But then, I remind myself, how often have I let Flo out of my sight because I was busy or distracted? No one is perfect. And we all think it will never happen to us. Bad stuff only ever happens to other people, right?

She shakes her head. "You try so hard as a mother, to keep them safe. And then, just one moment, and they can be snatched away."

"You couldn't have foreseen what would happen."

"But I should have." She looks at me more sharply. "Do you believe in evil, Reverend?"

I hesitate. "I believe in evil acts."

"You don't believe that someone can be born evil?"

I want to say no. I want to tell her that we are

born a blank canvas. That murderers, rapists and pe-dophiles are a product of their environment rather than some darkness of the soul. And yet, I have visited many offenders in prison. Some are victims of terrible circumstances and horrific upbringings. A pattern of abuse repeating again and again. But others? Others come from good homes with lov-ing parents and yet they still choose to kill, torture and maim.

"I think we all have the capacity for good and evil," I say. "But for some, one side is more preva-lent than the other."

She nods and bites her lip. I watch her carefully. There's something there. Just beneath the smooth, shiny surface. Barely contained by the Botox and the pills.

"Emma," I say, "if there's anything you want to talk about, you can always come to the chapel. I'd be—"

The door to the bar suddenly swings open. An old dear in tweed and wellies totters in, nods at us and lets herself into a cubicle.

"Emma?"

She smiles, mask firmly back in place. "Thanks for the chat, Reverend. And we really must get the girls together sometime. Bye."

And then she is gone, in a waft of perfume and pain.

I sigh and look back at myself in the mirror. My face surprises me sometimes. The bags beneath my eyes, the heaviness around my jowls. If Emma has chosen to disguise herself with needles and knives, I have done the opposite. I have let myself go. I have let the years erase the girl I used to be, hiding behind crow's feet and middle-age spread.

I think about what she said again. **Do you believe in evil?** Can someone be born bad? Nature versus nurture. And, if so, can they change? Or is the best they can ever hope for to deny their nature, hide the darkness inside, try and fit in, act just like anyone else? I don't have the answer, but I do wonder who she was talking about.

I walk back into the bar and sit down. Mike pushes my wine across the table.

"Here you go."

"Thanks."

"You were a long time."

"Queue."

He nods and picks up his orange juice. The not drinking makes sense now. Atonement. He blames himself for his daughter's death, even though it wasn't his fault. Just an unforeseeable tragedy. As all tragedies are. That's what makes them so hard to bear. The acceptance that life is random and often cruel. We seek to attribute blame. We cannot accept that things happen without reason. That not everything is within our control. We make ourselves small gods of our own universe without any of God's mercy, wisdom or grace.

I pick up my wine and take a swig.

"So, tell me, Jack?" Rushton says, interrupting my thoughts. "We were just discussing important theological matters."

"Oh. Really?"

"Yes. Who is the best on-screen devil? Al Pacino or Jack Nicholson?"

I smile. "Who says the devil has to be a man?"

THIRTY-ONE

"Stay the hell away from Wrigley. If you know what's good for you."

Fucking Rosie. The girl was a bitch and a bully, but was she also a liar? Flo was pretty sure Rosie Harper could twist the truth until it screamed. But there was something about her face when she issued her warning about Wrigley. Flo didn't like it.

Flo had found the story online. It had headlined the local rag. A fire had been deliberately set in the sports hall of Ferndown Academy. It had devastated the hall but hadn't reached the rest of the school. Firefighters had rescued a girl who had been trapped in a storeroom.

A pupil was arrested on suspicion of arson. There was no mention of the pupil being charged. Neither the alleged arsonist nor the girl were named. It might not even have been Wrigley. And, even if it was, if he hadn't been charged, they obviously didn't have enough evidence. It could all be gossip. Rumors spread like, well, wildfire, in schools.

Worst-case scenario, Wrigley **had** set the fire. That was bad, yes. But it didn't mean he knew there was someone in the storeroom. Perhaps it was an accident.

On the other hand, how well did she really know him?

"If I really wanted to murder you, I wouldn't have told you about the well."

She had tried to put it out of her mind when she got home, distracting herself with a book—an old Clive Barker. But it was no good. It was still there, like an itch. And then Mum had come in, rattling on about some stupid quiz at the pub. She had cracked. Lost her temper. She shouldn't have taken it out on her mum. It wasn't her fault, not really.

She lies back on her bed. What a shitshow. And the really, really crap thing? It isn't even the arson that bothers her the most. It's what Rosie had said about sucking Wrigley off. She's more bothered that Rosie sucked his dick than the fact he could have burned a girl to death. She's jealous. Stupid. She only spent a few hours with him. But she had thought he was different. He's the only friend she's made here. And now it turns out he's an arsonist and the sort of twat that would let a bitch like Rosie go down on him.

There's a soft knock on the bedroom door.

"Okay, I'm going."

She doesn't reply. Anger has filled her throat.

"Love you."

It's not her fault.

"Don't get too drunk," she calls gruffly back.

She hears her mum go back into her room and then trudge downstairs. The front door slams and Flo is alone. She rolls over and tries, again, to concentrate on her book. But it's too hot in the small room, even with the window open. And the claustrophobic silence of the cottage is distracting. She finds herself feeling tense, waiting for something to break it, even though she knows she is alone. **What's the scariest sound?** A stair creaking in an empty house. The soft tread of nonexistent feet. Perhaps belonging to a headless, armless, burning girl.

Give it a rest, brain! She reaches for her headphones and sticks them on, selecting something loud and punky to distract her. Frank Carter and The Rattlesnakes.

She manages most of the album and several more chapters of the book before her stomach starts to growl. Despite what she told her mum, she's starving. All she has eaten today is half a muffin.

She swings her legs out of bed and pushes open

the bedroom door. She pads downstairs. Even though it's not fully dark outside and all the lights are on, the cottage always feels full of shadows. Something about the rooms. The light never seems to stretch into all the crooked corners.

Despite the heat, she shivers. Reading too much horror again. She'll be seeing frigging clowns next. She walks into the kitchen and opens the fridge, surveying the contents. Mum's been shopping, but there still doesn't seem to be much here. Cooking and domesticity are not exactly her mum's strong points. She tries her best, but she is never going to be one of those TV mums who whips up a gourmet meal while spinning around the kitchen in an apron.

She spots some eggs, cheese and peppers. She could make an omelette, she supposes. She grabs the ingredients, slams the fridge shut and dumps them on the table. Then she goes over to the sink to get a knife out of the drainer.

Something catches her eye outside the window. A flash of movement. White between the grey headstones. From this angle, she can just make out a narrow strip of graveyard to the left of the chapel and then the chapel itself. She squints. There it is again. A figure. A girl? Moving swiftly from the graveyard toward the chapel. Instinctively, Flo turns and looks for her camera, then remembers that it's broken. When she looks back, the girl is gone. **If she was ever there at all.**

She debates. She has the strongest urge to follow her. But she's also well aware that following a ghostly girl into a deserted chapel at twilight is pretty much "Dumb Movie Heroine 101." She could only make it more clichéd if she was wearing a push-up bra and hot pants.

Still, something about the girl tugs at her. She grabs her phone and heads for the door. She is still holding the knife from the drainer: a small, sharp vegetable knife. She thinks about putting it back and then slips it into the back pocket of her jeans. Just in case.

It isn't much cooler outside. The air feels thick with trapped heat. She swats at a few midges. Thunder flies, her mum always calls them. The sign of a coming storm. In the city, the streetlights would just be starting to stutter on. Here, aside from the faint glow behind the cottage windows, there is only the muted grey of descending darkness; the silver and charcoal sky.

She stares over at the chapel. It looks a little like a ghost itself tonight. A specter of times past. She walks across the uneven path toward the door. It gapes open. Didn't Mum keep it locked in the evening?

She hesitates. She could call her mum, but then she would only freak and come rushing back. She was already on edge after the stuff with the airgun. Flo doesn't want to give her another excuse to treat her like a kid. Besides, the door looks fine. No one has forced it. And who broke into a chapel? What was there to steal? The moldy old curtains? The fake flowers by the altar? Mum probably just forgot. She's been preoccupied since they moved here, not herself.

Flo pushes the door open a little wider. It's much darker in the chapel. She pauses in the vestibule and lets her eyes adjust. Then she walks into the nave and looks around. Dim, dusty light drifts down in narrow shafts from the high windows. The pews are shadowy worshippers either side of the altar. They look empty. The whole nave looks empty. Of course, she can't see upstairs.

She takes a few more steps along the aisle. She is halfway down, her breathing steadying, when there is a heavy clunk that shakes the building. She jumps, spinning around. The door has slammed shut. She blinks. Dust spins in the air.

And then she sees her. Standing at the top of the aisle. White dress, dark hair. Not the same girl she saw before. This girl has a head and arms. Flo feels the hairs on her own arms quiver, her heart beats a little faster. She fumbles for her phone. She **will** get a picture this time.

The girl starts to walk slowly toward her, head down, tangled dark hair obscuring her face. She wears a dirty white smock, feet bare. Slight, but not a child.

"Are you all right?"

The girl remains silent.

"It's okay. I won't hurt you."

She still doesn't reply.

"I'm Flo. What's your—"

The girl looks up.

Flo screams. The girl's face is a mask of blackened and burnt flesh, melted away to bone and stubs of small teeth. Where her eyes should be there are just empty, dark craters. Flo stumbles backward, terror snatching her breath.

No, no, no. Not possible.

As she stares in horror, the girl's hair sparks and catches fire. More flames erupt at the tips of her hands and feet, creeping greedily along her limbs, darkening the skin until it peels away, like burnt paper.

A terrible dream. One that feels hideously real. She just has to wake up.

The girl draws closer, flaming hands outstretched. Flo can feel the heat, smell the stench of roasting flesh, hear the sizzle of her skin crisping.

Too real.

She takes another step backward. Her back hits the altar. The girl is still advancing. Flo's scalp prickles. Sweat dampens her underarms. This isn't a dream. She has to get out of here.

She darts blindly to the right, crashing into the makeshift barriers around the broken paving stones. She trips, regains her balance and jumps over the barriers. Her foot hits the floor . . . and plunges straight through.

She screams. Pain tears up her leg. Her phone flies from her hand.

Jesus Christ. Her leg is trapped. She can't move it. She stares around in panic. The chapel and her surroundings swim in and out of focus. Through the shock and pain, she realizes that the heat, the smell and the girl are all gone. She's alone.

She looks down. Her left leg has half disappeared through the chapel floor. The crumbling stone must have given way and her knee is now wedged between the cracked slabs. She tries to release it. Fresh, bright pain shoots up her leg. Her phone lies just out of reach. Of course. Probably no signal in here anyway, but still she strains for it, willing her fingertips to grow a few more inches. No good. Not even tantalizingly close.

She bites back a sob. Mum won't be back for another hour at least. What if she doesn't check Flo's room? No. She will. Of course she will. And then she'll check the chapel, surely? But what if she doesn't? What if she thinks Flo is in bed, asleep? **Stop it,** she tells herself. **Do not panic. Someone will come and . . . Wait!**

She can hear something. The creak of the chapel door? Footsteps. Yes, definitely footsteps. She tries to twist her body around. She can't see who it is from this angle, down on the floor. But it must be her mum. She must have come back early. Relief floods through her.

She's about to call out when the figure draws

into view around the end of the pews. The words shrivel on her tongue. She looks up and fear throbs in her throat.

"Flo."

She fumbles in her back pocket and pulls out the knife.

"Get back. Stay the hell away from me."

THIRTY-TWO

Rushton sinks his pint and looks around the table regretfully. "Well, this has been delightful, but we should probably get going."

Clara rises. "I'm so happy you came, Jack. Fresh blood."

"Yes, I think that was our best performance yet," Rushton adds, shrugging his arms into a worn blue anorak.

"I'd hate to have seen the worst," I say.

Rushton laughs. "We don't talk about it."

"I've had fun," I say, and realize I mean it. The evening, and company, have been enjoyable.

"Good. I'm glad to hear it, and we'll see you soon."

I watch Rushton and Clara leave and reach for my hoodie.

"Are you going?" Mike asks.

I hesitate. I should. I've had two glasses of wine.

Normally, my limit. Flo is waiting for me. On the other hand, I feel mellow, comfortable. It's only nine thirty. I suppose one more couldn't hurt.

"Well."

"I can give you a lift back."

"Just a small glass."

"Okay."

I slip my hoodie back over my stool and he saunters toward the bar. I note that Emma and Simon Harper have gone and wonder again about the conversation in the toilets. Emma had obviously had a drink, and maybe something else. Not that I'm judging her for that. Guilt is a little like grief. A cancer of the soul. They both hollow you out from the inside. But while you can learn to live with grief, guilt only grows as the years go by, spreading its tumorous tentacles. Who wouldn't take a pill for that?

Mike returns from the bar with a small wine for me and a black coffee for himself.

"No Cab Sav left. Hope Merlot is okay."

"Fine." I nod. "Call me a philistine but, after the first glass, I always think most wine tastes the same."

He smiles. "Been a while, but I tend to agree."

I raise my glass. "Well, here's to our uneducated palates."

He lifts his coffee cup. "Of course, I have now become a terrible coffee snob."

"How does that one measure up?"

He takes a sip. "Not bad. A little on the mellow side, but a good effort, considering I saw him spoon it out of a tin."

I laugh. We sip our drinks. There's an awkward pause, then we both start to speak at the same time.

"So—"

"After you," he says.

"Well, I wanted to apologize for getting off to a bad start the other day. I suffer from an appalling case of foot in mouth."

"That must be a bit of a problem, being a vicar."

"I get by on a wing and a prayer."

He mimes a cymbal bash. Then he looks at me more curiously. "Don't take this the wrong way, and I don't want to sound presumptuous, but you don't seem much like a vicar."

"Because I'm a woman?"

"No, no." He flushes.

"Joking."

"Right. I mean you just seem, sort of . . . less fuddy."

I chuckle. "Fuddy? Haven't heard that one before."

"I suppose, I mean, normally you can tell someone is a vicar even without the collar. Like Reverend Rushton. But you're more . . . normal. Oh God." He buries his head in his hands.

"Here," I say. "Let me take that shovel before you dig any further." I take a sip of my drink. "I do know what you mean."

"You do?"

"I meet a lot of vicars. Male and female. And you're right. Most of them are sort of . . . fuddy. A lot of the people who come into the church already come from religious backgrounds. Many also come from quite privileged backgrounds. They don't have a lot of life experience outside of the Church. That can make them a little disconnected from everyday life."

"That isn't your background?"

"No." I hesitate. "I didn't have a great childhood. Our mother was, well, I guess 'mentally unstable' is the best description. Home was not a good place. I left as soon as I could. Slept rough, begged. I could easily have become another statistic. And then a good man, who happened to be a vicar, helped me. He showed me that you can do a lot of good working for God. Helping the homeless, the lost, the abused."

"You can do that in other ways—working for charities, Social Services."

"True, but for me it was also about a sense of belonging. I'd never really had that before. God needed me, and it turned out that I needed him too."

He stares at me and I find myself dropping my eyes and taking a larger than intended sip of wine. I've told him more than most. But it's still a sanitized version. One without all the messy bits. **The only difference between a truth and a lie is how often you repeat it.**

"I used to be an atheist," he says.

"Used to be?"

"Yeah. Fervent. There is no God. Religion is the cause of all evil. We're just animals. There's nothing after death. Heaven and hell are just wishful thinking, et cetera."

"What changed your mind?"

His face clouds. "I had a child, a beautiful daughter . . . and I lost her."

"I'm so sorry," I say again.

"Suddenly I realized all that rhetoric, all that smug, clever conviction, was just bullshit. Because my daughter was not just flesh and blood. My joyful little mess of contradictions. Her glorious heart, her curiosity, her dreams, her vitality and energy. All of that couldn't just **disappear**. Like it meant nothing. Like **she** meant nothing. I have to believe that her soul still exists somewhere. I couldn't go on if I didn't."

His voice breaks. He looks down. Instinctively, I reach over and clasp his arm.

"Your daughter's soul is very much alive. I can feel her, in everything you just said. A wonderful energy that's all around us. That's how she lives on, in **you**."

He looks up and his eyes meet mine. I see something in them and, for a moment, I feel naked, exposed. Then he blinks.

"Thank you."

He picks up his coffee with a trembling hand. "Sorry. It still—"

"Of course."

It always will. The pain might get less sharp, less insistent. But it will always be there, until eventually he won't remember what life was like without it.

"So," he tries to gather himself, "that's me laying myself bare. What about you?"

"Me?"

"I sensed some hostility the other day—to journalists?"

"Oh, it's nothing, really."

"Really?"

"Drip, drip. You don't take my Ruby."

Maybe it's the wine, maybe I feel I owe him, but I find myself saying: "A terrible thing happened at my last church. A little girl died. The press weren't kind."

Vicar with Blood on Her Hands.

He looks down and then says, a little sheepishly, "I know."

I stare at him. **"You know?"**

"I googled you. Sorry. It didn't take long to find the story about your previous church. But also, I found this stuffed through my mailbox this morning." He reaches into his pocket and takes out a folded piece of paper. He places it on the table. "I didn't want to bring it up while the others were here."

I take the paper and unfold it. It's a photocopy of the same clipping I found pinned to the doll in the chapel. Underneath someone has typed:

Whoever conceals his transgressions will not prosper, but he who confesses and forsakes them will obtain mercy. (Proverbs 28:13)

The wine sours in my stomach. I look at Mike.

"D'you have any idea who it might be from?"

"No. But somehow, I doubt I'm the only person to receive one."

I swallow. Great.

"I was going to inform the police, but I thought you might like to know first."

"Thank you. I'd rather not involve the police."

"Okay."

"It's just, I don't really want it all dragged up again. Coming here, it was supposed to be a chance to put it behind us."

"Understood. How's that going?"

I smile thinly. "Not great."

"D'you want to talk about it?"

I look at him. And, actually, I find that I do.

THIRTY-THREE

"Flo?"

Wrigley draws closer, his face white.

"Get away from me!"

She tries to scrabble backward across the rough, damaged stone, but her leg is still stuck fast.

"Whoah. Don't try to move. You're going to hurt yourself."

"What are you doing here?"

"I was outside, and I heard you scream."

"What were you doing outside, creeping around the graveyard?"

"I wasn't creeping."

"So why are you here?"

"I came to see you."

"You couldn't call?"

"You never gave me your number."

"Oh."

"Why are you waving a knife at me?"

"Because I . . . was scared."

"Of me?"

She remembers Rosie's words: **"Stay the hell away from Wrigley."** But who does she really trust?

Slowly, she lowers the knife. "No."

He moves around and crouches down next to her. "What happened?"

"I . . . I thought there was someone in here and I . . . fell over and my foot just went through the floor."

"Shit." He tugs at a bit of the stone. "This must have been hollow underneath. No wonder they cordoned it off."

She tries to nod, but her head throbs. She feels exhausted and really, really cold. She starts to shiver.

"Here."

Wrigley pulls his hoodie off jerkily and gives it to her. Gratefully, she pulls it over her head.

"Thanks."

"Now, give me that knife."

"What? Why?"

"I'm going to try and use it to move this bit of paving."

Flo hesitates then hands him the knife.

"Why have you got a knife, anyway?"

"I thought there might be an intruder here."

"Was there?"

He wedges the knife under the stone slab and wiggles it. She thinks about the burning girl, arms outstretched.

"No."

He shrugs. "I used to carry a knife."

"What?"

"For protection."

The stone gives a little. She bites back a wince.

"From who?"

"Just kids. At school."

"You carried a knife **at school**?"

"It was stupid, I know. But you don't know what it was like. The stuff that happened."

The knife scrapes at the stone. It's very close to her leg, but she's sure she can feel the slab loosening.

"Was this at your old school?"

He tenses. "Who told you about that?"

"Rosie—"

"Of course."

"She said you tried to kill a girl."

"That's a lie."

"So you didn't set the school on fire?"

A pause. The only sound is the grating of the knife on stone. He isn't going to answer, she thinks.

He sighs and looks back at her. "No. I did try to burn down the school." A small, thin smile. "So, now you know. I'm a psycho."

"Why?"

"Just born that way, I guess."

"No. I mean, why did you try to burn down the school?"

Their eyes meet. Such odd eyes, she thinks. That strange silvery green. Weirdly hypnotic.

"Because I hated that place. I hated everything about it. The teachers, the other pupils. The smell. The rules. I hated the way they treated anyone who didn't fit their mold. Schools say all sorts of stuff about how they deal with bullying. But they don't. All they care about is the good, normal kids who boost their inspection reports.

"Once, this gang of kids surrounded me in the playing fields. They made me take my clothes off and crawl on my belly in the mud. Then they forced me to me eat worms. When I made it back to the school, covered in mud and naked, you know what the teachers did? They laughed."

"Christ."

"Even when Mum went up to the school to complain, nothing really changed. There weren't any good days. Not one. Just days they didn't torture me quite so much."

"I'm sorry."

"I just cracked. I . . . I wanted to obliterate that place."

"What about the girl?"

"I didn't know she was in there."

"So, what happened?"

"Someone called the fire brigade. They got her out. I felt terrible about it. I would never, ever hurt anyone."

"What about you?"

"I got off lightly. My mum paid for some fancy psychologist. I got counseling, supervision. We moved and I changed schools. Not that things are much better here." He turns back to the stone. "Almost there."

A chunk of the stone slab breaks away. Her leg is free. Painful, but free. She pulls it gingerly out. Her jeans are torn, and she can see a deep laceration and bruising through the ripped denim. She wiggles her foot. Hurts like hell. But it could have been worse.

"Thank you," she says to Wrigley.

"You should probably get that cleaned up."

"I should call my mum too."

He looks around and picks up her phone from the floor. "Not sure it'll work. Looks pretty badly smashed up."

He hands it to her. Their fingers brush. It suddenly strikes her that they are sitting close. Really close. She swallows. Then she thinks about what Rosie said.

"Wrigley—there's something else . . ."

But he's looking past her. "**Shit.** Have you seen this?"

He's peering into the hole where her leg was stuck.

"What?" she asks.

"This is really deep. You were lucky you didn't fall all the way through."

She turns stiffly and joins him. They stare down through the jagged hole in the floor. She can't see much, but she can tell Wrigley is right. The hole is deep. Far deeper than it should be, surely? Unless there's something underneath the church? Some kind of cellar?

"Have you got a light on your phone?" she asks.

Wrigley takes out his phone and shines it into the hole.

"Holy crap!"

Flo gasps. "Is that—"

They look at each other and then back down, into the hole.

Coffins.

THIRTY-FOUR

I first saw Ruby when her aunt brought her to be baptized. She had just turned five. Chubby-cheeked and the biggest brown eyes I'd ever seen. I didn't know her back story, not then, but it gradually came out through other parishioners. The church community was tightly knit. People knew each other's business. A bit like a small village.

Ruby's mother had died from a drug overdose. No father around. Her mother's sister had stepped in to foster her. Aunt Magdalene was a large, jovial woman who hadn't been able to have children of her own. She lived with her friend, Demi, a thin black lady, as skinny as Magdalene was fulsome.

I didn't know them particularly well. Prior to fostering Ruby, they had attended another church, but then decided to join my congregation. The two women brought Ruby to St. Anne's every Sunday for the family service and occasionally to the children's art group on Thursday evenings.

Lena (as I grew to know her) was chatty, always smiling and laughing. Demi was quieter, more reserved. However, they seemed a devoted couple, even if, sometimes, I got the impression that a child had perhaps been more Lena's desire than Demi's. But still, I didn't see any warning signs. Not at first. Or maybe I did, and I just tried to ignore them. Like we all do.

At the christening, I remember Lena saying she was relieved she had got it done. It seemed an odd choice of words, so I asked why.

"Her mother was godless," she told me. "She would have let her child die and Ruby would have remained in purgatory."

I had politely and gently said that God welcomes all children, even those who are not christened. She had looked at me strangely and said: "No, Reverend. They will forever wander the earth. I want my Ruby to go to heaven."

I had dismissed it. I shouldn't have done. I should have known that there is a fine line between being religious and religious fervor. But then, many of my congregation were far more "Old Testament" than me. I tried as much as I could to update their views, to encourage them to think more about love and tolerance than hellfire and damnation, but their views didn't mean that they were bad people.

Perhaps the first proper warning sign came when Ruby turned up to the art group with a large bruise on her forehead. **She fell,** Lena told me. And young children did fall. A lot. I knew this. Flo was always covered in bruises at Ruby's age. I remembered a time when Flo had run into the living room, tripped on the rug and headbutted the fireplace. Her head had immediately erupted into an egg-shaped lump and I had driven to A & E in a blind panic. Accidents happened.

But they seemed to happen to Ruby more and more. Bruises, scrapes. And then a broken arm. **She fell off the climbing frame in the garden,** Lena explained. All reasonable, plausible explanations delivered in Lena's reassuring, smiley tone.

I knew where they lived. Lena once invited me around for tea. It was a small council terrace on the edge of St. Anne's. Neatly kept when I visited. Ruby's toys stacked in pink plastic boxes. I was aware that by calling in again, unannounced, I was overstepping the mark. But my unease was growing. I couldn't ignore it any more. I bought some sweets for Ruby and told myself I was just putting my mind at rest.

When I reached the house, no one appeared to be home. And the house didn't look as neat and well kept as when I'd first visited several months earlier. Even from the outside. The curtains were pulled, but I could see through gaps in the falling-down fence that the garden was overgrown. Old toys lay discarded in the grass. Rubbish bins overflowed. More disconcertingly, there was no climbing frame.

That was when I first mentioned my concerns to Durkin. He had smiled (benevolently).

"I'm not sure an overgrown garden is proof of ill-doing."

"What about the climbing frame?"

"Maybe she meant a climbing frame at the park."

"She definitely said it was in the garden."

"Perhaps she misspoke."

"It's not just the bruises. I'm sure Ruby is getting thinner."

"Children go through growth spurts."

"I'm worried about her."

"Jack, if there was a problem, surely the child's school would have noticed? And if she's being fostered, Social Services must be making checks."

"I suppose so, but—"

"I know you have always taken a special interest in the welfare of young people in your parish, and that is admirable. But no parent is perfect, after all. Not even you, I'm sure. Has Flo never had an accident?"

Of course she had, but I still bristled.

"Judge not lest ye be judged," Durkin said.

"Of course."

Go to hell, I thought.

That afternoon I called Ruby's school to make an appointment to talk to her teacher. But I couldn't.

Because Ruby had been taken out of school several weeks ago. Her aunts were now home-schooling her, the headmistress told me. Lena had never mentioned it. Ruby had never mentioned it. But then, it seemed to me that Ruby had grown quieter of late. No longer the chubby-cheeked, smiling child she'd been when she joined the church.

Alarm bells were now well and truly ringing. Still, I tried to make excuses. Maybe Lena and Demi were struggling. A child is demanding. I tried to take Lena to one side after a service.

"Is everything all right, with Ruby?"

She gave me a wide beam and said, "Of course, Reverend. You must come round for tea again."

"That would be lovely," I said, knowing neither of us meant it. And then, casually, I asked: "How are things at school?"

Her face clouded. "Reverend, I must confess, we have been neglectful. Ruby was being bullied at school and we didn't know. Another child was hurting her, taking her lunch. We should have done something sooner, and we blame ourselves. But now we are schooling her at home, where we can look after her properly."

She smiled at me again, so widely, so sincerely. And her story was also so plausible and yet, I knew, in my heart, that she was lying through her gleaming teeth.

I made an anonymous call to Social Services. I waited. Nothing happened. Ruby continued to turn up to church, looking thinner each week. I couldn't talk to her because Lena or Demi was always there. I noted that Lena was wearing new clothes and Demi sported a new gold necklace around her scraggy neck.

I called Social Services again. Again, I waited. And then one day, during art class, while Lena was in the toilet, I took my chance and crouched down next to Ruby.

"Hey, sweetheart, how are you?"

She kept her eyes on her picture: a riot of glue and glitter. "Fine."

"Is everything all right at home? Are you eating okay?"

"Yes."

"Are you sure?"

She looked up. Her dark eyes swam with fear, hopelessness, desperation.

"I'm a bad girl. The devil is in me. It must be purged."

And then she burst into tears.

"Ruby—"

"What are you doing?"

I saw a swish of red fabric out of the corner of my eye. Lena had stormed across the room and swept me aside.

"What did you say? Why are you upsetting the child?"

"I'm worried about her, Lena."

She had seized Ruby's arm, hauling her up from her seat, and glared at me, eyes bright with hatred. "It's **you**, isn't it? Calling those people on us. Making trouble. You white bitch."

I had stared at her, aghast.

"I am a good woman, trying to bring this child up the right way, and you stand there, spreading lies about us. I love this child. I do what is best for her, you hear."

I tried to keep calm, aware now that everyone was staring at us. "I hear. But she doesn't look well, Lena."

"Is that what you think? That people like **us** can't raise our children properly? Not like you perfect white people, hey?"

"No. That's not it."

"How dare you. You don't take my Ruby, you understand. No one takes my Ruby."

And she had stormed out, dragging Ruby with her.

I should have gone to the police then. I should have hammered down Social Services' door to get them to listen. I should have gone after her. I should have done **something**. But I didn't. I was scared. I was scared of the looks the other parents had given me. I was scared that, in some way, what she had said might be true. Was I judging Lena and Demi more harshly because of their skin color, even subconsciously? Was I making a terrible mistake?

I didn't see Ruby at all the following week. I drove past the house and it looked shut up. Perhaps they had moved. I had lost her.

I came into church as usual the following Sunday. I liked to get there early to set up and to have some quiet contemplation time. In early February, the mornings were dark till around eight. I had unlocked the doors, stepped inside and, straightaway, I knew something was wrong.

The feel of the church. The smell. Metallic. A rich, sickly smell. I flicked on the lights and walked down the middle of the nave. I could see something lying on the steps beneath the altar. And I could hear something. A drip. Slow and steady. **Drip, drip, drip.**

Somehow, my legs carried me forward. I had to see. I had to know. Even though pretty much every fiber of my being was telling me I didn't want to see, I didn't want to know.

She lay, crumpled, beneath the altar. Naked, so thin that every rib protruded like a bicycle spoke, her limbs tiny, fragile matchsticks. She still clutched a worn toy bunny. Her eyes were wide open, and they stared at me accusingly. Her throat gaped in a vivid red mocking smile.

"Drip, drip, drip. You don't take my Ruby."

They arrested Lena and Demi at Toddington Services on the M1. They'd been pocketing the money they got for fostering Ruby. Buying themselves nice things and saving for a holiday. A getaway. She had been starved, beaten and then sacrificed. That was Lena's excuse.

"The child was possessed," she later told the police. "I had to exorcize the demons. Now her soul will go to heaven."

To this day, I don't know whether she truly believed it or whether it was simply the basis of an insanity plea. Either way, the papers had a field day. Because of Lena's ramblings, the church came under focus. I was held up as being the vicar who somehow let all of this happen on her watch. The community blamed me; the press blamed me. Most of all, I blamed myself. The vicar with blood on her hands.

Mike stares at me sympathetically.

"But it wasn't your fault. You did everything you could to help that little girl."

"It wasn't enough."

"Sometimes, nothing is." He looks down into his coffee. "I suppose Simon and Clara have told you how Tara died."

"They told me it was an accident."

He shakes his head. "An accident that wouldn't have happened, if it wasn't for me. I should have picked her up from school that day. But I was drunk. I couldn't drive. I asked Emma to look after her as a favor. Tara shouldn't have even been at their house."

"But it could have happened on another day.

You didn't cause the accident. It just happened. Accepting there is no blame, no reason for a tragedy, is the hardest thing we can do. But we have to, or we never move on."

"And have you done that, with Ruby?"

"Not yet." I smile thinly. "Like I said, it's the hardest thing we can do."

"What if you can never accept it?"

"Life goes on. It's our choice whether we go with it."

"And if we can't?"

"Mike—"

My phone buzzes on the table. I glance at the screen. A number I don't recognize. I frown. Only a few people have my number, and they're all saved in my contacts. I don't get calls from strange numbers.

Mike nods at the phone. "Do you want to get that?"

My hand hovers. And then I snatch the phone up and press accept.

"Hello?"

Breathing on the other end of the line. I tense.

"Mum?"

"**Flo?** What's going on. Whose phone is this?"

"Wrigley's."

I try not to bristle at hearing his name. But there's his name. Again.

"Why are you calling from Wrigley's phone?"

"Long story. Look, Mum, can you come back?"

"Why? What's happened? Are you okay?"

"Yes. I'm fine—well, I've hurt my leg a bit. But don't worry. There's something you need to see. In the chapel."

Questions tumble on my tongue. How did she hurt her leg? Why is Wrigley there? What were they doing in the chapel so late at night? But I try to keep my tone calm and reasonable.

"I'm on my way."

I put the phone into my pocket. Mike looks at me quizzically.

"Trouble?"

"My daughter. I need to get home."

"I'll give you a lift."

"Thank you."

I stand, and realize that my legs are shaking. I grip the edge of the table. Just for a moment, when that strange number came up, I had a terrible premonition that it might be **him**. That, somehow, he had found me. Just like he did before.

The man who murdered my husband.

My brother. Jacob.

THIRTY-FIVE

He lays his head down on the straw. Stars glint through the mosaic of holes in the rusted iron roof. The barn is cold, dirty and smells of cow shit. He's slept in worse places. And she is close; so close he can almost feel her.

It makes his predicament even more frustrating. His ankle throbs hotly. Sprained, not broken, he thinks. But still, a problem. His collar is dirty, and his suit torn. Another problem. And he has no money. She might be close, but she might as well be a million miles away. He feels the anger growing. He has come so far. Planned so well.

His train had arrived on time at St. Pancras. He had disembarked, into a throng of bustling bodies. He'd thought Nottingham was busy. Here, it was all he could do not to climb straight back on board and huddle in his seat.

Prison was full of people, but most hours were spent in your cell. Even in the mess hall and recreation area, the flow of bodies was ordered. Physical contact was limited. Indeed, accidental contact could result in a broken nose or worse.

The station was chaos. So many people rushing forward. Suitcases rumbling along the platform. Voices echoing off the high, arched roof. The squeal of train brakes, the robotic echo of the loudspeaker announcements.

He gritted his teeth and forced himself to walk slowly and calmly through the crowd, toward the ticket barriers. Here, he was momentarily confused. The barriers had been open at Nottingham. What was he supposed to do?

"Do you need some help, sir?"

He jumped. A small, dark-haired woman in a station uniform stared at him.

"Err, yes, sorry. I don't travel very often."

"Ticket?" she asked kindly.

He fished out his ticket and handed it to her. She glanced at it and then opened the barrier. "There you go, Reverend."

"Thank you. God bless."

He joined the throng of people heading down the escalator. A sign told him to stand to the right. He obeyed the instructions. Obeying instructions was something he was good at.

The people at the ticket office were helpful. Of course. A uniform—any uniform—gained you respect. The dog collar carried authority. Was that why his sister liked it? Or was it the anonymity? You weren't really a person in a dog collar. You were a priest.

He wondered idly if they had found the dead priest yet.

It was late afternoon by the time he boarded the train to Sussex. A much smaller train, half empty. He sat back, staring out of the window, as it rattled out of the tightly packed conurbations of London, through the sprawling suburbs and then out into the open countryside. He felt a stab, a strange yearning. It was so long since he had seen fields, livestock, clear skies.

An hour and a half later the train pulled into Beechgate station. Little more than a shed and a narrow platform with one solitary bench. He was the only one to disembark. Sheep grazed in the field next to the tracks. If the bustle of London had been disorienting, this much space, this much quiet, was overwhelming in its own way. He looked around, breathing in the air, staring up at the sky. So much sky.

A white wooden sign outside the station informed him that it was ten miles to Chapel Croft. There was no bus stop and he only had about fifty pence left in cash anyway. He straightened his collar and started to walk.

The road was narrow and twisty. There wasn't a proper pavement, so he walked on the tarmac and hopped on to the verge whenever he heard a car approaching. Fortunately, this wasn't very often. The road was virtually deserted.

An hour into his journey, the sky had started to darken. He didn't have a watch—he had never felt a need for one in prison—but he had become good at guessing the time. He thought it was probably about eight o'clock. He picked up his speed a little. He didn't want to be out on the road in the dark.

He was just rounding a particularly twisty bend when he heard the car approaching. Loud. Fast. Faster than the others. He turned and caught a flash of the large grille, heard the squeal of brakes as it cut the corner. He leaped back, but his ankle had twisted underneath him and he tumbled into the ditch. The four-by-four didn't stop. He wasn't even sure if the driver had seen him.

He lay there, in the muddy, stinking water of the ditch. His side hurt where he had landed. Worse, his ankle pulsated with hot white pain. He scrambled into a sitting position and managed to clamber from the ditch on to the verge. But when he tried to push himself to his feet, his ankle screamed, and he collapsed back on to his knees. He couldn't walk. What to do? Through a gap in the hedge he could see a farmhouse in the distance. Closer, in the next field, a dilapidated barn. It would do.

He started to crawl toward it.

· · ·

He closes his eyes now, wishing he had something to take the edge off the pain. Maybe his ankle **is** broken. He sits up and pulls up his trouser leg. It doesn't look good. It's more swollen than ever, the stretched skin a montage of black and purple and red. He groans and falls back on the straw.

He can't walk far on his busted ankle. And no one is going to give him a lift looking like this, even with the dog collar. He needs to clean himself up. He needs painkillers. He turns and stares through the gaping hole in the barn wall. Across the field, lights glow warmly through the windows of the farmhouse.

You're wearing a dog collar. Tell them you had an accident. They'll let you in.

And then what? I'm not going to hurt any-one else.

But they'll have painkillers. Alcohol. Maybe cash too.

No. They could also have children. They're in-nocent. He can't hurt innocent people.

No one is entirely innocent.

His ankle radiates pain. He tries to ignore it, but it's no good. He sits up. He looks back at the farm-house. **Painkillers. Alcohol**. Maybe he doesn't have to hurt them. Not much. Just enough to re-strain them. To take what he needs. How else is he going to reach her?

He forces himself to his feet.

THIRTY-SIX

I get down on my knees and point the flashlight down into the hole, which is about the circumference of a football. A vault, beneath the church. I can make out the curve of arched walls. Slightly to my left, what look like stone steps. And coffins. Three of them. Stacked haphazardly in one corner. The wood looks like it has rotted and warped. The lid on one coffin has cracked and I can just make out a leering skull peering out from within.

"Can I have a look?" Mike asks.

He accompanied me out to the chapel, even though I told him it was fine, I didn't need a chaperone. After tending to Flo's leg—which is badly scraped but not broken, fortunately—I left Flo and Wrigley in the cottage, drinking milk and eating biscuits. I'm presuming they can't do too much harm to themselves with a packet of chocolate Hobnobs.

Flo said she thought she saw someone going into the chapel, so she went to take a look around, tripped and put her foot through the crumbling paving slabs. Wrigley, who just happened to be passing (like pretty much everyone else in the village), heard her screams and came to her aid. The story has bigger holes than, well, the chapel floor, but the interrogation can wait, for now.

I hand Mike the flashlight. "Be my guest."

He kneels down and peers into the hole. "Wow. Quite a discovery. How old do you think this is?"

I consider. "Rushton mentioned that the original church was destroyed by a fire. The chapel was built on its footprint. The entrance to the vault must have been paved over."

Although, why seal off an old vault? If anything, a private vault would be a mark of prestige that the family of those buried there would want preserved.

Mike is still peering at the paving slabs. "I don't know. This looks like it's been done more recently. Look, this stone is much thinner, newer than the rest of the floor. And you can see the cement is fresher. This is a patch job."

"I didn't know you were an expert in flagstone flooring?"

"I am a man of many talents."

"Modesty not being one of them."

He grins. "Okay. I did a story about church restoration for the paper last year."

I raise an eyebrow. "Your days must simply fly."

"Ouch."

I stare at the hole in the floor, mind still churning. If he's right, and the floor was repaired at some point, then how come no one noticed the great big bloody vault underneath the chapel?

"What do you want to do?" Mike asks.

Tempting as it is to fetch a tire iron and find out exactly what's under there right now, I'm not sure that will endear me to the powers that be, and I don't mean God.

"I think I need to call out a qualified stonemason and get them to remove the slabs carefully, so we can investigate."

"Well, there, I can help—"

He gets out his phone. "I still have the number of the stonemason I followed around."

"Handy."

"Well, we went out for a drink a couple of times afterward."

"Oh."

I try to contain my surprise. Because he was previously married to a woman, I had presumed Mike was straight.

"She's really good," he adds.

"Right."

She. Stupid, Jack. Of all people, I should be used to people's presumptions.

"Have you got AirDrop?"

"Err, yes."

I get out my phone and it pings with Mike's message. I press accept.

"Thanks."

"What do you think is under there?" he asks.

"Well, usually vaults like this were built beneath churches for the wealthy and influential in the village."

"Right. Like their own private graves, away from all the peasants."

"Exactly."

We both look back at the vault.

"So, the question isn't really what, but who?"

I sit on the edge of Flo's bed, something I haven't done since she was a little girl. She's propped up on her pillows, her bandaged leg poking out of the duvet. Her face is pale, eyes circled with shadows.

"Are you mad at me?"

"I'm not mad," I say. "Not anymore. I just worry about you. I want to keep you safe."

"I know, Mum. But you can't protect me from everything. What happened in the chapel was just an accident."

"Right." I look at her more closely. "And the figure you followed in there?"

A hesitation. There it is. I knew there was something she wasn't telling me.

"Okay. Promise you won't think I'm crazy."

"I promise."

"I thought I saw another girl, like in the graveyard."

"The same girl."

"No, this girl had a head and arms—but she was on fire and all burnt up. It was horrible."

I just stare at her. **Burning girls.**

"I'm not making it up."

"I know." I sigh. "Are you sure no one else mentioned the story of the burning girls to you? Wrigley, perhaps?"

"Why? You think someone told me something and my mind somehow conjured these visions up?"

"I'm just looking for rational explanations. I've never believed in ghosts."

"Me neither."

"But I believe **you**."

What I don't add is that I also believe that the last few weeks have been traumatic. All the trouble in Nottingham. The sudden move here. Flo has never given me any cause to worry about her mental health. She's always been remarkably well balanced. But then, Jonathon was good at putting on an act. And there are some professionals who believe that mental health problems are hereditary.

"So, what are we going to do?" Flo asks.

"I don't know."

"Exorcism? I mean, you've got the kit."

I smile weakly. "If there are lost souls stuck on this earth, I don't think ripping them from it violently and in anger is the best way to treat them, do you?"

"I guess not."

"The folklore says the burning girls appear to those in trouble."

"So, you think I'm in trouble?"

I look pointedly at her leg.

"An accident," she says again.

"The second in two days."

"Here we go. I suppose you're going to blame Wrigley?"

"Both times you've met him, something bad has happened."

"He rescued me tonight."

"And I'm thankful he found you."

"But?"

"What if **he** was the person you saw going into the chapel?"

"He wasn't."

"Okay, but what do you really know about him?"

"He lives just outside the village with his mum."

"And?"

"Well, I didn't give him a whole interrogation."

"I'd still like to meet his mum."

"We're not dating."

I raise my eyebrows.

"It's not like that."

"Does **he** know that?"

"Yes. And what about you and that bloke, Mike?"

"Definitely not like that."

"Have you told **him**?"

"Okay, enough, young lady." I rise. "We'll chat about this in the morning."

She turns and reaches for her light, then pauses. "Mum, whose bodies do you think are in the vault?"

"I really don't know. We'll have to wait and see tomorrow. Get some rest. Do you think you'll sleep?"

She yawns. "The burning girls only haunt the chapel, right?"

"I suppose."

"Then I should be fine."

"Night. Love you to the moon and back."

A phrase we used to use when she was little.

"Love you to the whole universe and back."

"Love you to infinity and back."

"Love you to the Big Bang and back."

I smile and pad across to the bathroom. I wash, brush my teeth and get ready for bed. I feel exhausted but also on edge, as though I am teetering on the cusp of something; something bad. The feeling washes over me like vertigo.

Something wicked this way comes.

I reach for the silver chain I wear around my neck. And then I walk into the bedroom and kneel beside the bed. But I don't pray. I slide my hand beneath the mattress. My fingers fumble around, touching wooden slats. I frown. I lift the mattress and stare under it in disbelief.

The knife has gone.

THIRTY-SEVEN

Prayers should not be selfish. Something my old mentor, Blake, told me. **God is not a concierge. He's not here at your beck and call. By all means, ask for guidance, but if you need help, you must learn to help yourself.**

I've always tried to follow his advice. Along with his other important biblical teaching: everything looks better after a good night's sleep, a strong coffee and a cigarette.

I get dressed, go downstairs, make a very strong coffee and retrieve my tin of tobacco and papers. Then I take it all upstairs, open my bedroom window and sit on the windowsill. Smoking out of my bedroom window is neither safe nor hygienic, but I need to think, and I need to make some phone calls. Here is the only place I can do both.

I roll a cigarette, staring out at the fields across the road. The grass glints with dew. The sun is a silver disc in the misty blue sky. It's beautiful, but it does little to lighten my mood.

The knife has gone. I checked again when I got up. Not beneath the mattress. Not in my wardrobe, not in the case. How can it be gone? Who can have taken it? Well, basically only two people were alone in the house last night: Flo and Wrigley.

Could Flo have found it? Did she take it in the same way that she hides my tobacco? Perhaps for my own safety? Because she was worried about me? But how would she even have found it? Why would she have been looking beneath the mattress?

My first instinct was to confront her last night. But then I changed my mind. It was late. We were both tired. And if she hadn't taken it, that would have just led us on to a more uncomfortable discussion. Why had I hidden a knife under my mattress? And who else had been in the house today, perhaps with opportunity to go sneaking around? **Wrigley?**

This move was supposed to be a chance to get away from our problems. To escape. To set things right. But all I am finding are more worries, questions without answers. I feel like I've stepped into a puddle only to find that it's quicksand, and the more I try to drag myself out, the faster I'm hastening my descent into the quagmire.

The prison release letter still festers in my glovebox. The death of Reverend Bradley lurks at the back of my mind. Much as I keep trying to tell myself that the two are not connected, doubt lingers.

And what of the mysterious items left for me here? Not to mention the newspaper clipping? Who left them? What message are they trying to deliver?

I drag harder on the cigarette and take out my phone. Okay. First item of business. Call the stone-mason and ask them to find out exactly what is under the chapel, and why no one seems to have been aware of it. It's just after eight thirty. They're probably not open yet, but it's worth a try. I press call, half expecting it to go to voicemail but, to my surprise, a bright female voice answers:

"Hello, TPK."

"Oh, hello. This is Reverend Brooks at Chapel Croft."

"Hi."

"I was wondering if it might be possible for you to come and take a look at an area of damaged flooring in the chapel?"

"Yes. Of course. What sort of damage are we talking? Chipped, cracked?"

"More like a great big hole in the floor and a hidden vault underneath."

"Wow—now that sounds interesting! I've actually had a job cancel this morning. I could be with you in about half an hour, if that's convenient?"

"That would be great. Thank you."

"I'll see you shortly."

I put the phone down. One job done. Next, I cannot continue risking life and limb for three bars on my phone. I need to call BT and . . .

"Hello, up there!"

I jump, wobble on the windowsill and clutch at the frame.

"Jesus!"

I peer down. A bald man in what looks suspiciously like a BT uniform stands beneath the window. I was so preoccupied I hadn't noticed the van pull up.

"I'm looking for a Reverend Brooks? Are you Mrs. Brooks?"

I smile. **Thank you, God.**

"Actually, **I'm** Reverend Jack Brooks."

"Oh, right. I'm Frank, from BT."

"And **you,** quite literally, are the answer to my prayers."

While Frank the BT man fumbles around with connections and drills holes in the living-room wall, I shower and get dressed. I'm just heading downstairs when Flo pokes a disheveled head out of her bedroom.

"What's that noise?"

"That is the sound of us rejoining civilization."

"Internet?"

"Yep."

"Hallelujah."

I regard her for a moment. **The knife.**

"How's your leg?"

"A bit sore, but okay."

"Want a cup of tea or coffee?"

"Coffee would be good."

"Okay. I'll bring one up."

She stares at me suspiciously. "Why are you being so nice?"

"Because I love you."

"And?"

"Do I need another reason?" I smile, lovingly.

"You're being weird," she says, and retreats back into her room.

I walk downstairs and make her a milky coffee, one sugar. I pop my head into the living room and check on Frank.

"How's it going?"

"Almost done in here, love. Then I just need to go and check the connection up the road."

I smile politely and try to batten down my annoyance at being called "love."

"Thanks. I can't tell you how happy we'll be to have internet again."

"Funny. Never think of vicars using the internet."

"Well, sending prayers to Sainsbury's for the shopping doesn't work so well."

He stares at me and then laughs, awkwardly. "Oh, right. Good one." He looks around. "Y'know, I remember the other bloke who was here."

Of course. Small village. Even the BT man is local.

"Reverend Fletcher?"

"Yeah, decent fella. Shame what happened."

"Yes. Very sad."

"Thought that would be the end of it, to be honest."

"End of what?"

"Here. The chapel."

"Why?"

"Well, they had it up for sale at one point."

This is news to me. "Really?"

"Yeah. After the old vicar—Marsh—retired, it was closed for well over a year. Then Reverend Rushton started a campaign to save it. They got this big donation and decided to keep it open."

"Well, that was very fortunate. Who was the generous donor?"

"Local bloke. Simon Harper. Never had him down as the religious type, but I suppose it's village history, innit?"

"I suppose," I say.

"Right." He stands. "I'll just scoot up the road. Be back in a minute."

"Okay."

I take Flo's coffee upstairs, mind ticking over. So, Simon Harper made a large donation to the church. Rushton had mentioned the family "doing a lot" for the church. He obviously meant bailing it out. But why, I wonder? To make himself look good? Or something else?

I knock on Flo's door.

"Come in."

I walk in. She's sprawled on her bed, headphones on. I put the coffee down on her bedside table.

She mutters, "Thanks."

I wait. She notices me hovering and takes her headphones off.

"Yes?"

The knife.

"I just wanted to ask you something, about last night?"

"O-kay?"

"When you were in the house, with Wrigley, were you together all the time?"

"Yes. Why?"

Too quick. She's lying.

"So, he didn't use the toilet or anything?"

"Maybe. Why are you asking?"

I shrug. "He didn't put the seat down."

"Is that a crime?"

"It is in this house."

Her eyes narrow. "Why are you **really** asking?"

I hesitate. I don't want to accuse Wrigley without proof, and I don't want to start another argument. Fortunately, I'm saved by a knock on the front door. Frank.

"Better get that," I say.

"Knock yourself out." She puts her headphones back on.

I have my answer anyway. Looks like young Lucas Wrigley and I need to have another chat. I trot downstairs and open the door, expecting to see Frank's bald head gleaming in the sun. Instead, a young woman with short hair and a skull tattoo poking out from the arm of her T-shirt stands on the doorstep. She looks familiar.

"Hello again," she says.

And then it clicks. It's the same young woman I met in the village hall. Kirsty?

"Oh, hi. Can I help you?"

"I'm hoping I can help **you**." She holds up a large tool case with "**TPK Stonemasons**" written on the side.

She grins. "Something about a hidden vault?"

THIRTY-EIGHT

They don't have children.

They do have a dog, a small brown-and-white terrier who alternates between sitting at the man's feet, eyeing the bacon sandwich he is eating, and pawing agitatedly at the adjoining door to the living room.

"Settle down," he says, and chucks it a bit of bacon fat.

The dog looks at the door, whines and then trots over and eats the bacon.

Man's best friend, he thinks. **Yeah, right.** The extent of a dog's devotion begins and ends with food. Although, to be fair, the terrier probably doesn't quite understand that his owners will not be taking him for walkies ever again.

He glances at the door. He didn't mean to. But he had little choice. By the time he reached the farm his ankle was so painful he could barely hobble. Even if he could have managed to talk his way inside, there was no way he could overpower anyone. All he had was the element of surprise. He had found the axe embedded in some logs in a small shed outside. He could see the occupants through the patio doors. The doors hadn't even been locked. Old folk. Too trusting. Oblivious to the horrors that could be lurking outside, even here, in the middle of nowhere.

It had been quick. Bloody, but quick. They had both been sitting, backs to him, watching TV. One swipe had taken the wife's wispy grey head almost clean off. Her husband, equally grey and withered, had started to rise, but another swing had opened up his chest. The final blow had cleaved his skull almost in two. The terrier had yelped and yelped hysterically and then, when he turned toward it with the dripping axe, it had run and hidden in its crate.

He had stared at the bloody mess of bodies on the worn rug. Less than a couple of minutes for their lives to be snuffed out. But they were old, he reasoned. They had already lived their lives. He had probably only slashed them short by a few years. He didn't feel so bad. It was necessary.

He had gone upstairs and ransacked the bathroom for painkillers. Another benefit of them being old was a medicine cabinet crammed with drugs. He had necked four codeine tablets and then gone back downstairs in search of alcohol. He found two bottles of sherry and one decent brandy in the kitchen cupboard. He had opened the brandy and downed several glugs. Finally, he had lain down on their large double bed and closed his eyes.

He dreamed. About a house a long time ago. About his big sister. About how she would curl up in bed next to him when he cried, wrap her arms around him and sing to him about tomorrow. Until the night she left him. And never came back.

He finishes his sandwich and reaches for his mug of tea. Then he changes his mind and picks up the bottle of sherry he opened earlier. He takes a swig, savoring the sweet burn down his throat.

His ankle is still black and red, and more swollen than ever. The skin looks cracked and he's increasingly convinced it **is** broken after all. But, with the tablets and booze, he hardly notices the pain.

He **is** aware that he smells, quite badly. He needs to shower, he thinks. Then, he'll take the old couple's Toyota and drive over to Chapel Croft and take a look around. He's already got the keys out on the table. It's been a while since he drove. But it's a new car and he's hoping it's an automatic. Old people usually drive automatics, right?

He reaches for the sherry again . . . and tenses. He thought he heard something. Another car engine, tires crunching on the gravel driveway. The terrier runs from the kitchen, through the archway into the hall, yapping. He gets up from his chair and follows it. There's a small window to the side of the wooden front door. He peers through.

Sure enough, a silver Nissan has pulled up on the drive. **"Cathy's Cleaners"** is written down the side. What to do? He could just not answer the door, but she probably has a key. Plus, the damn dog is yapping up a storm. Fuck.

He watches as a slim woman—mid-thirties, dark blonde hair—climbs out of the car. He glances toward the living room. The axe is still embedded in the old man's head. He hobbles into the kitchen and pulls open the cutlery drawer. He selects a sharp bread knife and walks back to the front door, heart thudding.

He peers through the window. The woman goes to the trunk and takes out a Henry Hoover and a box of cleaning products. She carries the box up to the front door. His hand tightens on the knife. She puts the box down on the doorstep, then walks back to the car. She closes the trunk and picks up the vacuum cleaner. Then she stops, obviously re-membering something. She opens the back door and takes out a branded purple tunic, which she slips over her T-shirt. He stares. In the back of the car, there's a baby seat.

She locks the car and crunches up to the front door. He looks down at the knife. Back at the door. He sees there is a chain on it. He quickly loops it into place. Then he backs away. The doorbell rings.

The terrier scrabbles at the door, barking hysterically. He hears her say:

"Hello, Candy, are you okay?"

She rings the doorbell again. He climbs up the stairs and sits on the landing, out of sight. He hears her insert a key into the lock and push the door open. It jams against the chain.

"Hello—Roz, Geoff? The chain's on?"

The dog claws at the gap.

"Hey, Candy. It's okay, sweetheart."

She rattles the door again. He hears her tut. Why isn't she leaving? What's she doing? His question is answered as a mobile suddenly trills in the house. After five rings, it stops. He hears her voice outside:

"Hello, it's Cathy. I'm at the house, but I can't get in, the chain's on. Your car's here. Are you okay? Give me a call. I'm going to head off now, but I can always come back later. Okay. Bye."

He waits.

"Bye, Candy. Nose in."

She pulls the door shut and he listens as she crunches across the gravel to her car. A few seconds later he hears the car drive away again. He lets out a sigh of relief.

He walks into the kitchen and picks up the Toyota keys. There's a door from the kitchen to the side of the house. He eases it open and hobbles around the farmhouse.

You can't take the car.

Why?

Because it's the first thing the police will look for when they find the bodies.

His heart sinks. Of course. Right now, no one knows who he is or what he looks like. But if he takes the car, the police will be looking for it. Cars are not easy things to hide, even if you burn them out.

He looks around, and then he sees it. A bike. Propped against the log shed. He hurries across to it and swings his leg over the saddle. He can just about manage to pedal with his ankle. The terrier yaps and howls frantically from inside the house— loud enough to cause a small crowd of jackdaws to rise, squawking, from the rooftop. He should have killed the dog too.

He stares back at the farmhouse, considering. Then he cycles out of the driveway in a spit of gravel. The dog's howls echo after him.

THIRTY-NINE

"So, I thought you worked at the village hall?"

We walk across to the chapel from the cottage. I told Flo to let Frank know where we are if he needs me.

"I help out at the café as a favor, really," Kirsty says. "Nan enjoyed the coffee mornings when she was alive, so I feel I'm giving something back. Same with the youth club. I used to enjoy going there as a teenager."

"That's great. And this is your full-time job?"

"Mostly. I run the business with my dad and brother. Sometimes we're flat out on a big project, others we're twiddling our thumbs."

"Right. Well, I'm glad to have caught you twiddling."

I open the door to the chapel and we walk inside. Kirsty looks around. "Always thought this place was a bit weird and creepy." She glances at me. "Sorry. No offense."

"That's okay." I smile. "You're right."

We walk down the aisle of the nave and stare at the hole in the chapel floor. Kirsty draws in a breath.

"Whoah. Well, that's a mess."

"Yeah."

"I don't just mean the hole, although that **is** a mess, obviously." She kneels down. "I mean this stonework. Whoever tried to repair it did a really rubbish job."

She opens her toolbox, takes out a chisel and prods at the crumbling stone. "Total bodge job. The stone is cheap. Modern, not authentic, and the cement is poorly mixed." She frowns. "Also, I don't understand what they thought they were doing. It looks like the timber has rotted beneath the floor here. You shouldn't try to pave over rotten foundations. The floor will always give way again. Lucky someone didn't plunge all the way through."

"I almost did."

We both turn. Flo stands in the doorway. She limps toward us. "Put my foot right through the floor."

"Crap," Kirsty says. "Are you okay?"

"Yeah. Just scraped my leg, fortunately."

"You were lucky. This whole section of flooring could have given way at any time."

Flo sits down on a pew nearby.

"Has Frank gone?" I ask her.

"Yeah. Said the internet should be up and running in about an hour."

"Okay. Good."

Kirsty sits back on her haunches. "Right. First job. We need to get rid of these cheap slabs."

"Can we go down there then? I'd like to take a look at those coffins."

"I need to make sure it's safe. You don't want the whole ceiling caving in on you." She shines a flashlight down into the hole. "I can see some steps, so I would guess that the original entrance is slightly to our left. I still don't understand why this was paved over in the first place."

"Me neither," I say. "How recently d'you think it was done?"

"Within the last few months, from the looks of it."

Months? So, while Fletcher was still here. I suddenly think about the architectural plans in the box. Did he discover the vault? Maybe find a way down? But why pave over it again?

"Right." Kirsty takes a hammer and another chisel from the toolbox, as well as some protective goggles and a dust mask. "You might want to stand well back. Here we go."

The sound of the chisel striking stone echoes around the empty chapel. It reverberates through me, almost as if someone is taking the chisel to my own bones. I glance at Flo. She pulls a face and sticks her fingers in her ears.

Kirsty brings the hammer down on the chisel again then pulls away a chunk of stone paving slab. "Shouldn't take long," she says. "This stuff is like papier mâché."

It doesn't sound like it, unfortunately. I grimace as she whacks the hammer against the chisel on another corner of paving. This time, the whole lot crumbles and falls through what is now a much wider hole. I hear the bits of stone crash into the vault below.

Kirsty pulls her mask down and regards her handiwork. "Okay, I think if I just lift this older flag-stone here, we can expose the top of the stairway."

She bends and starts to lift the stone. I go to help.

"Careful," she says. "We don't want to dam-age it."

We wiggle the stone free of the loose cement.

"One, two, three . . ." Kirsty says. "Heave."

We lift the stone up—my back twinges—and place it down to one side.

"Whoah," Flo mutters, coming closer.

We stare into the hole. The removal of the pav-ing slabs has revealed a steep and uneven staircase that leads down to a vaulted tunnel.

Kirsty crouches right down, examining the tun-nel roof with her flashlight. "The rest of the founda-tions look okay. It's just this section that has rotted."

"Right," I say, pulling my own flashlight out

of my pocket. "I'll go down first. Flo, I think you should stay up here."

"No way." She folds her arms. "We go together."

There's no point arguing. I know that look. I invented that look.

"Fine. All together it is."

I snap the flashlight on and gingerly start down the stone steps. They are barely wide enough to fit half of my foot on and there is nothing to hold on to for balance, just the smooth and slightly damp curved wall. At some point there must have been a trapdoor here, I think.

"Mind your footing," I say to Flo and Kirsty, who are following closely behind me.

The flashlights illuminate about four or five steps ahead. My shoulders brush the brick. As I near the bottom, the vault opens out. I straighten and point the flashlight around. I hear Kirsty whistle. The underground room is small and narrow. The ceiling curves above us. Clustered in an arch on one side of the vault are three coffins.

Flo mutters. "Total Bram Stoker."

I feel a small chill. Which is ridiculous, of course. I'm a vicar. I deal with death and coffins pretty regularly. And yet, down here, beneath the ground, in the darkness . . .

"So, this is a crypt," Kirsty says.

"That's what most vaults are," I say. "Basically, fancy graves for those deemed of importance within the village or town."

Curiosity is now getting the better of claustrophobia. I walk up to the coffins and train my flashlight on them. They're all a bit moldy and warped, but only the uppermost one has completely cracked open, revealing its occupant.

Or perhaps the occupant was trying to claw his way out?

I shove that helpful thought aside and try to focus. Each coffin has a slightly corroded brass plaque on the top, engraved with the name of the deceased:

James Oswald Harper, 1531–1569. Isabel Harper, 1531–1570. And finally, **Andrew John Harper, 1533–1575**.

The Harper family vault. Except, something isn't right. Something is itching at the back of my mind.

"This doesn't make sense," I say.

"Why?" Flo asks. "You just said rich families had their coffins put into vaults?"

"Yes, but the story goes that the Harper family were Sussex Martyrs, burned at the stake for refusing to renounce their religion."

"That's right," Kirsty says. "Their names are on the memorial. We restored it only last year."

"That's what is bugging me. The names on the memorial. The same names. If the Harpers were burned at the stake, what are they doing buried down here?"

"When did the purge of Chapel Croft take place?"

"Oh, we did this in school," Kirsty says. "The Protestant Purge of Chapel Croft took place on the night of 17 September 1556."

I point at the plaques on the coffins. "So why are the dates of death different—over a decade later?"

We all stare at the coffins.

"So, you're thinking, they weren't burned as martyrs?" Flo says.

"It doesn't look like it."

It looks like, somewhere along the line, someone has decided to rewrite history. Easy enough to do. Record keeping was poor in the sixteenth century. And didn't Rushton say that the fire destroyed most of the parish records?

And history is written by the ruthless.

"But **everyone** knows that the Harpers were Sussex Martyrs," Kirsty says. "It's kind of a big deal. If it isn't true . . ." She trails off.

If it isn't true, then the Harper family name would be irrevocably tarnished. It might even mean **they** were the ones who betrayed the burning girls to save their own necks. And that **is** a big deal in a small village. Does Simon Harper know his family reputation is built on a lie? Is that why he "donated" money to the church? To keep it hidden? But, if that's the case, it would mean that someone **within** the church must have been complicit in covering it up.

I stare at the skull of James Oswald Harper. It's

in surprisingly good condition. I frown. And then I train my flashlight inside the coffin. **What the hell?**

"Kirsty, could you just point your flashlight over here?"

"Sure."

"What is it?" Flo asks.

I don't reply. I stick my flashlight in my mouth and, using both hands, tug at the cracked wood of the split coffin.

"Mum," Flo says, sounding worried. "What are you doing?"

I grunt and pull again. There's a **crrrrack** that echoes around the small chamber and the entire wooden coffin lid peels off. I stagger backward, clutching the broken lid. The coffin tips to one side and a skeletal body tumbles out.

Flo yelps. Even Kirsty mutters, "Shit!"

I stare at the remains on the ground. Then I look back at the coffin, where a far more decayed, brown skeleton rests inside. That's what I saw. A second skull. A second body inside the coffin.

"Wh—why are there two?" Kirsty gasps.

Good question. I crouch down beside the first skeleton. Only slightly yellowed. Dressed in a black priest's cassock and white dog collar. Strands of blond hair still cling to the scalp. And then I spot something else.

On one finger is a chunky silver signet ring.

I crawl forward and gently lift the skeletal

fingers, peering at the ring more closely. Engraved on the front is a saint wielding a cross and a sword. Words in Latin run around the circumference:

Sancte Michael Archangele, defende nos in proelio.

St. Michael, protect us in battle.

A wave of dizziness washes over me. I sit back on my haunches.

"Mum?" Flo's voice sounds distant. "Are you okay? What have you found?"

I nod, but I'm not okay.

I think we've just found the missing curate. Benjamin Grady.

A rattling at her window. Skeletal fingernails scratching the glass.

Merry sat up in bed, blinking blearily. Her room swelled with shadows. Moonlight wavered at the window.

Rattle, click. Rattle, click.

Not fingers. Pebbles. Stones.

She padded across the room and pulled the curtain aside, peering out. Her eyes widened as she spotted the figure standing beneath the window. Joy. She yanked it open.

"What are you doing here?"

"I needed to see you."

"In the middle of the night?"

"It was the only way. Please."

She debated with herself, and then nodded.

"Wait there."

She grabbed her dressing gown and tiptoed carefully out of her room. She could hear snoring next door. Mum had finished two bottles of wine after tea, so she should be out for the count. Still, Merry found herself holding her breath as she padded down the stairs and out of the back door. The night breeze felt cool through her thin pajamas.

"What's going on?"

Joy started to sob, noisily. "I'm so sorry. I let you down."

Merry glanced nervously back at the house. "Don't cry. Come on."

They walked to the end of the garden and sat down on the broken-down wall, near the well.

"I was so stupid," Joy sobbed. "I thought he was good, but he's the devil."

"Who? What are you talking about?"

But Joy just shook her head. "You know, what we talked about before? Running away?"

Merry did. But they hadn't talked about it much recently. They had barely seen each other.

"I thought you'd changed your mind."

"No. Do you still want to go?"

She thought about her mum. She was getting worse. The other night, she had become convinced that Merry was possessed and needed the devil driven out of her. When Merry had seen the full bath of ice-cold water, she had run and hidden in the woods.

"Yes," she said firmly.

"When?"

She considered. "Tomorrow night. Pack a bag. Meet me here."

"What about money?"

"I know where Mum has some hidden."

"Where will we go?"

Merry smiled. "Somewhere they'll never find us."

FORTY

It seems to take him a long time to cycle from the farmhouse to the outskirts of Chapel Croft, even though a weathered white sign informs him that it is only five miles.

His head throbs from the sherry (or rather, from stopping drinking the sherry) and his ankle feels like it's on fire. He stops several times, to catch his breath and rub uselessly at the ankle. The inflammation is spreading. Purply-red skin bulges over his sock and stretches up his calf. But he has to keep going.

At one point, he rests near a stile. He can see a trough for sheep on the other side. He clambers over, sticks his face in and drinks. The water is brown and sour, but it's relatively cold and it quenches some of his thirst.

Finally, he rounds a long bend and he sees it. A white chapel in the distance. That has to be it. His excitement rises. So near. And then he spots the row of police cars parked outside; officers in uniform, a roadside cordon.

What's going on? Why are they there? Has something happened to her?

He puts his head down and cycles on past. When he's at a safe distance, he stops, climbs off the bike, props it on its kickstand and crouches beside it, pretending to fiddle with the chain while stealing sly glances at the chapel.

And then he sees her. For the first time in fourteen years, walking across to the cottage with an old woman, a tall man and a teenage girl. **Her daughter.** Emotions flood through him. Shock. The daughter looks so much like she did as a girl. Relief. She is here, and she's okay. Confusion. **What is all the police activity about?**

It can't be connected to what he did at the farmhouse. It's too soon for them to have found the bodies. But he has a bad feeling. He messed up. He should have just stayed put in the barn. Out of people's way. Then no one would have got hurt. The only thing he has in his favor right now is that no one knows who he is or what he looks like. But that won't last. And he's hardly inconspicuous with his torn and dirty clothing and red, angry ankle. He needs somewhere else to lie low. Get himself together. Work out a plan.

What for? If she loves you, how you look won't matter. What are you scared of?

Nothing. He isn't scared of anything. He just wants it to be right. It has to be right. Or . . .

. . . she might reject you again. Leave you again?

No. He did a bad thing. He made a mistake. But now she's had time. To forgive him. Just like he has forgiven her.

He climbs back on the bike and cycles off again. This time, he doesn't stop until he is on the other side of the village. The road is deserted. Just fields and cows either side. And, to his left, a gate. Rusted, padlocked. A rutted, overgrown track leads away from the road and disappears into more tangled bushes. Just visible over their straggly branches, the tip of a weathered roof in the distance.

He wheels the bike up to the gate. After a moment's thought, he chucks it over. Then, he follows.

Every city, village and suburb has abandoned buildings. He learned that from his time on the streets. Places that, for some reason, no one has claimed or, perhaps more accurately, no one wants to claim.

Even in the richest neighborhoods there will be one dwelling that remains empty, never sold. Perhaps because of legalities or red tape, or perhaps because some buildings don't want to be lived in. Their walls have absorbed too much pain and misery. They brim with it. It seeps out of every cracked brick and warped floorboard. Inhabitable, inhospitable. Do not enter. You're not welcome. Stay away.

Like this place.

He stares up at the derelict house. The darkened windows glare back at him, the sagging roof like a glowering brow. The door gapes open in a silent scream.

He walks through the long grass toward it. He peers through the doorway and then steps inside. It's gloomy in the cottage. Even though the sun is high, the light doesn't stretch all the way into the rooms. The shadows are too deep. The darkness held too tightly within.

It doesn't bother him. Nor does the smell, the crushed cans and cigarettes butts on the floor, or the strange graffiti on the walls upstairs.

He smiles.

He's home.

FORTY-ONE

"Hard to be a hundred percent positive, but it certainly **looks** like the same ring."

The plainclothes detective, DI Derek, lays the photograph back down on the kitchen table and slips off his glasses. He's a tall, kind-faced man in his late fifties. He looks like he should be tending vegetables rather than investigating murders.

"So, it's him? Grady?" Joan peers at him over her coffee, her eyes bright.

I called her right after I called the police. She insisted on driving straight over. **"This is the most excitement I've had since someone drove a horse and cart into my front room."**

Derek smiles at Joan. "Grady might have given the ring away, or had it stolen—"

She gives a derisive snort. I suppress a smile. Sometimes, I long to be old enough to be unapologetically rude.

He concedes, "It's highly probable that the remains are those of Benjamin Grady. But, until the forensic team have had a chance to properly analyze the bones and clothing, we can't say for sure."

I glance out of the window. A uniformed police officer guards the entrance to the chapel, and another stands on the pavement, near the gate to the graveyard. A police cordon has been erected at the roadside. Earlier, I watched the forensic team march into the chapel, along with a photographer carrying portable lighting. I imagine them placing markers, snapping photos, gathering evidence. I doubt the chapel has seen this much activity since the days of the martyrs. Flo stands outside in the graveyard, watching everything that's going on and taking surreptitious pictures on her phone.

"Grady disappeared thirty years ago," Joan continues. "May 1990. Just after two local girls, Merry and Joy, also disappeared. Are you aware of that?"

"I know the case."

"Are you looking for other remains in the chapel?"

"The other skeletons in the vault appear to be historical."

"Will the case be reopened?" she presses.

"Unless we have new evidence—"

"You've got a dead priest in a church vault. How much more evidence do you need?"

This time, it's my turn to snort: coffee, out of my nose.

Derek's smile is more strained. "Right now, it's unhelpful to speculate. However, we will need the names of everyone who has worked here or had access to the chapel over the last thirty years."

"The church records are in a filing cabinet in the office," I say. "But I'm not sure they go back that far."

"Reverend Marsh was the vicar here from the eighties until five years ago," Joan says. "He's very ill with Huntington's, but he may have kept some paperwork."

"Aaron, his son, is the warden," I add. "He could help." I pause. "And Reverend Rushton has been a vicar at the neighboring church in Warblers Green for almost thirty years."

Derek writes all of this down. "Thank you. We'll speak to them both." He closes his notebook and turns to me. "This must have been a shock."

"You could say that."

"Quite a first week for you!"

"It's certainly been . . . eventful."

"Well, anything else you think of, this is my card."

He hands it to me, and I slip it in my pocket. "Thank you."

I walk him out of the cottage and watch as he strides back over to the chapel. I glance around the graveyard. And then I curse. The officer at the roadside seems to have been waylaid by a couple of curious villagers. Meanwhile, a battered MG has pulled up behind the police cars and a familiar figure is standing on the pavement snapping photos on his phone.

I march down the path toward Mike Sudduth. He smiles and waves.

"What are you doing here?" I ask brusquely.

The smile fades. "Err, my job. A body hidden in a church vault? Big news for the local paper."

"Who told you about the body?" I ask. "No, wait, let me guess—Kirsty?"

He has the good grace to look sheepish. "She may have mentioned it. Sorry—she didn't realize it was a secret."

"Right."

He regards me curiously. "What's wrong?"

"You mean—aside from all this?" I gesture toward the police cordon.

"Sorry. Stupid question."

I sigh. I'm being unfair. He **is** just doing his job. But police, the press. It's bringing back bad memories.

"Look—it's just a bit much to take in at the moment."

"I imagine. Do they have any idea who the body is yet?"

"No."

"So, it isn't Benjamin Grady, the curate who disappeared thirty years ago?"

I stare at him. "No comment."

"Was he murdered?"

"Is this an interview?"

"No. Well—"

I fold my arms. "I really don't know anything. So perhaps you should just take your pictures and go. Okay?"

His face closes. "Okay."

I turn and stomp back up the pathway and into the cottage. I handled that badly. I don't care right now. Joan looks up as I enter the kitchen: "Is everything all right?"

"Yes, fine." I manage a smile. "Would you like another coffee?"

She shakes her head. "No, I should be going. You've got enough to be dealing with here."

"You don't have to—"

"If I've learned one thing in eighty-five years, it's not to outstay my welcome."

She rises slowly, then glances out of the window. "I was wrong about Grady," she mutters.

"How?"

"All these years, I thought he had something do with the girls' disappearance. But if he's dead, then that rather rules him out, doesn't it?"

"I suppose so."

She turns, her face troubled. "But **someone** knew Grady was down there. Quite possibly someone within the church." She rests one bony hand on mine. "Be careful, Jack."

. . .

"What d'you think happened to him?"

Flo stares at me over her bowl of pasta. It's just after 7 p.m. The police and forensic teams finished their work at the chapel over an hour ago. Crime scene tape is still strung across the door and I've been told to keep it locked.

I spear a piece of broccoli with my fork. "Who?"

A slow eye roll. "The body. In the vault. Grady?"

I take a moment to answer. "Well, I think that's for the police to work out."

"Aren't you curious?"

"Of course."

"Was he murdered?"

"Well, he didn't climb in there by himself."

"I mean, who murders a **vicar**—" She suddenly catches herself and looks at me with shocked eyes. "Sorry, Mum. I didn't mean—"

I manage a faint smile. "It's okay. And, in answer to your question, people kill for all kinds of reasons. Some we can comprehend. Some we can't."

A long pause. Flo pushes pasta around her bowl. "If someone does something bad, does it mean they're always bad?"

"Well, that's the whole point Jesus makes about forgiveness."

"I'm not talking about Jesus or God. I'm asking what **you** think."

I put my fork down. "I think that **doing**

something bad is different from **being** bad. I think we all have the capability to do bad things, to do evil. It depends on the circumstances, how far we are pushed. But if you feel guilt, if you seek forgiveness and redemption, then that shows you're not a bad person. We should all be given the opportunity to change. To make amends for our mistakes."

"Even the man who killed Dad?"

We've only talked about what happened to Jonathon once before, when she was seven. A friend's mother had recently died from cancer. Flo wanted to know if her dad had been ill and died too. Tempting as it had been to lie and say yes, I had answered her questions as best I could, and that seemed to be the end of it. Flo was so young when Jonathon died she doesn't really remember him and I suppose that has distanced her from his death. But I admit, I sometimes wondered—and yes, dreaded—the day when she might start asking more questions.

"Yes," I say carefully. "Even him."

"Is that why you visited him in jail. To forgive him?"

I hesitate. "You have to want forgiveness. You have to want to change. The man who killed your dad, he wasn't able to do that."

"You said he was a drug addict."

"Yes."

"So, perhaps, once he kicked the drugs, he could have changed."

"Perhaps. Why are you asking about this now? What's on your mind?"

"Nothing really . . ."

"You can talk to me, you know."

"I know."

"Is this about Wrigley?"

The shutters go up. "Why would you say that?"

"I just wondered—"

"Here we go again. You don't like him, do you?"

"I haven't made my mind up yet."

"Is it because of his dystonia?"

"No."

"You think he's not normal, not good enough."

"**No**. And don't put words into my mouth."

"He rescued me last night."

Because he was creeping around the chapel, up to no good, I want to say, but don't. I think about the knife again.

"Flo, I wasn't sure whether to mention this, but last night, something went missing from my room."

"What?"

"The knife from the exorcism kit. You and Wrigley were the only ones alone in the house."

Her eyes widen. "And you think **Wrigley** took it?"

"Well, I'm presuming **you** didn't take it?"

"No. But it's not like he's the only one who could have stolen it. You were out all night. I was stuck in the chapel. The cottage wasn't locked. Anyone could have walked in."

She has a point. "But why would someone break in and steal a knife?"

"Why would Wrigley steal it?"

"I don't know."

She stares at me. Her face is full of hurt and confusion and my heart aches. Oh, it's all so hard when you're fifteen. You want to believe the world is black and white. But, as an adult, you realize that most people exist in the grey area in between. All just stuck in the middle and bumbling through.

"Flo—"

"He didn't take it, okay? He thinks carrying knives is stupid. **Okay?**"

No. Not okay. But I can't prove it. Not right now.

"Okay."

She shoves her chair back from the table. "I'm going to my room."

"You haven't finished."

"Not hungry."

I watch helplessly as she stomps from the kitchen. The staircase creaks and I hear a door slam upstairs. Great. I run my hands through my hair. Flo and I don't argue much, not usually. But since we came here, it feels like everything is fraying, my life unraveling around me. I pick up the bowls, scrape off the uneaten pasta into the bin and stick them in the sink.

I need a cigarette. I fetch my tin, roll one quickly at the kitchen table and open the back door. I step outside and then jerk back.

There's something on the doorstep. Two more twig dolls. Bigger than the others and crafted into a sitting position, twig legs outstretched, arms entwined. Strands of blonde hair have been woven into the head of one doll; dark hair into the other. And they're moving. Shifting slightly from side to side, as though restless.

What the hell?

Heart thudding, I bend down to pick them up. As I do, something fat and white wriggles out of one doll and plops to the floor.

"Shit!"

I drop the dolls again with a shriek of disgust, wiping my hands on my jeans.

They're full of maggots.

FORTY-TWO

The bedroom is hot and stuffy. I'm lying on top of the sheets, naked. Sweat still trickles down my neck and between my breasts. I try to turn, to find a cooler patch to lie on. But I can't. My wrists and ankles are bound to the bedposts. I'm captive. A prisoner.

And someone is coming.

I can hear their footsteps, climbing slowly up the stairs. Growing closer and closer. Panic grips me. I twist against the restraints, but it's no good. I watch as the door handle turns. The door opens. A figure in dark clothes walks in, a flash of white at their neck and a glint of something sharp and silver in one hand. A knife.

I hear them whisper: **"Sancte Michael Archangele, defende nos in proelio."**

St. Michael, protect us in battle.

I look up, pleading. **Please, no. Please let me go**. They bend over me. My eyes find their face in the darkness and horror engulfs me as I see that they have no face. Just a mass of squirming, wriggling maggots . . .

"**Aahhh!**"

I wake with a start, brushing at my bedclothes, sweaty and disoriented. I roll over. The clock tells me it's 5:33 a.m. I pull on my joggers and pad downstairs. Instead of getting out my rolling tin, I grab the heavy iron key, open the door and walk across the short path to the chapel. The sun is a faint silver disc in the hazy sky. The warm air nuzzles my bare arms. I can smell jasmine, the faint tang of compost, dry grass. It yanks me back to another morning, a long time ago. Standing at the side of a road, scared, alone, wondering where to go.

The police told me not to let anyone into the chapel, but they didn't say whether that included me. I turn the key in the lock and shove the heavy door open. Inside, it's gratifyingly cool. I walk down the nave and sit on a pew near the end. The entrance to the vault gapes darkly. Crime scene tape is still strung around the edge. I stare at it. The final resting place of Benjamin Grady. How did he end up here? And who knew?

Whoever conceals his transgressions will not prosper, but he who confesses and forsakes them will obtain mercy.

I turn back toward the altar, bow my head and pray.

After a while, I feel calmer, restored. Faith is not an infinite resource. It can run dry. Even priests need to recharge it sometimes. Eventually, I stand, make the sign of the cross, and leave the chapel.

I know what I have to do.

The description "chocolate box" could have been invented for the Rushtons' cottage. Warm red brick glows in the mid-morning sun. The roof is neatly thatched. Small leaded windows sparkle with light, and climbers trail flowers over the walls. It nestles up to Warblers Green village church on one side and, on the other, a small stream gurgles past the local pub—the Black Duck.

I can see why Rushton loves this place. And why he might do anything to protect his comfortable life here.

When he opens the door, his normally jolly face is somber, even his curls deflated. He doesn't look surprised to see me.

"Come through. Clara's just gone out for a walk."

He leads me into a large, sun-dappled kitchen at the back of the house. French doors open out on to a sprawling garden, blooming with bright flowers. A cool breeze wafts through. providing welcome relief from the heat of the day.

"Coffee?"

"No, thanks."

He sits down at the table opposite me and offers a rueful smile. "Before you ask, I've already spoken to the police . . . and I owe you an apology."

"You knew about the vault?"

"Yes. But as I told the police, I had absolutely no idea about the body. That was"—he shakes his head—"a terrible, terrible shock."

"How long have you known?"

He sighs heavily. "Reverend Marsh told me when I started my tenure. He explained that they had uncovered the vault the previous year, when they were relaying some damaged flagstones. But they wouldn't be making it public, because it would hurt the reputation of the Harper family."

"Because their ancestors weren't martyrs?"

He nods. "It might seem odd to you, but it means a lot in Chapel Croft. Even now, those with lineage to the martyrs are respected. Those without are seen as poor relations."

"Surely the truth is more important than one family's ego?"

"I may have said much the same. Reverend Marsh asked me who I thought had paid for the repairs to the chapel's roof. Who sponsored the church fete? Who paid for the supplies and equipment for the children's club?"

"The Harpers."

He nods. "Every year they make a sizeable donation to the church. To preserve its history."

"So, you agreed to cover it up?"

Another deep sigh. "I agreed to not **uncover** it."

But a lie by omission is still a lie. And then I wonder, who am I to judge?

"Who else knows?" I ask.

"Until recently, only me, Aaron and Simon Harper." He pauses. "But then Reverend Fletcher started looking into the history of the chapel."

"He found a copy of the architectural plans?"

"Yes. He was very excited about the possibility of a hidden vault. Aaron came into the chapel one morning to find he had taken up half the floor, uncovered the old entrance."

"What did you do?"

"Well, I tried to persuade him not to tell anyone. But he felt the vault and coffins were an important historical discovery. So, I asked Simon Harper to speak to him. Whatever he said, it seemed to make a difference. Fletcher agreed to keep quiet and, not long afterward, he handed in his resignation."

"Just like that?"

"Yes. I arranged for a tiler I know to come and cover up the entrance. I thought that was the end of it."

"And then Fletcher killed himself?"

"Sadly, yes."

"Do you still think it was suicide?"

"Yes. I do." His tone is firm, verging on annoyed. "You can't seriously think that someone killed him because of the vault?"

"If they knew what was hidden inside, maybe. Maybe they were worried he was getting too close."

Rushton shakes his head. "I know this village. The people. No one here is capable of murder."

"The body in the vault would suggest otherwise." Before he can retort, I ask: "Do you think Marsh knew the body was down there?"

"The police asked the same thing, and I will tell you what I told them. Marsh was an honorable man. Deeply religious. Why would he cover up a murder?"

Why indeed? I think about the timeline. Marsh must have discovered the vault around the same time Merry and Joy disappeared, and Grady (supposedly) left the village. At some point before it was paved over, Grady's body was hidden inside. A narrow window. And if no one else knew about the vault outside of the church, a small number of suspects.

"Joan told me about the disappearance of Merry and Joy," I say. "Benjamin Grady allegedly left the village around the same time. Except now we know he didn't. Could the two things be connected?"

"I don't see how. The girls ran away."

"But did they?"

"Jack, please, stop." His voice rises. His face is growing red. "This is exactly what happened with

Matthew. Joan spinning her yarns. He became obsessed. And we both know how that ended up."

I stare at him, wondering if that is an oblique threat.

He takes a breath, tries to offer a smile, but the jolly-reverend act isn't cutting it any more. "I understand your interest. Naturally, you have questions. But we must leave the investigating to the police. At times like this, we must all stick together. For the good of the church and the village."

"And the good of the Harpers?"

"Whether you like it or not, in a village like Chapel Croft we need families like the Harpers. Their business sustains a lot of jobs. They give to charities—"

"I understand that. But in trying to appease one family, you covered up a crime."

Possibly more than one.

Rushton levels a hard stare at me. "And have you never sought to bury some small truths, Jack, to make things easier on yourself or someone else?"

"This isn't about me." I stand. "I should get going."

He moves to rise.

"It's okay," I say. "I can see myself out."

I walk out of the cottage, back into the hot, bright sunshine. I parked my car under a shady tree just down the lane from the Rushtons'. Even so, when I climb into the driver's seat it's like climbing into a microwave oven. I roll the windows down, feeling hot, angry and, worse, let down. I liked Rushton. I wanted to trust him. I was wrong.

I'm just about to pull off when I see Clara walking down the road. She's dressed in shorts and hiking boots. A large canvas tote bag is hooked over one shoulder. She stops just before the gate to the cottage. Her chest is hitching. Her eyes are red. She's crying. Instinct tells me to go and comfort her. Something else tells me not to. She has stopped outside the cottage deliberately. She doesn't want her husband to see her.

Of course, there could be lots of reasons why she is so upset. But bearing in mind the recent discovery at the chapel, I can think of only one. **Grady**. And you don't shed tears like that over someone who was just a friend.

I watch as she wipes at her eyes, adjusts her snowy hair and pushes the gate open. As she does, the canvas bag slips off her shoulder, gaping open.

Inside are bundles of twigs.

FORTY-THREE

Flo tacks cardboard up at the bathroom window. Her mum had gone out, so she decided she night as well develop the second canister of film while she has the cottage to herself.

She thought it might take her mind off things, but it hasn't really helped. Perhaps it isn't surprising. She's been terrorized by burning apparitions, almost killed herself falling through the chapel floor and then discovered a bunch of ancient skeletons and a murdered vicar in the vault. Just your average week in Salem, right?

She climbs down carefully from the bath—her left leg is still a bit stiff—and arranges her developing trays on the loo seat and the floor. Part of her wishes they could just move the hell away from this place, back to Nottingham, and some sanity. Another part is kind of relishing the weirdness. Stumbling over skeletons in a vault is certainly a step up from finding used needles on the church doorstep. And maybe, just maybe, there's another reason she'd like to stay. A dark-haired, green-eyed reason. **Wrigley**.

She likes him. And, although she's certainly not some damsel in distress, he **did** rescue her last night. But can she really trust a boy who has confessed to trying to burn down his last school? That's pretty hardcore. And what about the knife? She told Mum he definitely didn't take it, but she can't quite crush that tiny kernel of doubt. She finds herself worrying at it, like a hangnail. Maybe that's why she got so mad at her mum. She didn't want to admit that she could, possibly, be right.

They had managed to maintain an uneasy truce over breakfast this morning. To be fair, her mum had looked worn out and Flo had felt a bit bad. Flo doesn't like things being weird between them, but Mum is **so** uptight about Wrigley. Flo doesn't understand why she can't give him a chance. Perhaps she'd be the same with any boy Flo liked. But she senses there's something more. Something about being **here**.

Flo wishes she had someone she could talk to about it all. She'd thought about messaging Kayleigh, but then realized she didn't know what to say. Everything going on here, it's all so different from Nottingham. It's like they're in separate worlds.

When she finally got around to messaging her

friends on Snapchat in the café the other day, she found herself feeling oddly detached from all the stuff they were rattling on about. It had seemed inconsequential, uninteresting even. And she had got the feeling that they felt the same about the stuff she had told them about Chapel Croft. Leon hadn't even pretended to be interested. He was too busy filling her in on gossip: a girl in Year 11 had got herself up the duff, their chemistry teacher had been spotted in a park smoking dope and two girls she barely knew were in a same-sex relationship. In the end, she wished she hadn't bothered. Instead of feeling closer, it had made her feel more distant than ever.

She sighs and sets her equipment out. And then she pauses. She thought she heard something. A banging. There it is again. Someone is knocking on the front door.

Christ. What now?

She steps over the tray, opens the door and walks downstairs. She tiptoes into the living room and peers between the curtains. A familiar skinny black-clad figure hovers outside, hopping from foot to foot. She debates with herself for a moment. Then she walks back into the hall and pulls open the door.

"I'm starting to think if I look in a mirror and say your name three times you'll appear."

Wrigley grins. "Funny."

"What are you doing here?"

"Just wanted to see how you are. And I thought you might want to borrow this." He holds out an old iPhone. "It's a spare. You just need to put your SIM card in."

"Oh, thanks."

"I wiped it last night."

"In case of anything incriminating?"

"Actually, it's my mum's old one, so . . ."

"She doesn't mind me borrowing it?"

"I might not have told her. But she won't notice. It was only in a drawer." He twitches, pushing his black hair out of his eyes. "So, are you okay?"

"I'm fine. Thanks."

"Right. Good."

She hesitates. Her mum wouldn't be happy about her inviting Wrigley in when she's out, but he's brought her a phone, and it would be rude to leave him outside. And, well, her mum's out.

"D'you want to come in for a bit?"

"Well, I can't stay too long, but yeah, for a bit."

She stands aside and he walks into the small hall. They face each other awkwardly.

"I'm just developing some photos," she says.

"Oh, right."

"D'you want to come and see?"

"Yeah, that would be cool."

He follows her up the stairs. At the top, she pauses. "Just try not to touch anything, okay?"

"Okay."

She opens the door a crack and they slip inside.

She shuts it again quickly and flicks on the safety light.

"So, this is your darkroom?" Wrigley asks.

"It's only temporary," she says. "Long term, I need to find a better solution."

"No, I mean, it's great." He stares around.

She picks up the canister containing the roll of film and takes it out.

"Don't you have to do that in, like, total dark?"

"No, it's black-and-white film so it's not sensitive to red light. If it was color, I'd need to take the film out in a block bag."

"I didn't know people still did this stuff."

He comes over and stands closer as she unspools the film.

"Not so many people do now. Kind of a dying art. Everyone wants everything instantly. Why spend time doing all this when you can just take a photo on a phone and stick a filter on it?"

"So, why do you?"

She snips the negatives. "I like not having the answers right away. There's something in waiting, not knowing how things are going to turn out. Actually watching the images develop. It's more satisfying than taking endless pictures on a phone and then leaving them sitting on a computer and never looking at them again."

She turns. Wrigley is right behind her. Almost too close.

"You're right," he says. "Everything is kind of

disposable these days. There's no appreciation of things . . . no anticipation."

She looks at him. The red light throws his face into a strange kind of anime, the jet black of his hair, the green of his eyes more intense than ever. **Crap,** she thinks. **Are we going to** . . . and suddenly, they are. His lips are on hers and it feels good and weird and exciting all at once. He presses her back against the wall. Their hands entwine and he pushes them up above her head. She feels something catch around her wrist. Too late, she realizes it's the light cord. She hears a click.

"Shit!"

Harsh fluorescent light floods the bathroom. No, no, no. She turns and grabs for the cord, tugging it back off again. Only a couple of seconds, but . . .

"The negatives."

She pushes Wrigley away and darts over to the roll of film.

"I'm sorry—" he stutters.

She can already see that about half of the negatives are completely leached out. Shit.

"Will they be okay?"

"No. They're ruined."

"I'm really sorry. I shouldn't have—"

"It isn't your fault. It doesn't matter."

But it did matter. The negatives were screwed and the moment—whatever it was—has gone.

"I should go."

"Okay."

He turns for the door.

"Wait," Flo says. "Look, it's not that I don't want . . . that I don't like you."

"Right." He shuffles and spasms. "Then let me make it up to you."

"How?"

"Meet me, tonight."

"Where?"

"The house by the woods."

"I don't know—"

"Why?"

"What do I tell my mum?"

"Tell her we're going to the youth club."

She debates with herself. Wrigley's phone buzzes. He takes it out of his pocket and glances at it.

"It's **my** mum. I have to go."

"Okay."

"So, I'll see you tonight?"

"I guess."

"Seven p.m."

"Okay."

"You trust me, right?"

"Ye-es. But if we get attacked by zombies—"

He grins. "I'll bring a shovel."

She's wrong about the photos. Only half are ruined. She can save the rest. She sets about slipping them under the enlarger, then dipping them into the developing fluids. In fact, the light might even give a cool effect to some of the photos. Sometimes a flaw can be what makes something beautiful.

"Stay the hell away from Wrigley."

But she can't. Sometimes, you don't have any choice.

Finally finished, she trots downstairs into the kitchen. She's thirsty. She grabs a glass and goes to the sink. She turns on the cold tap and then yelps, jumping backward, heart pounding.

There's a man standing outside the kitchen window, staring in.

Dishevelled, dirty-looking, baggy dark circles under his eyes. As soon as he sees her, he backs off, turns and starts to lope away.

Without even thinking, Flo puts down the glass, sprints to the door, unlocks it and races outside. She looks around, squinting in the sunshine. She spots him, disappearing around the back of the cottage, into the graveyard.

"Hey!"

She follows, jogging around the corner. He's halfway up the slope, limping between the headstones. He looks like he has an injured ankle and, she can't be sure, but he also looks like he's wearing a vicar's tunic.

She starts up the hill after him, and she's gaining when she catches her foot on something poking up from the ground. She trips, her arms windmill, but she has too much forward momentum and she crashes to the ground. Her breath **whoomps** out of her. Pain shoots up her bad leg.

"Owww. Shit."

She lies there for a moment, shaken, trying to catch her breath. Eventually, she pushes herself up, but the man has disappeared over the small stone wall and into the fields. She won't catch him now. Even if she did, what exactly was she planning to do? She hasn't even got her phone to call the police. Not her best-made plan. But something about him had angered her, staring in like that.

She sits up on the dry grass and turns to see what tripped her. It's the same bloody toppled headstone she almost fell over the other day. The one she was about to photograph when she was distracted by the headless, armless girl.

She glares at the headstone, as if it has some-how booby-trapped her on purpose, and then spots something else, half hidden in the long grass. She reaches forward and picks it up. It's a photo in a tarnished frame. A teenage girl and a young boy. Familiar, but she can't quite place it. And then she remembers. It's the same picture she stood on in the old, derelict house. She frowns. Did the home-less guy drop it? Did he steal it from the house? Perhaps that was what he was doing here—casing the cottage?

She stares at the picture. There's something else. Something that didn't really register before. It's kind of weird but . . . she feels a shiver ripple over her skin.

The girl in the picture looks a lot like her.

FORTY-FOUR

Emma Harper doesn't look happy to see me. I get the feeling she knows she said too much the other night in the pub, but she can't remember what.

Of course, I shouldn't really be here. It's probably not what Rushton meant when he talked about all sticking together. But something struck me as I drove away from the Rushtons' cottage. Fletcher spent a lot of time and effort looking into the history of the chapel and the girls who disappeared. And yet, one word from Simon Harper and he quietly agreed to say nothing and resign. I'm wondering exactly what Simon Harper said to him.

"I'm sorry to bother you," I say.

She holds the door, half open, primed to shut it in my face. "It's not a good time, I'm afraid. I'm rather busy—"

"Actually, it was Simon I wanted to talk to."

"Simon? Oh, well, he's out on the farm."

"Is it okay if I go and find him?"

"Is it anything I can help you with?"

"It's to do with the chapel. The vault?"

She looks at me blankly. Obviously, Simon never mentioned the hidden vault to his wife.

"Oh, well, if it's church stuff, probably best to talk to Simon. Let me call him, find out where he is or if he's on his way back." She looks around. "I think my phone is upstairs. Come on in."

She trots up the staircase. I walk into the massive hallway. Through the doors to the left I can see Poppy playing with dolls on the floor of the conservatory. She doesn't look up as I enter. Once again, I think how solemn she seems and, also, how oddly childish. At ten, dolls are normally replaced by iPads.

I walk over and crouch down beside her.

"Hiya."

She doesn't look up.

"What are you playing?"

A small shrug.

"Are these your favorite dolls?"

A nod.

"What are they called?"

"Poppy and Tara."

Tara. The little girl who died.

"Are they friends?"

"Best friends."

"That's nice. Do they play together a lot?"

"All the time."

"Do you have any other friends?"

"No. No one wants to play with me."

"Why?"

"In case they die, like Tara did."

I stare at her, feeling a chill.

"Reverend Brooks?"

I jump, and then straighten as Emma emerges in the hall. "Simon's just in the sheep barn. You can either pop down or wait here."

"I'll pop down. The barn's just around the corner?"

"Yes."

"Thanks."

I walk toward the door. And pause. An airgun is propped by the umbrella stand.

"Is that an airgun?"

"Oh yes. It's Tom's."

"Tom?"

"Rosie's cousin. They're upstairs now, playing Xbox."

"Likes to shoot things, does he?"

"Shooting is a way of life in the country."

I smile thinly. "Apparently so."

I walk down the muddy track, away from the farmhouse, quietly fuming. The airgun could be a coincidence. But I don't think so. Not in this small village. Tom is the one who shot Flo. But was it really an accident? I wouldn't put anything past this family. I think about Poppy again. She's clearly still traumatized by the death of her best friend. But there's something else, something **wrong** in this house. It's a gut reaction. But, when it comes to dysfunctional families, I have some experience.

The barn draws into view. A corrugated, weathered structure. The scent of manure and rotting vegetables hangs in the air. I walk inside. Rows of sheep pens line either side of the barn. Simon Harper, clad in a Barbour jacket and wellies, is forking fresh straw into them.

"Hello?" I call out.

He chucks the straw into a pen, props the fork on the metal railing and brushes his hands off on his jacket.

"Reverend Brooks? To what do I owe the pleasure?"

"I wanted to talk to you about the chapel."

"What about it?"

"We've found the hidden burial vault."

"How remarkable." He turns and picks up the fork. "Seal it back up."

"I'm sorry?"

"You heard me. Seal it back up again. I'll pay for the new floor, whatever else the chapel needs."

"I can't—"

"Yes, you can. I own the vault. They're my ancestors."

"And once they are interred, they become the property of the church."

He turns back toward me. "I own most of that

bloody chapel. Seal the vault up and I'll write the diocese another check."

"I'm afraid I'm not going to be able do that."

He stabs the fork into the mound of straw. "What **is** your problem?"

"My problem is that we found a body hidden in the vault. It appears to be that of Benjamin Grady, a young curate who went missing thirty years ago."

He spins around. "**What?**"

"You didn't know?"

"Of course I didn't bloody know. **Jesus!**" He runs a hand through his hair. "So, what, he was murdered?"

"It looks that way."

"Great. So, I suppose this will be all over the news now."

"Probably," I say, realizing that I hadn't thought of that myself.

"Is there any way you can keep the Harper name out of it?"

I stare at him. "A body has been discovered, and that's all you care about? Good to know where your priorities lie."

"My **priorities** are my family and my business. This could ruin both."

"Why is it **so** important to you that your ancestors are martyrs? It was hundreds of years ago."

A bitter smile. "As **martyrs,** they're part of history. As cowards who renounced their faith to save their skins, they're nothing. The Harper **name** means nothing. Do you know how hard it is to run a business in the country, Reverend?"

"No."

"Bloody hard. We succeed because of our reputation. We've been here generations. People trust us."

"And I'm sure they still will."

"You don't know what villages like Chapel Croft are like. You couldn't possibly understand."

"You don't know me."

"I know your sort."

"My sort?"

"A busybody. Sticking your nose in where it doesn't belong." He takes a step toward me. "I know all about what happened at your last church, with that little black girl."

I note the redundant adjective. "You got sent a clipping?"

"Yeah." He sneers. "Interfering didn't work out so well for you there, did it?"

I fight to keep my temper in check. "Is this what you did to Reverend Fletcher? Bullied him? Threatened him? Is that why he agreed to keep quiet about the vault?"

He shakes his head. "I liked Matthew. He was a decent bloke. But he was stubborn. So I simply pointed out to him that he had some secrets of his own he might want to protect."

"Such as?"

"A relationship he didn't want people knowing about."

I remember what Joan had said, about the author. "With Saffron Winter?"

He laughs, unpleasantly. "That might have been what he wanted people to think."

"I don't follow?"

"Saffron Winter wasn't really Fletcher's type, if you get what I mean."

I'm pretty sure the sheep **get what he means**. But now, despite myself, I'm curious.

"So, who was?"

FORTY-FIVE

The old Victorian house is situated a mile or so down the road from the chapel. It might have been a handsome home once. Now, the garden is overgrown and neglected, the window frames are rotten, and it looks like one gust of strong wind might cause the tilting chimney to come tumbling down.

We sit in the dining room at the back of the house. It's dark and cluttered. Boxes of medical supplies cover most of the table. Books, magazines and tinned goods take up the space on a cabinet and sideboard. There is also a smell. Institutional. The sort you always get in school dining rooms or hospitals. Stale cooking, urine, feces.

I'm trying not to pity Aaron. But it's hard.

"If you wish me to hand in my resignation," he says stiffly, "I'll understand."

"I don't want you to resign, Aaron. Although I wish you had told me about the vault."

"I'm sorry. I thought I was doing the right thing for the church."

"Is that why you hid your relationship with Matthew too?"

He stares at me. I see his Adam's apple bob as he swallows.

"I don't care about your sexuality," I say softly. "I **do** care that Simon Harper used it to bully Reverend Fletcher into keeping quiet about the vault."

"What?"

"Simon Harper found out about your relationship somehow. The reason Matthew resigned was because Simon Harper threatened to expose it."

His face trembles and he looks down. "I . . . I didn't know."

"I think Matthew wanted to protect you, even though being in a same-sex relationship is nothing to be ashamed of."

"It's a sin."

"Nowhere in the Bible does Jesus say homosexuality is a sin."

"In the Old Testament—"

"The Old Testament is crap. It's full of misogyny, torture and inconsistencies. Jesus preached about love. All love."

He smiles oddly. "What if I told you it wasn't love, Reverend. It was just sex. What does Jesus say about that?"

"I don't think God or Jesus would care."

"But plenty of people in this village would."

"People are often more open-minded than you give them credit for."

But even as I say it, I realize I'm not sure. Not here in Chapel Croft.

Aaron shakes his head. "My father brought me up after my mother died. He's always been a good parent: kind, patient. But he's traditional. He would never accept me. And I can't let him down. He's lost everything. How can I take away the only thing he has left—pride in his child?"

I sigh. I understand. People are made to feel guilty for "living a lie," but who hasn't hidden parts of themselves from those they love? Because we don't want to hurt them. Because we don't want to see the disappointment in their eyes. We talk about love being unconditional, but very few of us ever want to put that to the test.

"Aaron," I say slowly. "I'm sorry to have to ask you this but—do you think your father could have known about the body in the vault?"

He hesitates. I see him debate with himself. Finally, he says: "If I tell you this, I expect it to go no further."

"You have my word."

"One night, when I was about four years old, I woke up to hear my father returning to the house."

"From where?"

"I don't know. My father never went out at night.

It was most unusual. I crept downstairs. I could see my father in the kitchen. He had taken off all his clothes—I had never, ever seen him without his priest's cassock—and he was stuffing them into the washing machine like he didn't want my mother to see them. And the oddest thing—he was crying."

"This was around the time the girls and Grady disappeared?"

"I can't be sure of the date."

"Did you tell this to the police?"

He shakes his head. "**No**. Because I **know** my father. He couldn't hurt a soul. His whole life has been devoted to the church, the community and his family. Why would he risk all of that to help cover up a murder?"

It's a good question and I'm not able to give him an answer.

Instead, I say: "Can I see him?"

He stares at me for a moment. And then he nods. He leads me down the hall, to a door which is half open. The institutional smell is worse here.

"A few years ago, I moved him downstairs, converted the front room into a bedroom for him."

Aaron pushes open the door and we step inside.

The room is large. Bookcases line one wall. A large cross hangs on another wall. In the center of the room, Reverend Marsh lies in a hospital bed. I can hear the faint wheeze of the pressure mattress as it undulates to prevent bed sores. I can smell the sour urine from the catheter, the faint odor of the commode. Smells I'm familiar with from visits to nursing homes and hospitals.

Marsh is a pale, thin shadow of himself. The shock of dark hair has bleached to white and is as fine as candyfloss. Veins protrude starkly beneath his skin. His eyes are closed and the paper-thin lids tremble gently as he sleeps.

"They keep him dosed up on a lot of drugs," Aaron says quietly. "He sleeps a lot now. It's about the only time I feel he's at peace."

"Is he in pain?"

"Not so much. It's more frustration, fear. He's still aware enough to understand that his body is failing around him, becoming a prison of flesh and blood. He's trapped within himself. Helpless."

A phone rings from another room. Aaron makes a small bow. "Excuse me. That will probably be the hospital."

I nod, and then I walk toward the bed. I stand, staring down at Marsh. I think again how unprepared we are for illness and old age. How we trundle toward it unthinkingly, like lemmings toward the edge of a cliff. The tiny humans we coo over at the start of their lives, we shudder to look upon at the end.

"I'm sorry," I whisper. "I wish things could have turned out differently."

He opens his eyes. I jump. They meet mine and

widen. One hand lifts from the sheet, crooked fingers pointing.

"It's okay," I say. "I'm—"

A gurgling groan emits from his throat. He's trying to speak, but it sounds more like he's choking.

"Meh . . . Meeehhh."

I back away, legs shaky. The door bursts open and Aaron rushes back in.

"What happened?"

"I'm sorry," I say. "He woke up and started crying out."

"He doesn't see many new faces. It's probably just shock."

He goes to his father's side and gently takes his arm. "It's all right, Dad. It's all right. This is Reverend Brooks. The new vicar."

Marsh tries to pull his arm away. "Meh, meh."

"I should probably wait outside," I say, and hurry out of the door. I stand in the hallway, gathering myself, still feeling a little shaken. That look in his eyes. The choking cry. A few minutes later, Aaron steps out to join me, closing the door behind him.

"He's calmer again now."

"Good. I'm sorry for upsetting him."

"It wasn't your fault." He clears his throat. "I appreciate your visit, and your support."

We smile at each other uneasily.

"I'd better get going," I say.

Aaron walks me down the hall. I'm eager to

escape this house now. The smell, the misery, the memories. But at the door, Aaron hesitates.

"Reverend Brooks?"

I look at him inquiringly.

"I can think of only one reason why my father would hide a body, and that's if he was protecting someone else."

"Who?"

His eyes meet mine. "That's the question, isn't it?"

FORTY-SIX

What tangled webs we weave. Except we don't, not really. We're more like unfortunate flies than spiders, never seeing the sticky trap we've wandered into until it's too late.

I pull up outside the chapel and walk up the uneven path to the cottage. At the door, I pause. My neck prickles. That odd sensation you get when you feel like you're being watched. I turn and scan the road and surrounding fields. No cars. No people. The distant sound of farm machinery. Nothing else.

Maybe I'm just twitchy, on edge. My brain is still processing all the new information that's been thrown at it. Changing presumptions I've made about people. Although not Simon Harper. He's still a dick. I also have a strange feeling that I'm on the verge of answers, but unsure whether I really want to know what they are.

I frown, look around one final time, and then I push open the door.

"Hello?"

No reply. I poke my head into the living room. Flo is sprawled on the sofa, legs hanging over one arm, staring at her phone. She looks up. "Hi."

"Miss me?"

"Not really."

"Charming."

She swings her legs around and sits up. "Mum, I'm sorry about last night."

"Me too."

I perch on the edge of the sofa. "Look, I don't want to be one of those interfering mums who treats you like a child."

"You're not. Most of the time. Well, sometimes you are. A bit."

I smile. "I'm a **mum**. And I'm old. Believe it or not, I was a teenager once and I did a lot of stupid things."

"Like what?"

"I'm not giving you tips."

She grins.

"But, as a mum," I continue, "my job is to try and keep you safe."

"I **am** safe. I know you want to look out for me, but you have to trust my judgment, too."

"It's just, sometimes, you make friends and they get you into trouble."

A raised eyebrow. "Wrigley didn't get me into

trouble. I got myself into trouble and he helped me out."

"Maybe you're right."

"I am. Please, Mum. I don't want us to keep arguing about this."

Neither do I. But I can't tell her why the thought of her and boys fills me with dread. How there are predatory males everywhere. How it doesn't matter if you are clever, eloquent, kind, talented—a man can still use his physical strength to take all of that from you, degrade you, abuse you and turn you into a victim.

"I'm sorry," I say. "I'll try to make an effort with Wrigley, okay?"

"Good." She sits up. "Because he's asked me to go to the youth club with him tonight."

And there it is.

"A youth club?"

"Yes."

"With Wrigley?"

"Yes."

"When did he ask you?"

"He called round earlier."

"He did **what?**"

"He came to bring me a phone to replace mine. That's kind."

But he also came around here when I was out. I try to rein in my annoyance.

"Where is this youth club?"

"Henfield."

"How are you planning to get there?"

"Bus."

"I'm not sure."

"Mum? Please?"

I don't want her to go. But neither do I want to give her something else to kick back against.

I say: "You can go, on one condition."

"What?"

"I want to clear it with his mum."

"Not treating me like a kid didn't last long."

"Well, until you're sixteen, legally, you are."

She gives me a look that could pierce steel. I stare back steadily. "Message him and get his mum's number."

"Jeeessus."

But she picks up her phone and taps out a message.

I walk into the hall and kick off my boots. Flo's phone pings.

"AirDropping it to you," she says.

I take out my phone and accept the WhatsApp link. The tiny picture in the corner shows a woman in a large sunhat holding up a cocktail of some sort. I can't really make out her face.

Flo smiles sweetly. "Happy now?"

No, but it's a start. I tap out a message.

"Hi, I'm Jack Brooks, Florence's mum. As Flo and Lucas seem to have made friends, I thought it might be nice to get to know each other. Maybe a coffee sometime? Also, just wanted to check that you're okay with the pair of them going to the youth club tonight?"

It pings almost immediately with a reply. I pick it up.

"Hi, Jack, thanks for your message. Yes, I was thinking exactly the same thing. Lucas mentioned the youth club. I'm sure they'll have a lovely time. Would you like me to pick them up later?"

I feel my worry ease a little. I type back:

"If you don't mind?"

"No trouble! xx."

"So?" Flo is regarding me sulkily.

"Wrigley's mum says she'll pick you up afterward."

"I can go?"

"I suppose so."

Her face lights up and my heart gives. "Thanks, Mum."

"Are you sure you don't want me to drop you?"

"No, it's fine. Have a bath or something this evening. Chill."

Fat chance.

"I'll try."

"Oh, I almost forgot," she says. "Something weird happened this afternoon—"

"Weird? How?"

"There was this man hanging around."

I stare at her. "A man. What sort of man?"

"Like a homeless man."

"What did he look like?"

"Scruffy, dark hair."

My nerves jangle. It **could** be Jacob. But then, it could be anyone. And how would he find me here?

"Did he talk to you?"

"No. He was just hanging around in the grave-yard, and then he disappeared."

I'm probably being paranoid. On the other hand, he found me last time.

"Have you seen him before?"

"No!"

I try to batten down my panic. "I just don't like the thought of strange men hanging around."

"Maybe he wanted to get into the church, but it was locked."

"Maybe."

She gives me a worried look. "I **can** still go to-night, can't I? You're not going to go all weird about this?"

I don't like it, but it would be unfair to go back on what I've said.

"You can still go but, please, be careful."

Her face relaxes. "I will. Thanks, Mum."

I stand. "I need a coffee and then I'll make some dinner. Chili okay?"

"Yeah. And then I have to get ready if I'm going to catch the bus."

"Okay."

I walk into the kitchen and take two mugs out of the cupboard. I'm trembling with adrenaline. **A**

man. A strange man. As I reach to put the mugs on the counter, one slips from my fingers and smashes, jagged pieces of pottery flying across the worn linoleum.

"What was that?" Flo calls from the living room.

"Just dropped a mug. No worries."

I breathe heavily, staring at the bits of broken mug, imagining for a moment jumping up and down barefoot on the razor-sharp shards. Then I fetch the dustpan and brush. **Chill**.

Flo saunters down the pathway and along the road toward the bus stop. She looks beautiful in skinny jeans, purple Docs and a baggy vest top. She would look beautiful in a sack. My heart aches. Wrigley isn't good enough for her. No one is good enough for her. Least of all me.

I slowly close the door, fighting the urge to follow her and make sure she gets on the bus safely. I'm worried about the man she saw. Even if it's not Jacob, any strange man hanging around is a potential threat. I try to tell myself that it's still light outside. The bus stop is right outside a house. She'll be back by ten at the latest. She's only going to a youth club. Not a nightclub. Or a pub. And Flo knows how to defend herself. She'll be fine.

But I can't shift the lump of unease in my stomach. Was she a bit too keen to refuse a lift? Or am I just being overly suspicious? There will be other teenagers at the youth club. Other adults. And Wrigley's mum is picking them up. Isn't she? I didn't actually speak to her. What if it wasn't her messaging?

Oh, for goodness' sake, Jack. Get a grip.

Or rather, don't. Teenagers are like sand. The tighter you try and hold on to them, the more they slip through your fingers. I have to give her her freedom. Let her choose her own friends, and boyfriends. **But does it have to be Wrigley?**

I walk into the kitchen and pick up a bottle of red wine from the counter. I don't drink much at home, but this evening, I could do with it. I open the bottle and pour out half a glass.

My voice of reason tries to tell me that there are only a couple of weeks of the summer holidays left. Once Flo starts school, she'll make new friends. Hanging out with Wrigley might not seem so cool. Unfortunately, I also know my daughter. She's loyal and, like me, she has a thing for underdogs.

Speaking of which, my mind drifts back to Aaron. **Did** his father hide Grady's body? It seems the most likely scenario. Marsh had access. He knew about the vault. And if he thought he was protecting someone, then there's motive. He was also best placed to cover up Grady's sudden disappearance. But there's still something about it that doesn't quite gel. I just can't think what.

And what of Reverend Fletcher? A man haunted

in more ways than one. An illicit relationship, black-mailed by Harper, conflicted by his faith. Perhaps his death had nothing to do with the discovery in the vault.

I take my wine over to the kitchen table and sit down. There is still one person I haven't spoken to who might be able to shed some light on things. The elusive Saffron Winter.

I open up my ancient laptop. Internet, at last. "At last" being the operative term, as it is still pain-fully slow. But beggars, choosers, et cetera. I google Saffron's name. Fletcher supposedly confided in her, but I still don't know anything much about the reclusive author.

The picture on the website is a larger version of the photo from the back of her books. There is a short bio, telling me not very much about her at all, and a link to her titles. Five YA novels about a school for witches. There's also an email link, and I send a quick message, explaining who I am and ask-ing if she has time for a chat. Just on the off chance, I search for her name on Twitter, Facebook and Instagram. Nothing. No social media, which is un-usual, and especially so for a writer.

I stare at my laptop thoughtfully. I'm pretty sure Joan will know where Saffron lives, but although I am making my peace with this whole "turning up on people's doorsteps unannounced" way of life in the country, I'm getting the impression that Saffron Winter is a private person. Which is fair enough.

Although, in that case, moving to the country was a bad idea.

In fiction, if people want to hide out, they always move to a small village somewhere. Big mistake. One thing you can count on in a small village is that everyone will want to know your business. If you want anonymity, live in a big city. In a city, you can lose the old you like loose change down a drain. Change your name, change your clothes. Reappear as a different person. If you want to.

I close my laptop. What to do now? TV? A film? Maybe I should actually take Flo's advice and have a long bath and chill. I've done precious little of that since getting here. I make my way up the narrow stairs and push open the bathroom door.

"Ah."

Now I remember that Flo has been using the bathroom as a darkroom again. I had to move some of the equipment when I nipped up to use the loo before dinner. She's cleared some of it away, but that has really just involved dumping it in the bath. There are also two stacks of photos piled on top of the loo.

I pick up the first stack. These are the ones she took of the chapel and the graveyard. No sign of the burning girl. I place them to one side and reach for the second stack. My heart tumbles down the hill.

The first photo shows a derelict-looking building. The empty windows gaze out darkly, the roof is pitted with holes. You can tell, just from the pictures, **this is a bad place**. When did Flo take these? It must have been when she **said** that she and Wrigley were in the woods.

I start to work my way through the photos, from the exterior of the house to some obviously taken inside. I stare at the ruined rooms, the smashed-up furniture. Walls covered with graffiti. Pagan symbols. Evil eyes. Signs of Satanic worship.

I sit down heavily on the closed loo seat. What was Flo thinking, creeping around some deserted old building? I know what teenagers are like, but still, I'm angry. With Flo. With myself. I brought her here. This is on me too.

I flick through the rest of the photos. About halfway through, it looks like the negatives must have been exposed to the light. The photos are partially bleached out. The final picture is almost abstract. I can tell it has been taken from inside, looking out of an upstairs window. The woods are a dark ink blot. The fields a grey mass. At the edge is a slightly more distinct white streak. I squint at it. Something unfurls in my stomach.

I take the photo into my bedroom and grab my glasses from the bedside table. I slip them on and peer at it more closely. Not a trick of the light. A figure, standing between the woods and the house's boundary wall. Almost spectral. But this figure isn't a ghost. This person is very much alive.

And I know them.

FORTY-SEVEN

The sky is tracing-paper grey. It won't get dark for another couple of hours. But the forest is already in night-time mode. The trees' overhanging branches block out the light like a large leafy blanket. Flo flicks on the iPhone's flashlight as she walks along the narrow path and wonders again just how sensible—or stupid—this is.

Of course, she tries to tell herself, she was probably in far more danger walking through Nottingham city center than she is walking through the woods here. Potential rapists, murderers or muggers were more likely to be found in bustling metropolitan streets than in a field in the middle of nowhere, and yet, still . . . just because a place is pretty and quaint doesn't mean that bad stuff doesn't happen.

She thinks about the man at the window. Could he still be around, somewhere? **No.** He was probably just some chancer, checking for empty houses and unlocked doors, on the lookout for something to steal. And the picture? She had left it in the graveyard eventually, telling herself it was just a freaky coincidence. A vague similarity. Her mind was making too much of it. This goddamn place was making everything seem weird and creepy.

She reaches the wooden bridge over the small stream, crosses it and is halfway over the stile when she pauses. She thought she heard something. Movement ahead. More rustling. A deer bursts out of the undergrowth and stops, startled.

"Hey there."

The deer stares at her with wide, glowing eyes and then, with a flick of its tail, it's off, bounding away through the fields. She waits and, sure enough, another three or four follow, fast, light hooves barely touching the ground.

She wonders what's scared them. And then realizes it's probably her. Sometimes you're the predator. Sometimes the prey. Just depends on the perspective.

She hitches her other leg over the stile and looks around. The fields appear deserted, but she gets the feeling she's not alone. Animals hide in the undergrowth. Hidden eyes peer from the leafy trees.

She shivers a little, wishing she'd worn her hoodie now, and traipses through the long grass toward the old house. The empty windows glower darkly. Except, in one upstairs window, lights flicker. She picks up her pace, jumping over the broken-down wall, holding out her phone to illuminate the old well, and skirting around it. She jogs up the stairs and reaches the master bedroom.

"Wrigley?"

Through the half-open door she can see flames flickering off the walls. **Oh God**. **Surely, he hasn't?**

She bursts into the bedroom . . . and then she stops.

An array of candles has been arranged around the room. Wedged into old bottles and cans. Wrigley sits on a blanket spread out on the dirty floor. He's laid out crisps, chocolate, a bottle of wine and two plastic cups.

He spreads his arms wide and she can sense the effort he is making in controlling the shaking.

"Welcome!"

"Wow! What romantic teen shit have you been watching?"

"Glad to see you're impressed."

"I am. It's just—"

"Too much?"

"A bit."

"Right."

He lowers his head.

She says hastily: "But I like it. I mean, no one has ever burned a house down for me—" She catches herself. "Sorry. I didn't mean—"

"I know."

She plonks herself down next to him. "So, are you going to pour me a drink?"

He tips some wine into one of the plastic cups and hands it to her.

She takes a swig. It's bitter and warm, but she feels a slow heat spread through her. She takes another swig.

"Don't go mad."

She wipes her mouth. "I'm fine."

He pours a cup and takes a smaller sip himself. He pulls a face. "Not sure why people drink this stuff."

"To get drunk, usually."

He smiles. "Yeah." The silver flecks in his eyes glint. He tips his cup up again, but a spasm jerks his hand, spilling wine down his chin and hoodie.

"Shit!" He wipes at it with his sleeve. "**Fucking** spasms. What a joke."

"Hey, it's okay."

"No. It's not. I wanted this to be right, and—"

She leans forward and presses her lips to his. He tastes of salt and sour wine. He hesitates and then he kisses her back hungrily, wrapping a hand around her neck, catching her hair. And this is different from before, in the bathroom. Or with other boys at parties, where it was all vodka and beer and spit. This feels real and urgent and, for the first time, she feels something other than a mild revulsion. Desire.

She lets him push her down on the blanket and, fleetingly, she thinks that her mum would kill her and are they going to go all the way, and did he have any protection? His hands run over her breasts, pushing up her vest top. She reaches down to fumble with his jeans. And then she hears a noise from downstairs. She sits up and pushes him away.

"What's that?"

"What?"

It comes again. A thud. Like a door being shoved open. They look at each other.

"Is someone else here?"

"I don't know. Hang on."

He stands, shoving his hair out of his eyes. "I'll go and check."

"I'll come with you."

"No, you stay here."

She wants to point out that she's the one who knows self-defense and that she totally kicked his arse. But she doesn't want to humiliate him. Let him go. She can follow. It's probably nothing, anyway. The wind. Birds. Animals.

He looks around then snatches a candle out of one of the empty wine bottles. He blows out the flame and drops it to the ground. Then he holds up the bottle by the neck. "Just in case."

She nods and watches him tiptoe out on to the landing. She strains her ears. Was that a creak? A voice? She stands, starting to feel a little nervous. Not that she actually thinks some crazed **Texas**

Chainsaw–style serial killer is lurking outside, or a nutter in a **Scream** mask, or zombies, or . . . **Christ, just stop it.**

"Wrigley?"

The distinct sound of glass breaking. She jumps.

"Wrigley?"

She pounds down the stairs, taking them two at a time. At the bottom, she flicks the phone flashlight on. She points it around. She can't see Wrigley. And then she can't see anything as someone grabs her from behind and yanks a sack over her head.

FORTY-EIGHT

"Hope you don't mind me dropping by?"

Joan places two cups of coffee on the kitchen table in front of us.

"And distracting me from an exciting evening of **Coronation Street**? No, dear, I don't."

I smile and reach for my coffee. "Thanks."

I had debated with myself about driving over, but when Joan opened the door she didn't seem surprised to see me.

"So, any more news on the body in the vault?"

"Reverend Rushton knew about the vault, but not the body. He accepted donations from the Harpers to cover it up."

Her lips purse and then she sighs. "That surprises me less than it should."

"Why?"

"Reverend Rushton doesn't like to rock the boat.

His first thought is always to protect the church, and himself."

I sip my coffee. "I think Marsh knew about Grady's body, maybe even hid it there."

"I see."

"You still don't sound shocked."

"Well, there can't have been many people who knew about the existence of the vault or had easy access to it. The real question is: what would drive a devoted minister to hide a dead body—and, of course, who killed Grady?"

That **is** the question. And one I can't answer. Not yet.

She smiles. "There's something else?" she asks.

"I wanted to show you this."

I take Flo's photos of the derelict house out of my pocket and spread them out on the table.

Joan stares at them. Her face seems to pale a little.

"Who took these?"

"My daughter, Flo."

"That's the old Lane house. Where Merry lived. You should tell your daughter to stay away from that place."

"I'm surprised it's never been sold."

"Well, legally, Merry's mother still owns it. But I think after a certain period of time it's possible to lay claim to an abandoned property. Mike Sudduth and his wife were looking into it, but then they lost their daughter and it all fell through. More recently, I think Simon Harper has made some claim on the place."

"Really?"

"He's never one to miss a money-making opportunity. The house is in a prime position, plenty of land. I imagine his long-term aim would be to knock it down and sell the land to developers—and maybe that would be for the best."

I slide the photos to one side and slip out the final one, capturing the figure standing between the woods and the broken-down wall, staring toward the house. I tap it with my finger.

"Look familiar?"

She squints at the photo. Her wispy white eyebrows rise. "Interesting. And odd. It's not easy to get to the Lane house. Simon Harper put up new fencing and gates at the entrance from the road, to stop teenagers going up there. The only other way is up through the woods and fields behind the chapel. You don't pass casually by."

I look back at the photo. That's what I thought. Of course, there are innocent reasons why someone might be there. An interest in old buildings, perhaps? But something about it niggles at me.

"What are you thinking?" Joan asks.

"I don't know. I feel like I'm picking up bread-crumbs to see if I can make a loaf."

"And how's that going?"

"At the moment—I'm a sandwich short of a picnic."

"Have you spoken to Saffron yet?"

I shake my head. "No. I sent her a message, but she hasn't replied."

"She's quite a private person."

"Have you seen her recently?"

"No. She didn't come to Matthew's funeral. I presumed she was too upset."

I swig my coffee. I'm not convinced that speaking to Saffron will get me anywhere. On the other hand, if I do speak to her, at least I can tell myself I've followed every crumb and, if I'm still no closer to the gingerbread house, then maybe it's time to get the hell out of the woods.

I look at Joan. "I don't suppose you happen to know where she lives?"

She smiles again. "Well, funny you should ask."

FORTY-NINE

She can't breathe. The hood is thick and coarse and stinks of hay and manure. It's been pulled tight around her neck. Hands grab her wrists before she has a chance to fight back, snapping a plastic tie around them. Panic bubbles in her throat. She tries to summon up what she learned in self-defense, but that's okay when you're facing your attacker with all your limbs in play. When you're ambushed, blind, struggling to breathe, you're helpless.

Someone pushes her roughly forward.

"Let me go," she tries to shout, but the sack suffocates her words.

Keep calm, she tells herself. **Remember, if you can't fight, try to gain knowledge of your attacker and your surroundings till you get a chance to escape. Try and work out what's going on.** She is being pushed out of the cottage. That means her attacker probably isn't going to rape her.

Why take her outside for that? So, what's going on, and where's Wrigley?

"Move," a male voice hisses. A familiar voice? Maybe. She can't be totally sure with the hood over her head. It muffles everything.

Another shove, and she stumbles forward.

"What are you doing?" she pants, trying to get him to speak again, to confirm her suspicions. **Know your attacker**. That way you have a better chance of either reasoning with them or finding a weak spot.

"You'll see."

A shove so hard that she almost trips over the tangled weeds of the garden.

"Wrigley!" she yells through the sack. "Where are you?"

"Flo," a strangled voice cries in return, from somewhere ahead, to her right. "Over here."

"Shut up," a second voice snaps. A female voice. And now she's sure she knows who their attackers are. **Rosie and Tom**. She's just not sure if that makes things better, or worse.

"Please." She tries to keep her voice calm, reasonable. "This is enough. You scared us. Now just let us go."

"Oh, you're going. **Down the well**."

Oh God. Jesus. Panic coats her body in sweat. "Are you insane?"

"Scared, Vampirina?" Rosie's voice, closer now.

"Please, don't."

"Say bye to your boyfriend."

She hears scuffling. A struggle. And then a scream. Panicked, primal. It rises high into the night air and then falls away to silence.

"**WRIGLEY!**"

"One down," Tom chuckles.

She tries to struggle, digging in her heels, pushing back against the sturdy body behind her. But then another set of hands grabs her and shoves her forward and she can't fight against two of them. She feels the toes of her Docs stub the stone lip of the well. They really are going to do this. She closes her eyes, bracing for the fall.

"NOOOOO!"

The roar comes out of nowhere. Angry, animalistic. Heavy feet pound the ground.

"**What the fuck?**"

"**Run!**"

She's shoved roughly to one side. She trips, losing her balance. Unable to put her hands out, she hits the ground hard, the side of her head smacking into the earth, dazing her. She lies on the scrubby grass, breathing hard, disoriented.

Have Rosie and Tom gone? She tries to push herself up and then she hears someone approaching again. Dry grass crunches underfoot. She tenses as the person crouches down next to her. They radiate a hot, dank heat and smell bad. Really bad. Sweat, alcohol and something else, kind of sickly sweet and rotten. **Oh God**. Has she been left here to meet an even worse fate?

"Don't move."

The man's voice is gruff, with the hint of a northern accent. She feels him grab her wrists. And then there's a snap as the bindings on her hands are released.

"Stay there. Count to ten. Then take the hood off."

She counts to thirty, just to be sure. Then she slowly sits up and tugs the sack off her head. Weakness washes over her. She feels dizzy and sick. She leans over and retches. Then she looks around. The garden is empty. No sign of Rosie and Tom. Or her rescuer.

Her heart is pounding. She wouldn't be surprised if she had peed her pants a little. Fear. Like she had never known. Not even when she saw the burning girls. She thought she was going down the well. She thought she might die. **Wrigley.**

She scrambles over to the well's open mouth. "Wrigley!!"

Her own voice echoes back. **Christ**. Is he down there? Is he even alive?

She fumbles in her jeans pocket for the phone and flicks on the flashlight. She points it down the well. It's not strong enough to illuminate all the way down, but she thinks she can just make out a shadow.

And then, weakly, croakily, she hears his voice:

"Flo?"

"Oh, thank God. Are you hurt?"

"My ankle's busted, but otherwise I'm okay."

Christ. Talk about miracles.

"Jesus. You could have broken your neck. Fucking psychos."

"I know. What happened? Where did they go?"

"I don't know. Someone . . . scared them off. Maybe a tramp or something?"

"Shit."

"Look, I'm going to call for help. Just hang tight, okay?"

"I'm not going anywhere."

She smiles through the fear.

"Flo?"

"Yes."

"There's something else."

"What?"

"There's something down here, with me."

"What? Spiders? Rats?"

"No. I think it's . . . a body."

FIFTY

Never have children, a friend once told me. Not if you want to finish a cup of coffee, get to see the end of a film or enjoy a full night's sleep ever again.

It's not just the first few months, when you hover over their cot, listening to check that they're still breathing. Nor the toddler years, when you turn away for a second to find them launching themselves off the back of the sofa at an open window, or even the school years, full of friendships, fallouts and first loves.

It's the years when they're teenagers and you're waiting for them to get home safely, knowing you need to give them their independence, knowing you can't clip their wings, telling yourself that the reason you can't get hold of them is because they're having too much fun, not that they're lying dead in an alley somewhere. Praying you never get **that** call . . .

My mobile trills in my pocket. I've only just got back home, after deciding not to visit Saffron Winter tonight. I'm still holding my car keys. I pull my phone out and stare at the screen. Unknown number. Another one? I press accept.

"Hello?"

"Hello, am I speaking to Reverend Brooks?"

A young male voice, polite, officious. Police. My body goes limp.

"Yes."

"My name is PC Ackroyd—"

"What's happened? Is it my daughter? Is it Flo?"

"There's nothing to panic about, ma'am."

"I'm not **panicking**. I'm asking a question."

"Your daughter is fine, but there has been an incident."

"What sort of incident?"

"Your daughter and her boyfriend have been victims of an assault."

"An assault? Jesus. Is she injured or—"

"No, no. She's not injured, just a little shaken up, but if you could come and pick her up."

"From the youth club—"

"No." A note of puzzlement. "The old Lane house, off Merkle Road. Do you know it?"

The Lane house. I grip the phone so tightly I'm surprised the casing doesn't crack. "I know it. I'm on my way."

. . .

I bump the car up a rutted track that has obviously not been used in years and screech to a halt outside the derelict house. The gate is open, the padlock hanging off. The place buzzes with frenetic activity.

Two police cars and a Scientific Support van are parked outside. Blue lights illuminate the darkness. I can see people in uniforms and, once again, more people in white suits. Behind the house, floodlights are being set up. It seems a lot of activity for an assault. My panic notches up.

"Excuse me, ma'am?" A uniformed police officer approaches.

"I'm Reverend Jack Brooks. I'm looking for my daughter, Flo."

"Oh yes. I'm PC Ackroyd. She's just over here."

He leads me around the side of the van. Flo is perched in the back of a police car, door open, legs outside, wrapped in a silver foil blanket.

"Oh my God. Flo."

I run over. She stands and hugs me, tears starting to well. "I'm sorry."

I smooth her hair. "I'm just glad you're safe. What happened?"

She looks down. I see guilt writ large across her pale face.

"Wrigley and I—we arranged to meet up here tonight."

Wrigley. Goddamn Wrigley. I will kill that boy.

"So you never went to the youth club?"

"No. I'm sorry."

I bite back the anger. "We'll talk about it later. Go on."

"We were in the house, upstairs, when I heard a noise, and Wrigley went to look and he didn't come back, so I went to find him and that's when someone pulled this bag over my head and tied my arms."

"Oh God." I feel sick. "You didn't see who?"

She shakes her head.

"They didn't do anything else—"

"**No,** Mum. Nothing like that. They just shoved me outside into the garden."

"Where was Wrigley?"

"They must have grabbed him first. I heard a scream and that's when they pushed him into the well. They were going to do the same to me, but then there was this man. He just came out of no-where and scared them off. He released my wrists, but when I pulled the sack off, he was gone again."

"So you didn't see who attacked you or who rescued you?"

"No."

"What about Wrigley?"

"He didn't see anything either."

"Where is he?"

"They checked him over, to make sure he hadn't broken his ankle. Then the paramedics dropped him home."

A shame. I was planning on breaking his neck.

"And you don't have **any** idea who your attackers were?"

A hesitation. She twists the hem of her vest top.

"Flo," I say. "If you have any suspicions, you have to tell the police. You could both have been killed."

"I know, and I **have** told them but—" I see her wrestle with it and sigh. "I don't know for sure it's them."

"Who?"

"Rosie and Tom."

"Rosie **Harper**?"

"Yeah."

I feel the rage surge so fast and hard I think I'll lose it. The façade I work so hard to maintain will just shatter, like volcanic lava bursting through its crust. I clench my fists tight.

"I will kill her."

"What about forgiveness?"

"I'll forgive her and then I'll kill her."

"I'm sorry, Mum. **Really**."

"I know."

"You're not mad?"

"Of course I'm mad. I'm mad you lied. I'm mad you went somewhere I would have told you not to." I sigh. "But all I really care about is that you are safe. I know there's stuff you don't want to talk to me about. I know even mentioning sex to your mum is embarrassing and gross, especially when your mum is a vicar—"

"And yet, here you go."

"**But** I just want you to know that I'm here if you do want to talk, and I will never judge and—"

"I get it, Mum. But just for the record, that's not what we went there to do. It was just, like, a date."

"A date?"

"Yes."

"So why not go to a café, or the cinema or . . . oooh, I don't know, the youth club?"

She gives me a caustic look. "Have you ever thought that maybe it's difficult for Wrigley, with his condition?"

"Fair enough, but there are safer places to hang out than a deserted, derelict house in the middle of the woods. Have you not seen **Evil Dead**?"

"No."

"Okay. Well, maybe another night."

"We just wanted to be alone."

"Right."

"Do you want me to stop seeing him?"

Yes.

"No. But I do want you to be honest with me. No more secrets."

She stares at me, and for a moment, I think she is going to demand the same in return, and that's a whole other can of rotten worms.

"Okay." She nods.

"Okay." I hug her tight. "And I wish you had told me before about Rosie and Tom."

"I thought I could handle it."

"Well, the police can deal with them now."

"Excuse me?"

I turn. The same plainclothes detective from yesterday—Derek—is hovering. "Erm . . . Reverend Brooks?"

"DI Derek." I hold out my hand and he shakes it. "Are we all right here?"

"Yes. Flo was just explaining what happened."

"Right. Good. Well, we've taken a statement. We may need to ask some more questions later, but you can take Flo home for now."

"Thank you."

He looks back at Flo. "You were both very lucky. Hanging around an old building like this, it's dangerous."

My hackles rise. "You're trying to blame my daughter for being attacked?"

"No, of course not. I'm just saying that this is not a place for kids to hang out . . . not that anyone is going to be coming up here for a while, not after what your daughter's boyfriend found."

I wish he wouldn't call Wrigley that.

"So it's real?" Flo asks.

"Forensics believe so." He smiles. "We might need to employ you and your young fellow. Two bodies unearthed in two days. Must be some kind of record."

"**Bodies**." I stare at Derek. "What are you talking about?"

"When your daughter's boyfriend—"

"**Wrigley.**"

"When Wrigley fell down the well, he found something down there."

"What?"

"A human skull . . . we're retrieving the rest of the bones now."

She waited. First sitting on the broken-down wall, then pacing. They had arranged to meet at eight. Sneak out, hop on a bus to Henfield and from there to Brighton. You could catch a train to anywhere from Brighton.

She checked her watch. Almost quarter past. Clouds scudded across the darkening sky. Time hurrying by. Where was she?

Finally, heart sinking, she realized.

She wasn't coming.

Tears pricked at her eyes. She picked up her small rucksack and started to turn. An owl hooted, disguising the soft rustle of grass behind her.

Someone grabbed her by the hair and yanked her backward.

FIFTY-ONE

I'm dreaming about girls. Always girls. Mutilated. Abused. Tortured. Killed. I see their faces; their sad, broken bodies. Why do we hate our girls so much that history echoes with their screams and the earth is pitted with their unmarked graves?

I watch them advance through the wet grass of the graveyard: Ruby with her wide, scarlet smile; the burning girls, trailing flames, skin blackened to a crisp; and Merry and Joy, holding hands, silver necklaces glinting around their necks—M and J. Best friends forever.

I'm standing outside the chapel and I'm trying to pray, to call for God's mercy. But they don't hear me, and I realize that they are not seeing a priest, just another devil. God has no meaning for them because he has deserted them. I turn and run inside, pulling the door closed on their grasping hands, sliding the bolt shut. But they're still clamoring, clawing and thumping at the wood.

Thud, thud, thud.

I blearily blink my eyes open. They flop shut again.

Thud, thud, thud.

I try again, using my fingers to prop them open. The dream is fading, the girls' faces disintegrating, floating away like ash on the breeze. I glance at the clock: 8:30 a.m. A human-ish hour. But only just. I yawn and clamber out of bed.

"Coming," I call, as I yank on some clothes and pad down the stairs.

I reach the front door, unlock it and pull it open.

Simon Harper stands on my doorstep. Red-faced, hair tousled, breath rank with stale alcohol. He jabs a calloused finger at me.

"I hope you're happy now!"

"Well, when I'm actually awake I'll let you know. Church hours are from 10 a.m."

I move to shut the door. He sticks one muddy boot in it.

"Could you please remove your foot from my door, Mr. Harper?"

"Not until you listen to what I have to say."

I fold my arms. "Go on."

"The police came around to my house last night."

"Really?"

"Your daughter accused Rosie of assaulting her."

"Someone put a bag over my daughter's head, tied her wrists and pushed her friend down a well."

"It wasn't Rosie."

"Really? It seems she and her cousin have form."

"What?"

"The other day, someone shot at Flo with an airgun. Tom owns an airgun, doesn't he?"

"My daughter was home all last night, like I told the police."

"I see lying really is a family tradition."

He leans in toward me. "Leave my family alone."

"With pleasure. Now get your foot out of my door before **I** call the police."

He takes a step back. "The chapel won't be seeing any more donations from me. See how long you last without my family propping this place up."

"I'm sure the discovery of the vault will prompt renewed interest and investment. Everyone loves a good historical scandal, don't they?"

His face flames even redder and then he smiles nastily. "I know who your daughter was with last night. That twisted little freak Lucas Wrigley. Perhaps you should worry less about **my** daughter and more about him."

"If you have a point, could you lumber toward it?"

"Lucas Wrigley was expelled from his last school."

"And?"

"He tried to burn it down and almost killed a girl."

It derails me. I try to keep my voice steady.

"Why should I believe you?"

He sticks his hand in his pocket and pulls out a crumpled piece of paper. He thrusts it at me.

"What's that?"

"The number of Inez Harrington. The former head of the school. She'll tell you."

I keep my arms folded.

"Suit yourself." He smirks and lets the paper flutter to the ground. "But if it was me, I'd want to know who my daughter was screwing."

He turns and strides back to his Range Rover. It takes all my self-control not to run after him, leap on his back and pound his head to a pulp with my fists. I watch as he revs his engine and pulls off down the road. Then I bend and pick up the piece of paper from the ground. My hands are shaking. I should really rip it up. Bin it. Burn it.

But I don't. I slip it into my pocket and go and fetch my rolling tin.

I'm halfway down my second cigarette when Flo walks into the kitchen, yawning and stretching. She stares at me.

"You're smoking!"

"Yep."

"In front of me."

"Yep." I regard her from eyes baggy with sleep. "You were going to have sex last night . . . oh, and you almost got yourself killed."

She smiles over-brightly. "Coffee?"

"Black."

I take a final drag of the cigarette and stub it out on the wall of the cottage. Then I close the door and walk back inside. The piece of paper rustles in my pocket. I sit down at the kitchen table as Flo boils the kettle.

"How are you feeling this morning?" I ask.

"Okay. It all feels like some kind of bad dream."

"Yeah."

"D'you think Wrigley's okay?"

"I'm sure he's fine."

"I should text him."

"Maybe it might be wise to keep a little distance for a while."

"Why?"

"You have to ask?"

She gives me a hurt look and picks up her coffee. "Fine. I'll be in my room."

She disappears upstairs and I flop back in my chair. I can feel the phone number burning a hole in my pocket. I'm itching to call Inez Harrington. To arrange a time to talk. But if she agrees to meet, I don't want to leave Flo on her own. I hate to say I don't trust my daughter but, especially after last night, I don't trust my daughter. I take a sip of coffee. My mobile rings. Mike Sudduth.

"Hello."

The phone crackles.

"Hi. It . . . om."

"Hang on."

I take the phone upstairs, open the window and poke my head out.

"Hi. Can you hear me?"

"Much better—how are you?"

"I'm okay. I'm sorry if I was rude the other day."

"It's fine. I understand. It was a bad time."

"And not getting any better."

"Yeah." He pauses. "I heard about what happened last night."

"Already? That was fast."

"We might have rubbish broadband, but the village grapevine is like lightning."

And he works at a newspaper.

"Is Flo okay?" he asks.

"She's fine. I suppose you heard about the discovery in the well too?"

"The skeletons. Yeah."

I freeze. "Skeletons, **plural**?"

"Ah, you see, this is why I'm usually consigned to covering village fetes and hog roasts. Not exactly good at being discreet."

"So, they found more than one?"

"Two."

"Do the police know who they are?"

"They're still testing, but you'd have to assume they're the two girls who disappeared in the nineties. Merry and Joy."

"Right," I say slowly. "You probably would assume that."

"And this is really going to blow up, if so. The case will be reopened. National press will be all over it."

I hadn't thought about that. Journalists swarming over the village, raking up the past.

"Jack. Are you still there?" Mike asks.

"Yes. Just thinking how awful it is."

"And even worse, if they were murdered, which looks likely, it means that someone here, in this village, knows what happened to them."

"I suppose it does."

It also means that more than one person here is lying. And I feel like I'm running out of time to get to the truth. I glance toward the stairs.

"Mike, could you do me a favor?"

"Of course. I still owe you for the tire."

"D'you have a couple of hours free?"

FIFTY-TWO

I have arranged to meet Inez Harrington near her home in Lewes, at an artisan café on the high street.

Everything in Lewes appears to be artisan, hand-made or individually crafted. The place is awash with artistically ruffled women in flowered dresses and wellies, herding up children with names like Apollo, Benedictine and Amaretto.

I order a black coffee and settle down at a table in the corner of the café, feeling conspicuous and scruffy. I debated about losing the clerical collar but then decided that it would give me more authority, especially as I'm meeting a teacher. Teachers always make me feel vulnerable. Like they are about to pick me up on not using the correct form of a verb. Or tell me to stop lying. Somewhat ironic, I know, considering my own profession.

I googled Inez Harrington before I came, so I

know who to look out for. Her picture showed a square-faced woman in her fifties with short grey hair and a wide smile. A face for which the term "no-nonsense" was invented. I scan the people coming and going from the coffee shop. I'm a few minutes early. And then I spot her, coming through the door. She looks a little older than the picture, and a little stouter. She walks over.

"Reverend Brooks?"

"Yes. Jack, please."

She holds out a hand. "Inez."

We shake. Her grip is firm and warm.

"Thanks for coming," I say.

She smiles and it immediately shaves years off her. "You're welcome."

A waitress wanders over. "Can I get you a drink?"

"A latte, please."

She turns back to me. Her gaze is direct. "You should know, I don't normally discuss former pupils with anyone."

"Okay."

"I'm making an exception because Simon Harper asked me to."

"He's a friend?"

"No. I used to provide extra English tutoring to his daughter, Rosie. His wife, Emma, is a friend."

"Right."

"I understand your daughter, Flo, is the same age as Rosie."

"Yes."

"Then you'll know that the teenage years are tough."

"Oh, yes."

"It's a confusing time. They have all these raging hormones. I'm not sure if they even understand themselves why they do things sometimes."

The waitress brings over the latte and sets it down.

"Thank you."

"I know what you mean. Teaching secondary must be a tough job."

"But rewarding too. I've seen teenagers who were total delinquents turn into the most kind and lovely adults. Similarly, I have seen perfect A-star students go off the rails completely. Our teenage selves do not define us."

"I couldn't agree more. I'm a completely different person from the teenager I used to be."

"Well, you understand then."

I do. I also sense there is a very big "but" coming.

"But, once in a while, you encounter a teenager who confounds you."

"Lucas Wrigley?"

She nods and, when she lifts the coffee cup, I notice a slight tremble.

"Tell me about him?"

"At first, I felt sorry for him. His parents died when he was quite young. He was adopted when he was nine. Not that that makes a difference. I'm just saying he didn't have the easiest start. And then, of course, there's the dystonia."

"Yes, some kind of neurological condition."

She nods. "Inevitably, it made him a target. Difference is a teenager's greatest enemy. There was some name-calling, bullying."

I bristle slightly at the use of the word "inevitably." I don't think that cruelty is inevitable. It's a choice, nurtured by parents and environment. But I let it slide.

"The school did what it could to help him. **I** went out of my way to support him and talk to the bullies, but some children don't help themselves."

"How do you mean?"

"It was almost like Lucas would invite other children to pick on him, provoke fights, deliberately put himself in the path of the bullies. He **wanted** conflict."

"I find it hard to believe any child **wants** to be bullied."

"So would I, normally."

"Tell me about the fire."

"Lucas became friends with a girl called Evie. She was a bit of a misfit too. Quiet, shy. They hung around together. I thought the relationship might be good for them both."

"And then?"

"She dropped him—another group of girls took her under their wing. She didn't want to know Lucas Wrigley any more. You know how girls are at that age."

I don't really, because Flo has never been part

of that girly type of clique. And she is loyal to her friends, fiercely so. I used to be the same.

"Lucas was upset," Inez continues. "His behavior became more erratic. He missed school. Got into trouble. Evie complained that he was following her home, hanging around outside her house."

"What has this got to do with the fire?"

"**Evie** was the girl who almost died in the fire."

It stops me in my tracks.

"It was a Wednesday. Evie had been tasked with putting away some equipment after PE—the last lesson. Someone shut her in the storeroom."

"Where was the teacher?"

"The teacher didn't realize she was in there. She thought that all the pupils had gone."

"Responsible."

"No. But we all make mistakes. Later, Lucas broke into the school and started a fire in the gym."

"And you know for a fact that it was Wrigley?"

"Someone spotted him running away, became suspicious and investigated. Fortunately, the fire hadn't spread to the storeroom and they heard Evie shouting for help."

"What about physical evidence? Matches. Petrol on his clothes."

She sighs. "By the time he was questioned he had been home. He could have changed clothes, washed."

"So, in other words, no real evidence."

"Evie told me it was him. She said that a few

days before, he had cornered her in the playground and told her she was going to burn."

"Kids say bad stuff sometimes."

"Yes. And some kids are just bad."

I stare at her, shocked. "What happened to 'our teenage selves do not define us'?"

"Most of the time, they don't. But sometimes, you meet a child who isn't just suffering the usual teenage angst. It isn't their background, their up-bringing. They're simply put together wrong. You can't fix it. To put it bluntly, Lucas Wrigley scared me. I worried about what he might do next."

"And that's why he was expelled?"

"He wasn't expelled. After careful discussion with his mother and Evie's parents, it was agreed it would be best if he moved to another school."

"And Evie?"

"She stayed at the school, but her schoolwork went downhill. She became withdrawn, depressed. Her mother went to wake her up one morning and she wasn't in her room. She'd hanged herself in a small copse at the bottom of their garden."

"Oh God." I feel a shiver ripple through me. "How tragic."

"It was all kept very quiet. The family moved away soon afterward."

"Yet you told Emma Harper. Why?"

"A few months later, I was visiting a friend in Henfield and I saw Rosie with a boy."

"Lucas Wrigley?"

"Yes. And they looked . . . friendly."

I frown. Queen Bee **Rosie** hanging out with awkward, twitchy Wrigley? It didn't make any sense. Didn't she and Tom just throw him down a well?

"When was this?"

"It would have been just after he started at his new school."

"So, you were scared of what Wrigley might do to Rosie?"

She laughs. "No."

"Sorry?"

"Rosie Harper can look after herself. I was scared about what they might do **together**."

I let this sink in. "What did Emma do?"

"I believe she stopped Rosie from seeing him."

"Just like that?"

A small shrug. "I never saw them together again, but teenagers can be devious."

They can indeed.

"What about Wrigley's mother?"

"Like many mothers, she struggled to see fault with her child. To be honest, I found her a little odd, preoccupied with her writing. She seemed to spend more time with her fictional coven of witches than with her son."

Something shifts rustily into place in my brain. **Clunk**.

"Sorry, you said **writing**? She's an author?"

"Yes. YA. Popular with some of the children at school."

"What's her name?"

"Annette Wrigley, but you'd probably know her by her pen name—Saffron Winter."

FIFTY-THREE

A sign hangs beside the front door. **"No canvassers or unsolicited callers."** They'd have to be pretty determined salesmen to traipse all the way out here. I'm not even sure a Jehovah's Witness would make the effort.

Saffron Winter's house isn't visible from the lane, not even a sign. Just a battered postbox at the bottom of the long, rutted path. A car is parked outside. A dusty red Volvo. So, someone is home.

Even though I am most definitely an unsolicited caller, I ring the front doorbell. No answer. But the car is here. I look back at it, and something catches my eye. Weeds around the tires, which both look a little flat. Okay. So, Saffron hasn't driven anywhere in a while. Perhaps she walked or caught a bus. Not necessarily suspicious, but still.

I look back at the house. It doesn't look obviously neglected. The grass is cut, curtains open.

But it doesn't feel obviously lived-in either. There's a hollow feel about it. Like one of those cut-outs they use in films. Convincing from a distance but, up close, you can tell it's just a façade. I try the bell again. Then I knock three times, briskly.

I step back, searching the windows for a face or a twitch of curtains. Maybe she isn't home after all. And yet, something is bothering me. About Saffron Winter. About Wrigley. About all of this. If she received my message about Reverend Fletcher, she must have known who I was, so why didn't she reply? Why hasn't she been in touch since everything that happened last night? Why has no one seen her since before Fletcher's funeral? Well over a month.

I walk around the side of the house. There's a gate, but it doesn't have a lock on it. I unlatch it and walk down a narrow path to the back garden. I'm immediately struck by the fact that the back of the house is far less well maintained than the front. The grass is overgrown and the small patio area outside the back door is littered with cigarette butts. So Saffron is a smoker. Perhaps, like me, she enjoys standing outside of an evening, savoring a ciggie or two. Perhaps we could have been friends. And then I wonder why I am thinking of her in the past tense.

I try the back door. Locked. Of course. People are more trusting in the countryside, but most aren't careless enough to leave their doors unlocked.

Especially not private people who don't want any-one poking about in their home.

I peer in the kitchen window. I'm not the tidiest person, but wow. The sink is piled with dirty plates. Packets and tins are stacked on every surface, along with pizza boxes and takeout containers.

I step back, feeling even more uneasy, and glance at the cigarette butts again. The back door, like the front, has a Yale lock. We had them in our old house in Nottingham. One thing I do know about Yale locks is that it's all too easy to lock yourself out, especially if you regularly nip outside for a cigarette and forget to pick up your keys. You don't do it more than once without learning to give yourself an insurance policy.

I look around and my eyes fall on an upturned garden pot. I pick it up. Nada. Okay, too easy. Where did I use to hide my keys? I walk back around to the front of the house. Then I kneel down by the rear bumper of the car and peer in the exhaust. **Bingo**. I hook the keys out. Back and front, from the looks of it. I regard the front door. Perhaps I should knock once more. I mean, I have keys so, strictly speaking, I'm not "breaking," but I am still entering, uninvited.

I raise my fist and hammer on the door once more.

"Hello? Saffron? My name's Jack Brooks, I'm the new vicar. Could I talk to you?"

No reply. Except, did I see the net twitch upstairs?

I debate. And then I stick the key into the lock. The door opens.

"Hello? Is anyone home?"

Silence. I step tentatively into the hall and immediately raise a hand to my nose. Urgh. It stinks. Stale and sour. Unclean. I take a few steps forward.

"Saffron? My name is—shiiit!"

A small black shape darts down the stairs and between my legs. Crap. My heart catapults itself into my mouth. Frigging hell. A bloody cat. And now I've let the damn thing out.

I walk into the kitchen. I might need to find some food to tempt it back in. Now I'm inside, the kitchen looks even more like a bomb has gone off in it. I stare around. The piles of dishes in the sink are congealed with mold. The bin is overflowing on to the filthy floor. A cat-litter tray is piled with excrement.

Christ. This is the sort of detritus that I might expect in student digs, not the home of a middle-aged woman. And a mother. I back out, wrinkling my nose.

The living room is on my right. I peer in. Not as bad as the kitchen, but still pretty high on the disgusting scale. Pizza cartons, dirty plates and empty cans litter the wooden floorboards. Clothes have been piled in one corner. A sleeping bag is crumpled on the sofa and, all around, scattered over the floor, the chairs, stuck on the walls, there are drawings. They'd be good drawings if it weren't for the subject matter. Graphic depictions of murder, mutilation, rape and torture. Satanic symbols. Pentagrams, the Leviathan cross, demons, devils. I stare at them, feeling my skin crawl.

Is this Wrigley's room? Is he sleeping down here? It certainly smells like it. There is the pungent aroma of sweat and hormones. But why would Saffron let him, unless she isn't around? Unless she has left him here, on his own.

I walk back into the hall and look up the stairs. I place a hand on the banister and start upward. My bad feeling increases. The awful smell—more unpleasant than stale food, sweat and hormones—is worse up here. Almost unbearable. I stick my arm in front of my nose as I reach the landing. Three rooms. To my left, I see a bathroom. To my right, a teenage boy's room. And now I understand why Wrigley isn't sleeping up here. It would be impossible with that smell. A smell which is coming from the room in front of me. The one with the closed door. **Of course**.

I tell myself I don't need to open it. I don't need to know. I could call the police right now and let them deal with it. But I **do** need to know. I steel myself and push the door open.

"Jesus Christ."

I turn and throw up. Without even thinking about it. A reflex reaction. I remain, bent over, saliva spooling from my mouth, for several minutes. Trying to regain control of my stomach, trying to stop myself from screaming.

Finally, I straighten and turn back to the room. A body lies on the double bed. Or what remains of a body. Much has soaked into the mattress, bodily fluids pooling on the floor. The rest is a barely identifiable mess of rotting flesh and stained clothing. Pajamas. Strands of tangled dark dreadlocks.

Saffron Winter.

She must have been dead for at least a couple of months. Not much mystery as to how. The wall behind the bed is stained with a pattern of dark maroon flecks and splodges. On the floor, I can see a sharp knife, similarly stained russet.

He killed her while she slept, I think. **Slaughtered her. How many times did he stab her?**

I need to get out of here. I need to call the police. I need to . . . A floorboard creaks behind me. **No.** I turn. Seconds too late. Something heavy crashes into my skull. So hard my spine cracks and my legs buckle. A moment of blinding pain. A realization that I am in big trouble. And then, darkness.

FIFTY-FOUR

A babysitter. Flo fumes. She lies on her bed, listening to Nine Inch Nails thrash in her ears. Mike Sudduth is downstairs. She presumes. She hasn't been down to see him or say hello. Why should she? She doesn't want him here. She doesn't need him here. Whatever her mum might think.

She knows that she has let her mum down, but she still feels furious. Screw this place and this shithole village. Screw Rosie and her inbred cousin. Screw her mum for bringing them here and screw you too, God.

She messaged Wrigley again, but he hasn't replied. She feels sick and angry about that too. Is he ghosting her? Is he embarrassed? Maybe his mum won't let him. Or maybe he is just like every other boy, who goes cold after they get their way—not that he **got** his way, but she had hardly been unwilling.

She thinks about going on to Snapchat and chewing Kayleigh's ear off about it, but right now she doesn't really want to reveal just how crap her life has become. That's the problem with social media. It's not designed for negatives. It's all about people showing their best side. Posing with filters, creating some sort of fake perfect life. But what do you do when life isn't perfect? When everything feels shit. When you feel like you're sinking into a deep, black hole and you can't crawl your way out. LOFL.

And then her phone buzzes with a message. She grabs it up. **Yes**. Wrigley.

"How r you?"

She smiles and messages back, "Okay. How's your ankle?"

"Not bad."

"Good."

"R u grounded?"

"No, but Mum thinks you're a jinx!"

"Maybe she's right."

"No. It wasn't your fault."

"Still feel bad. My idea to go up there."

"I wanted to go."

"I really like you."

"I like you too."

"Is your mum there now?"

"No. But her boyfriend is here, keeping an eye on me."

"Boyfriend?"

"Not really. Just a friend."

"Okay. Well, hang tight. I'll see you soon."

He signs off with two black hearts.

She stares at the phone, feeling kind of warm inside. Okay, maybe all this would work out after all. She sits up and realizes she feels hungry. She missed breakfast and lunch and it's almost five o'clock.

She switches her music off and climbs off the bed. She opens the door and pads downstairs. She can hear Mike talking on his phone in the kitchen.

"Two bodies. The next village. **Christ**. Well, it's not strictly my . . . well, yes, I get it. I am just down the road. But I'm kind of in the middle of something right now. What d'you mean—'what'? Writing up the story about the skeletons in the well!"

She walks into the kitchen. He's sitting at the table, laptop open in front of him, a cup of coffee steaming at his side. **Make yourself at home,** she thinks.

He glances up as she walks in. "Look, I'll call you back." He puts his phone down and smiles at her. "Hi. How are you?"

She stares at him. It occurs to her that Mum could do worse. He's kind of good-looking in an old, craggy kind of way. Stubble. Dark hair that's a bit long and streaked with grey. Lines radiating from pale blue eyes.

"I'm fine." She walks past him to the fridge. "But I don't need a babysitter."

"I'm sure you don't. But your mum asked me for a favor and I still owe her one for helping me out the other day."

She notices him glance at his phone.

"Not keeping you from anything, am I?"

"No, no. It's fine."

"I heard you on the phone. Something about more bodies?"

"Eavesdropping?"

"You have a loud voice."

"Okay. The newspaper wants me to go and cover a story."

"A murder?"

"Yeah. Two pensioners in the next village."

"Wow. It's all kicking off in Nothing Happensville."

"There's not been this much murder and mayhem since someone sabotaged the prize marrow at the Chapel Croft village fair."

She can't help a small smile. "You should go."

"I promised your mum."

"I'll be **fine**."

"No."

"Look, why don't you text her and ask?"

"I'm not sure."

She pulls her own phone out of her pocket. "Shall I do it?"

"No. I can do it. It's not like I'm scared of your mum or anything."

"Really?"

"Well, maybe just a bit." He picks up his phone and types a message.

Flo grabs some cheese, tomatoes and butter from the fridge and starts to prepare a sandwich. She hears his phone ping with a reply.

"What does she say?"

"She says she's on her way back. Ten minutes away. So, I don't need to hang around if I need to go."

"There you are then." She glances over her shoulder. She can see he's debating with himself. "I'll be **fine** for ten minutes."

"O-kay." He closes his laptop and slips it into his bag. "But I want you to promise you'll keep the door locked, and don't open it to anyone you don't know."

"I'm not stupid."

"Far from it." He slings his bag over his shoulder and grabs his coat. "Tell your mum I'll call her later, okay?"

"Okay."

"Lock the door after me. Yes?"

"**Yes**."

"Okay."

She sees him out of the front door then locks it firmly behind him. **Jeez**. She walks back into the kitchen and pours a glass of orange juice. She brings it over to the table and sits down with her sandwich. She's just about to take a bite when there's a knock at the front door. Seriously? She puts her sandwich down. It's probably Mike, she thinks. He's probably forgotten something. Still, she should check.

She gets up and walks through the hall, into the living room. She peers out the window. Her eyebrows rise. **Really?**

She walks to the front door.

Don't open it to anyone you don't know.

She unlocks the door and yanks it open.

"What are you doing here?"

FIFTY-FIVE

When I was a child, my favorite book was **The Owl Who Was Afraid of the Dark.**

I used to repeat it to myself when Mum punished me. I would recite: **"Darkness is exciting, darkness is fun, darkness is beautiful, darkness is kind."**

Of course, as I grew older, I saw through the lie.

Darkness is only exciting and fun when you're the owl. A hunter, a predator.

If you're the prey, helpless and alone, darkness is death.

I blink my eyes open. All around me, thick, impenetrable black. I'm lying on my side, my shoulder cramped under me. My cheek is pressed into rough, bristly carpet. I can feel the fibers tickling at my nose, some trapped in my throat. I cough. Hot, sharp pain envelops one side of my head. Something sticky is crusted around my ear and neck. I want to raise a hand to touch the pain, but I can't move it. My wrists are bound behind me. I can't feel my feet but I'm pretty sure they're similarly restricted. **Hog-tied. Helpless in the dark.**

I try to quell the panic. Move a little. Fresh pain shoots through my skull as it connects with metal. Only a few inches above me. I roll the other way and my nose bumps into more coarse fabric. I try to straighten my legs and find I can't.

I'm trapped, confined. In a coffin. Buried alive. The panic swells and threatens to bubble over. No. Push it down. Stop it. Not possible. There isn't much air, but there's still air coming in from **some-where**. And a smell . . . grease and oil.

I strain my ears. Outside, I can hear something. Birds. Evening song. I'm above ground. Confined. And the realization is not as horrific as being buried alive, but almost. I am in a car trunk. **Saffron's car trunk**. My brain draws on foggy memory. Standing, staring at her body. Hearing a noise behind me. Starting to turn, and then the blow. A crippling pain in my head as something crashed into my skull. But just before the blackness, a glimpse. Silvery-green eyes.

Wrigley killed his mother. And he's been living with her body, pretending she's still alive. The messages I received must have been from Wrigley. My stomach rolls. Not just at the thought of Saffron's decomposing corpse but at the thought of that boy—that **psychopath**—touching my daughter. **Flo. Oh God. Flo**. I need to warn Flo.

And then I hear another sound. Footsteps crunching on the shingle driveway. Getting closer. A **clunk**. I squint against the sudden shaft of sunlight. A tall silhouette stands over me. My vision adjusts.

For a moment, I don't recognize this stranger. Through my fog of fear and pain I realize that his hair is shorter, shorn right down to his skull. It makes him look older. The baggy hoodie has gone too. He wears a charcoal T-shirt and his arms are sinewy with muscle.

"Hi, Reverend Brooks."

"Wrigley."

Except my tongue is sluggish and it comes out, "Wugglah."

He smiles. And I notice what else is different. The twitching, the strange jerking movements, have stopped. He stands, tall and perfectly still.

"Your twutch?"

"Oh, that. Yeah."

He suddenly convulses. Limbs jerking uncontrollably. Then he straightens and laughs.

"Good act, right? Poor wriggly Wrigley." He perches on the edge of the trunk. "You ever see the film **The Usual Suspects**? Great film." He leans in and whispers, "The greatest trick the devil ever pulled was pretending he didn't exist."

He hops off the trunk. "People don't like to stare at a cripple. They're embarrassed. All they feel is pity." He winks. "You can get away with a lot that way."

I stare at him helplessly. "What uh you gunna do?"

"Well, we're going to wait till it's darker and **then** we're going for a drive. Just got to get one more thing."

He disappears from my sight, leaving the trunk open. I twist and turn, wriggling from side to side, tugging at my restraints, but it's no good. I think about screaming, but who would hear me, apart from Wrigley, and I don't want to make him angry. I hear whistling. Wrigley is already returning. He's limping very slightly—so he did actually hurt his ankle—and he's carrying a long shape wrapped in stained bedsheets.

My stomach lurches and my heart fills with horror.

"No."

He smiles. "Sorry, Reverend. It's going to be a bit cramped."

And then he lays Saffron's rotting corpse in the trunk next to me and slams the lid closed.

FIFTY-SIX

Her blonde hair is pulled back. She's dressed down in jeans and a baggy hoodie, hands shoved deep in her pockets. Her face looks pale and contrite.

Flo stares at Rosie. "You know this could be seen as intimidating a witness."

"That's not why I'm here. Honestly. I just need to talk."

"Why?"

"I . . . I want to say sorry."

"Fine. You've said it. Bye."

"Wait!"

Against her better judgment, Flo keeps the door open, just a wedge. "What?"

"Look, I never meant for things to go this far. Really. It wasn't my idea."

"I find it hard to believe **Tom** has any ideas."

"I'm not talking about Tom."

"Then what **are** you talking about?"

"Can I come in?"

"Can't you tell me out here?"

"Please? I brought you this back."

Rosie holds out a Jack Skellington sweatshirt. The one Flo lent Poppy on their first day here. It feels like a lifetime ago.

Flo debates with herself. One on one, she can take this bitch. "Fine." She snatches the sweatshirt and opens the door wider. "But make it quick. My mum will be back in five minutes—and if she finds you here, she'll actually kill you."

They walk into the kitchen and stand stiffly.

"Well?" Flo says.

"Look, I know you hate me."

"Can't imagine why. Shooting at me and Wrigley. Throwing him down a well."

"I didn't throw him down a well."

"Oh, yeah. It was all Tom, right?"

"No."

"What?"

"No one threw Wrigley down the well."

"What the hell are you talking about?"

"Did you **see** us throw him down the well?"

"No, but—"

"Don't you think it was a bit odd that he didn't hurt himself?"

"Maybe he was just lucky."

"Whose idea was it to meet up there? Wrigley's, right?"

Flo stares at her, a horrible dry feeling in her throat. "Yeah."

"It was all planned. The bag over your head. The attack. We tied a rope around him and lowered him down into the well. It was a big wind-up."

"No."

"Yes."

"Why? Why would you do that? Why would Tom do that?"

"Because you broke his nose."

"But you hate Wrigley."

"Oh, you are so fucking stupid."

She moves closer. Instinctively, Flo backs away.

"Wrigley and me. We're together. Soulmates." She smiles. "If it's any consolation, he did kind of like you. But I couldn't have that. So, I made him prove himself to me. By fucking with you."

"I don't believe you."

"He told me to come around here."

"And I told you—my mum will be home any minute."

"No, she won't."

Rosie pulls her hand out of her pocket. She holds the serrated knife. The one from the exorcism kit. The one Flo swore to her mum that Wrigley didn't steal. Fear crushes Flo's insides.

"We're going to have so much fun, Vampirina."

FIFTY-SEVEN

He watches the chapel. He is lying belly-down in the grass behind a tall headstone. He doesn't dare get any closer. Not yet. Not till it's darker. Not after her daughter saw him at the window yesterday.

He mustn't make any more mistakes. But it's difficult. He's in constant pain. He's tired. His head feels odd, thoughts slumbering around sluggishly. His whole body feels like it's slowing down on him, stuttering to a halt.

Earlier, he heard the drone of the police helicopter. Searching. They must have found the bodies. So far, they've missed him. But he can't keep hidden for long. With his filthy clothes, stench and festering ankle, he's not exactly indistinctive.

But he's come so far.

He needs to see her, to talk to her. That's all.

He messed it up last time. Badly. All those years looking for her—his only clue the one letter she had sent him and a faded postmark. And then, he had found her by chance. In a soup kitchen. He had been shuffling along with the other homeless and suddenly she had been there. Smiling, happy, with her white collar gleaming around her neck. He could barely believe it, but he would know his sister anywhere.

He hadn't dared talk to her. He had bided his time, watching her, working out the best approach. He had always been like that. A watcher. Slow to act, except when the anger took over. Like with Mum. She had pushed him too far and he had lashed out. Only afterward did he become aware that he had lashed out with a bread knife in his hand.

It was the same with the husband. That night in the church. He hadn't meant to hurt him. Well, maybe just a little. After all, he had seen how he treated his sister. How he shouted at her, hit her. He had wanted to punish him. But he went too far.

When she came to visit him in prison, she had told him she forgave him. But she made him promise not to tell anyone about them. And he had agreed. He knew he had let her down. She had said she would come back. She never did. But he forgives her for that too.

She's not there at the moment. Just the daughter. And a girl has arrived. He's not sure, but he thinks she's the same girl from last night.

When the boy first turned up at the derelict

house, he had hidden in the cellar. He'd heard voices above him. And then a scream. He had rushed out. Chased off the attackers and freed the girl. When he realized who she was, he had hidden again. She couldn't see him. Not yet.

Confusingly, the daughter has just let her attacker inside. He wonders whether he should do something but, for now, he just watches. Watching over his niece, he thinks. His family. He smiles, then yawns. Soon she'll be home. They'll be together. At last.

FIFTY-EIGHT

I'm not sure how long I lie there, in the darkness, lover-close with Saffron's rotting remains. At first, I lose it. I scream. I kick my heels against the trunk. I feel the fine threads that tether me to sanity snapping one by one.

And then a tiny part of my brain reaches out and clutches on. **You've been here before. You survived then. You will survive now. You have to. For Flo.**

I need to keep calm. Focus on something other than the heat, the smell, the irrational fear of movement in the darkness next to me. The sound of gasping, wet breath and skeletal hands fumbling to pull away the soiled sheet.

Stop it. Just stop it.

Saffron is dead. And I need to stay alive. For my daughter. Is she still at home with Mike? Have they tried to get hold of me? Are they starting to worry, perhaps thinking about looking for me, calling the police? Or are they giving it more time?

Time. How long have I been here? I got to the house around four. My perception is warped. Time moves more slowly in the dark, in fear, in pain. But it must be several hours since I arrived. Eight or nine o'clock. The light outside will be fading. Wrigley said he wanted to wait until it was dark.

Then we're going for a drive.

Can he drive? I have to presume so. Not so unusual in the country. Lots of parents have private land and kids start to learn before seventeen. But where are we going? What is he planning?

I tense. Footsteps on gravel again, the **clunk** of car doors opening. Something being shoved on to the backseat. A door slams. Then a creak and lowering in the suspension as someone climbs into the front. The engine starts. We're moving. I'm bashed and bumped around in the trunk, feeling every pothole in the road through the deflated tires. Thrown together with Saffron's soft, decomposing body, the damp of bodily fluids seeping into my clothes. Then, finally, it's over. The car lurches to a stop. I lie, breathing harshly, listening. Wrigley climbs out. He's taking something out of the back. Then suddenly the trunk opens. Fresh air. I breathe it in hungrily.

Wrigley reaches in and lifts out Saffron's body. I try to focus my eyes. It isn't quite dark. Twilight. He's putting her body in . . . a wheelbarrow.

Draping a blanket over her. But where are we? I can see sky, a sprinkling of stars. To my right, a fence, a gate. I recognize it. **The chapel**. We're at the chapel.

I should scream, cry for help. My tongue feels like it's working again. Someone might be passing and hear me. As if reading my mind, Wrigley turns and pulls something out of his pocket. He leans in, grabs my hair and stuffs a dirty rag in my mouth.

"Be right back."

The trunk slams shut again. I scream my frustration through the rag. Although Saffron's body has gone, the smell remains. I try to roll myself into a better position, to ease the cramp in my arms and legs. Why has he brought us here? What the hell is he doing? And what about Flo and Mike? Fear gnaws hungrily at my guts.

A few minutes later the trunk opens again.

"Your turn."

He is surprisingly strong. I find myself lifted and dumped into the wheelbarrow. With my legs and arms bound and the rag in my mouth, I can do little to resist. I try to look around. We're in the driveway outside the chapel. The rear of the car is turned toward the church. In the near dark, the quiet of this country lane, you'd be hard-pressed to see anything, except perhaps a shadowy figure pushing a dark lump in a wheelbarrow up the path. There are no lights, only a faint sliver of moon. I feel despair lie heavy in my chest.

Wrigley pushes the wheelbarrow toward the chapel. My bones rattle. I glance toward the cottage. The lights are on. But is anyone home?

"Y'know, this has all worked out really well," Wrigley says conversationally. "I'd been wondering how to get rid of Mum's body, but discovering the vault was a gift. Where better to dump a body than in a burial chamber, right?"

The door to the chapel is open. He must have taken my key. He bumps the wheelbarrow over the threshold and wheels me inside.

"Home sweet home."

There is a **clunk** as the door shuts behind us, the rattle of the key.

I stare around. The chapel has been lit with candles. Stuffed into bottles and propped on pews, the altar and the floor. I can smell melting wax and another, harsher, chemical smell.

But that's not what causes my bladder to loosen.

A plastic chair has been placed in front of the altar. Above it, draped over the upper banister, dangles a noose.

Wrigley plucks the gag from my mouth.

"Now might be a good time to pray."

FIFTY-NINE

I stare at the dangling noose, realization dawning.

"It was you. You killed Reverend Fletcher."

"Well, technically, he killed himself. Just like you're going to."

He pulls a small sharp knife out of his pocket, bends and slices the plastic tie around my ankles. "Stand up."

"No."

He tips the wheelbarrow up, and I fall face-first on to the floor, managing to turn at the last moment and land on my side, just missing a lit candle. I can feel the heat from the flame close to my wrist.

"How? How did you convince him to do it?"

Wrigley grins, then sticks his fingers in his mouth and whistles. A figure emerges from the small office. Rosie Harper. **What the hell?** She walks over to Wrigley's side. He grabs her, hooks an arm around her throat and presses the knife against the soft flesh.

"Get up on the chair, put the noose around your neck or I'll kill her."

"Please. Don't hurt me." Rosie's eyes fill with tears.

"Do it," Wrigley snarls. "Or I'll make it slow."

I stare at them both in horror. Then suddenly, Wrigley spins Rosie around and they kiss, long and hard. My limbs feel weak. They both burst into laughter.

"Her face," Rosie says.

Wrigley turns back to me. "It was so easy. That dozy old goat got right up there and strung himself up. You should have seen the look in his eyes when he understood he'd been played."

I push myself into a sitting position, wrist hovering over the flame of the candle behind me.

"Why?"

"Because when I was in care, before I was adopted, a priest abused me. Is that what you want to hear? You want reasons? You want a neat confession. Like in the movies. Will that make it easier?"

"Maybe."

"Fine. I'll play. Fletcher was a faggot and a liar. It used to be just me and Mum, but suddenly he's around the house all the time, talking to her about books and history and shit. Pretending he's interested in her."

"You were jealous?"

"No. He was using her. He didn't like her in that way and she couldn't see it. Stupid bitch. Then, one day, Mum was out and I was in the garden, doing push-ups. Fletcher walked round the back and saw me."

"He realized you were faking the dystonia?"

"Yeah. He said he'd tell Mum, if I didn't."

"She never suspected?"

"Mum was so wrapped up in her writing I could have grown another fucking head and she wouldn't have noticed. Plus, she liked the idea of adopting a 'broken' one. It's why I started faking it to start with—to stand out from all the other unwanted brats. But now Fletcher was going to ruin every-thing."

"And he had to die, for that?"

"I tried to warn him off, to get him to leave—"

Something else clicks into place. "The Burning Girls pinned to his door. The fire in the chapel?"

"Stupid fucker wouldn't take a hint."

"And what about Saffron? Why kill her?"

"The lying faggot told her anyway. She knew something was up when he died. Kept asking all these questions." He shrugs. "She was just doing my fucking head in—"

I can feel the skin of my wrists tightening in the heat, but I can also feel the plastic of the thin cable tie softening.

"I'm not getting up there. I'm not going to make it easy."

"Yeah, you are."

He nods at Rosie and she disappears back into the office. A moment later she reemerges with another thin, pale figure.

And I realize that he's right. I'm going to kill myself here tonight.

SIXTY

He must have fallen asleep (or maybe passed out) for a while. When he opens his eyes, it's dark. He's cramped and cold. Shivering. Apart from his ankle, which feels like a lump of molten lava on the end of his leg.

It occurs to him dimly that passing out, shivering and burning are all signs of an infection running rampant in his body.

But he can't deal with that now. He sits up, orienting himself.

The graveyard. Yes. That's where he is. Watching out for her. Is she home? His eyes search the cottage. It's in darkness. But he can see lights flickering in the chapel. No, not lights. Flames. Like candles.

Why would there be candles in the chapel? Something is wrong. He can feel it in his gut.

He fights through the lethargy and pain, pushes himself to his feet and starts to limp, slowly, across the graveyard.

SIXTY-ONE

"Mum!"

I stare at my daughter. "It's okay, sweetheart. Are you all right?"

Her arms are bound behind her. Rosie has a knife pressed into her back. The serrated knife from the exorcism kit.

"You were right, Mum. All along."

I smile sadly. "I hate to say I told you so—"

"Sweet," Wrigley says.

Rosie shoves Flo toward him and he wraps his arm around her neck. He holds out his other hand to Rosie.

"Honey, I think I'm going to need a bigger knife."

She smiles, taking the small knife off him and handing him the serrated one. He presses the blade to Flo's eye. And, this time, I know he's not faking.

"Now get up on the chair."

"Mum," Flo whimpers. "He's going to kill me anyway."

"And I can do it fast or slow. I can cut her up bit by bit while you watch."

"Then what? You think you'll convince people that I killed my own daughter, set fire to the chapel and hanged myself?"

"You've found it hard to settle here, Reverend. You still feel so guilty about what happened at your old church. Really, it was inevitable." He shrugs. "You know why I like fire? Fire fucks everything up. By the time the police start to piece it all together, we'll be long gone."

"Sussex's own Bonnie and Clyde." I look at Rosie. "You really think someone who can do all of this will think twice about getting rid of you?"

She snarls, "Shut up and get up on the chair."

The flame is so hot against my wrists I want to scream, but I feel the tie give. I tug my wrists apart but keep them behind me. Then I get to my feet and shuffle backward toward the chair.

Wrigley smiles. "See. Told you you'd do it."

I turn. But instead of climbing on to the seat, I grab the chair and fling it at Wrigley.

Throw something and the person will try to deflect it. Instinctively, Wrigley raises his arm. The chair strikes his wrist and the knife flies from his hand. Flo takes advantage. She stamps hard on his foot and slips from his grip. The chair crashes into several candles. They fall to the floor and flames spring up all around. I remember the harsh chemical smell. **Accelerant.**

"Run!" I scream at my daughter.

She turns and sprints for the door. Rosie runs after her and grabs her arm, but before she can raise the knife Flo headbutts her. Rosie screams and doubles over. Flo knees her in the face and she crumples. **Good girl.** Flo fumbles with the key, and then she's out, into the darkness.

My relief is short-lived. Wrigley is still blocking my escape route. He advances toward me. I back up, knocking over another candle. He lunges for me. I try to dart around him, but he's quicker. He punches me in the face. I stumble and trip, falling backward, head smacking hard into the stone slabs. Sparkling motes spin in front of my eyes. Wrigley throws himself on top of me, his hands around my throat.

"You **fucking** bitch."

I buck and twist, trying to throw him off. More candles topple. His grip is tight. I'm struggling to breathe. I grab at his hands, trying to prize his fingers loose. I can feel the heat of the fire all around us. I only have one advantage. My body weight. I roll to the right, taking Wrigley with me, toward the flames. He screams as his T-shirt catches alight.

The grip on my throat is released. I gasp and sit up. Wrigley is batting at the flames, rolling around on the floor to put them out. I start to crawl away. Beneath the pews I can see a glint of metal. The serrated knife. I reach for it. A hand grabs me by the hair and yanks me back.

His breath is hot in my ear. "I'm going to fuck you up like you wouldn't believe."

My fingers touch the worn bone handle . . . and close over it.

"Too late for that."

I turn and thrust out wildly. By luck more than judgment, I feel the blade plunge into firm flesh and hear him grunt in pain. His eyes widen. He looks down, clutches at his stomach and sinks to the floor.

I push myself to my feet, panting. The flames are spreading rapidly, licking at the pews, eating up the old, dry wood. Rosie is gone. I need to get out of here. To find my daughter.

"Please," Wrigley moans from behind me. "Help me."

I look back. He's curled on the floor, holding his stomach. A darker stain is spreading out over the charcoal T-shirt. Parts of it have melted into his scorched flesh. He looks thin and young and scared.

"You can't leave me here. You're a priest."

He's right. Reluctantly, I walk back and crouch down next to him. I lay one hand on his brow. I am a priest. A woman of God.

But I'm also a mother.

"I'm sorry."

I raise the knife and plunge it into his stomach

again. Hard. Up to its hilt. And I watch as the darkness reclaims him.

I stand. My muscles don't want to support me. I stagger and reach for a pew to hold on to, but they are all on fire. The air is thick with smoke. My throat is swollen, tight with heat. The door seems so far away. I feel weary.

I take a step forward, but my legs give beneath my own weight and I find myself on my knees, staring into the fire. My eyes water and burn. Through the tears, I see something.

Two figures. Girls. **Always girls**. Standing side by side. Whole again. Flames halo their heads and sprout like wings from their backs. They hold out their arms. I reach for them, barely feeling the flames crisping the tips of my fingers.

They tried to warn Flo, I think. **Just like they tried to warn Reverend Fletcher.**

They appear to those in trouble.

"Thank you," I murmur.

My eyelids start to close. And then I see another figure, striding between the girls. Huge and dark, reeking of something sour and foul. He looms over me, like a vengeful demon.

I stare up at his face. I know him.

As I fall back, his arms seize me and lift me from the flames.

SIXTY-TWO

A memory. Standing outside the chapel with his mum and sister. His sister held his hand. The night air was cool and acrid with the stench of smoke.

A fire had been lit at the base of the big monument in the graveyard and a large crowd stood around it, chatting and laughing. Flames leaped up toward the night sky, painting their faces in orange, distorting smiles into crazy leers.

On a trestle table, big urns of warm cider steamed, sweet and pungent. Villagers ladled the cider into crude clay mugs and drank heartily. The clock above the chapel struck the hour and the vicar walked out, stern-faced and somber in his dark robes. He stared around at the gathering.

"Thank you, everyone, for coming to our annual Burning Girls commemoration. Tonight, we remember our ancestors who died here for their beliefs. We give thanks for their sacrifice and say prayers for their souls. And, just as the Sussex Martyrs gave their bodies to the flame so that they might enjoy everlasting life, we make offerings in remembrance. Please join me in the Martyr's Recitation."

The group chanted: **"For martyrs are we. In fire our end. Souls set free. To heaven we ascend."**

"And now, please cast your Burning Girls to the flame."

As he watched, one by one, each villager held up a small twig doll and threw it on to the pyre. His mum nudged him. He took his own crude creation out of his pocket. But he didn't want to let her go. Didn't want her to burn. Eventually, his mum snatched the doll from his hands and flung her into the fire.

The tiny twig body twisted and blackened and finally whitened to ash. Eaten alive by the hungry flames.

He felt the heat course through his own body. He closed his eyes. A tear ran down his cheek.

SIXTY-THREE

(Two weeks later)

"Chips."

Flo plonks herself down next to me on the bench and shoves a tray of greasy chips into my lap. An aroma of frying and vinegar rises into my nostrils.

"Yum," I say, even though I'm not feeling remotely hungry.

I prong a soggy bit of potato with my wooden fork and stare out at the sea. It's a peaky kind of day. Washed-out grey sky, the sea an inhospitable mucky-brown color. It looks more like ridges of mud than water. Like you could walk over them, all the way to the horizon.

We're staying in a tatty B&B just outside Eastbourne. It is not glamorous or particularly comfortable, but it's all the Church would stump up for and it's kept us away from the press intrusion around Chapel Croft. I couldn't protect my daughter from Wrigley, but at least I can protect her from the fallout.

Mike has been keeping us updated with events, although even he doesn't know where we're staying. I haven't quite forgiven him for leaving Flo alone, at the mercy of psychopaths, although I understand how he was tricked by the message Wrigley sent from my phone, just as plenty of us were fooled by the messages sent from his dead mother's phone.

I think how easy it is to be someone else these days, with our reluctance to engage in person, to even talk to people. We rely upon texts and emails and never question who might be on the other end. Passwords can be worked out. Wrigley just had to use my thumb while I was unconscious to open my phone. But then, I suppose Wrigley fooled everyone face to face too.

The greatest trick the devil ever pulled was pretending he didn't exist.

Rosie has confessed but is claiming that it was all Wrigley's idea. She was scared of him. He manipulated and controlled her. She was a victim herself. She has perfected the wide-eyed-innocent act. I hope she doesn't get away with it. But she's a good actress, and Simon Harper has deep pockets to pay for the best defense. Sometimes, justice isn't always played out in the courts.

Rosie's cousin, Tom, has denied knowledge of everything apart from the "pranks" on Flo. I tend to believe him. There's a big difference between a bully and a killer.

The police questioned me, but there's nothing to refute my claim of self-defense. As Wrigley himself proclaimed—**"fire fucks everything up."**

There are still loose ends. Like the murder of the couple in the next village. Not all resolutions are neat and tidy. Nor people's motives. Although Wrigley was regarded as a troubled child, none of the experts who assessed him ever noticed any psychopathic traits.

"They're simply put together wrong. You can't fix it."

I glance at Flo. I hope I can fix her. She hasn't talked much about what happened. Outwardly, she seems fine, if a little quiet. But I can see the damage in her eyes. I just hope it's not permanent. She's still young. There's time to heal. Although we can never really erase trauma, our mind is good at repairing it, layering it over with new experiences, like fresh skin growing over an old wound. The scar remains. It just hurts less and becomes harder to see.

She glances at me. "Aren't you eating your chips?"

I grimace. "Actually, I'm not that hungry."

She smiles wanly. "Me neither."

We sit for a moment and stare out at the sea.

"Why does the sea here always look like manky tea?"

"No idea. Still nice to see it, though?"

"Meh."

"And sea air is good for you."

"Smells of sewage and seagull crap."

"You're sounding better."

"Sort of." She looks down. "I still think about Wrigley."

"Well, it's only been a couple of weeks."

"Is it weird that I feel sad he's dead even after everything he did?"

"No. I think maybe it's harder to accept what he did **because** he's dead. You never had a chance to deal with it."

"Yeah, maybe. When I think about him, I still see the Wrigley I thought I knew. The one I liked. Who made me laugh and quoted Bill Hicks."

"That's natural. But it'll fade."

I hope.

"Did Dad fade?"

I stiffen. "Yes. But, to be honest, he had faded a long time before he died."

"How d'you mean?"

"It wasn't a great marriage, Flo. He was an unhappy man and sometimes he took that out on me. I wasn't sad when he died. I was shocked and angry, but he wasn't the man I fell in love with." I wait for this to settle. "I'm sorry. I should have been more honest with you before."

"It's okay," Flo says eventually. "Life is complicated, isn't it?"

I wrap an arm around her shoulders. "Yeah, but I think ours has been more complicated than most, and I don't want you to think you can't trust people ever again."

"I know. But I might give dating a rest for a while."

"Well, as your mum, obviously, I'm thrilled to hear that."

Another small smile. "Mum, when can we go home?"

"Well, the chapel isn't going to be rebuilt for a while, if ever, so—"

"No, I meant, **home,** to Nottingham."

"Right. Well—" I take a breath and get ready to broach something I've been thinking about. "I need to speak to Bishop Durkin before we can really decide, but . . . what if we didn't go back to Nottingham? What if we went somewhere else? Further away?"

"Like where?"

"Australia."

Before she can reply, my phone vibrates in my pocket. I pluck it out and glance at Flo. "It's Mike."

She nods to say I should answer it.

"Hello?"

"Hi."

"How are you both doing?"

"We're okay."

"Good."

"How are things there?"

"Calming down a bit. Fewer press. Most of the police work is in the lab now, and that will take weeks."

"It's a lot faster on **CSI**."

He chuckles. "Who'd have thought that wasn't wholly realistic?"

There's a pause.

"And how are you?" I ask.

The revelations about Rosie have sparked renewed interest in his daughter's death. Poppy has started to open up about some of the cruelties her sister inflicted upon her, including being forced into the abattoir on the day I first met her. I wonder if the scales are finally falling from Simon and Emma's eyes when it comes to their elder daughter, and what she's capable of.

"I'm okay," he says. "Whatever the truth, it doesn't bring her back, does it? Nothing changes that."

"No."

A longer pause. Then he says: "Anyway, another interesting development. The skeletons in the well? The police are pretty sure one is Merry. Right age, and they found a necklace with the initial M. Apparently, both Merry and Joy wore necklaces with their initials on them."

"And the other one?"

"It isn't Joy. It's an older woman who had been

through childbirth. They think it could be Merry's mother. Murdered sometime later and dumped there."

"I see," I say flatly. "Guess a well is a good hiding place for bodies."

"Yeah. The police are very eager to trace Merry's younger brother."

"Right."

"**And** there's one more thing."

"What?"

"Merry was pregnant."

SIXTY-FOUR

They say not knowing is worse. But sometimes, knowing is just as bad. Knowing is finally finding that elusive needle in the haystack, only to discover that the needle was the very thing stopping the entire haystack from collapsing and burying you.

I make some phone calls. My first is to Bishop Durkin:

"I just need you to tell me something, honestly."

"Is that really necessary?"

"When did my name come up in connection with the position at Chapel Croft?"

"Not long after Reverend Fletcher's resignation."

"So, before his death?"

"Yes."

"And who suggested me?"

"Well, as you know, I had a conversation with Bishop Gordon at the Weldon diocese."

"Yes, I know that. I want to know who gave **him** my name."

"Does it matter?"

"Yes. It does."

Something in my tone must convince him. He considers for a moment and then he tells me.

My next call is to Kayleigh's mother, Linda. I ask for a favor. She is happy to oblige.

When I tell Flo, she looks at me suspiciously. "So, I'm going to stay with Kayleigh for a couple of nights. What about you?"

"I just have a few things to tie up here. Boring stuff."

She continues to stare at me and then she suddenly lunges forward and hugs me so tightly I can't breathe. "I love you."

"I love you too."

"Don't do anything stupid."

"Me? Who do you think I am?"

She pulls back and stares at me. "My mum."

I wave Flo off on the train and then I get into my car and head back to Chapel Croft. I drive through the village and pull up outside the same decrepit Victorian house I visited just over two weeks ago. A lot has happened since then. And I have been giving things a lot of thought.

I walk up to the door, but it opens before I can knock.

"Reverend Brooks."

"Aaron."

"I got your call."

He opens the door and I step inside.

"How are you and your daughter?"

"We're getting there. I never had a chance to thank you for calling 999."

When Flo bolted into the night, she managed to flag down a car. It happened to be Aaron. Turns out that he drove around every night to check on the chapel. Obsessive, odd, but on this occasion, no pun intended, a godsend.

"You're welcome. And how are you, Reverend? It must be hard to reconcile your faith with what you did."

"Sometimes there is no choice," I say tightly.

"I've been praying for you."

"Thanks." I smile briskly. "Now, like I said on the phone, I'd like to talk to your father."

"And like I said, you've seen him. He can't talk."

"But he can listen."

I stare at him pleadingly. Finally, he nods.

"Five minutes."

Marsh is awake, just. His breathing is labored. The institutional smell is stronger than ever. And there's something else. Not specific. But anyone who has been with an ill person toward the end will recognize it. It's the smell of death.

I sit on a chair beside his bed and I think how life and illness can be so cruel. Would any of us choose to continue with our life if we knew this might be our fate? And then I remind myself that at least Marsh had a choice. At least his life was not taken away by someone else before it had even started.

"Hello, Reverend Marsh."

He blinks at me.

"You remember me, don't you?"

A small head movement. Maybe a nod. Maybe an involuntary twitch. Hard to tell.

"Good. Then I'll keep this brief. We uncovered the vault beneath the chapel. We found Benjamin Grady's body."

A slight hitch in his breathing. I lean closer.

"I know you were involved in hiding it there. I think you did it to protect the Church, and your family, from scandal. I'd like to think you also did it to protect someone else. A young, frightened girl. Is that true?"

Another small head movement.

"But here's the thing. We both know that Grady wasn't killed in the church. His body was moved there from somewhere else. And I remembered something Joan Hartman said: **you can't drive**. So you must have had help that night."

His eyes stare at me helplessly.

"I'm pretty sure I already know who it was. So, I'm just going to say a name and you can let me know if I'm right." I smile. "Time to confess."

SIXTY-FIVE

"Jack, it is so good to see you. My goodness, what a time it has been for you."

I allow Rushton to envelop me in a warm, slightly musty hug.

He steps back. "I have to say, I didn't think you would be coming back, not after everything that's happened."

"No. Me neither. But there were just a few things I needed to get straight."

We walk inside.

"Is Clara here?" I ask.

"No, she's gone out." He rolls his eyes. "Running, walking. No wonder she keeps so thin. Of course, I work hard to stay in my best shape too." He chortles and pats his stomach.

I smile, feeling sad.

"So, to what do I owe the pleasure?" he asks now.

"I wondered if I could talk to you—about Benjamin Grady."

He stares at me for a long time. And then he says:

"It's a lovely day. Why don't we go in the garden?"

We sit at a small wrought-iron table in the shade of a weeping willow.

All around us wildflowers bloom in a riot of color. Bees buzz lazily between them. Birds chirrup in the trees.

"It's beautiful out here."

"Yes, Clara and I have been very happy here. I always used to say that the only way I would leave this place would be in a coffin, or maybe not even then. I always quite fancied being buried under this tree."

"Nice spot."

"Yes." He sighs. "Perhaps that's my weakness. I love it here too much. My life, my wife, my work. My complacency has been my greatest sin."

"The curse of being a priest—the need to confess our sins."

"And we're not even Catholic."

A small smile.

"Why did you recommend me for the position here?" I ask.

"Actually, I didn't."

"When Fletcher resigned, you put my name forward to Bishop Gordon?"

"Clara asked me to. She'd read about you, in a newspaper. She said that as soon as she saw your picture she knew you were the one. Very insistent, she was."

I feel something settle inside. A final missing piece slotting into place.

"Did you know that Clara and Benjamin Grady were friends, that they grew up together?"

"Yes. I did." He regards me with a small, rueful smile. "And yes, before you ask, I have always known that Clara was in love with him."

I stare at him in surprise. "She told you."

"She didn't have to. I could see it in her face whenever his name was mentioned—not that anyone mentioned him very much. She keeps a picture of him. Hidden in a book. I found it once, by accident. She doesn't know."

"You don't mind?"

"First love is a powerful thing, especially when it never has a chance to grow old, to disappoint or become dull. I adore Clara. I know she doesn't love me as much, but she loves me **enough**."

"And you're happy with that?"

"I'm content—and that is all most of us can hope for, don't you think?"

Maybe, I think. **But maybe some of us need something more.**

"I need to speak to Clara," I say. "You said she'd gone out?"

"Yes, although I've no idea where she goes when she takes off on one of her rambles."

But I think I do.

SIXTY-SIX

She stands, just as she does in Flo's picture. Still and silent, staring toward the house. Crime scene tape flutters around the well nearby.

"Clara!"

She turns. "Jack. What are you doing up here?"

"I could ask you the same."

"Oh, I'm just taking a walk."

"You come up here a lot?"

She smiles at me, wrinkles crinkling around those enviable cheekbones. A woman who has become more beautiful in her later years. Nothing like the awkward schoolteacher who was never enough for a handsome young priest.

Sometimes our desires run to darker pleasures.

"Why would you think that?"

"Well, it took me a while to work it out. Why come up here to the house? I understand why you want to stay close to the chapel. Because that's where his body is buried. But here—where he died?"

Her smile falters.

"Then I realized," I continue. "It's not the house you visit. It's the well."

She shakes her head. "I'm sorry, Jack. I really have no idea what you're talking about."

"Yes, you do. You knew about the body in the well. You've known for thirty years."

"And how on earth would I know that Merry's body was in the well?"

"Because it's not Merry. It's Joy. And you killed her."

She was early.

They had agreed to meet at eight o'clock. It wasn't quite ten to.

Joy waited by the broken-down stone wall at the edge of the garden, just out of sight of the house. She checked her watch, willing Merry to emerge from the back door.

Please hurry, **she thought.** Please. We can leave this place. Start a new life.

She touched her stomach.

And then she heard a sound behind her.

She turned. Her eyes widened.

"You? Why are you here?"

SIXTY-SEVEN

"It was an accident."

"Really?"

"We argued. She tripped and fell."

"What did you argue about?"

"What do you think?"

"Grady. You loved him. But he wasn't interested in a plain, twenty-something teacher, was he? He preferred them younger. Pretty little things he could subjugate, dominate, hurt."

"Joy seduced him."

"She was fifteen."

Her lip curls. "She knew what she was doing. I **saw** what they were doing when he was supposed to be teaching her the Bible."

"You saw what he was doing to **her**."

"I told Marsh. I thought that would put an end to it. But then, I spotted her that night, sneaking up here with a rucksack. I thought she was on her way to the chapel to meet him. I followed her."

"She wasn't meeting Grady. She was meeting Merry. They had planned to run away together."

"I didn't mean for it to happen."

"Then why didn't you go for help? You could have walked right up to the house, knocked on the door."

"I was scared."

"She was pregnant. Did you know that?"

She looks down. "No, I didn't."

"She was fifteen and pregnant and you left her in a hole to die."

"It was an accident."

"Really. Or did you think, with Joy out of the way, that Grady might finally notice you? But he didn't, did he? He just moved on to another young victim."

She sneers. "Merry was no victim. That girl was always trouble. Benjamin was just trying to save her. He was a man of God."

"If you really believe that, why did you help Marsh to hide his body?"

She hesitates. "Marsh called me that night. Panicked. Desperate. He told me that Benjamin had been performing exorcisms without the

Church's permission. This one had got out of hand. Something terrible had happened—"

She looks down, voice catching. I'd feel sorry for her if I didn't know that she had no pity for the girls Grady had been abusing.

"Benjamin was dead, and Merry had run away. Her mother had begged Marsh not to involve the police."

"So, Marsh agreed and you just went along with it?"

Her eyes flash. "I'd have killed Merry Lane if I could. But Marsh told me that if anyone found out what had happened it would destroy the church. Benjamin would be vilified, disgraced. I couldn't bear that. I wasn't able to save his life, so I chose to save his name."

"And cover up what he'd been doing."

"He was doing God's work."

"You really believe that?"

I reach into my pocket and take out the tape recorder. The cassette is inside. I finally fixed it. In some ways I wish I hadn't. The contents are hard to listen to.

Clara frowns. "What's that?"

"The truth about your precious Grady. Everything that happened that night. Everything he did. All on here. I could take this to the police right now."

Clara stares at it and then smiles coldly.

"You could . . . but we both know you won't."

"Really? And why's that?"

"Because if the body in the well is Joy, then that must mean that Merry is still alive, out there, somewhere." Her grey eyes fix on mine. "And I'll tell them who you really are."

She lay on the bed, spread-eagled, caked in her own filth. Her mum had caught her trying to run. Now, this was her punishment. Imprisoned. Alone in this room.

Apart from his visits.

She was possessed, her mother had told him. The devil was making her behave this way. She needed his help.

He stared down at her. Her hands and ankles were secured. She was naked, ribs sharp ripples beneath her skin. The bruises from their last encounter lay stark against the white of her flesh. Fingerprints traced in purple and black. Angry red welts from where he had heated his silver signet ring over a flame and pressed it into the tender spots of her body.

Grady smiled. "Tonight, Merry, we must work harder to expel your demons."

He turned and opened his case. It was lined with red silk. Sturdy straps held the contents in place: a heavy crucifix, holy water, a Bible, muslin cloths. His tools. His playthings. On the other side of the case: a scalpel, a sharp serrated knife and one more item, a small black box.

He removed this first, checked the contents and pressed a button along the side. He laid the tape recorder on the bedside table beside her.

He liked to relive their encounters.

"Please," she begged. "Please don't hurt me again."

"Oh, I will only do what is necessary."

He took a rag, walked over and, seizing her by the roots of her greasy hair, stuffed it deep into her mouth. She choked, bucking and fighting against the restraints. He laid his hands on her. It seemed to go on forever. She twisted and spat. The gag flew from her mouth and thick spittle hit his cheeks.

Grady wiped at his face. "I can feel the devil inside you. He must be purged."

He turned to his case, reaching for the serrated knife.

The knife wasn't there.

Her brother stood in front of him, the heavy blade clasped in his hands.

"Son —"

Jacob plunged the knife into the curate's chest. Grady staggered, twisting back toward the bed.

Merry sat up. Her bindings hung loose. Her brother had untied them earlier. She watched as the curate's eyes registered the deception, then his legs gave way and he crumpled to his knees.

She climbed out of the bed and padded across the floorboards. Grady clutched at the handle of the knife, wheezing hotly. She took the scalpel from the case and crouched down beside him.

"Please," he whispered. "I am a man of God."

Merry smiled and pressed the sharp tip into the soft flesh beneath his left eye.

"You're a sick bastard."

She drove the blade into his eyeball. Grady screamed.

And then she raised the scalpel again . . .

SIXTY-EIGHT

"You're wrong."

"No." Clara shakes her head. "You've changed. A lot. But I spent a lifetime wondering what happened to Merry Lane. And suddenly, there you were. Your picture in the newspaper: '**Vicar with Blood on Her Hands**.' Appropriate, don't you think?"

I don't bite. "You persuaded Brian to ask Bishop Gordon to offer me the job here."

"I wasn't sure you'd do it. I was surprised when you accepted. And then I got angry. That you could just waltz back here, guilt free."

"You left the exorcism kit, the Bible, the Burning Girls. You sent those letters—"

She nods. "The case and Bible were among Fletcher's things. He must have found them in the vault, where Marsh hid them with Benjamin's body."

"**Why,** Clara? After all this time?"

"I could ask you the same thing. Why come back?"

I hesitate, and then I say: "Because of Joy. I thought I might finally have a chance to find out what happened to her."

"And I thought I'd finally have a chance to make you pay for what you did to Benjamin."

"Benjamin Grady was a pedophile and an abuser. He deserved to die. Joy didn't."

Clara smiles another of her chill smiles. "We can both find ways to justify our actions. But ultimately, we're both killers."

It occurs to me that I could grab her. Pull her off balance. It wouldn't take much to yank her down into the darkness. To leave her to die there. Like Joy.

Then our eyes meet. And I know she's thinking the same thing.

"How do you live with yourself?"

"The same way you do, I imagine."

We stare at each other. I take a step forward . . . and drop the tape down the well.

"Merry's dead. And you can go to hell, Clara."

And then I turn and walk away.

For the last time.

SIXTY-NINE

"I'll be sad to see you go."

I smile at Joan across the kitchen table. "I'll miss you too."

"We haven't had this much excitement here for years."

"I imagine the police investigation will continue for a while. There's still a lot to work out."

Not least, who killed Grady.

"I doubt they'll ever get to the truth of it."

"I'm sorry—I know you were hoping for answers."

She reaches for her sherry. "Don't be. When you get to my age, you understand there are more un-answered questions in life than not. The best you can hope for is a resolution you can live with. And at least I know the truth about Matthew."

"How are the Harpers coping?"

"Emma has moved back to her mother's with

Poppy for a while. Simon is still finding it hard to believe Rosie's guilt. All of this, it's broken him."

I almost feel sorry for him. Almost.

"We all try to do our best for our family," I say.

"And do you think this move will be best for you and Flo?"

"I hope so."

"Do you think you'll come back?"

"Maybe."

"Well, don't leave it so long next time."

I stare at her. She smiles and pats my hand. "I don't need all the answers."

SEVENTY

What kind of woman am I?

I would like to answer that at heart I am a good woman, a woman who has tried to make the best of her life, to help others, to spread kindness.

But I am also a woman who has lied, stolen and killed.

We all have the capability to do evil. And most of us could find a reason to justify it. I don't believe that people are simply born "bad." Nurture trumps nature. However, I do believe that some of us are born with a greater **potential** to do wrong. Perhaps something genetic, when combined with environment, produces monsters. Like Grady. Like Wrigley.

Like me?

Do I feel guilt for the lives I have taken, the lies I have told? Does it keep me awake at night?

Sometimes. But not often. Does that make me a psychopath? Or a survivor?

I stare at myself in the bathroom mirror. Jack stares back. It's not that difficult to get a new identity. An old name from a gravestone. Begging and stealing until I could afford to pay for some good forged documents. Escaping a place is not enough. You need to escape yourself. You need to leave everything behind, including those you love. Like my brother.

I never intended to go into the church. But some of what I told Mike is true. I did meet a priest. Blake. A good man. He helped me understand that I could make a difference. Make amends. He also made me realize that the best place to hide is in plain sight. People don't look past a clerical collar. And if they do, they are still blinded by their presumptions.

I unclip the collar now and slip it into my pocket. Then I reach into my shirt and lift out the cheap silver chain that I always wear. For over thirty years. Dangling from it, a slightly tarnished letter J.

Because best friends swap things: mix tapes, clothes, jewelry.

I hold on to the necklace for just a moment, then I grasp it between my fingers and yank it off. I drop it down the sink and run the tap until it's washed away.

The toilet flushes from the cubicle behind me. I tuck my hair behind my ears, shorter now, the roots touched up. I step back and smile. Then I push open the door and step back into the throng of the airport.

Mike and Flo are sitting at a table in a busy café. Mike insisted upon driving us here. He's been around quite a bit since that night at the chapel. I'll miss him. But I'll also be glad to say goodbye. Sometimes, when he looks at me, I feel he's almost on the verge of saying something. Something that wouldn't be good. For me. Or him.

"Hey," Mike says as I approach. "Okay?"

"Yeah. Good."

"I'm just going to get another coffee," Flo says. "Want one?"

"Yes, thanks."

She walks off to join the queue at the counter.

"So," Mike says. "Feeling nervous about Australia?"

"Yeah—mostly about how I'll pay off the credit card."

"You deserve this."

"Thanks. But it's only for a month. To check a few places out."

Maybe.

"I meant to ask," I say. "Did the police ever find the person who pulled me from the chapel?"

"No. I mean, nobody came forward."

"Right."

"And if they were injured—they'd have showed up at a hospital, right?"

"Right." I smile quickly. "Maybe I imagined it."

"It was a traumatic night."

"Yes."

But I didn't imagine it. I know it was him. Jacob. My brother. He found me again. He saved me. And he's still out there, somewhere.

"Here we go. Two Americanos." Flo dumps two coffees on the table. "I got double shots, so that should see us through half the journey to Oz."

"I should get going," Mike says.

"Oh. Okay."

We both stand, a little awkwardly.

"Thanks for the lift," I say. "And, well, you know."

"I know. Remember the stuffed koala."

"Will do."

"Okay then."

Flo rolls her eyes. "Painful."

Mike leans forward and embraces me in a quick, clumsy hug. "Take care, and look after yourselves."

He straightens, smiles and then turns and ambles away.

"Such a loser," Flo says, taking the lid off her coffee. "He's perfect for you."

"I don't think so."

"Why?"

"Just not my type."

"Holding out for Hugh Jackman?"

"I think he's holding out for me."

She smiles. "I love you, Mum."

I reach over and squeeze her hand.

"And I love you."

She suddenly frowns. "You've taken your collar off."

"Oh, yes. Thought it might be more comfortable. For the flight."

"Oh. Okay."

We sip our coffees. Flo checks her phone. When we rise to leave, I let Flo walk ahead and I take the collar out of my pocket. After a moment's hesitation, I stuff it into the empty coffee cup, pop the lid back on and leave it on the table.

What kind of woman am I?

Perhaps it's time to find out.

EPILOGUE

The patient had come to them a few weeks ago. Found barely alive in a ditch, not far from Hastings. No ID. In a bad way. He'd obviously been there a while.

He had burns to a large area of his right side and cellulitis had spread from an injured ankle, up his leg. He'd been placed in an induced coma. He had battled back from sepsis. But the leg couldn't be saved. It was amputated below the knee. Rehabilitation had been slow. He couldn't or wouldn't talk.

"But we're making some progress," Nurse Mitchell says as she leads the new doctor (all shiny hair and earnest enthusiasm) down the corridor, rubber-soled shoes squeaking. "He's been engaging in art therapy recently and that seems to have helped."

"Good."

You might not say that when you see it, she thinks.

She pushes open the door to the therapy room. The doctor blinks. The tables at the side of the room display the patients' work. Amid the woven baskets, papier mâché models and painted plates, pretty much every surface is covered in small twig dolls.

The doctor walks over and peers at them. "Interesting."

One word for it.

"They're all he makes," Nurse Mitchell says. "Obsessively."

The doctor picks up one of the dolls, stares at it, and then quickly puts it down again. "And has he said what they represent?"

"He's only spoken two words since he's been here."

She glances back at the twig dolls, trying to contain a shudder.

"Burning Girls."

ACKNOWLEDGMENTS

I'm not a religious person—my only experience of churches is sitting through a few bum-numbing christenings and harvest festivals—so writing a book where the main character is a vicar was always going to be an interesting proposition.

Therefore, I owe a big thanks to Mark Townsend for his insight into small rural churches and the day-to-day life of a vicar—although obviously I've used some, ahem, creative license!

It seemed to take me an eternity to finish this, my fourth book. It really does get tougher each time! So, I'd like to give a shout out to my always supportive agent, Maddy, my ever-patient editors, Max and Anne, and to everyone at my publishers who has worked so hard, even over lockdown, to polish, promote and finally get the book out there.

It goes without saying—but he might sulk if I don't—that my husband, Neil, is a constant source of love and tech support. And, of course, I have to thank my little girl, Betty, for filling my days with joy—and Lego.

I'd also like to thank everyone in the village where we now live for being so welcoming and supportive. I've made some lovely friends here, whose tales about the area's history helped to inspire this story.

As always, thank you wonderful readers for picking this book up. I couldn't do it without you. So—same time next year?

ABOUT THE AUTHOR

C. J. Tudor is the author of **The Other People,
The Hiding Place,** and **The Chalk Man,** which
won the International Thriller Writers Award for
Best First Novel and the Strand Magazine Award
for Best Debut Novel. Over the years she has
worked as a copywriter, television presenter, voice-
over artist, and dog walker. She is now thrilled to
be able to write full-time, and doesn't miss chasing
wet dogs through muddy fields all that much. She
lives in England with her partner and daughter.

Facebook.com/CJTudorOfficial
Twitter: @cjtudor

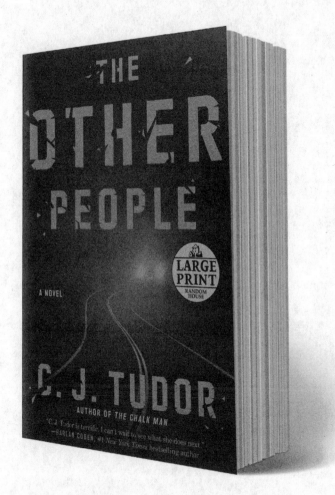

LP
The burning girls